BLOOD AND THE FOREST

A Novel Of The Maya World.

Rich Orman

Copyright © 2012 by Rich Orman.

All rights reserved

Without limiting the rights under the copyright reserved above, no part of this publication may be reproduced, stored in or introduced into a retreival system or transmitted, in any form or any means (electronic, mechanical, photocopying, recording, or otherwise), without the prior written consent of the author of this books. This excludes brief quotes used in reviews.

Scanning, uploading and distribution of this book via the Internet or via any other means without the consent of the author or is illegal and punishable by law.

For information, contact bloodandtheforest@gmail.com.

ISBN 978-1449598914

PROLOGUE

My vision is fading, but I can still see it.
Soon it will be gone from my sight entirely, but for now I hang on to each moment of blessed perception, knowing that it will all end soon.
It is all around us.
It flows.
It creeps.
It gurgles.
It glistens.
It whispers.
It sighs.
Its branches reach high into the heavens.
Its roots dig deep into the depths of the Underworld.
It is sky.
It is air.
It is the clouds.
It is earth.
It is the sea.
It is the rivers.
It is the jaguar.
It is the rubber tree.
It is the cacao bean.
It is maize.
It is rock.
It is the mountains.
It is the temples.
It is the cities.
It is everything.
It is nothing.
It is everywhere.
It is nowhere.

    My lips would tell you that there are many worlds, many places. The place where we live and draw our breath is merely one of the realms that the Gods have constructed–for whatever reasons compel them. The Council Book tells us that we live in the fourth manifestation of the Earth—that the Gods made three mistakes before they were finally pleased with their handicraft.

Unlike our world, the Gods did not err when they created the other realms of the cosmos—they were created only once. There is the Underworld, where the dead speak quietly in the darkness, and where the ancestors await our blood for their sustenance. There is the Overworld, where the Hero Twins, and those few men and women who prove their worth through great deeds, look down upon us from the night sky. There is the Otherworld, the land of Gods and departed kings, the land that is both the Underworld and the Overworld, and yet it is neither of them. All these worlds are different, yet all are part of It, all part of the Great Tree. The Great Tree is the connection, it is the bond, it is the glue that holds the many worlds together.

When I was a child and my father first told me of the Great Tree, it seemed like a fantasy—a tall tale that old men told to young boys and then laughed at their gullibility. As I came of age and the priests described its most arcane details with absolute clarity, I started to see it as a metaphor, a means by which men described the world to suit their own purposes. One night when I was still an apprentice scribe I looked into the summer sky and saw the Milky Way, which the books told me was the actual trunk of the Great Tree. At that moment I knew that it was real, something that I could see and touch. The next day, when my Master released me from my duties, I went into his library and read about the Great Tree. When that resource was exhausted I went to the house of every scribe I knew and devoured every book in the city that I could lay my hands on, and—so I thought—my understanding grew. I now know that I understood *nothing*. Nothing of life. Nothing of the Gods. Nothing of the true nature of our world. And though I would have punched you in the nose for saying so when I was thirteen years of age, I understood less than nothing of the Great Tree.

No, the Gods did not choose to grace me with true understanding until Fireborn took the blinders from my eyes and showed me the truth. Fireborn the ballplayer. Fireborn the trader. Fireborn the conqueror. Fireborn the king.

Oh how I love him and hate him both. Like the Great Tree, he is my protector. Like the Great Tree, I go to sleep each night thankful that he did not kill me during the day. Yes, he and the Great Tree have at least that much in common. And now as I lay dying in the house of my father, I find that I understand them both. I understand them perfectly.

But this understanding has come at a heavy price—a price so high that not even the ruler of the great city of Teotihuacan, with his limitless wealth, with mountains of cacao beans at his fingertips, would be willing to pay it. Indeed, knowing what I now know, and given a chance, I would have spurned this knowledge and gone on in blissful ignorance for the rest of my days.

But enough of this. The journey is what is important. Anticipation is so much better than the completed act. In the end the journey is all that matters. Let me show you my journey, for we will surely arrive at the same destination, as all of us must. Let us go back to those days of my youth, when the Great Tree was still a wonder before my eyes, and when honor and fidelity still had meaning. Back to the days when the name Fireborn wasn't even a figment of my imagination.

Imagine now that Eight *baktuns*, Sixteen *katuns*, Eight *tuns*, Zero *uinals* and Zero days have passed since the moment when Lord Sun first looked down upon on the face of our world.

Chapter One
THE GAME

8.16.8.0.0. December 23, 364 A.D.

As much as he tried to think back farther, Jaguar Spot's earliest memory was of the ballcourt in his home city of Uaxactun. It seemed like every important event, every relationship, and every chapter of Jaguar Spot's life was somehow connected to the ballgame, to the ballcourt, or a to ballplayer. The ballgame had started as his passion, it had become his savior, and, as it seemed that he knew from the very beginning, it would ultimately be his demise.

Jaguar Spot walked to the ballcourt behind his father and the other *ahauob* of the city carrying a wooden trumpet not much larger than a coconut. It was a child's trumpet. It had once been his father's, and his grandfather's before that. His father had stayed up late the night before trying to teach him how to play it, and when this failed he at least tried to teach him to make a steady tone. If he could do that, if at least he could teach the boy that much, maybe his son could blend in with the other children's playing and not embarrass the family. But it was not to be. Much to his father's consternation, after half an evening's tutoring Jaguar Spot could still blow little more than a quiet, wavering, buzz. His father was a patient man, but was bedridden from his wounds and was not as much help as he would have liked. Finally Jaguar Spot's eldest sister Orchid shooed him out of his father's bedchamber and made him go to bed well past midnight. Hopefully there would be enough other noise that day to drown out Jaguar Spot's lousy trumpeting.

Orchid woke him up long before sunrise for a breakfast of corn tortillas and venison. Venison was a rare treat in the household, and was a gift from His Lordship for his father's prowess in battle. Spirit Dog, the fifth son of a *cahel*, and a man who, to put it politely, "claimed" to be a doctor, walked into the house just as they were finishing breakfast and went straight to their father's bedchamber. He shook his head when he looked at the wounds in Toucan Claw's arm and chest. He knelt down and sniffed at the wounds before he spoke. "You should stay home, Your Lordship," Spirit Dog said. "You really should. These wounds are healing quite nicely with no sign or scent of infection at all. Getting out of bed and moving around can do no good for you, even if the *Ch'ul Ahau* expects you to march with him today."

"I will march," Toucan Claw replied brusquely. "No matter what you or my daughter think. And I will thank you to mind our own business and let me get on with mine." Toucan Claw started moving to rise out of his bed. Spirit Dog clicked his tongue and spoke quickly, as if he did not think that he would have enough time to get all the words out. "It is not just the marching, Your Lordship. If yesterday's weather is any guide it will be a hot day today, and sitting for half the day in the hot sun would only make things worse. Please take my advice. Send your boy to the palace to extend your apologies to the *Ch'ul Ahau*."

Orchid knew Spirt Dog to be a pompous ass. She was normally dubious of his medical pronouncements, but on this occasion she was in complete agreement with his advice—her father had to stay home. Toucan Claw would have none of it. He called over to Jaguar Spot. "Boy, get me my clothes and equipment, we have a ballgame to attend." As Jaguar Spot left the room he heard Orchid arguing with his father. "But Father, you heard what the doctor said!" Jaguar Spot thought that he heard his father say "Ha!" when Orchid uttered the word "doctor." Orchid kept pleading. "You can't go! You must stay home! I beg you!" Orchid's voice faded into the background as Jaguar Spot searched through the house for the special clothes that his father would need that day. Orchid and Spirit Dog were still pleading with his father when Jaguar Spot returned. As he gave his father the clothes and left to get the ballgame equipment, it seemed that the adults had reached some kind of consensus, as Spirit Dog sounded mollified. "Okay, as long as he promises not to do something as foolish as to actually go down onto the ballcourt and play in a game, he will probably be all right. Still, I want it understood that I can give no guarantees."

Orchid was helping Toucan Claw into his clothes when Jaguar Spot came back with the special pads and other equipment, much of it ceremonial, that all the *ahauob* would be expected to wear that day. Spirit Dog was gone; no doubt off to gather his own family for the day's festivities. Toucan Claw pushed away Orchid's offers of help as he walked into the kitchen and grabbed some tortillas and meat. "You two," he said to Orchid and Jaguar Spot, "get ready to go. We leave as soon as possible." They both ran to their respective bedchambers to put on their ceremonial garb and jewelry. When Jaguar Spot returned to the kitchen all three of his sisters were already there and his father was looking antsy. Toucan Claw chided him severely. "Come on, come on, you idiot boy, you will make us late! As if being late under ordinary circumstances isn't bad enough, we will be late to join His Lordship on the journey to a ceremonial ballgame! Why, I will be the laughingstock of all the other *ahauob*! Can you imagine the disgrace?"

For all of his father's worries, they were not late when they arrived at the palace of the *Ch'ul Ahau* just as the first glimmer of the dawn could be seen in the Eastern sky. They led a procession of seventy or so members of the extended clan who who had started following them as they walked through the clan's compound while Jaguar Spot, by tradition, tried to call them out with the trumpet. For most of the attempts his trumpet playing was so quiet that no one could hear it. On the few occasions when he was able to make an appreciable noise, it was so different from what the clan members expected that they did not recognize it as trumpet playing at all, thinking perhaps that a large bird or wild animal was loose in the compound. Toucan Claw was forced to yell to announce his presence in order to get his kinsmen to leave their houses.

Apart from Jaguar Spot's immediate family, there were seven *cahelob* subservient to his father, and their wives, sons and daughters. There were another thirty or so citizens who came at Toucan Claw's invitation, as a reward for years of loyal service. , Jaguar Spot and Toucan Claw left the rest of the group as they entered the palace plaza and walked to the waiting throng of *ahauob* and their eldest sons. Even though they had arrived just in time, they were still the last two members of the *ahau* class unaccounted for, much to Toucan Claw's chagrin. A waiting palace guard nodded up the stairs toward the palace's main door. Five guards at the top of the stairs blew blasts on conch-shell trumpets as the *Ch'ul Ahau* and twenty bodyguards—all of them the *Ch'ul Ahau's* close relatives—walked past the group of *ahauob* and their sons and made their way to the residential quarter of the city. Like a great snake, the assembled nobility and honored guests followed. The line slithered and crawled as it went through all the quarters of the city—past the houses of the poorest, past the temples, past the residential compounds of the noble houses and their vassals, past government buildings, and past empty farm fields waiting to be planted with maize and beans. All along the way the snake was joined by more and more people, always at the end. To Jaguar Spot it seemed like the entire city was there, although less than one in thirty would be allowed to attend the day's main event.

As eldest son of an *ahau* Jaguar Spot had an honored status in the city. Even *cahelob* would be expected to call him "Master Jaguar Spot" or "Your Lordship" until he reached the age of ascension. After that, everyone in the city other than the *ahauob* and their eldest sons would have no choice–they would call him "Your Lordship" and nothing else. Even his sisters would be expected to call him "Your Lordship" when, some day in a future so far off that it was difficult for Jaguar Spot to imagine, he succeeded his father as *ahau*.

The eldest sons of the other *ahauob* walked around Jaguar Spot in a tight group, some of them carrying musical instruments like Jaguar Spot's, many of the others dressed for the ballgame. The eldest of the boys, and the sons of the highest ranking *ahauob* who had passed the age of ascension, were carrying ritual obsidian blades above their heads with both hands. Such blades were priceless in Uaxactun. Like conch shells and stingray spines, the *Ch'ul Ahau* purchased the blades from traders who traveled many months to reach Uaxactun. Jaguar Spot had never seen anything like them.

The blades were made of green obsidian and were almost a foot long. They blades were smooth, as if a craftsman had chipped them off a mountain in a single hit. The blades were fresh, as was dictated by the Gods for such an occasion, and had not yet tasted men's blood. Jaguar Spot suspected that the blades would have their fill of blood by the end of the day.

The *cahelob* and their eldest sons walked behind Jaguar Spot, followed by the other members of the noble houses of the city–the women, the younger sons, and the daughters. This was a ballgame of special significance, even for a ceremonial contest. Normally everyone wore their finest clothes to a ceremonial ballgame, but this was not an ordinary day. The people of the city, if they were lucky, might see three or four days like this in their entire lifetime. Because of the rarity and added importance of the occasion, most of the nobility, and many of the common citizens, long ago had clothes specially made for this day, back when the possibility of such a ballgame was purely theoretical. Once made, the clothes were hidden in quiet corners of the house, or buried in large earthen pots, awaiting the day that they would be called into service. At day's end the clothes, the costumes, all of it, would be burned as a sacrifice to the Gods. Many that day wore plumed hats, colorful clothes, or dressed as ballplayers as part of the ritual. Even some of the women chose to dress as ballplayers, although none of them had ever so much as served a ball in a match. Of course Toucan Claw would never allow his daughters to act as vain and vulgar as to dress like that. That was for the commoners, and maybe for the families of the *cahelob*, at least those *cahelob* who did not have to report to Toucan Claw.

By the time Jaguar Spot arrived at the procession's destination there were more than one thousand people in the line, all of whom wanted to watch the spectacle. Of course that was not possible. Only a few hundred at most would be able to watch. Everyone present was either a noble of the city or had been invited by an *ahau* or by the *Ch'ul Ahau* himself. There were many rewards for loyalty and service in the city, but nothing save a title of nobility or a mountain of cacao beans came close to an invitation to such a ceremonial ballgame. Everyone quietly filed into the respective spots assigned to their social class in total silence. Apart from the occasional cough or whimper from a stubbed toe, the only sound came from twenty priests beating drums in unison. The priests stood next to twenty long wooden stakes that lined the top of the ballcourt. The priests would scream "blood" after every twenty beats so as to awaken the Gods of the city and the ancestors of the *Ch'ul Ahau* and let them know that feeding time was about to begin.

The *ahauob* sat on edge of the ballcourt's north wall. Their legs rested on the incline, which pitched steeply to the floor of the court. A man could walk down the incline to the bottom, but just barely. This was a dangerous spot, for the ball was heavy and could bounce higher than the ballcourt ledge. Many had been maimed, and some killed, from a surprise bounce of the ball. Sitting on the edge was a test of courage, and of manhood. As the eldest son of an *ahau*, Jaguar Spot was expected to sit there stoically, seemingly oblivious to the danger. Men who feared being hit by the ball were hardly considered to be men at all, and were deemed totally unfit to be leaders. If an *ahau* exhibited such fear his honor, and his title, could be stripped away from him. His family would be disgraced, and might have to leave the city forever to avoid a life of shame and humiliation. If the son of an *ahau* showed fear, his chances of ever inheriting the title for himself, even if he was the eldest son, were absolutely nil. He would certainly lose any inheritance from his father, and would likely be disowned entirely, left to wander the countryside begging for food in disgrace. He might even be sacrificed to the Gods as an orphan might be. Even at five and half years old Jaguar Spot knew his duty, his role, and the consequences of failing to meet expectations.

When they arrived at the ballcourt the *Ch'ul Ahau* went straight down to the playing area in his full ceremonial ballplayer regalia, complete with hip pad, knee pad, and arm protector. He stood there alone as citizens of all ranks crowded behind the seated *Ahauob* in absolute silence, but for the beating of the priests' drums. Jaguar Spot began to whisper a question to his father about the rules of the game, but the *ahau* to the other side of him shushed him into silence: "Not now boy, you must remain silent. Do you want to shame your father?" Jaguar Spot looked down at his feet as those of lesser rank standing behind him struggled for a view. Toucan Claw stared into the distance with a studied disinterest.

The *Ch'ul Ahau* broke the silence. "Citizens of Uaxactun, hear my words." As the *Ch'ul Ahau* started speaking, the drums stopped. His voice was strong and loud, and Jaguar Spot had no doubt that everyone in vicinity of the ballcourt could hear him clearly. "It has now been eight years since I ascended to the throne of this city and first looked into the Otherworld as your king. I have done my duty as your ruler. I have spoken to the Gods. I have fed them with my blood and beseeched them on behalf of our city. I have built monuments to the Gods and our ancestors. All this you have seen. But two days ago we had something different. We had victory!" The *Ch'ul Ahau* stood silent as everyone else present at the ballcourt broke into a deafening cheer. The crowd only fell quiet when the *Ch'ul Ahau* raised his arms and spoke again. "We had a glorious victory against the self-satisfied so-called warriors from the oh-so-superior city of Tikal! Against our so-called betters, against people who just *know* that they are better than us. They teach their own sense of superiority to their children when they are weaned from mother's milk, sometimes even before. There is not a doubt in their minds that we are little more than a loose tribe of country bumpkins who, truth be told, shouldn't be an independent city at all." The crowd laughed lustfully at the *Ch'ul Ahau*'s imitation of a Tikal accent. They quieted down as the *Ch'ul Ahau* continued. "Well, we have shown them! We have a victory over Tikal that our descendants will speak of until the turn of the next ten *baktuns*!"

"Two days ago we met the army of Tikal in battle. The battle was hard, and we lost some good men to the Underworld. I learned something interesting from the priests before the battle. They told me that the people of Tikal call their city 'First Prophesy.' Well, if the Gods give them the power of prophecy, their *Ch'ul Ahau* must have been mighty stingy with his blood of late, because there was no evidence of divine intervention on behalf of Tikal two days ago!" The crowd broke into uproarious laughter, which seemed to go forever. The crowd fell silent as he continued. "The enemy fought well. They fought honorably, but in the end, they ran from us as a tapir runs from a jaguar. They fled into the woods and skulked back to their city, but not before we captured five of their *ahauob* and fifteen of their *cahelob*–twenty nobles altogether."

As if on cue the crowd again screamed adulation for the divine lord of the city. The *Ch'ul Ahau* motioned to the palace guards who stood in a circle in the East endzone. They quickly moved to the center with twenty bound prisoners at spear point.

The prisoners from Tikal were stripped naked. They staggered into the center of the ballcourt with their hands bound behind their backs, weak from their wounds and from two days without food or water. The five *ahauob* were the first brought to the center. The *Ch'ul Ahau* had two of those five brought over to him. The men did not resist, but at the same time they did not acknowledge the *Ch'ul Ahau* or his taunts–they simply stared into space. Even though these men were the enemy, Jaguar Spot found himself admiring their nobility and grace under pressure. They acted as if they grew up in the same house, andwith the same father, that he had.

The *Ch'ul Ahau* pulled a green obsidian blade from his waist and held it to the neck of the older of the two prisoners, who must have been sixty years old, and again he addressed the crowd. "This man is Gray Thunder, the brother of the *Ch'ul Ahau* of Tikal. He was Tikal's battle master, in charge of the field. This man led his army with courage and intelligence. He fought bravely in battle and he is a noble warrior. Yet I captured him with my own hands." The *Ch'ul Ahau* moved over to the second of the two men, who was much younger than the first, and had the muscles and demeanor of a seasoned ballplayer. "And this is Fireborn, the half-brother of the *Ch'ul Ahau* of Tikal. He is likewise a cunning warrior, a man who is to be respected on the field of battle, yet we defeated him and his brother, and defeated them soundly. We gained an honorable victory, and to show for it we captured two members of Tikal's royal family. Now our captives, at least those of them who show their worth, will have the honor of feeding the Gods and all of our ancestors." The *Ch'ul Ahau* waved his right arm with flourish and the palace guards led all twenty captives into the West endzone, where they forced them up the wall to be made to watch the day's festivities.

Once the twenty prisoners from Tikal were removed, the *Ch'ul Ahau* pointed to three *cahelob* in quick succession. They quickly made their way to the Eastern side of the ballcourt, while the *Ch'ul Ahau* instructed his palace guards to bring three of the Tikal men of similar rank to the West playing area. As the guards dressed the captives in waist pads, knee pads and arm pads, the *Ch'ul Ahau* walked up lip of the North side. All thirty-five of the city's *ahauob* held their breath. All of them had fought in the battle that had produced these captives. Many of them, like Jaguar Spot's father, had been injured. Even those who had suffered the gravest of injuries had come to this game, as had been the case with Toucan Claw. The possibility that the *Ch'ul Ahau* would honor them was just too enticing, and the idea that he would honor someone else because of an absence was too revolting, to even consider staying at home that day. Tradition required that the *Ch'ul Ahau* would sit beside one of them—an act of grace that would show the others that the selected *ahau* was held in the highest esteem, an honor reserved for the bravest warrior of the *ahau* class. The *Ch'ul Ahau* would in this fashion select his playing partner for the day. Playing in a ballgame with the divine lord of the city was an honor on any occasion, but today they would face off against the two highest ranked captured Tikal *ahauob*. The honor gained would be immeasurable.

The *Ch'ul Ahau* walked along the row of *ahauob*. Jaguar Spot silently prayed to the Hero Twins that the High Lord would pick his father—he prayed over and over in his mind. Orchid would have smacked him on the head had she known. Standing behind them, she silently prayed to the Maize god that the *Ch'ul Ahau* would pass her father by, saving him from possible further injury and death. Finally the *Ch'ul Ahau* came to a stop—right next to Jaguar Spot—and looked straight down at him. "My, how you have grown since I last saw you, young Jaguar Spot."

Jaguar Spot felt as if a tree frog had crawled down his throat. He could barely whisper out a reply. "Thank you, Your Lordship."

The *Ch'ul Ahau* chuckled at Jaguar Spot's nervousness and looked over at Jaguar Spot's father. "So, Toucan Claw, are you up for some two-on-two later today? That is, if you have recovered enough from your wounds for it to be safe. I would hate to lose one of my most valued *ahauob* on something as avoidable as a ballgame." Orchid could hear the conversation quite clearly and silently hoped that her father would decline the *Ch'ul Ahau*'s offer as a result of his injuries, but she knew better. Admitting fear or frailty on such an occasion would cause her father to lose face in front of the *Ch'ul Ahau* and all the other *ahauob*. Certainly, Toucan Claw would not be stripped of this title or shamed into leaving the city for truthfully answering the *Ch'ul Ahau's* question and declining the invitation, but he knew that if he did his colleagues would snigger and laugh behind his back for years to come. Jaguar Spot's father smiled at the *Ch'ul Ahau*. He said that he was feeling in excellent health and would be delighted to join His Lordship in the ballgame. Orchid stoically maintained her composure–Jaguar Spot barely suppressed his joy.

With Toucan Claw's acceptance the Divine Lord of Uaxactun sat down between Toucan Claw and Jaguar Spot. A priest brought the ball to the *Ch'ul Ahau* for inspection. The ball for three-on-three was large, about twice the size of a man's skull and four times as heavy. This ball, like most of the others, was made from solid rubber and was kept in a special ball-shaped container whenever not in play to keep its shape.

The *Ch'ul Ahau* looked down at Jaguar Spot and tickled him on the waist. "So, young man, do you like to watch the ballgame?" Jaguar Spot laughed at the tickling and only settled down to answer after the *Ch'ul Ahau* stopped.

"Yes, Your Lordship, but I don't understand the rules very well. It looks like fun."

The *Ch'ul Ahau* nodded, humoring the child. "Fun? Yes, I suppose that it is fun. But not today. Today is not for fun. What we do today we do for honor, and for the Gods." Jaguar Spot looked up at the *Ch'ul Ahau*. "Whose honor, Your Lordship, for ours or for the men from Tikal?" Toucan Claw immediately reached his hand behind the *Ch'ul Ahau's* back to slap his son on the head. "Don't bother His Lordship with such idiotic questions! Of course it is for the honor of His Lordship and of our city," he whispered.

The *Ch'ul Ahau* good naturedly let Toucan Claw discipline his son, then looked down at the boy. "Your father is right, it is for our honor. After all we had victory. But we are also here to let the Tikal men regain their honor. It is a shameful thing to be captured in battle, more shameful still if you are an *ahau*. By participating in this ritual they can regain what they have lost in defeat and can die with honor. You see, there is no real game here. The results are predetermined; this is why we deprive the captives of food and drink. They can't win, but once they lose and are sacrificed to the Gods and to our ancestors, they will have again found honor."

The ballcourt was the largest in all the domains of Uaxactun. The central playing area was 70 paces long and 8 paces wide with endzones fifteen paces square. The ball could bounce anywhere.

The three Uaxactun ballplayers stood in a line from the center of the ballcourt back to the East endzone, their faces looking as if they were girding for battle. The Tikal players stood in a similar formation to the West, but they looked tired and seemed barely able to stand. A priest took the ball to the center of the court, handed it to the closest Tikal player, and then ran off to the side. As the priest cleared the playing surface, the referee priest blew a conch shell trumpet–a priceless gift from the *Ch'ul Ahau's* father many years before–to start the game. The Tikal player took the ball in his left hand and hit it with is right forearm, barely sending it into the Uaxactun forecourt. The *Ch'ul Ahau* joked that a child of Jaguar Spot's age could have made a better serve. After the first bounce the middle Uaxactun player met the ball with his waist, sending it flying into the Tikal endzone. The Tikal players were too slow, and too weak, to get to the ball before the second bounce. Uaxactun won the point and the serve. The forward Uaxactun player served the ball deep into the Tikal backcourt and it landed where Tikal had no chance whatsoever of making a play for the ball. The crowd roared in triumph and the *Ch'ul Ahau* patted Jaguar Spot on the back. "Like I said, my boy, this is not a contest at all. There is no sport in what you see today. You will notice that the common people and the *cahelob* scream and yell when our players score a point. As you can see, the *ahauob* remain silent. They do not cheer because they understand the true nature of this game. No one but the uninformed, or an idiot, would want to watch such a mismatch for its own merit. This is about honor, not competition. Here we relive the glorious victory we had over Tikal two days ago, and those men down there," the *Ch'ul Ahau* pointed down at the Tikal men, "their families will rest easier knowing that their kinsmen died here, today, and didn't have to endure years of captivity and pain."

Jaguar Spot stared at the ballgame as if in a trance as Uaxactun scored the fifth point in a row. The *Ch'ul Ahau* rubbed his hands together and looked over at Toucan Claw. "Only one more point to go, my friend. Who shall have the honor of sending these brave men from Tikal into the Underworld? Name a worthy *cahel* of the city. Make it a member of your clan, if you wish. You will make the choice. It is my gift to you." The referee gave three blasts from his trumpet as Uaxactun scored the winning point and the players from both teams walked over to the North wall and stood right below the *Ch'ul Ahau*. The *Ch'ul Ahau* whispered to Toucan Claw. "Come now my friend, give me a name."

As Toucan Claw turned around he tried to hide the pain that his wounds caused him. He looked at the ranks of *cahelob* and their families standing six rows deep behind him. There were many of the lesser noble ranks that he knew well. Many were his kinsmen, who looked up to him as the leader of the clan, and who collected taxes or managed tribute labor for him. All of them looked at him in silence, knowing that the *Ch'ul Ahau* had given him the choice. He had to select carefully, mindful not to give the honor to someone who was unworthy, for that would cause resentment in the more upright members of the clan. Likewise he couldn't pick a braggart or a drunkard, no matter how efficient and law abiding they might be. Nor could he point to any man who would boast of the honor to the other *cahelob* of the city. There were some in the clan, Toucan Claw was forced to admit to himself, who would act in so disgraceful a manner. Of course the *cahelob* knew better than to appear eager to be selected or to call out to Toucan Claw to choose them. It went without saying that they should simply wait in silence, appearing to be oblivious to the fact that one of them was about to receive a great honor. Toucan Claw's eye stopped at Blue Squirrel, who unlike the other *cahelob* of the clan appeared to be silently begging to be selected. He smiled at Toucan Claw and nodded his head as if the two of them recognized some secret that they had together. Toucan Claw could not think of a worse *cahel* to select. Blue Squirrel was new to the ranks of the *cahelob*, even though he was close to forty years old. He had always fancied himself an intellectual, much to the bemusement of anyone that knew him. He collected taxes and administered labor with unequaled inefficiency. When he and Toucan Claw were young men they had been close friends, and Toucan Claw had once considered him to be an honored confidante. But that was a long time ago. Toucan Claw decided to choose Sharp Blade, a different kinsman who was sitting right next to Blue Squirrel. Sharp Blade was not as close a relative as Blue Squirrel, but he was respected by the entire nobility of the city as a man of great probity and depth of character. Toucan Claw pointed over to Sharp Blade and whispered to the *Ch'ul Ahau*. "Your Lordship, I would select..." Before Toucan Claw finished, Blue Squirrel stood up and shouted. "Thank you, Your Lordship. It is a great honor!"

Whether Blue Squirrel suffered from delusions of grandeur and thus really believed that he had been chosen, or whether he was attempting to steal the honor from Sharp Blade, Toucan Claw would never know. He opened his mouth to clarify his choice, but before he could do so, the *Ch'ul Ahau* had wormed his way over to Blue Squirrel and took an obsidian ax from the bodyguard who accompanied him. Toucan Claw had no choice but to go along with Blue Squirrel's usurpation. At this point issuing a correction would have been tantamount to saying that the *Ch'ul Ahau* had made a mistake, which in this public place was out of the question. So Toucan Claw ground his teeth as Blue Squirrel kneeled before the *Ch'ul Ahau*, who shouted out what amounted to a blessing. "Blue Squirrel, I have selected you to feed the Gods and our ancestors with the blood of the brave warriors from Tikal. Your *ahau* has selected you for this great honor, so take this ax and go."

Blue Squirrel took the ax and looked straight at Toucan Claw, who had never seen him look so happy in his entire life. Blue Squirrel was practically giddy when he answered the *Ch'ul Ahau*. "Thank you for this honor, Your Lordship." The crowd silently made a path for Blue Squirrel as he walked down to the ballcourt. He totally ignored Toucan Claw as he passed. He did not give so much as a nod of recognition or thanks. Toucan Claw knew for certain that moment that this "selection" would be disaster, and that his kinsman would bring dishonor to the clan and to himself by loudly bragging about his role in the sacrifice for years to come.

Once the *Ch'ul Ahau* had retaken his seat next to Jaguar Spot, Blue Squirrel stood behind the first of the Tikal men. The man placed him self on the stone surface with his face straight down and his arms to his sides. He knew exactly what his fate was to be, and knew that there was absolutely nothing that he could do to avoid it. Blue Squirrel raised the ax handle high above his head and brought the obsidian blade down quickly onto the back of the man's neck. The other Tikal men stood silently, as if not even noticing the bleeding head that rolled at their feet. Their fathers, Jaguar Spot thought, had raised them well. Blue Squirrel quickly dispatched the other two men in the same fashion. Palace guards came out to carry away the bodies. Three *ahauob* scrambled down the wall, picked up the dismembered heads, and threw them to the crowd at the top. The crowd started cheering again as the heads were handed from person to person, slowly moving through the crowd. Citizens handed the heads to priests who put them on top of three of the tall wooden stakes. Soon, everyone knew, there would be many more more heads next to them.

At last the time came for Toucan Claw and the *Ch'ul Ahau* to play the day's final game. Jaguar Spot could barely contain his excitement as his father walked down to the ballcourt, but he had been raised too well to show a break in his composure. He sat silently with the *ahauob* and the other eldest sons as the two last Tikal prisoners were brought to the center of the court. The *cahelob* and the commoners started chanting the name of the *Ch'ul Ahau*. "Speaking Macaw, Speaking Macaw Speaking Macaw," they said quietly at first. As the prisoners were brought forward the crowd started screaming the name in unison, while Jaguar Spot and those sitting with him silently regarded the *Ch'ul Ahau* and Toucan Claw. The roar of the crowd was deafening when a priest finally brought out the ball and handed it to the forward Tikal player, Gray Thunder, the brother of Tikal's *Ch'ul Ahau*. This ball was much larger than the others, but the Tikal player served it deep into the Uaxactun backcourt with seeming ease. The ball bounced once and flew up out of the ballcourt where it knocked a woman down to the ground. The referee blew five sharp blows from his trumpet. "Foul ball," the *ahau* next to Jaguar Spot whispered to him, "it is now our serve." Jaguar Spot whispered back to the man, who was a close friend of his father. "Uncle, how does the ball bounce so high? It must weigh more than I do, and those men look so weak." By tradition the eldest sons of the all the *ahauob* called any of the men of that rank "uncle." The *ahau* leaned over and whispered straight into Jaguar Spot's ear. "That is a special ball. Inside it is a man's skull, from a noble of another city who the *Ch'ul Ahau*'s father captured years ago in battle and bested in a ceremonial ballgame. The ball is manufactured around the skull, so it has an air pocket inside. This makes the ball deceptively light, which makes it bounce very far. I doubt that the Tikal player knew that he was playing with such a ball, hence the foul. Now hush! The *Ch'ul Ahau* is going to serve." While the two of them had been whispering, Speaking Macaw had retrieved the errant ball and made his way to the center of the ballcourt. He bounced the ball and hit it with his right forearm. The ball flew far towards the Tikal endzone. It bounced to the left, making any chance of a return impossible. The *Ch'ul Ahau* knew this particular ball very well. He served it with a precision that amazed everyone watching. In five successive serves the *Ch'ul Ahau* was able to best the two brothers from Tikal single-handedly. Toucan Claw only had to stand and watch, although he fully shared in the honor of the victory. Orchid was never as happy in her life as the moment that the game was over without her father suffering any injury.

The two Tikal players, prodded by the spears of palace guards who had come down onto the surface of the ballcourt, slowly walked over to the now blood-drenched spot where their compatriots had been slain.

They both stood and defiantly faced the *ahauob* of Uaxactun. The *Ch'ul Ahau* took a clean ceremonial ax from a nearby palace guard and gave it to Toucan Claw as the crowd quieted down. Toucan Claw walked behind Gray Thunder and put his arm on the captive's right shoulder. Gray Thunder stood there, refusing to submit himself to sacrifice, saying nothing. The nobles and citizens of Uaxactun gasped at the insult to their city and to the *Ch'ul Ahau*. This was unheard of. Captives knew their roles in these rituals as well as anyone. They were hardly in a position to express moral outrage at their fate, as they had almost certainly participated in such sacrifices in their own city with captives from Uaxactun and other places. If they fought the sacrifice, if they resisted, they would die without honor. Not only that, but their defiance would undo all the previous sacrifices of the day, spoiling the blood that had already been spilled, and depriving their departed comrades in arms of an honorable death. If this kept up, the Gods and the ancestors of Uaxactun would go hungry that night.

Speaking Macaw walked up to Gray Thunder and spoke in stern tone. "Why do you dishonor yourself so?" Gray Thunder continued to stare ahead, not even acknowledging the *Ch'ul Ahau's* presence. The *Ch'ul Ahau* started showing his temper. The *ahauob* looked down on him with bewilderment. An *ahau* should always be in control of his feelings, to make his emotions serve him, not the other way around. Now the *Ch'ul Ahau* was on the verge of losing his composure in front of the *cahelob* and the commoners. Did these men from Tikal somehow know of a defect in the *Ch'ul Ahau's* character? Was this part of some master plan to bring shame and humiliation the entire City of Uaxactun? As much as they might want to, it would have meant instant death for any of the *ahauob* to intervene with His Lordship to tell him to snap out of it. All they could do was watch, biting their tongues, hoping against hope that the *Ch'ul Ahau* would not shame the city.

Speaking Macaw showed no sign of calming down. He grabbed Gray Thunder's neck and almost spat in his face as he spoke. "You are an *ahau* of Tikal! Act like it! Be proud of who you are. Be proud of your rank. Show these people that an *ahau* of Tikal can die an honorable death." Gray Thunder simply stood there as if not hearing the *Ch'ul Ahau's* words. Speaking Macaw then seemed to calm down. He turned to Toucan Claw and shook his head in resignation, as if saying that there was nothing that he could do to save the honor of the brothers from Tikal. Speaking Macaw took an obsidian blade from his waist pad and pointed it at Gray Thunder's stomach. He moved forward to whisper. "If you do not lie down, if you do not submit to the sacrifice, if you continue to disgrace yourself and your city in his fashion, I will stab you in the belly right here as we speak. You will lie here, writhing in pain, slowly bleeding to death perhaps until long after sunset, if not for days. Your brother here will not die today. He will remain my captive for years on end. His life will be one of never ending humiliation. He will be led around as if a dog on a leash, tortured, made to stand before young children at festivals as they throw rotten fruit at him and spit in his face. That is what your defiance today will buy you if you choose not to die with honor. It is your choice. Make it now." Speaking Macaw took a step back to give the man room to kneel down and meet his doom, but he still stood there, staring at the horrified *ahauob* of Uaxactun. The *Ch'ul Ahau* motioned to the palace guards and pointed to Fireborn. "Tie that one up and take him to the palace. He will remain our captive. I will have scribes carve stone-trees showing him bound under my feet. Perhaps I will even send one to his dear half-brother back home." The guards pushed Fireborn to the ground and tied his hands and legs together behind his back. They then carried him up the South wall and out of the ballcourt. The *Ch'ul Ahau* waited for them to be out of sight before he again whispered to Gray Thunder. "This is your last chance, old man. Do you really want your brother to live a life of misery and humiliation?" As before, Gray Thunder gave no answer. The *Ch'ul Ahau* whispered to him one last time. "Before I kill you, will you at least tell my why you have decided to disgrace yourself and your comrades in this fashion?"

Gray Thunder looked at the *Ch'ul Ahau* and smirked, which Jaguar Spot thought was not becoming for a man of his age. "Your Lordship," Gray Thunder said in a loud voice, "before this battle I bled myself for the sacrament of purification. I ate the holy mushrooms and I had a vision. It was a vision of unparalleled vividity and depth. The Great Tree spoke to me. It told me that my brother would some day kill you with his own hands. My only regret is that I will not see that day come. Now, if you are going to kill me, why don't you go ahead and get it over with. I grow weary of listening to your girlish voice."

Speaking Macaw thrust the knife into Gray Thunder's belly and let go. Gray Thunder had a face of stone as he fell to the ground. More than two hundred saw that he was in great pain, but he was not about to let the eyes of his enemy have the satisfaction of seeing him suffer. With the face of a stoic, he took the blade from his stomach, putting it to his own throat before Speaking Macaw could stop him. He died almost instantly. A group of priests started walking over to the body, but the *Ch'ul Ahau* stopped them. "Leave his body for the buzzards and the ants," he said to them before turning away and muttering to Toucan Claw. "At least *they* will get some nourishment out of this disgrace."

Chapter Two
SCRIBE APPRENTICE

8.16.13.11.10. July 15, 370 A.D.

"Do you understand the Great Tree, Jaguar Spot?" Master Snail raised his eyebrow as he walked around the room asking random questions to the seven scribe-apprentices who, moments before, had been busy copying pages of the Council Book. The Master liked to burst in to the workshop at irregular intervals to test whether his students were gleaning anything from the texts that they copied. Jaguar Spot looked up from the paper in front of him and put down his brush. The other apprentices were studiously looking at their work, hoping not to catch the Master's eye, lest they be called upon next. Jaguar Spot had learned enough in his five years as one of Master Snail's apprentices to know that you never told the Master that you understood *anything*. A scribe should always be humble, according to Master Snail. Standing up in front of the other scribe-apprentices and professing understanding of the Great Tree, even if true, would not meet Master Snail's expectation of proper humility. Once, two years before, Jaguar Spot had truthfully admitted to Master Snail that he completely understood all the major glyph forms. Thus ensued half a morning's inquisition about the fundamentals of grammar and combining sounds into glyphs. Master Snail's questions had been so hard, and the information he sought so arcane, that the most senior scribes in the city would have had to rack their brains to come up with the right answers. When Jaguar Spot was unable to provide answers to even the most basic of Master Snail's questions, Master Snail heaped piles of scorn on Jaguar Spot's worthiness to be a scribe-apprentice, his ability to read the glyphs, and, for added measure, his general intelligence. Jaguar Spot had seen other scribe-apprentices storm out of the room in tears after receiving such treatment from Master Snail, but he retained his composure. Throughout his childhood he had withstood far worse tongue lashings from his father and his uncles.

Ahauob were never supposed to show weakness at any time. Starting when he was three years old, Jaguar Spot's family had trained him to withstand abuse and insults of all kinds without appearing to take notice of any of it. As a result there was very little that anyone could say to Jaguar Spot that could achieve any type of emotional reaction, and he was thus totally immune to any of the normal insults and taunts that Master Snail used to keep the other boys in line. Jaguar Spot knew this. Master Snail knew this. The other scribe-apprentices knew it. But Master Snail was not a simpleton, and knew how to adapt. After years of failing to humiliate Jaguar Spot by berating him in front of his colleagues, he then switched tactics. Instead of his normal methods, he started giving regular reports to Jaguar Spot's father of the boy's slightest transgressions. Toucan Claw had thus learned of the day that Jaguar Spot had left the workshop early to watch a ballgame. He learned of the day that Jaguar Spot had lost a paintbrush. To Jaguar Spot's horror, his father had even learned of the day that he spilled ink on one of the city's oldest copies of the Council Book, a copy so old, and written in a hand so arcane, that no one could even decipher the name-glyph of the scribe who had originally copied it. Although the anger was unpleasant, Jaguar Spot could deal with his father's reaction to such minor misdeeds. A report of bragging would be quite another issue entirely. Anything so antithetical to the Maya ideal of an *ahau* as a lack of humility or, horror of horrors, self-congratulation, would result in his father expressing *disappointment* in Jaguar Spot. Even the most mild words of disappointment from his father made Jaguar Spot wish that he could fade into invisibility and walk into the forest.

Still, Jaguar Spot knew that to profess absolute ignorance of the subject of the Great Tree would bring far worse than a report of boasting from the Master. After all, he had spent much of the last five years studying everything that had ever been written about the Great Tree. If he said that he knew nothing, Master Snail might very well report this to his father, who would no doubt quiz his son on why he had spent five years studying and yet remained completely ignorant of such an important subject. Jaguar Spot thus had to be careful in his answer.

Master," he said. "The Great Tree is the tie that binds the different worlds together. Its trunk is the path that men take when they go to the Underworld after death . . . ." Master Snail waved his hand and stared at Jaguar Spot until he fell silent. "Jaguar Spot," he whispered, "I did not ask you to give me a rote recitation from some dusty old book. I asked you a yes or no question. Do you understand the Great Tree? Give me a yes or no answer." The other apprentices looked at their work in an even more studious manner than before, which Jaguar Spot would not previously believed to be possible. Jaguar Spot stuttered out an answer to Master Snail. "Master, I think that no one but the Gods completely understands the Great Tree."

Master Snail appeared to think about Jaguar Spot's answer for a couple of breaths and, for the first time in Jaguar Spot's memory, smiled. The other students were only able to see the smile out of their peripheral vision. None of them had ever seen the like before, and most thought that Master Snail was about to take special delight in doing his best to humiliate Jaguar Spot. Knowing that it was more likely than not that they would be next, the other scribe-apprentices waited with nervous anticipation as Master Snail spoke again. "That is a good answer, Jaguar Spot. A very good answer indeed. Tell me though, do you think that *I* understand the Great Tree?"

Jaguar Spot's heart skipped a beat. Apprentices were supposed to revere their masters almost to the point of gods themselves, more even than their fathers, and almost as much as the *Ch'ul Ahau*. And yet, sycophancy did not become the eldest son of an *ahau*. Jaguar Spot answered the Master carefully. "Master, compared to the Gods, not even you understand the Great Tree completely."

Jaguar Spot's heart now raced as he waited for Master Snail's reaction. Master Snail stood in his place, frowned, and looked like he was considering his words before he answered. Jaguar Spot felt as if his heart might explode at any second when the Master finally spoke again. "Very good answer, Jaguar Spot. Most impressive, in fact. I am quite pleased. You may actually be learning something after all." Jaguar Spot felt as if he might collapse in relief as the Master turned to another apprentice and asked a question about the calendar round. Finally, after questioning all seven of his apprentices and expressing no satisfaction with any of their responses other than Jaguar Spot's, he looked over their shoulders and examined their handiwork one by one. Jaguar Spot picked up his brush and resumed copying the Council Book that the Master had set before him four months before. He was less than half finished, but when the work was complete Jaguar Spot would have his own Council Book.

"Very nice work, Jaguar Spot, very nice indeed." The Master sounded genuinely impressed as he looked over the latest folds that Jaguar Spot had finished in the book. "Your glyphs are quite legible and the illustrations are verging, dare I say it, on excellent. I doubt very much that I could do a better job of illustration myself." Jaguar Spot thanked Master Snail for the complement and went back to his work while the Master moved on to the next scribe-apprentice.

Half way between mid-day and sunset Master Snail released his charges and Jaguar Spot walked home. He would have run, but such a public display of impatience would not have become the son of an *ahau*, and numerous citizens of the city would be only too happy to make a personal report to his father in the event of such a transgression. Toucan Claw might even give them a handful of cacao beans as a reward for providing the information. He might even give some cotton cloth. If the person provided information valuable enough, Toucan Claw might be willing just to owe the citizen a favor.

So Jaguar Spot walked as fast as possible into the residential district. By the time he walked two thousand paces he would be home, which would leave him plenty of time to gather his ball clothes and equipment and get to the ballcourt for the afternoon's game. Jaguar Spot had been looking forward to this game for quite some time, as it would be his first with juvenile boys, as opposed to the young children that he had played with for all of his life. Instead of being the oldest player on the court and thus having no way to really test his skills, he would now be playing with larger boys, some of them four years his senior. At last he would finally have a test for his talents. He could think of little else as he walked through the market, although he did notice new paint on a large wall as he walked by. When Jaguar Spot had walked to Master Snail's in the morning, the wall had been covered with the traditional red stucco of the city. There were now ten or so painters and other artisans working on the wall, which was covered with blue paint and an almost finished mural of a ballgame. The artwork was very beautiful, showing four ballplayers in the throes of an epic struggle. Jaguar Spot lost all concentration and stared at the mural as he continued to walk by. One of the men depicted in the mural was clearly the *Ch'ul Ahau*, although the painting made His Lordship appear more handsome than he really was. Jaguar Spot could not recognize two of the others, but he thought that man that the artisans were painting behind the *Ch'ul Ahau* was . . . no it couldn't be . . . could it? He looked closer at the face in the mural and thought that it bore a strong resemblance to . . . his own father! The image was clearly that of a ceremonial ballgame. Could it have been the game where his father and the *Ch'ul Ahau* had bested the brothers of Tikal's *Ch'ul Ahau* some five years before? Probably. After all, the *Ch'ul Ahau* often commissioned public works of art to commemorate his triumphs. As opposed to an ordinary *ahau*, the *Ch'ul Ahau* was expected to gloat over his achievements.

As he reached the end of the wall, Jaguar Spot craned his neck as far as he could for one last look at the mural. It was definitely the *Ch'ul Ahau* and his father. The next thing that Jaguar Spot knew, he was flat on his back, looking up into the sky. He saw the profile of a man looking down at him, apparently the same man that he had just absentmindedly walked into. The glare from Lord Sun obscured the man's features, and before Jaguar Spot could even mouth an apology a pair of large and powerful hands picked him up from behind and pushed him against the newly painted wall. The man who picked him up was, as Jaguar Spot quickly noticed, a palace guard. The guard screamed at Jaguar Spot as he pushed him. "Look where you are going, you little pipsqueak! Your next mistake like that might well be fatal." The man that Jaguar Spot had walked into was standing behind the guard, laughing quietly. Now that he was no longer on his back, Jaguar Spot could see that, gods forbid, he had walked straight into the *Ch'ul Ahau*. Jaguar Spot tried to get down on his knees and bow to His Lordship but the guard was still holding him against the wall, so he stammered out an apology. "Your Lordship, I beg your pardon for my carelessness. . ." As Jaguar Spot hesitantly spit out his words the *Ch'ul Ahau* laughed louder, so loud that Jaguar Spot stopped his apology in mid-sentence. The *Ch'ul Ahau* motioned to the guard to release Jaguar Spot and pulled him away from the wall.

Jaguar Spot felt a sticky wetness on his back. He knew that he would have a lot of explaining to do to his father, not only about walking in to the *Ch'ul Ahau*, but also why he had gotten paint all over a perfectly good set of clothes. The *Ch'ul Ahau* rustled Jaguar Spot's hair and pinched his cheek. Jaguar Spot always hated it when adults did that. Without saying another word the *Ch'ul Ahau* laughed again and walked away with a group of palace guards in tow. The guard who had pushed Jaguar Spot against the wall gave him long glare as he moved off after His Lordship.

Jaguar Spot skulked into his house, his backside covered with the blue paint. He had hoped that his father would be off on business, collecting taxes or something. He had hoped that he might be able to sneak into the kitchen, make his way across the courtyard into his bedchamber, quickly collect his ballclothes and equipment, and sneak out of the house to the ballcourt unnoticed. No such luck. Orchid spotted him when he came through the door of the main hall and immediately started questioning him in a loud voice about why he had blue paint all over his back. Jaguar Spot raised his hands and grimaced in an effort to quiet her down, but she kept questioning him about the paint, and kept getting louder and louder. Finally Jaguar Spot saw his father walking across the courtyard. Toucan Claw walked into the hall in a huff. Or what passed for huff when an *ahau* of the city was involved. Servants long accustomed to their master's moods scattered into the kitchen and other subsidiary halls. To an outside observer, even one of Toucan Claw's closest friends, he would have appeared perfectly calm and collected, not showing so much as a hint of emotion. Those that lived with him knew different. An inflection of voice here, a slight emphasis on a particular word there, or an affect even colder than normal–those were the key signs of anger in a man like Toucan Claw. And once his father got angry there was little, if anything, that could be done to calm him down. Moreover, his ire seemed to be transferable from one person to another without so much as a whim. Jaguar Spot had half a mind to follow the servants and leave the room quietly, but Orchid had a firm grip on his arm.

Toucan Claw's eye turned to Orchid after he lost sight of the fleeing servants. "Daughter, what in the Underworld is that infernal noise that you are making?" For a split second Jaguar Spot thought that he might escape his father's notice and sneak away while his attention was diverted. He started slinking toward the kitchen when his father's attention shifted to him. "Not so fast, boy. What happened to your backside?"

"I was pushed into a wall, Father."

"Pushed?"

"Yes."

"On purpose?"

"Yes."

"By whom?"

"By a palace guard. I don't know his name."

His father's countenance slowly changed. He closed his eyes and took a deep breath. It was obvious to Jaguar Spot and Orchid that he was making an effort to curb his temper and avoid an outburst that he would regret later. "Why," he almost whispered, "did a palace guard see fit to push my son into a wall covered with blue paint? Please tell me that it was some kind of passing fancy on the part of the guard."

Jaguar Spot looked down at his feet as he half-whispered back. "Not on a passing fancy, Father. I . . ." He stopped, unable to finish his statement.

His father's face showed that he was now making a supreme effort to maintain his composure. If he had not been an *ahau*, he would have screamed and beat an answer out of his son, as any father in the city had the right to do. His position would not allow him to do that, not even in his own house. Finally, he opened his eyes and spoke in a calm voice. "What did you do, son? Tell us what you did that would elicit such a reaction in a palace guard."

Jaguar Spot stood there looking as if he was trying to speak. He wanted to tell his father and Orchid what he had done, but no words came out of his mouth. It was as if he was paralyzed by his fear. He knew that the son of an *ahau* was not supposed to let fear stop him from doing anything, that he was supposed to control his fear, and to use it to his advantage, but to know that was not the same as doing it. Finally, he was able to utter a few words. "I, I, I was careless."

His father looked grim. He did not need to say anything to let Jaguar Spot know that there was no option but to provide a full explanation, and quick. Jaguar Spot tried to speak again. "Father, I was walking home from Master Snail's workshop. I was walking through the market when I saw that some men were painting a new mural. I think that you were one of the characters in the mural." Jaguar Spot stopped speaking. It took everything in him to keep from breaking into tears, but years of training from his father had managed to drive the normal instincts of a boy out of him. He stood there mouthing words, but again he was unable to speak. Toucan Claw's expression began to soften. He understood what his son was going through. He had once been the eldest son of an *ahau*. He had vivid memories of standing before Jaguar Spot's grandfather on similar occasions. He was one of the few people in the city with a true understanding of what it was like to grow up with the demands and expectations that everyone put on a boy like Jaguar Spot. "Come on son," he said, "out with it."

"Father, the mural caught my attention. I looked at it while I was walking through the market. I wasn't watching where I was going. I walked straight into him. I fell flat on my back." Jaguar Spot was relieved that he was finally able tell his father what happened. Toucan Claw looked relieved as well, and rubbed Jaguar Spot's hair in the same way the *Ch'ul Ahau* had earlier in the afternoon. "Well boy, there are worst things in the world than walking into a palace guard in the market. Just be more careful in the future. They can have a temper, as is evidenced by the state of your backside." His father started walking out of the room, apparently satisfied with the results of his interview with Jaguar Spot.

Jaguar Spot's instincts told him to leave well enough alone, and to let his father go. After all, maybe the *Ch'ul Ahau* would put it all up to youthful folly and not even speak to Toucan Claw about the incident. His Lordship did not seem all that upset over it. He did laugh, didn't he? Yes, that was it, he laughed. It was nothing. Leave it be. Jaguar Spot's mind raced as his father got closer and closer to the door. On the other hand if his father ever found out the truth he would think that Jaguar Spot had purposefully deceived him. In his upbringing Jaguar Spot could only remember one time when his father had caught him in a lie. There was nothing pleasant about that experience, and Jaguar Spot did not want to go through it again. "Father."

Toucan Claw stopped and turned around.

"Yes, son."

"It wasn't the guard. It was. . It was. . It was the . . . It was the *Ch'ul Ahau*."

Toucan Claw's jaw dropped. Orchid let out a short breath and sat down. Both of them seemed too shocked for words. Embarrassed by the silence, Jaguar Spot kept talking. "I mean, I didn't mean to walk into him. He was just there. He didn't seem angry. He laughed and pinched my cheek . . ." Finally, Toucan Claw raised up his hand to quiet the boy.

"You walked into the *Ch'ul Ahau*?"

"Yes, Father."

"You did this blindly, in the public market?"

"Yes, Father."

"You fell to the ground. Did the *Ch'ul Ahau* also fall?"

"No, Father."

"And this is when the palace guard pushed you into the wall."

"Yes, Father."

"And, as you say, His Lordship did not seem angry, but he was amused?"

"Yes, Father."

"He seemed to recognize you?"

"Oh yes, Father."

"He pinched your cheek?"

"Yes, Father."

"Did he say anything?"

"He told the guard to let me go."

"Anything else?"

"No, Father. He just walked away."

"Walked away?"

"Yes, father. He walked away. Oh, and he laughed."

Toucan Claw turned to Orchid, apparently no longer wanting Jaguar Spot's attention. "Daughter, have your heard our discussion?" Orchid nodded, unable to speak. "Well," Father continued, "I don't think that it is all that bad. It's not like His Lordship was hurt, and according to the boy, His Lordship wasn't even angry. Even so, I will probably face some ribbing from His Lordship in front of the other *ahauob*. This is something that I would like to avoid. I would like to avoid it very much. If we give it a few days His Lordship will probably forget all about it and I can avoid embarrassment." Toucan Claw turned back to his son. "Boy, I think that it is about time that you accompany me on my rounds. Yes, yes, yes. Come to think of it I am days overdue for a tour of the countryside, so as soon as you change we will be off. Orchid," he said, shifting his attention, "we will be gone for a few days. If anyone asks, tell them that I have gone on my rounds, and I have taken the boy with me. Get the boy cleaned up and changed into some suitable clothes. Perhaps a cotton tunic and a feather headdress." With that, his father made an about face and stormed back into the courtyard.

Jaguar Spot called after him. "Father, what about the ballgame?"

Toucan Claw stopped for a moment, as if thinking about turning around to tell his son not to argue with him, but after a moment started walking again without saying a word.

"And what about Master Snail?"

Toucan Claw turned around and came back.

"What did you say, boy?"

"What about Master Snail? He won't like me missing my studies."

Toucan Claw looked down at Orchid, who was still sitting, seemingly immobilized from shock. "Daughter, go. Prepare clothes for your brother and myself." Orchid left the room, staring at Jaguar Spot with a blank look. Once she crossed the courtyard, Toucan Claw walked right next to Jaguar Spot and spoke so that only the two of them could hear.

"Son, I will only say this once, so remember what I say. Snail isn't even a *cahel*. I understand that you are his apprentice, but you must never call him 'Master' anymore, except in his workshop, or when speaking to him directly."

"Father?"

"Son, the eldest son of an *ahau* only has two masters: his father and His Lordship. Even the other *ahauob* are not your lords. Everyone in the City calls the *ahauob* 'Lordship' except for the *Ch'ul Ahau*, the other *ahauob*, and the eldest sons of the *ahauob*. This is why you call the other *ahauob* 'uncle.' It is beneath your station to call Snail 'Master,' except under the circumstances that I have described to you. After all, you will be *his* master some day, just as I am."

"Yes, Father."

Jaguar Spot seemed terrified at the thought of speaking about the Master in anything other than the proper mode of respect expected of an apprentice for his teacher. He said so to Toucan Claw. For the first time that afternoon, Toucan Claw laughed.

"Son," he said, "why have I apprenticed you to Snail?"

"To learn to be a scribe, Father."

"No."

"No?"

"No. I have sent you to him to learn to read and write, and to know what it is to be a scribe, but you will never make your living the same way as your friends in Snail's workshop."

"Father?"

"Son, what is my job?"

"You are an *ahau*. You oversee farms, villages. You collect taxes and make sure that people do their work for the city and His Lordship."

"All *ahauob* do that. What is my specific job for His Lordship, over and above my duties as an *ahau*?"

"You oversee the installation of stone-trees. You make sure that glyphs in murals depicting His Lordship's ancestors and achievements are correct. Oh, I see."

Toucan Claw rubbed his son's hair again, happy that he understood. "Good. Now you understand. I was an apprentice to Snail's grandfather. I can read and write as well as any scribe in the city, yet the only time I actually act as a scribe is to draft the most sacred of texts for His Lordship, and that is on very rare occasions. When I write something, it is at the express command of the *Ch'ul Ahau*, usually a message for him to take into the Otherworld when he is in a trance. Only his most trusted *ahau* can be given the responsibility for such a task. Like me, you will some day perform this duty for the divine lord of this city. You will oversee the stone-trees. You will make sure that the scribes of the city are correct in their listings of His Lordship's achievements. Never forget this. That is why you are training as a scribe. That is the only reason that you are training to be a scribe. Now go and get changed. No ballgame for you today."

Jaguar Spot got up and kissed his father. Thoughts of the ballgame still held his attention, but he knew that whining to his father would not become the eldest son of an *ahau*. He left and went to his room to change his clothes.

When Jaguar Spot returned to the great hall he found that pompous twit Blue Squirrel waiting there with three bags made from red cotton cloth. Cotton was a rare commodity, and Jaguar Spot had never seen it used for anything except fine clothes. Even as the son of an *ahau* he had only one set of cotton clothes, and he was wearing them right now. Even *cahelob* usually did not wear cotton clothes. This was reserved solely for the *ahauob*, their families, and the household of the *Ch'ul Ahau*. Cotton was sometimes even traded as currency, especially when the cacao beans were scarce. And here was a *cahel* of the city with large three bags made of cotton—a treasure in its own right.

Blue Squirrel was fussing inside one of the bags when Jaguar Spot entered the room. The sounds of objects rubbing against each other were easy to hear, but Jaguar Spot could not discern the contents of the bags from listening. It was obvious that Blue Squirrel had not heard Jaguar Spot's approach, as he was still shuffling items inside the largest of the bags. Jaguar Spot stood behind him in silence, trying to catch a glimpse at what he was doing, but the room was dark, and inside of the bag even darker. After a few futile moments of this Jaguar Spot cleared his throat. The *cahel* on the floor in front of him gave a start. He dropped the bag, bolted up, and spun around to face Jaguar Spot in less time than it took to draw one breath. "Oh, it's you!" he said, with relief in his voice, but also a tinge of nervousness. "What I meant to say, of course, is that it's nice to see you, Your Lordship. You gave me quite a fright right there, I'll tell you. You shouldn't sneak up on people like that, Your Lordship! I . . ." Blue Squirrel's voice faded into silence as he looked into the courtyard over Jaguar Spot's shoulder. He pushed past Jaguar Spot, almost shoving him to the ground, and fell to his knees.

Jaguar Spot had just regained his balance when his father entered the great hall. Blue Squirrel immediately started speaking, this time with the nervousness painfully clear in his voice. "Your Lordship, thank you! Thank you! Thank you! This is such an honor! Such an honor! Never since the day that you selected me at the ceremonial ballgame have I had such an honor! The gods have indeed been kind to my house on this day!" Toucan Claw walked past Blue Squirrel without notice. After looking in all three bags Toucan Claw stood up and turned to Jaguar Spot. "Stop that drivel, Blue Squirrel" he said over his shoulder. Blue Squirrel shut up immediately and Toucan Claw looked at his son. "You look fine, boy. You look as the son of an *ahau* should look for such an occasion." While Toucan Claw had been speaking, Blue Squirrel came behind Jaguar Spot and stood there with a dreamy look on his face, as if he were staring into the eyes of one of the Hero Twins and was completely taken by the transcendence of the moment. "And you, my *cahel*," said Toucan Claw, shifting his attention yet again. "What was that nonsense I was just hearing? I have never heard the like from a *cahel* in all my days. Not even the *Ch'ul Ahau* expects, or even desires, such fawning obsequiousness. Loyalty? Yes. Devotion? Certainly. Respect? Definitely. But a display such as I just saw? The day that the *Ch'ul Ahau* or any of the *ahauob* of this City come to expect, or even openly tolerate such a degradation, is the day that me and my family leave for good. If you had acted in such a manner in front of anyone but me and the boy I would have had you stripped of your rank! Do you understand me? Stripped you of your rank!"

"Yes, Your Lordship."

"As it is, I am half inclined to rescind my invitation and take someone else."

"Oh, please don't do that, Your Lordship. I have already told my family. Think of what it would mean to my reputation if you . . ."

"Shut up."

"Yes, Your Lordship."

"I'm serious, Blue Squirrel; I don't know what has gotten into you. To be certain, I have never considered you to be the best of my *cahelob*"

"Yes, Your Lordship. I am certainly not the best."

"Blue Squirrel?"

"Yes, Your Lordship?"

"Shut up and let me talk."

"Yes, Your Lordship."

"As I was saying, even though you are sometimes a sluggard and a nincompoop, you usually know what is expected of a man of your position. But yet I find you on the floor, acting like a dog to which I have just given a choice morsel of meat. Wait. I have it! Holy mushrooms! Yes. That must be it. You have been eating holy mushrooms, haven't you?"

"No, Your Lordship."

"Bloodletting? Is that it? Are you weak from too much bloodletting? Because if you are I will have to select someone else."

"No, Your Lordship. I assure you that I am in perfect physical condition. I fed my ancestors yesterday, but it was a modest amount. I am not weak."

"Then what, pray tell, is the explanation for your behavior? And in front of my son, no less! What is the boy to think? Seeing a *cahel* of the city acting in such a fashion? You have shamed yourself. You have shamed your family. You have shamed me. You have shamed my son. And all of that in the same day! That was quite an achievement even for you. So tell me, what is the explanation?"

"I have none, Your Lordship."

"Then you better come up with one, and quick."

"Perhaps I let my gratitude at Your Lordship's largess take control of me. I realize now that I behaved disgracefully. I apologize to Your Lordship and to your son. I will redouble my efforts to act as a *cahel* should in all of my affairs."

Toucan Claw grunted and carefully inspected all three of the bags. His manner showed that he was not entirely pleased with Blue Squirrel's response, but he chose to say nothing else. Blue Squirrel and Jaguar Spot watched Toucan Claw in silence. When he was finally done he turned back to Blue Squirrel it was as if their conversation had not been interrupted. "And where did you pick that up? That's what I want to know. Where did that come from?"

"Your Lordship?"

"You know what I mean, Blue Squirrel! Don't act like you don't. That nonsense of groveling on the floor like a dog. I have never seen anything like that in you before. Nothing even close. What is the source? Have all the *cahelob* taken to acting is such a fashion without my notice?"

"No, Your Lordship."

"Then what? Pray tell."

"The only explanation that I can give is that I have spent too much time among the common farmers, as Your Lordship directed. Perhaps their country manners have rubbed off on me. I will endeavor to correct it, Your Lordship. Also, if I may say, you have never graced any of the *cahelob* with an invitation to accompany you and your son when you inspect all of your districts. I was quite moved. Almost to tears, Your Lordship."

"Well, keep the tears to yourself. Don't thank me with words. Thank me with the gifts of hard work and efficiency–I seek nothing else from you. I will forgive this transgression. One time only. Don't ask me to do it again."

"Oh no, Your Lordship. Never again."

Throughout the exchange of the adults Jaguar Spot became increasingly uncomfortable at seeing the humiliation of Blue Squirrel, even though he was a man for whom Jaguar Spot had nothing but contempt. True, he had been surprised when Blue Squirrel had fallen to his knees and debased himself. But he had never seen his father deliver such a dressing down at the expense of even a house servant, much less a *cahel*. He wanted to leave the room, but his father would glance at him occasionally, as if to make sure that he was paying attention. Perhaps this was meant to be a lesson.

Toucan Claw gave one bag each to Blue Squirrel and Jaguar Spot. He hoisted the largest bag, almost double the length of Toucan Claw's right arm, over his shoulder and moved toward the front door. "Come on, lets go. Enough of this dawdling," he said and walked out. They wormed their way through the compound of houses belonging to the clan. Every householder that was home stood in front of his house and bowed his head as his *ahau* passed by. Those of the *cahel* rank offered a quiet greeting, usually just "good afternoon, Your Lordship." Those of lesser rank, or no rank at all, stood in silence for Toucan Claw. There were fifty-seven households in the clan compound, all of them owing allegiance to Toucan Claw, either by heritage or by mutual interest. Toucan Claw kept his right hand on Jaguar Spot's shoulder as he walked beside him. While the members of the clan were careful to avoid uninvited eye contact with the *ahau*, they had no reluctance to look at his son. Jaguar Spot felt their eyes on him with every step he took. It was as if they looked straight through his body, seeing every weakness, every fear. He knew that they were surveying him as a future *ahau* of the city, as *their* future *ahau*.

None too soon for Jaguar Spot's taste, they left the compound and walked in the comparative anonymity of a public street near a market.

Of course many of the citizens of the city personally knew Toucan Claw. Those that did not recognized his clothing and thus knew his rank. Everyone gave the respect due to a man of his position, but seeing an *ahau* was an everyday occurrence, and Jaguar Spot did not notice any special attention paid to him or his father. Nonetheless, with every new face he saw, with every person that came into view, Jaguar Spot prayed to the Hero Twins that he would not see one of the palace guards approaching. The thought of coming across the *Ch'ul Ahau* was too terrifying for him to even consider. Although Jaguar Spot did not know it, a similar uneasiness had befallen his father. With every step, Toucan Claw silently prayed to every god that he could think of that the face of the *Ch'ul Ahau* or one of the *ahauob* would not materialize in the distance.

Reputation, dignity, and service to the city. These were the touchstones of Toucan Claw's life, the centers of his universe. He would have gladly sacrificed a year's collection of taxes rather than see his son the brunt of a joke on the lips of the *ahauob*. As the three traveled north out of the market area and people became increasingly scarce, his fears finally began to subside. Finally the houses, small temples and occasional shrines that they had been passing for a few thousand paces dwindled in number until they faded into virtual nonexistence. The road became a narrow track, with barely enough room for two people to pass. At last they had reached the fields, canals and open swampland that marked the beginning of Uaxactun's farm country.

Compared to the city this was a silent land, virtually without noise of any kind. Jaguar Spot heard little other than the group's footsteps and the calls of birds as he passed field after field planted with maize and beans. From time to time there would be sound of activity, but with the plants high and almost ready for harvest, not even the farmers had much occasion to do anything that would make much noise. Those farmers that were tending the crops, at least the few that Jaguar Spot could see, turned toward he and his father and bowed their heads. Other farmers continued to toil in the heat, seeming not to notice the passing of a high nobleman and his small entourage.

After they were in the open country for a while, the fields to the right of the track dwindled into nonexistence and they saw swampland ahead, thick with small plants and trees. The calls of the birds were becoming more numerous, and the air became thick with moisture. Toucan Claw led his son and his *cahel* off the track to the edge of the swamp. One hundred or so men were laboring in the swamp or on its periphery, digging, dredging, and felling trees. Jaguar Spot saw the beginnings of a canal forming where the land met the water's edge. They walked up to a *cahel* who was overseeing the work. Jaguar Spot had seen him before in passing, but did not know his name. He was a *cahel* of lesser rank, not under the direction of Toucan Claw, although they seemed to know each other well enough to be on friendly terms.

His name turned out to be Mak. He was a *cahel* in the clan of Buried Tapir, who was probably Toucan Claw's best friend among the *ahauob*. Jaguar Spot had seen Buried Tapir on a regular basis ever since he could remember. He came over to the house at least once a week to speak to Toucan Claw, although lately they had been meeting far more often, meetings conducted in secret, in far off recesses of the family home. A week before, Jaguar Spot had walked in on them by accident, searching for some trinket for Orchid. From the little that Jaguar Spot could hear, they sounded like they were negotiating over something, but when he entered the room both men fell into silence. They refused to continue their discussion until Jaguar Spot found what he was looking for and left.

Mak and Toucan Claw walked off south and spoke among themselves. Like the incident with his father and Buried Tapir, Jaguar Spot could not tell what they were talking about specifically, but it sounded like a business transaction. Blue Squirrel took it upon himself to show Jaguar Spot the work that the men were doing clearing the swamp, digging canals, and creating farmland. Apparently he had been doing a similar job overseeing swamp clearing for Toucan Claw over the past few years. He waved his arm at the farm fields to the south of them. "Does Your Lordship see all of these fields?" he asked. "I see nothing else," Jaguar Spot replied. "Good, good," Blue Squirrel chuckled, "all of these fields were once swamp like this. All of them. Men like me and Mak cleared them for men like your father and the *Ch'ul Ahau*. We cleared them, and now men like your father have all of this farmland. Such incredible wealth." Blue Squirrel's speech faded into a mumble as he spoke in an almost wistful tone. They stood there silently surveying the farm fields. Blue Squirrel sighed, and Jaguar Spot thought that he could hear him whisper: "such wealth, such incredible wealth."

Lord Sun was starting to set when Toucan Claw and Mak returned from their discussions. The men working on the swamp had already gone home to their families, and Mak invited the travelers to his country home for the night. The house was a simple affair, typical for a *cahel*'s house in the country. Jaguar Spot knew that Mak would have a proper home in the city where his family lived. This house was more typical of what a country farmer would live in. Its walls were adobe, without even the traditional red stucco of the city. The roof, like almost every roof that Jaguar Spot had ever seen, was thatch. There was a cook fire in the center of the room, burning in a pit dug into the house's dirt floor. Jaguar Spot had never seen a dirt floor in the city. Even the homes of the city's poorest had foundations of stone, with the floor raised above the house's surroundings by more than the length of a grown man's forearm.

A teenage daughters of one of Mak's workers came in to cook their dinner. Her brother came along to act as chaperone. Mak quietly explained to Jaguar Spot that the he and the teenagers' father got along quite well. When the boy first accompanied the girl Mak went to their father and told him that he could trust a *cahel* of the city not to violate one of his men's daughters. The boy should be out on the work crews with his father. Mak whispered to Jaguar Spot that the father agreed, but said that his daughter was very beautiful. Mak admitted that she was lovely, but said that he was quite too busy to flirt with a child. The father again agreed with his *cahel*, and said that under normal circumstances he would have no compunction about trusting the girl to Mak. However, he had to consider her physical beauty. Many men, if left to their devices, would have tried to rob the girl of her virtue, especially a man who had to leave his wife and family for weeks on end. Mak relented. He needed a cook more than he needed the boy to work in the swamps, and he could not force the man to send his daughter into another man's house without a chaperone. Mak told Jaguar Spot that he believed that the father silently hoped that Mak's loneliness would cause him to fall in love with the girl, and that he would come to the father and ask to take her as his second wife. The father would then demand a high dowry, as if the increase in the family's social standing would not be enough compensation for the loss of his daughter.

The girl took some ground maize flower that she mixed with water to make tortillas, which she fried on a cook-stone next to the fire. On another stone she cooked some fish, which she put into a bowl with chilies and honey. Mak poured maize beer for everybody out of a large jug as the girl handed them the food. Once she and the boy left, Jaguar Spot and the others started eating.

The food was excellent, much different from what Jaguar Spot was used to in the city. Mak explained that the fish had been caught that afternoon from one of the canals running through the farmland. He expounded that this was one of the main food sources for the farmers in the area. For a while after that they munched their food in silence. Jaguar Spot was the first one done with his meal. "Father," he said, "Blue Squirrel and I were talking about what we saw today."

"What we saw?" asked Toucan Claw with food in his mouth, looking at Blue Squirrel. "Tell me, my *cahel*, what exactly did you say to my son about the things that we saw today?"

Blue Squirrel nodded his head in excitement, as if he thought that his *ahau* was praising him for assisting in the education of his son. "Yes, Your Lordship. It is quite interesting, what we saw. The fields, the crops. Oh the crops. Such a bounty, such a continual source of wealth and power. I explained to Master Jaguar Spot that these fields around here are the true source of the *Ch'ul Ahau's* wealth, and the wealth of the *ahauob* as well. A lesson well learned, if I may say so myself."

Toucan Claw looked at Blue Squirrel in silence as he ate the last of his tortilla, which seemed to take forever. He took a long drink of the maize beer before he spoke to Jaguar Spot, ignoring Blue Squirrel. "All the fields that we have seen, every one of them, belong to the *Ch'ul Ahau*. That's a lot of farmland, wouldn't you agree?" he asked.

"Yes, Father."

"It is the main source of his wealth, the crops from these fields. But the land itself gives him no wealth at all."

"I don't understand, Father."

"No, I expect that you don't. I *am* surprised that Blue Squirrel shares your lack of understanding. I would think that a *cahel* would have more sense than to think that the land gives the *Ch'ul Ahau*, or me for that matter, any wealth at all."

Blue Squirrel was aghast. To his mind, he had given quite a sensible explanation, one that should have served to engender respect. Instead, here he was sitting in the home of that idiot Mak having his *ahau* call him nothing short of a halfwit. And to make matters worse, there was Mak looking at him with that smug look on his face. That smug look of superiority that he always had. That look that Blue Squirrel had been forced to endure for years on end every time that he had seen him, whether at the ballgame, in the market, or just passing on the street. My how he hated that man. And there he was, present at another moment of humiliation. This was almost too much to bear. "Your Lordship!" Blue Squirrel croaked, "Why do you defame me so?"

Toucan Claw finished his beer while looking straight at Blue Squirrel. He handed the bowl to Mak, who refilled it and handed it back. Toucan Claw took another drink, never taking his eyes off of his *cahel.* After finishing off half the bowl he looked at Jaguar Spot, not bothering to respond to Blue Squirrel's plea. "Tell me son, what did you see after we left the city?"

"I saw maize. I saw beans. I saw farmers. I saw the men in the swamp."

"Ah, there is you answer. Farmers. Men in the swamp. Tell me, why do these men work the fields? Why do they dig in the swamp?"

"I don't know."

Blue Squirrel laughed and rested his right hand on the boy's shoulder. Here he saw his chance for redemption, his chance to save himself in the eyes of his *ahau.* "Oh come now," he said, "even a child should know that. They do so because they have to. Because they owe the *Ch'ul Ahau* and the city a certain amount of service each year, payable in labor or money. What His Lordship is telling you is that the labor of these farmers is the source of the *Ch'ul Ahau's* wealth."

Again all of them fell into silence as Toucan Claw took another long drink of maize beer, finishing off his second bowl. He wiped his mouth with the back of his forearm before he broke the silence. "Blue Squirrel, sometimes you can say the most idiotic things. Please leave the education of my son to myself and those in whom I choose to entrust it. And when I refer to 'those in whom I trust,' that group does not include yourself. Do you understand?"

"Your Lordship?" Blue Squirrel had now passed from being aghast to a state verging on terror. It showed. He knew it showed. He saw that the idiot Mak now had a look on his face verging on gloating.

"Stop trying to put ideas into the boy's head," Toucan Claw answered. "Do you understand me?"

"Yes, Your Lordship," said Blue Squirrel, now looking as if all hope of redemption had been lost. He had lost face in front of his *ahau.* He had lost face in front of the boy. And to make matters worse, far worse in fact, he had lost face in front of that insufferable, intolerable, Mak. He was sure that Mak would spread stories about this disgrace among the other *cahelob*, and that soon he would be a laughingstock. Him! A laughingstock! He, whom the *Ch'ul Ahau* and Toucan Claw had honored in the ballgame against the prisoners from Tikal years before! He, who had managed an entire farming district for Toucan Claw for the past two years, and had done so very well, thank you very much! If *anyone* deserved to be a laughingstock it was that idiot Mak! And to add insult to injury, he had no idea what he was supposed to have done. "But, what did I say that gave offense to Your Lordship?" he asked.

"You understand nothing of the matters on which you choose to educate my son. You try to fill his head with idiotic tripe."

"Oh. I see, Your Lordship."

"You see nothing."

"Yes, Your Lordship."

"Tell me, do these men that we saw today have a choice whether they provide labor or taxes to the *Ch'ul Ahau*? Or for one of the *ahauob* if they tend other lands? What if they simply said 'no, I won't do it.'?"

"They wouldn't. Everyone knows that." Blue Squirrel looked around the room for support. Toucan Claw was staring him straight in the eye with the same expressionless look that he always had in such situations. Mak was now looking at the floor, embarrassed that a *cahel* was making such a fool of himself. Blue Squirrel took it as a lame attempt by Mak to hide his laughter. Jaguar Spot was looking at his father, as if Blue Squirrel was not even in the room. Blue Squirrel was desperate. He had to try to find a way out of his predicament. He adopted an almost pleading tone with Toucan Claw. "After all, you and the other *ahauob* wouldn't let them farm their land anymore. They can only farm at your sufferance. They would be outcasts. They would have to leave the boundaries of the city."

Toucan Claw continued his iron lock on Blue Squirrel's eyes as he dissected his argument. "They wouldn't. That's what you say? That's your answer? They wouldn't stop doing the work and paying the taxes. As simple as that. They wouldn't. Actually, now that I think about it, it is not a bad answer." Blue Squirrel started to look relieved. Finally there was a potential light at the end of the tunnel.

Toucan Claw continued. "You say that they wouldn't refuse to do the work, or pay the taxes. They just . . . wouldn't. True. Very true. After all, the *Ch'ul Ahau* wisely governs the city, does he not? He makes the expected sacrifices to the Gods and to his ancestors, as well he should. He has good relations with the Otherworld. He trades wisely with other cities and with those who live as far away as the Valley of Mexico. We have plentiful obsidian. Even the common people sometimes get stingray spines so they can feed their ancestors with a small pinprick. The rains come when we need them. The rains stop when they are supposed to. And we have had numerous victories in battle. In short, life in our city is good. But what if none of this were true? What if we had a bad *Ch'ul Ahau*? What if we had year after year of drought and famine? What if our city went into a state of decay? Would our loyal citizens continue to provide the labor if that happened?"

Blue Squirrel's mouth opened and closed, but not a sound emanated from his throat. He looked as if he had been hit on the head with a blunt object, and had yet to recover from the blow. Toucan Claw's words bordered on heresy. They were certainly no less. To imply that some day the Gods might no longer favor Uaxactun? This was not only heresy, it was verging on treason. He had never heard the like spoken by a common farmer, much less an *ahau* of Toucan Claw's standing. Still staring at Blue Squirrel, Toucan Claw asked him to answer the question.

"I cannot ever imagine that happening, Your Lordship. To even speak of such a thing . . . I can't do it."

"Answer me, Blue Squirrel. Tell me what would happen. Tell me now."

It was Jaguar Spot who stepped in to rescue Blue Squirrel from the ever deepening hole that he had been digging himself. "Father," he said, "I think that I can answer that question." Without taking his eyes off of Blue Squirrel, Toucan Claw nodded his ascent.

"Father, I think that they might not do the work. I think that many would leave."

Toucan Claw smiled in satisfaction as he had gotten his son to understand his point when a *cahel* many years his senior was still befuddled. "Exactly," he said, closing his eyes in satisfaction. "And never forget it. Power, wealth, nobility, all these things come from one source. A leader must provide those under him with something that they want, something that they *need*, in return for their loyalty. This is true for our *Ch'ul Ahau*. It is true for me. It will someday be true for you. If you don't give them what they need, they will leave. They might need food during tough times. They might need protection from marauders. They might just need their spirits lifted when all hope seems lost. Once you stop, once you forget your purpose as a leader, once you no longer provide them with that special intangible *thing* that they need, they will just walk away. They will pick up and leave the city. It has happened before. There are whole cities in the jungle, deserted, their temples defaced, their palaces abandoned. I have seen these places. With my own eyes I have seen them. I have walked down boulevards lined with great houses and monuments where no one treads anymore except the beasts of the forest.

The buildings are covered with plants and trees and dirt. The holy places are no longer even holy. The inner sanctums of the temples are no longer even pathways into the Otherworld. The temples have been subjected to the rituals of de-sacrament."

Blue Squirrel had never heard of anything so awful in his life. The very thought...unimaginable. He started breathing quickly, the images of lost and deserted cities floating through his head. "Your Lordship," he whispered "please tell me that Your Lordship is pulling my leg. Please tell me that Your Lordship is mocking my ignorance by telling a tall tale. This cannot be true. Please tell me that this is not true." Blue Squirrel was now on the verge of tears. He now spoke in a soft whisper. "Please, please, please."

Toucan Claw looked over at Mak and nodded. Mak now spoke. "It is true, my friend. I have seen these places too. It is just as His Lordship says, whole cities, deserted. No voices, no children, no ballgames, nothing except desolation." Blue Squirrel now closed his eyes and held his head in his hands. His whisper now became horse. "This is unimaginable. Horrific. What happened to the people? Where did they go?"

Toucan Claw raised his hand to silence Mak, who was about to answer. He answered instead. "A good question, my *cahel*. What of the people? That is the true question, the true lesson that my son needs to learn. Their fate varies. Some of them moved to other cities where they found leadership more to their suiting. Some of them chose to live in squalor in the jungle, without a city, without a *ch'ul ahau*, without anyone to perform the proper rituals and sacrifices. This is the result of bad leadership, the result of lax self-discipline on the part of the ruling classes. This is what every *ahau* must avoid. Hundreds of years of men's labor can come to nothing within the space of a generation, or even less time."

Jaguar Spot looked over at Blue Squirrel. The *cahel* now seemed to have almost passed into a trance, a trance deeper than any that Jaguar Spot had ever seen, deeper even than those from bloodletting or eating holy mushrooms. Blue Squirrel finally looked up after more than thirty breaths passed, tears streaming from his eyes. "I must thank Your Lordship," he said. "I must thank you most sincerely for this lesson. I will not forget it. I promise you that."

Toucan Claw grinned; the broadest smile that Jaguar Spot remembered seeing for quite some time. "There may be hope for you yet, my *cahel*. There may be hope for you yet."

Chapter Three
THE SECRET

8.16.13.11.11. July 16, 370 A.D.

Jaguar Spot woke up early in the morning, when everyone else in Mak's house was still asleep. He rose as quietly as he could to go outside and relieve himself. Toucan Claw slept on his back on the only sleeping mat in the house, Mak having given up his usual sleeping place for his distinguished visitor. Mak and Blue Squirrel were sleeping on the floor near the door. Jaguar Spot had to step over them. The air was already hot outside, even though Jaguar Spot could barely perceive the first faint glimmers of dawn in the sky to the East.

Jaguar Spot could hear stirring coming from most of the neighboring houses. No one in the city ever got up this early unless they absolutely had to. Here, it seemed that everyone leapt into industry long before Lord Sun showed his face for the day. Strange people, these farmers.

Mak was up and outside the house when Jaguar Spot returned. "Ah, Your Lordship," he whispered. "You are up early. It is good to see. Too often sons of the *ahauob* are so lazy and indolent that they don't wake up before the workers here take their midday meal. And here you are, up before Lord Sun. Your Father will be proud when I tell him. And I assure you, I *will* tell him the first thing when I see him. You must be up because you want to see how I get the men ready for their work for the day, yes? So admirable in a young man. Come, come. Follow me and I will show you everything." Mak walked over to a nearby house and beckoned Jaguar Spot to follow. What Jaguar Spot really wanted to do was to go back to sleep, but Mak had not let him get a word in edgewise. He stood there, watching Mak walk away, hoping that the *cahel* would forget about him and just go about his morning routine. When Mak got about 50 paces away, he turned around and saw that Jaguar Spot had not moved a single step. He quietly came back and pulled on Jaguar Spot's arm. "Come, come Your Lordship. You will miss the best part of the day." Jaguar Spot knew what his father's response would be if he broke free from Mak's grip and went back to the house for some more rest. Not only would his father have thought that Mak's idea was a good one, but more importantly he would have skinned Jaguar Spot alive for showing anything even approaching rudeness to a *cahel.* "But, but . ." was all that Jaguar Spot could manage to say as Mak pulled him along, no longer whispering as they got farther from his house. "Oh come on, Your Lordship, no need to be shy," Mak said. "I know, you must be worried that the men will be embarrassed that the son of an *ahau* sees their humble dwellings, but nothing could be further from the truth. They are proud of their houses out here in the country. Still, I must admit that your worries about the feelings of the farmers here is a credit to your clan. Come on, Your Lordship, I don't want to keep the men waiting."

Mak's increasingly common references to Jaguar Spot's sterling character were making it harder and harder for Jaguar Spot to figure out a way to escape, but just as they were about to enter one of the larger houses in the area he came up with an idea. "But sir," he said. "What about my father? If I am missing when he wakes up, won't he be concerned about my absence?" Mak stopped pulling Jaguar Spot and let go of his arm. He rubbed his chin and mumbled something so low that Jaguar Spot could barely make it out. "Hmmm," he said mostly to himself. "Young Master Jaguar Spot has a pretty good point. I could have one of the women tell His Lordship Toucan Claw about our whereabouts when he wakes up. But no. The women will be gone at the cacao plantation all day, and I can't waste the manpower to have one of the men wait around to deliver the news. Hold on! I have an idea! Yes! Yes, that might just work." Mak looked down at Jaguar Spot. "Am I correct in remembering that Your Lordship is a scribe-apprentice?"

"Yes," answered Jaguar Spot.

"And, of course, Your Lordship can read and write the glyphs?"

"Yes."

"And His Lordship your Father is the *ahau* responsible for all the scribes in the City, yes?"

"Yes, everybody knows that."

"Then there is our answer!"

"I beg your pardon?"

"You will write a . . . oh what is the word I am searching for, a. . .a message, yes, a message for His Lordship telling him where we have gone. I will leave it where he will see it."

Jaguar Spot was intrigued. As far as he knew, glyphs were inscribed on monuments to commemorate the accomplishments of a city's leaders or to establish their lineage. Glyphs were sometimes glazed onto pottery, usually to commemorate a date or something similar. Of course they were written into books of tree bark paper so that the priests and the nobility could have a reference and a depository of their knowledge. Sometimes the *Ch'ul Ahau* would have Toucan Claw write a prayer on a piece of bark paper so that he could take it with him into the Otherworld. All of these uses for the glyphs were well known and widely accepted. What Mak was suggesting, on the other hand, was unknown, at least to Jaguar Spot.

To use the glyphs to relay a particular message from one person to another person in order to eliminate the need for face-to-face conversation or a human intermediary–what a fascinating idea. At once, all kinds of ideas spilled into Jaguar Spot's mind. Writing could be used to relay a message across the city, or even between cities. Merchants might be able to actually hire a scribe to write down their agreements, instead of just scrawling numbers in the dirt. He would have to tell Master Snail of this idea when he got back to the city. Mak's plan did seem to have one flaw. He had no paper, brush, or ink. Mak was nonplussed. "I have already thought of that, Your Lordship. Come inside and I will show you what to do."

The house that Mak led him into was little different from Mak's own country house, except for its larger size. The thatch roof was supported by four solid beams of a dark wood, which Jaguar Spot thought to be mahogany. The walls, which formed a circle, were made of narrow slats of wood, which were separated with gaps and openings to assure ventilation. Sleeping mats, which Jaguar Spot knew had just recently covered almost the entire floor as the family slept, were now stacked in a neat pile next to the wall. There was a fire pit in the center, surrounded by three large flattened stones. There were nets and baskets hanging from the ceiling, filled with food and tools. Inside, a family of eight was preparing for the day. Two girls, not more than ten years old, were starting a cook fire. Another girl and a woman in early middle-age, presumably the children's mother, were preparing maize dough for tortillas. Three boys, ranging from about five to thirteen, sat with their father carving something out of a large block of wood, about two foot lengths by four foot lengths, and one foot length thick. Upon seeing Mak enter the house, the entire family immediately stood up and faced Mak and Jaguar Spot. "Sir!" the father said, looking at Mak. "Your Lordship!" he said, noticing Jaguar Spot's clothes. "You honor us with your presence. Will you join my family for breakfast?"

"The honor is ours, citizen" replied Jaguar Spot. Mak looked at Jaguar Spot, and with a nod of approval led Jaguar Spot over to some chairs and a wooden table. One of the girls soon brought over the tortillas and some unknown meat, and the entire family joined Jaguar Spot and Mak for the meal. The boys and their father sat or knelt around Jaguar Spot, the boys staring at him. Mak and the father were having a general conversation about the upcoming work for the day when the middle of the three boys, who was about eight years old, spoke to Jaguar Spot. "Are you an *ahau*? Where is your umbilicus buried?" he asked. Before Jaguar Spot could answer, the boy's father slapped the boy across the face. "You call him 'Your Lordship,'" he said. "Do you understand, you don't just talk to him as if he were a common citizen. He is nobility. His father is an *ahau*, and not just any *ahau* at that. Remember that; always call any of the *ahauob* and their sons 'Your Lordship' just as you call Mak or any of the *cahelob* 'Sir.'"

The boy's father was visibly shaking as he spoke. At first, Jaguar Spot thought that it was out of anger, but it quickly became clear that he was shaking out of fear. The man turned to Jaguar Spot and got on his knees. "Your Lordship," he whispered, "please take no offense at my son's slight. He is a good boy, and I will punish him for this transgression. Please hold my family harmless from your ire and exact any vengeance that you have on me and me alone."

Jaguar Spot looked at Mak, but his face showed as little emotion as if it were made from solid obsidian. He could see no hint of feelings there. He looked back at the father, who was now prostrate on the floor. "Citizen," said Jaguar Spot. He didn't know what to say. "Citizen," he repeated, then stopped. He looked again over at Mak, who still showed no emotion whatsoever. He looked back at the father, who was still face down on the ground, crying. He looked around at the family, all of whom were looking at the ground. The mother let out a sob, and one of her daughters tried to comfort her, putting her arm around her back. "Citizen," Jaguar Spot said again, "I don't understand. Why are you on the floor? Why is your wife crying? Mak, what is going on here?" Mak was still exercising his extreme self-control and showed not even a hint of feeling as he replied. "Your Lordship, this man is worried that you will have him beheaded and fed to Lord Crocodile. Or worse, that you will have his son taken to the city and sacrificed in the manner of an orphan, to feed the Gods. He awaits Your Lordship's decision. It is a hard decision for anyone to make, much less a boy of your age. But you must announce what you have decided. I hope that I am not being presumptuous when I beg Your Lordship not to make any rash decisions."

"Mak," Jaguar Spot asked, "is this about the boy forgetting to call me 'Your Lordship'?"

"Of course, Your Lordship."

"And this man thinks that I will have him killed for this, or have his son killed?"

"Of course, Your Lordship."

Jaguar Spot was very confused. He knew that the unwritten laws of Uaxactun required all citizens to afford the nobility the expected salutations of respect. This was why the *ahauob* and their sons wore distinctive clothing. On occasion he had seen people forget to use the proper terms of respect when speaking to his father. A gentle throat clearing here, a noted raising of an eyebrow there, or some other kind of unspoken reminder was the only action that Jaguar Spot had ever seen his father take. It was the only thing that ever needed to be done, and it always worked. Now, these people thought that this relatively minor transgression was a capital offense. There was something very wrong in this place. "Citizen," Jaguar Spot said and then turned to Mak, "Mak, I don't want to have anyone killed. I don't want to have anyone punished. This man's apology was more than adequate, although even that was probably not necessary. Sir, please stand up and finish your breakfast."

When the man got up, Jaguar Spot believed that he had never seen such a feeling of relief in his entire life. Everyone except Mak resumed eating breakfast. Mak sat there and looked at Jaguar Spot for a while, with that same stone-faced expression. He then left. The boys were still staring at Jaguar Spot, although now they were joined by the entire family. Soon no one ate, no one drank, they just stared at Jaguar Spot. He could not discern what emotion this family was feeling, and the looks on their respective faces were almost as blank as Mak's had been. Jaguar Spot felt very uncomfortable, so he spoke to the child that had asked him if he was an ahau. "To answer your question," he said, "I am not an *ahau*. My father, Toucan Claw, is an *ahau*. My umbilicus is buried in my father's house in the city, where I was born." The boy just sat there and stared at Jaguar Spot, along with the rest of his family, in silence. Because he hated the silence, Jaguar Spot kept talking. "Citizen, this is a very impressive home you have here. Very . . . clean, yes, very clean. The food is . . . good, yes, good. Your daughters make very good tortillas." The family still sat there in silence, not taking their eyes off of Jaguar Spot. Finally, Mak came back in the house with a cylindrical pot. He stopped at the fire and picked up a cold piece of charcoal and placed both items on the table in front of Jaguar Spot. "Here," he said. "Your Lordship can use this charcoal to write a message on this pot, which we will leave for your father."

Jaguar Spot picked up the pot and rubbed the surface with his hand. It was certainly smooth enough to write on, but he had never before used charcoal on pottery to make glyphs. He took the charcoal and wrote a line on the bottom of the pot. The line was legible and perfectly straight. There were various styles of glyph writing that Jaguar Spot had learned. Portions of the Council Book were written the same way that a man would tell a story to his children. Jaguar Spot could read those portions aloud, and it was just as if he were speaking naturally. Other portions of the Council Book were more like lists, describing good days and bad days. Jaguar Spot decided on the third style of writing that he had seen, but had not had much occasion to actually write himself. This was the writing found on the great stone-trees, monuments and buildings of the city, describing the military victories and the other great deeds of great men. He hoped that his father would not be offended by this whimsical, and almost satirical, use of the ancient writing. With the charcoal he wrote the following message.

"8.16.13.11.10 12 Ok 8 Sotz'

Jaguar Spot, son of great *ahau*

Toucan Claw.

Left before Lord Sun.

Seeking knowledge.

Cahel Mak.

Takes the son away.

Off to the fields.

Toucan Claw will follow."

Jaguar Spot handed the pot to Mak, who inspected it. "This is beautiful, Your Lordship," Mak said. "My knowledge of reading is very limited. I have never seen glyphs like this before. Are they different from the normal writing that I have seen?" Jaguar Spot asked the woman of the house to give him some dry corn meal, which he spread over the table. "Mak, I will show you," he said. Jaguar spot drew the outlines of several glyphs in the cornmeal on the table. "Here, this is the glyph for the word 'mountain,' do you recognize it?" The glyph that Jaguar Spot pointed to showed the face of a monster with his eyes closed, which was meant to be the personified mountain monster. Mak gave a tentative nod of understanding. Jaguar Spot continued. "Of course, the word 'mountain' can have several different meanings, such as 'hill', or even 'temple.' So, to be more precise, I put the sound symbol 'mo' over the monster face. Since 'mountain' is the only word associated with the symbol that starts with the sound 'mo,' anyone reading this glyph will know what it means. Do you understand?" Mak now looked confused. "But Your Lordship, what you have written on the pottery looks nothing like this." Jaguar Spot nodded. "Exactly! Here I have strung the symbols for the sounds together to sound out the words. It is a longer form of writing that takes more space, so we generally only use it for very important inscriptions when we seek extra precision." Mak let out a "huh" of astonishment and turned around to leave the house with the pot under his arm. Before he left, he came back and whispered in Jaguar Spot's ear. "His Lordship your father is right when he tells me that you are a child of special intelligence and ability. He is right to be as proud of you as he is." Mak stood up and left the house as the father and the boys started gathering tools from the nets hanging from the ceiling. The woman and her daughters gathered and inspected some strange tools that Jaguar Spot had never seen before. Just as he was about to ask what they were, Mak came back in. "Come on, Your Lordship, it is time to make our way to the swamp. I need to get there before everyone else to decide what work needs to get done today." Jaguar Spot barely had time to thank the family for their hospitality when Mak dragged him by the arm out of the house.

The sky to the East was almost totally light, although the Lord Sun had not yet appeared. Jaguar Spot could see fires through the walls of all the houses except Mak's, and the sounds coming from the houses indicated that the little village was coming to life for day. The village was next to the edge of the forest. Instead of taking Jaguar Spot over to the fields where the men had been working on clearing the swamp the day before, Mak led Jaguar Spot down a path into the forest. The air was dark and heavy as they went deeper and deeper into the woods. With the light of the day starting to stream in through the tops of the trees, Jaguar Spot saw a pair of macaws sitting on a tree branch about twenty feet away. He had never seen a macaw so close. They were so *big*. And so *red*. Jaguar Spot had seen macaw feathers on his father's headdress almost every day, but they were pallid compared to seeing the animals themselves in the forest. Jaguar Spot stopped Mak and pointed to the birds. "Look, macaws! They are beautiful." Mak pushed Jaguar Spot along the trail, telling him that they had no time to stop and look at birds. After another few thousand paces, Mak stopped at a small stone-tree that someone had placed beside the path. Every other stone-tree that Jaguar Spot had ever seen was roughly the height of a grown man, sometimes almost twice as tall, and covered with glyphs and images. This one was only as tall as a ten year old boy. "There," Mak said, pointing at the stone-tree, "do you see that glyph, Your Lordship?" The stone-tree was covered with two large glyphs, almost twenty times larger than normal. The top glyph was the emblem glyph for the city of Uaxactun, the only glyph that even the most illiterate citizen would know. Jaguar Spot had seen this glyph virtually every day of his life as far back as his memory went. As the symbol of the Uaxactun city-state, the glyph appeared all over the city, and in every town of consequence in the area ruled by the *Ch'ul Ahau*. The glyph marked the borders, it marked royal property, and it symbolized the power of the *Ch'ul Ahau*. Thus, whatever lay ahead had to be the property of the *Ch'ul Ahau* and of the City itself. Underneath the emblem glyph was an emphatic symbol for death, not so much a glyph as a talisman denoting a forbidden zone. Anyone who came across this small stone-tree would know that to continue down the path without the consent of the *Ch'ul Ahau* was a serious offense, meriting a sentence of death.

While the meaning of the stone-tree was clear enough, Jaguar Spot had never seen the like before. There were plenty of places in the city where he was not supposed to go, but neither he nor anyone else needed reminding of that fact. A person just *knew* that they were not supposed to go into the royal palace, or someone else's house, without permission. Whatever lay on the other side of the stone-tree must have been of such great importance that the *Ch'ul Ahau* did not even want to take the chance that a random person, unaccustomed to this area, would wander down this forest path and blunder into whatever secret His Lordship wanted to protect.

Jaguar Spot took a step back. His father would not like to hear that he had ventured into the exclusive property of the *Ch'ul Ahau* without permission. Mak pulled on his arm again and led him past the stone-tree. "Your Lordship need not worry about the stone-tree. His Lordship the *Ch'ul Ahau* has entrusted the management of this enterprise to me and His Lordship Buried Tapir. Come on, there is much to see."

Mak led Jaguar Spot to a strange sort of clearing. A few of the large canopy trees had been left to provide shade. The ground underneath was covered with strange broadleaf evergreen trees, each of them only three to four times as tall as a grown man. The bark of the trees was mottled, in some parts white, in some parts almost black, and in some parts brown. The trees bore a strange fruit, unlike any fruit that Jaguar Spot had ever seen. The fruit, ovoid pods really, were about a forearm long and a hand's width across. The pods varied in color from green to almost black, and had deep grooves running the long way down the sides. All the trees had this fruit in different stages of development, and there must have been more than five hundred of the trees. "What is this place?" asked Jaguar Spot.

Mak pulled Jaguar Spot right up to one of the trees and pointed to one of the darker pods. "This," he said, "is the best kept secret in all the land of Uaxactun. These are cacao trees. Inside these pods are cacao beans, waiting to be harvested. There are somewhere between twenty and sixty cacao beans inside each pod. There are dozens of pods on each tree, and hundreds of trees. We take these pods and pull them off the tree. We let the seeds and the pods ferment, and then cut them open and take the beans out. We roast the beans, and there you have it. Cacao."

Mak pointed off to the side of the plantation to a pile of the pods so large that it seemed to tower over Jaguar Spot. He took Jaguar Spot over to large fire pits where the beans were roasted. There was a small hut off to the side, where Mak showed Jaguar Spot bag upon bag of roasted cacao beans. He had never seen the like. "Mak," he asked, "is this where all the cacao beans come from?" Mak scoffed at the question. "No, Your Lordship. This is one of many such plantations in the land of Uaxactun. This one, however, makes the best cacao. The families who work here keep a portion of the production. His Lordship Buried Tapir and myself keep a portion of the production. The rest goes to the *Ch'ul Ahau* for his household use."

"Household use?" Jaguar Spot asked himself. "Household use? All of this just for the royal palace?" Mak started looking through the stacks of cacao sacks, counting them. Jaguar Spot helped him, counting a separate group of sacks. They made notations of the number of sacks with a stick in the dirt. After a while they had counted almost two hundred sacks, each weighing about as much a seven year old boy. By this point Lord Sun was high in the Eastern Sky. The cacao plantation, even though somewhat protected by the forest canopy overhead, was getting very hot. They went to a nearby stream for a drink. When they returned to the plantation, thirty or so women and girls were busy working in the trees, inspecting the pods, cutting some down, leaving others to grow. They used the strange tools that Jaguar Spot had seen in the house earlier that morning. Mak and Jaguar went from tree to tree, watching the women at their work. There seemed little for Mak to do here, as he was satisfied with what he saw. Mak soon led Jaguar Spot away from the plantation up the same path that they had taken from the village. "That's a lot of cacao," Jaguar Spot said. "All of that is for the *Ch'ul Ahau*'s household? How can he use all of that?"

"What did Your Lordship eat for breakfast this morning?" Mak asked in return.

"You know what I ate. You were there."

"Humor me, Your Lordship."

"Tortillas and meat."

"Tortillas and meat. Exactly. And at home, what does Your Lordship normally eat for breakfast?"

"Tortillas and meat. Sometimes some chilies, sometimes some beans."

"Any flavorings? Any spices?"

"Some cilantro, some pimenta, chilies of course."

"And for lunch, and dinner, Your Lordship eats roughly the same?"

"Yes, of course."

"And chocolate. Does Your Lordship often drink chocolate?"

"Sometimes."

"How often, if I may ask, Your Lordship?"

"Once or twice a month."

"And His Lordship your father, how often does he drink chocolate?"

"Maybe once every few days, when we have an important visitor."

"What would Your Lordship say if I told you that in the household of the *Ch'ul Ahau*, everyone drinks chocolate at every meal? And I mean everyone, from His Lordship to his family to the palace guards to the people who clean the rooms. What would Your Lordship say to that?"

Jaguar Spot did not answer for a while. The idea was almost ludicrous. Chocolate at every meal? He had no idea that such opulence was even possible. Mak led him off of the main path onto a much smaller trail through the forest. A toucan landed on the trail in front of them. It was a small bird, its beak as long as its body, which was covered in white feathers. Jaguar Spot had only seen a toucan twice before in his life. Once was a captive toucan that a man was selling in the market, the other time was a dead toucan that someone had brought to his father to use as a sacrifice. Mak and Jaguar Spot stopped and observed the bird. Jaguar Spot could not remember seeing such beauty in his life. There was something in the little bird that seemed different from any bird that Jaguar Spot had seen before. An intelligence, perhaps? Jaguar Spot did not know, but there was definitely something unusual. Mak leaned down towards the bird and made a strange sound, as if he himself were a bird. The toucan squawked back at him and flew off. Mak again pulled on Jaguar Spot's arm. "We will have to tell His Lordship your father about that. We don't often see a toucan in these parts."

As they continued down the path, the forest seemed to draw in closer. The air became thicker, more musty. Little shafts of sunlight penetrated the canopy above, their rays visible in the air, but it was getting darker and darker. The noise of the birds and the insects became increasingly quiet. Finally, the only sounds that Jaguar Spot could hear were his and Mak's footsteps and breathing. Jaguar Spot wanted to ask Mak question, but it felt wrong to disturb the silence of the forest. "Mak," he finally whispered, "there is something strange about this place. It's creepy. I want to leave." Mak stopped and kneeled down next to Jaguar Spot. He whispered too. "Your Lordship is very observant. This is a strange place. Every time that I come here, something different, something strange, happens. Sometimes it is quiet like this. Sometimes it is the most noisy place in the forest. Sometimes it is filled with birds. Sometimes it seems almost barren of life. I think that perhaps this place is haunted by the ghost of a god. But do not fear, my young Lordship. Do not fear, for you are safe with me. I have been to this place many times, but have never seen anything dangerous."

Mak moved to stand up, but Jaguar Spot pulled him back down. "Mak," he asked, "I have been wondering about the cacao."

"Yes, Your Lordship?"

"The *Ch'ul Ahau* must have other such plantations, yes?"

"Of course, Your Lordship. But they are not secret. They do not produce cacao of this quality, and they do not supply the royal household. They are for people like you and me, and for the ordinary citizens of our city, and for export, and for the merchants to use in their trading. There are many such plantations. What you saw this morning, you must never speak of it to anyone but myself, His Lordship your father, and his Lordship Buried Tapir. Especially don't mention it to that imbecile Blue Squirrel. Do you understand me? Never!"

Jaguar Spot nodded ascent and Mak continued leading him down the path. They passed what looked to be a small hill. Mak said that this used to be a town, long ago, before the city was built. From the large mound in the center, Jaguar Spot could see that they once had a pyramid-temple, and from the look of the smaller mounds in the area, some other buildings as well. Everything was completely overgrown with grass and trees. "You see, Your Lordship," Mak whispered. "I think that these ruins are old. Very old. Many, many katuns old, perhaps even more than a *baktun* old. This was once a holy place. The Lord of this place, I don't even know if he called himself an *ahau*, I think that he would use that ruined pyramid to enter the Otherworld. To these long dead people, that pyramid represented a mountain, a real mountain that was a passageway to another place, another world. Is this not the way that we look at our pyramids and temples in our city?" Jaguar Spot nodded, staring at the ruins. Mak continued whispering. "I don't know, but I think that some of the holiness remains. When I am here, sometimes I feel like I am walking with the Gods. I feel that if I ever needed a place of safety and refuge, I could come here, isn't that strange? Oh my! Your Lordship, get down, get down!" Mak put his hands on Jaguar Spot's left shoulder and pushed him down to the ground. Mak put a hand across Jaguar Spot's mouth and whispered as quietly as possible right in his ear. "Your Lordship must remain as quiet and as still as possible, do you understand." Jaguar Spot nodded, Mak's hand still over his mouth. "I am going to take my hand off of Your Lordship's mouth, but you must promise to remain as silent and as still as possible. Do you understand?" Jaguar Spot nodded again.

Mak took his hand off of Jaguar Spot's mouth and pointed up to a tree about 75 paces away. "Do you see it, Your Lordship?" Mak whispered. Jaguar Spot saw nothing. "Up there," Mak pointed. "Up in the tree about thirty feet up, where the two large branches separate, do you see it?" Jaguar Spot still saw nothing. Mak was getting a little frustrated. "Your Lordship, there is a jaguar in that tree. He is sleeping, as jaguars do during the day. There, do you see him?" All the sudden, there it was. Jaguar Spot had been looking right at the jaguar without seeing it, but in an instant it appeared to him as if from thin air. The jaguar was sleeping at the base of two large branches. Two of its legs were hanging down, as was its tail. "It is beautiful," Jaguar Spot whispered. "I have never seen a live jaguar before." Mak appeared to be getting a little antsy. "Beautiful? Yes, it is beautiful. But it is valuable, too. The pelt from that animal is a treasure. Alas, I have no weapons to take it today. Still, seeing it is a good omen, that is for sure."

They knelt there on the path for at least a hundred breaths, looking at the jaguar. Finally, they snuck off, not waking it. After a few hundred paces, the forest widened from the path a bit, and the thickness began to dissipate from the air. The forest became brighter and brighter until they came out of it, a few hundred paces from where the men of the village were working on the project that Jaguar Spot had seen the day before. Toucan Claw was there, closely observing the men at their work. Blue Squirrel sat under a tree, apparently sleeping. Toucan Claw saw them as they approached, and met them about 200 paces from where the men were working. "You have a good crew of men here, Mak," he said upon greeting them. "Very good. So, my son, did you learn anything from your sojourn?" Jaguar Spot told his father about the cacao plantation, about the toucan, about the ruined town, and the jaguar in the tree. Toucan Claw looked at Mak with a slightly raised eyebrow. "It appears that you have taught my son much this morning, perhaps too much, but I think that it is all for the best. That pot with the writing on it, whose idea was that?" Jaguar Spot pointed at Mak. "Good idea," said Toucan Claw. "A very good idea, in fact. I will have to tell the *Ch'ul Ahau* about it when I next see him. You are doing very well out here, Mak, very well indeed. Thank you for your hospitality, but I must now continue on my rounds. Come on boy, lets go."

Toucan Claw led his son back to the main road while Mak went to inspect the work that the men had done so far that day. Blue Squirrel still appeared to be sleeping when they made their way to his tree. "Blue Squirrel, " Toucan Claw yelled. "Get up. We've got to get going. I can't wait around for you all day." Blue Squirrel shot up and noticed Jaguar Spot. "I hope that Your Lordship had a good morning?" he asked. "Never mind that," Toucan Claw said before Jaguar Spot could answer. "Just give him his bag and let's get on our way."

Blue Squirrel picked up two bags and handed the smaller to Jaguar Spot. Together, the three of them continued their journey north on the main road. Occasionally, they would stop at a stream or a canal and drink some water. They passed numerous small villages, each with its cluster of thatch-roofed houses, some of them made of wood, some of adobe. Most of the villages had an open plaza in the center, with one or more small shrines to different gods. Around midday they passed into the domain under the direct jurisdiction of Toucan Claw. As they walked, Toucan Claw would point out different farms and what they produced. The farmers grew mostly maize and beans, of course, but some of them planted chilies and squash. A few of the fields were even planted with cotton, and were covered with cotton flowers bursting with white fiber. Toucan Claw knew every farm, every inch of the land. He knew the exact boundaries of each farmer's plot, and explained to Jaguar Spot why each farmer was assigned a particular piece of land. Those who provided the most meritorious service to Toucan Claw were allowed to farm the largest and best plots. Those who shirked their responsibility to provide either work or taxes were assigned plots so small that they could barely support a man's family. In this way, Toucan Claw explained, the men had an incentive to provide the necessary labor or taxes to their *ahau* and to the city. Toucan Claw could then fulfill his requirements to supply labor and money to the *Ch'ul Ahau*.

As they passed each group of farms, one or more men would approach Toucan Claw, and they would discuss various issues of agriculture and local politics. Toucan Claw introduced all of these men to Jaguar Spot. They were local leaders, overseeing the everyday work of the farmers and the labor that they provided for Toucan Claw's own farms, which were interspersed throughout the area. Sometimes the men gave Toucan Claw money, in the form of greenstone beads, strips of cotton cloth, or cacao beans. Each time that the travelers encountered such men, Toucan Claw would reach into the bag he carried and hand the men small bags of salt. Sometimes, no more than every fifth man or so, Toucan Claw distributed used obsidian blades, still covered with the blood of whoever used the blade to feed the Gods.

By mid-afternoon the largest of Toucan Claw's bags was empty and Jaguar Spot was famished. They stopped in one of the larger villages that they had passed, where they were approached by an old man of about sixty-five years. The man led them to a shrine at in the village plaza where a large tree provided shade from Lord Sun. He left them for a moment and brought tortillas, beans, and maize beer, and then left again. Jaguar Spot reached to grab a tortilla when he noticed a raised eyebrow from his father. He pulled his hand back and waited for Blue Squirrel to take his portion. Toucan Claw then waved his hand for Jaguar Spot to help himself, and then Toucan Claw began to eat in silence. When the meal was almost done, Jaguar Spot asked his father why he was handing out valuable obsidian and salt to the men in the villages. "Where does obsidian come from, Jaguar Spot?" was his answer.

"I don't know, father."

"Well, suffice it to say, it comes from a place that is a long way off. It has to be imported into Uaxactun. The *Ch'ul Ahau* uses merchants to trade for the obsidian, and for the salt. The only way that the people can acquire these goods is through the *Ch'ul Ahau*, who distributes them through me. If I provide adequate labor to His Lordship, and enough tribute, he gives me enough so that everyone has enough salt, and that the worthy have obsidian."

"So it is a reward?"

"No. It is a gift. A gift for the worthy and a gift for the loyal."

Toucan Claw took the bag that Jaguar Spot had been carrying and they started walking east on another road. He continued to hand out obsidian and salt until nightfall, when they reached Ixan, the first actual town that Jaguar Spot had seen on their trip. Ixan was a large town for the countryside of Uaxactun, with what appeared to be almost 150 houses arranged in a number of circles surrounding plazas, with a large plaza in the center. When they got to the central plaza, Jaguar Spot saw that there were a few stone temples and one large stone residence, with a thatch roof. The temples and the stone residence bore the emblem glyph of Uaxactun and were painted with red stucco. Near the central plaza of Uaxactun, the buildings were literally covered with pictures and glyphs. In the city, all the stairs leading up the temples had carvings of the Gods and of the royal lineage, so that everyone could see it. Even the ballcourt was studded with carved shrines for the Gods, for departed ballplayers, and with carvings of the royal house's history. Not so here. All the stone buildings were painted with red stucco and nothing else.

Toucan Claw led Jaguar Spot and Blue Squirrel through the front door of the stone residence. There was no need to knock or announce their presence before entering. An *ahau* and his entourage could enter such a house almost at will. There was no mechanism on the door to keep out intruders–there did not need to be.

Unlike the other houses of Ixan, which were round with one room, this house was long and rectangular, and was separated into different areas by internal walls. The main entrance led into the largest room, where a woman was making tortillas at a large cook-fire, and where about ten people, both men and women, sat in a rough circle eating their evening meal. A number of women toiled away to one side, leaning over roughly made clay bowls, which were full of maize soaking in lime. The next morning, they would make it into dough for the tortillas. Upon seeing Toucan Claw enter the room, a very large man stood up immediately. Jaguar Spot had never seen a man this tall–he was almost half again as tall as Toucan Claw. The man was also very, very fat. He must have weighed more than three times the weight of a normal man his age. His clothing suggested that he was an *ahau* of very low rank, barely an *ahau* at all, in reality something between a high ranking *cahel* and a lower *ahau*. Jaguar Spot had never seen him in the city, and did not recognize his name, which turned out to be Fifteen Crocodile. Fifteen Crocodile invited them to sit at what was the room's only table, and a small table at that. The people who had been eating with Fifteen Crocodile went into a flurry of activity as he instructed them to bring food and drink for the visitors. They brought tortillas, various kinds of meat, fish, beans, and chilies.

Before Blue Squirrel could take the first bite, Fifteen Crocodile instructed the woman who had been tending the fire to bring chocolate. Even though the three travelers were famished, Blue Squirrel reluctantly put down the tortilla that he had in his hand and waited. Chocolate was best enjoyed on an empty stomach, and their host might feel slighted if any of his guests started eating the other food before the chocolate was prepared. The woman reached into a basket that was hanging from the ceiling and brought out a bowl filled with a dark paste made of ground cacao beans that had been allowed to sit and ferment. She added some ground chilies and a little bit of water until the mixture had the consistency of warm honey. Fifteen Crocodile took the bowl while the woman reached into another hanging basket and produced four smaller bowls. She put one of the smaller bowls on the floor under Fifteen Crocodile, and he reached his hand above his head and poured the mixture from the large bowl into the smaller one. One by one, he filled the four small bowls with a dark froth, which he handed to his guests, keeping one for himself. "My friends," he said, raising his bowl. "Let us drink to the Maize Gods and to Lord Sun for a good harvest this year."

Jaguar Spot took the chocolate and slurped at the foam. Toucan Claw and Blue Squirrel did the same. When they were finished, Fifteen Crocodile sat down with them. As they ate, he regaled them with the history of the town of Ixan. "Older even than the city of Uaxactun, it is," he said. "My ancestors have lived in this town for close to six hundred years. They watched as the ruling dynasty built Uaxactun, and made it into a city. We just stayed a town. Eventually, of course, my ancestors had to accept dominance from Uaxactun, and we became *ahauob* of the city, ruling our little town in the name of the *Ch'ul Ahau*. Still, I am the fifteenth male heir in my family's line," Fifteen Crocodile went on and on like this for quite some time. After a while, Jaguar Spot stopped listening and let his thoughts wander. He thought of the ballgame that he had missed by coming out into the country with his father. He thought about the plays that he would have made, about playing with the older boys. He thought of the lessons in the workshop of Master Snail. He thought about his mother, who died at his birth, and what she would have been like.

Suddenly everyone else at the table was looking at Jaguar Spot, and it was clear that Fifteen Crocodile had asked him a question of some sort and was awaiting a response. Jaguar Spot had no idea whatsoever what had been asked of him. He looked at his father, but that did not provide any hint as to the relevant subject matter. Likewise, looking at Blue Squirrel did not yield any useful information. Fifteen Crocodile was looking at him with such good natured earnestness that he did not have the heart to tell him that he had not been paying attention. He tried for a middle ground. "Uncle?" he asked Fifteen Crocodile, who squinted his eyes and then burst into laughter. "You weren't listening to me at all, were you my boy?" asked Fifteen Crocodile in between his laughs. Jaguar Spot had to admit the truth. "No, Uncle," he said and then looked at Toucan Claw. "I am sorry, Father." If anything, Jaguar Spot's answer made Fifteen Crocodile even more jolly, and he let out a great belly laugh. "I can't say that I blame you, my boy. I wouldn't listen to me, either!" he said before he almost fell to the floor in laughter. "What a bore I am!" At this point Fifteen Crocodile actually did fall to the floor, where he writhed in laughter for quite some time. Toucan Claw, and then Blue Squirrel, started laughing in response. Jaguar Spot looked at them feeling like he was the brunt of whatever joke was causing all of this hilarity.

Eventually Fifteen Crocodile managed to pull himself together and got back in his chair. His eyes were still moist from the laughter. "Your father tells me that you are a scribe-apprentice. Tell me, how are your studies coming along? Can you read the glyphs?" Jaguar Spot looked over to his father. Answering the question truthfully might seem like bragging, and he was inclined to prevaricate and say that he was just starting his studies. Toucan Claw nodded, which Jaguar Spot took to be an invitation to tell the truth. "Uncle," Jaguar Spot said, "I can read the glyphs." Fifteen Crocodile slapped his leg and stood up. "Capital!" he said. "Let me show you something, something that I am quite proud of, and something that very few people outside of my family have ever seen. Come along, all of you, if you wish."

He led them through a door which led into a courtyard, all four sides of which were bounded by internal walls of the stone house. In reality, Fifteen Crocodile's house was created from many different stone buildings constructed over the centuries, all joined together into the residence's present form. The buildings appeared to be of various ages. The one that they were headed to seemed to be the oldest, possibly as old as the 600 years that Fifteen Crocodile ascribed to the age of the town. Fifteen Crocodile explained that the older buildings had once been the principal house of the *ahau* of the village from time to time. His father, Fourteen Crocodile, had some thirty years before built the portion of the residence where they had eaten dinner. The building that they entered was dark and musty. To Jaguar Spot, it smelt, well, *old*. The baskets and nets hanging from the thatch ceiling seemed to be covered with dust, as were the scattered items laying about the floor. Fifteen Crocodile pulled away a curtain that had been hanging in front of a window and led them to the East wall, which was made of finely cut limestone blocks, installed so that they made an almost seamless surface. The wall was covered with carvings, about half writing and half pictures. Fifteen Crocodile suddenly became very serious and quiet as he walked over to the wall and pointed to the glyphs. "As far as I know, this right here is the oldest writing in all the domains of Uaxactun." He was pointing at the upper left corner of the wall. He moved his arm down and to the right as continued with his explanation. "This is the story of my ancestors in this town, how they built it up from nothing, how son followed after father, about great deeds in battle in the service of the *Ch'ul Ahau*, about death, and birth, and children." Jaguar Spot walked up to the wall and studied the writing. He found some of it to be quite difficult to read, not because the rock had weathered or eroded, but because the style of the glyphs had apparently changed over the course of the centuries. The wall told how Fifteen Crocodile's ancestors had come to Ixan from a far off place, that they were just a few people and that they started a village. After a few generations the village became a town, with an *ahau*. At this point the glyphs became much easier to read, and it was obvious to Jaguar Spot that there was a different person responsible for writing this portion of the narrative. As he continued, he saw that the wall had been carved by as many as twenty different people. The last entry depicted the death or capture of Fourteen Crocodile in battle and Fifteen Crocodile taking over as *ahau* at 14 years of age. Jaguar Spot rubbed his hands against the carvings as the light in the room began to dim with the sunset. "Uncle," he said, "this is the story of your family. Why is it here where no one can see it?" Fifteen Crocodile didn't answer the question, and looked over at Toucan Claw. "Son," said Toucan Claw, "this is the story of the lineage of the noble family of this town."

"Yes, I know that, Father."

"Okay, good. Do you know why this record is kept?"

"No, Father."

"This carving, this information, establishes the historical legitimacy of Fifteen Crocodile's dynasty. It shows why he, and some day his sons, rule this town. It is meant to anchor them to the past to ensure their survival in the future. Do you understand?"

"I think so."

"You have seen other carvings like this in the plaza in the city, depicting the history of the *Ch'ul Ahau*'s dynasty, haven't you? He does that so that people respect his right to rule over the city and its lands. This does the same thing."

"Yes, father, I understand. But why is this in here where no one can see it?"

"This is private, Jaguar Spot. Only the *Ch'ul Ahau* proclaims such things in public. Our friend Fifteen Crocodile shows this to us so that we will have greater respect for his family and him. He probably shows this to any *ahau* that visits his house, am I right Fifteen Crocodile?" Fifteen Crocodile nodded, and they started walking out of the old building. As the light diminished to almost nothing, Jaguar Spot looked back at the wall and tried to remember the story of the town of Ixan. "When I die," he asked himself silently, "will my ancestors write carvings about me?"

Chapter Four
The Palace

8.16.13.11.14. July 19, 370 A.D.

A palace guard was waiting at the entrance to the residential compound when Toucan Claw, Jaguar Spot, and Blue Squirrel arrived back in the city after their three days journey. His name was Gray Sky, and he was one of the more senior palace guards, well into his fifties. Jaguar Spot had seen him many times before, and had always admired his strong physique. He knew that Gray Sky had once been the most preeminent ballplayer in the city, perhaps the best in all the cities known to the people of Uaxactun. Gray Sky approached Toucan Claw as they reached the compound portal. "Your Lordship, I have a message. You are requested by his Supreme Lordship the *Ch'ul Ahau* to accompany me to the palace upon your return to the city."

Toucan Claw had started feeling queasy from the moment that he saw Gray Sky waiting by the compound. Palace guards were not in the habit of loitering around the city without a purpose, and Toucan Claw had a strong suspicion as to why His Lordship had sent Gray Sky on this particular mission. When Gray Sky confirmed his initial concern Toucan Claw dismissed Blue Squirrel and told Jaguar Spot that he would meet him at home later. "Oh no, Your Lordship, I am instructed to bring the boy along as well," said Gray Sky. So the three of them walked through the red stucco covered corridors of the city to the royal palace with Gray Sky leading the way. Both Jaguar Spot and Toucan Claw shared the same fear that the *Ch'ul Ahau* had called them to the palace in relation Jaguar Spot's carelessness of a few days before. Jaguar Spot particularly dreaded the upcoming audience, and tried hard to hear as Toucan Claw indirectly questioned Gray Sky on the purpose of the meeting.

"So my old friend, has anything interesting happened in the city in the past few days? You know that me and the boy were in the country doing my rounds."

"Interesting, Your Lordship? Nothing particularly interesting that I can think of."

"And how is His Lordship the *Ch'ul Ahau*?"

"Fine, Your Lordship, just fine."

"He is in good spirits, I trust?"

"As always, Your Lordship, as always."

"Has he been seeing many visitors? Have the *ahauob* been coming by?"

"Just the usual, Your Lordship, just the usual."

The conversation continued in a similar vein all the way to the palace, with Gray Sky providing Toucan Claw with nothing but vague generalities in answer to his equally vague questions. Finally, they arrived at the main plaza for the city, a sight that always awed Jaguar Spot. The temples lining three sides seemed to soar straight into the heavens, their steps rising steeper than any hill or mountain that Jaguar Spot had ever seen or read about. The rooms on the top, which were the only structures in the city that had a stone roof, were almost pitch dark beyond their open doors. Jaguar Spot knew from Master Snail that this was by design, to increase the air of mystery surrounding the temples, and to make them more like the entrances to the caves that they were meant to represent. Jaguar Spot knew that some day in the distant future he would accompany the *Ch'ul Ahau* up those stairs and into the darkness, where they would give their blood to the Gods together. Only the *ahauob* were granted that privilege, and it would only come to Jaguar Spot upon the death of his father. He wanted to ask his father what it was like in those rooms, but Toucan Claw was still trying to prize information out of the tight lipped Gray Sky.

When they finally reached the royal palace they took the stairs straight up to the second floor. The palace was the only two storied dwelling in the city, and there were only two ways into the second floor. One was the stairway on the outside, and the other was a much smaller set of stairs in the inner courtyard. The outside stairway was not nearly as steep as the stairs on a temple, and it extended from the palace for more than twenty paces. Two palace guards stood at the top of the stairway with spears, although their presence was purely ceremonial. No one in the city had ever tried to trespass in the residence of the *Ch'ul Ahau*. The guard on the right was the same one who had pushed Jaguar Spot against the wall a few days before, but he gave no sign of recognition as they entered the palace. The air inside was heavy with the smell of incense. Toucan Claw had once explained to Jaguar Spot that the incense was made from the sap of a particular tree that grew near the city, sometimes mixed with raw rubber. This sap was a symbol of the blood of the Great Tree, which nourished and fed the world every time that the rain fell. By burning the incense, Toucan Claw had explained, the *Ch'ul Ahau* paid homage to the Great Tree and to the Gods.

Gray Sky led them through a number of doors into a large chamber which was bright with the light from torches which lined the walls. Gray Sky waited outside the door as Toucan Claw led Jaguar Spot into the room. There, in the center of the room, the *Ch'ul Ahau* knelt over a bowl with a stingray spine in his right hand. Blood dripped from his mouth onto a piece of paper that lay in the bowl. Toucan Claw grabbed Jaguar Spot to stop him and they waited just inside the door. The *Ch'ul Ahau* sat there in silence for more than twenty breaths, not paying any attention to his visitors as the blood dripped from his mouth. Finally, when the small piece of paper was almost totally covered with blood, he picked up the bowl and put the stingray spine on top of a knee-high platform that sat beside him. He stood up with the bowl and noticed his visitors. "Ah, Toucan Claw, how long have you been standing there, my friend?" he asked, appearing startled at the sight of father and son. "Not very long, Your Lordship. I did not want to interrupt your ceremony," Toucan Claw answered. The *Ch'ul Ahau* turned around and started walking toward the room's second door, which led into another large chamber. "Ah, never mind, never mind, come follow me, both of you," he said as he walked through the door.

The room that the *Ch'ul Ahau* led them into was covered with painted glyphs and pictures describing various ceremonies and offerings for the Gods. It was almost as if someone had copied an entire Council Book for the *Ch'ul Ahau* on the walls so that His Lordship would know exactly what to do for each ceremony required of him. Jaguar Spot had never seen anything like it. The writing was many times larger than any painted writing that Jaguar Spot had ever seen, and the walls seemed to be covered with the same type of plaster that covered the tree bark paper of a Council Book. The *Ch'ul Ahau* took the bowl that he was still carrying and placed it on a long table that ran the entire length of one of the walls. There was a brazier of sorts on the table, essentially an almost spherical shaped item about half the size of a man's head with three legs protruding from the bottom. The top had a small opening about the size of a toddler's fist, and there was a fire inside with flames that barely rose above the opening. The *Ch'ul Ahau* took the blood-soaked paper from the bowl and held it over the flame. As the paper began to burn the smell of incense became even stronger, as if the paper itself was made from the bark of the same tree from whose sap the artisans made His Lordship's incense. The *Ch'ul Ahau* stared at the paper as it burned, and finally dropped in the brazier just as the fire was about to reach his fingertips. When the paper was completely burned, the *Ch'ul Ahau* turned around and let out a deep sigh. "My friends, it always makes me a little blue when I have to feed my father like this. I know that his soul needs the nourishment, and I am happy to be dutiful to my obligations, but do you know what I think of?"

Toucan Claw, who had much more experience with the *Ch'ul Ahau* and was well versed in his mannerisms, knew that this was an entirely rhetorical question and that His Lordship neither sought nor desired any response. Jaguar Spot, not having the benefit of his father's knowledge, nor the opportunity to receive his advice, answered. "No, Your Lordship," he said. The *Ch'ul Ahau* pretended to ignore the child and continued with his intended monologue. "I think of the fact that someday I will reside in the Otherworld full time, and that my descendants will be doing the same for me. Still, that's a much better thought than the idea that my decedents *won't* do this for me, or dare I say it, that I won't have *any* male decedents at all." The *Ch'ul Ahau* then led them into a third room, this one richly appointed with furniture and textiles. He asked them to sit down. "That's where you come in, my friend," he said to Toucan Claw.

"Your Lordship?"

"I need your help. I need a son."

"I hardly think that I can offer Your Lordship any assistance in that area. I wouldn't even know where to start. Perhaps an extract of rubber, melted with honey, applied to the. . ."

The *Ch'ul Ahau* cut Toucan Claw off in mid-sentence. "Oh don't be daft! *I'm* not the problem. I am perfectly fine. It's my wife, who for some reason that the Gods only know, has decided to bear me nothing but daughters, six of them! Six! And not one son! I think that it is time that I took a second wife. And that is where you come in." Toucan Claw could hardly believe what he was hearing. Was His Lordship actually going to ask him for one of his daughters as a second wife? If one of his daughters bore the *Ch'ul Ahau* a son, then Toucan Claw's own grandson would some day be the *Ch'ul Ahau*. This was a boon beyond his wildest dreams, almost too good to be true. The *Ch'ul Ahau* continued. "I need you to help me pick a wife."

Toucan Claw paused, his dreams of glory tumbling down before him. "Your Lordship?" he asked with a quavering voice.

"You know that my father arranged for my marriage when I was a boy."

"Yes, Your Lordship."

"Do you know that he picked her simply on the basis of political expediency without consulting with the priests, and without considering the auguries? He didn't even *consider* whether our birthdays portended a good match. Did you know that?"

"No, Your Lordship. But if I may say so, I think that Her Ladyship is a most admirable wife for any *Ch'ul Ahau*. Even if he did not consider the auguries, His Lordship your father made a most excellent choice."

"True" said the *Ch'ul Ahau*, calming down. "She is an excellent wife in all respects except her inability to provide me with a male heir. But I must have an heir. I must! I have decided to choose a second wife based on nothing but the auguries. Do you hear me, nothing! Not beauty, not intelligence, not social graces, not even the absence of an offensive body odor. I will choose my second wife entirely on the basis of our respective dates of birth. And that is where you come in."

"Me, Your Lordship? What do you want me to do?"

At this point the *Ch'ul Ahau* snapped his fingers and an attendant walked in with jug of maize beer and stood silently off to the side while she poured three bowls full. Once she handed out the bowls and left the *Ch'ul Ahau* answered Toucan Claw's question. "Well, here's what I am thinking, there must be a couple of hundred unmarried girls of the *ahau* and the *cahel* classes, including those who are, as yet, too young to bear children. Would you agree that this is a roughly accurate count?"

"Yes, Your Lordship."

"Good. What I want you to do is to get a date of birth for each and every one of them. And I want you to compare it to my birth day and then consult the auguries. Find me the girl or woman that augers best to be my wife."

Toucan Claw was disappointed and astounded at the same time. The disappointment that His Lordship did not intend to marry one of his daughters, as he had been hoping, was now beginning to fade. He was astounded by the *Ch'ul Ahau*'s lack of understanding of how the auguries worked. He did not want to contradict his *Ch'ul Ahau*, but he could not agree to undertake an impossible task. "Your Lordship, I am somewhat confused by your request. If I may ask . ." The *Ch'ul Ahau* began speaking again before Toucan Claw could ask his question. Toucan Claw stopped speaking immediately as soon as the *Ch'ul Ahau* opened his mouth. "Yes, yes, yes. You were about to tell me that this is basically an impossible task, because there are only 260 days in the sacred calendar, each day being either good, bad, or neutral. You were then going to tell me that out of such a large group of girls, a great many would come back when matched to my birthday as a good match, and that the matches would either be good, bad, or neutral. One good match would be roughly equivalent to another, yes? Was this not what you were going to say?"

"It was indeed, Your Lordship."

"I thought of that, of course. But here is what I am thinking, the sacred calendar repeats itself every 260 days, right?"

"Yes, Your Lordship."

"And the civil calendar repeats itself every 365 days, yes?"

"Yes, Your Lordship."

"Well, when we combine a civil calendar date and a sacred calendar date we have a cycle that repeats itself how often? I mean if you start with a sacred calendar date of, say 4 *Ahau*, and you combine it with a civil calendar date, say the 8th day of the month of *Cumku*, how long does it take before the two calendars coincide and give us the same date combination?"

"Roughly every 52 civil years, Your Lordship."

"Roughly nothing! I'll tell you, exactly 18,980 days. 18,980 possible date combinations. What I am thinking is this, when we combine these dates we can get various grades of augury. From very bad to very good. Hundreds of grades, perhaps thousands. I want you to dig deep in the Council Book, to talk to all the priests, and to divine the auguries of all of the possible date combinations, and compare them with my birthday and find me the wife that augers well."

"Your Lordship, I would hardly know where to begin on such an undertaking, it might take years."

"Years! Hah! You are my best *ahau*. You are the smartest, the most loyal, simply the best. Not only that, you are a scribe. You are a scholar. You are a priest. I can only trust an *ahau* with this task. None of the other *ahauob* have anywhere near your knowledge or ability in these matters. And anyway, it's not as bad as it seems. You are only going to look at girls from age, let's say eight years old at the youngest to women aged, let's say 18 years at the oldest. Ten years. That's only a maximum range of 3650 possible date combinations to augur, plus I don't need you to bother to augur combinations for anything other than the exact birthdays of the girls at issue. It shouldn't take more than a month, two at most."

Toucan Claw was left almost speechless. Speechless not only at the scale of the undertaking, but at something else that His Lordship said. "Your Lordship," Toucan Claw almost whispered, "Eight years old? Surely a girl that young cannot. . ." Once again the *Ch'ul Ahau* cut Toucan Claw off. "Oh come now, my friend! I haven't turned into a pedophile all of the sudden. I just want to cast my net as wide as possible. If you find me a prepubescent girl we will simply announce the engagement and then schedule the wedding on the most auspicious day after she comes of age. She can bear my son then. I can wait. I just can't wait forever. Of course this may mean some inconvenience to all the families of the *ahauob* and the *cahelob* classes."

"Your Lordship?" Toucan Claw was once again confused. Surely this would inconvenience him, along with whichever scholars and priests he dragooned into helping him with this project, but the all of the *ahauob* and *cahelob*?

"Yes, yes, I understand your confusion," said the *Ch'ul Ahau*. "You see, since we don't know who the lucky woman is going to be yet, I can't go and have the perfect bride for me up and marry someone else while you are still looking. So from this moment forward, until you determine the auguries for my perfect bride, all planned or future weddings involving daughters of the *ahauob* and the *cahelob* are hereby suspended. All engagements, too. Everyone will have to wait. Once you complete this task for me life as normal can continue."

"Your Lordship, it. . it . .it is midsummer. The wedding season is about to begin. There must be twenty or more weddings planned. The outcry from the nobility will be. . . " The *Ch'ul Ahau* waved off Toucan Claw's concern. "There will be no outcry. There will be no complaints. There will be no hard feelings. Can you imagine? Almost every noble family will have chance of marrying into my dynasty! I think that everyone will be satisfied that this possible benefit outweighs any inconvenience. You agree, don't you?" Toucan Claw was forced to concede the *Ch'ul Ahau*'s point. He himself had been almost overjoyed when he thought that His Lordship wanted to marry one of his daughters. Even so, he did not look forward to the task that the *Ch'ul Ahau* had in store for him, and to whatever feelings it might engender among the other *ahauob*.

From the start of the *Ch'ul Ahau's* discussion with his father, Jaguar Spot began to wonder why he was there. It was readily apparent that the meeting had little, if anything, to do with his carelessness in walking into His Lordship a few days before. It was likewise clear that topic of the discussion was of such a high level of importance that his presence bordered on the absurd. Here they were, discussing the issue of succession of the royal dynasty, and they had a child sitting there hearing every word. The *Ch'ul Ahau* must have noticed his discomfort. "Well good then," he said to Toucan Claw, "that's settled. Get me a list of names and the auguries as soon as you can. Now, both of you are probably wondering why I asked you to bring Jaguar Spot along for this little meeting, am I right?" Father and son answered the *Ch'ul Ahau* in unison: "Yes, Your Lordship." The *Ch'ul Ahau* drank some more maize beer before answering. "Recently I was speaking to the scribe Snail. I believe that you are apprenticed in his workshop, aren't you?"

Jaguar Spot gulped. The *Ch'ul Ahau* was talking to *Master Snail?* Talking to Master Snail *about him?* What on Earth could the two of them have to talk about? The idea that he was the topic of such discussions outside of his presence was almost enough to make Jaguar Spot physically ill. He felt sweat starting to form on his forehead. He sat there, unable to speak until his father prodded him with a finger in the ribs. "Yes, Your Lordship," Jaguar Spot said meekly, the words coming out almost as if they were a question. The *Ch'ul Ahau* seemed pleased with the answer. "Yes, of course you are. Silly question, really. After all, we all knew the answer. Anyway, Snail says that you are the best apprentice that he has ever had, bar none." Jaguar Spot and Toucan Claw both experienced profound feelings of relief that the report from Snail had been positive, although Toucan Claw was nervous about what his son's response would be. Praise from the *Ch'ul Ahau*, even second hand praise such as his, could go right to a young boy's head.

Toucan Claw's fears were allayed when Jaguar Spot finally responded to the *Ch'ul Ahau*'s statement. "Well, I am sure that Snail is just saying that because my father is an *ahau*. I doubt that I am even one of his better students, much less the best." Toucan Claw almost beamed in pride at his son's modesty, but the *Ch'ul Ahau* brushed Jaguar Spot's protests aside. "Nonsense. I don't know what has gotten into the nobility of late, all of this false modesty is so, well, false. Be proud of what you have done! But I digress. In speaking with Snail, I asked him if you would be an appropriate candidate for a special job that I want completed, a job that will take several months, if not more than a year.

He said that you were admirably qualified. He released you from your apprenticeship at my request, and I hereby appoint you a scribe of the city." The *Ch'ul Ahau* snapped his fingers and a servant brought in a child-sized set of a scribe's garments, fringed with special fabric so that anyone would know that this scribe was the eldest son of an *ahau*. The servant knelt in front of Jaguar Spot gave him the clothes. After the servant left the *Ch'ul Ahau* told Jaguar Spot to get dressed. All Jaguar Spot could do was stare at his lap admiring the garments, uncertain what to do. Toucan Claw tried to intervene. "Your Lordship, if I may..." The *Ch'ul Ahau* grimaced and quickly waved his arms high into the air to silence Toucan Claw. "You may not! You will listen to me! I am the *Ch'ul Ahau* of this city. Anyway, I already knew what you were going to say. You were going to express some banalities about how you are the father of this child and that by right you are the one responsible for his education, am I right?"

"Yes, Your Lordship."

"Well, here I am going to override you. That's that. You were probably also going to say that his training is incomplete and that he should stay with Snail, right?"

"Yes, Your Lordship."

"Well, Snail says that he is ready. That's good enough for me. And anyway, this boy was never going to be an actual scribe in the first place, any more than you were in the days of your own apprenticeship. He has certainly learned enough to fulfill his duties as *ahau* in the event of your untimely demise, hasn't he?"

"Yes, Your Lordship."

"And anyway, you were not much older than him when you left the scribe's workshop, were you?"

"I was eleven, Your Lordship."

"Ten, eleven, what's the difference. And plus, he will be doing important work for me. Me! What better learning experience could you even ask for?"

"Nothing that I can think of, Your Lordship."

"So its settled then, is it?"

Toucan Claw paused and looked over at the boy before answering the *Ch'ul Ahau*'s question. Jaguar Spot was still staring at the clothes that lay in his lap, seemingly oblivious to the conversation, if one wanted to call it a conversation, that Toucan Claw had been having with the *Ch'ul Ahau*.

Toucan Claw looked back at the *Ch'ul Ahau*, who had an expectant look on his face. "Yes, Your Lordship, it is settled. Son, please change into the clothes that His Lordship has provided." Jaguar Spot slowly stood up and stripped naked before he put on the new clothes. He almost appeared to be beaming with pride, a sight which made Toucan Claw wince like a dog whose master beats him too often. "You look fine, just fine," said the *Ch'ul Ahau*. "Now sit down and I will explain what I want you to do. Good. Now, you know that a little more than five years ago I won a glorious victory over those monkeys in Tikal." Jaguar Spot nodded. The *Ch'ul Ahau* continued. "Good. In this palace there is a room with a bare wall, completely bare. It is, in fact, my new bedchamber. I have had that wall covered with white plaster. What I want you to do is to paint the story of that victory, complete with a history of my family, the details of the victory, and even include something about that miserable cur Fireborn, his family, about his brother, the disgrace at the ceremonial ballgame, and such. Do you understand?" Jaguar Spot nodded again, but Toucan Claw was not convinced that this was the right job for his son. "Your Lordship," he said gently, "shouldn't this be done be someone who was actually there at the site of the battle? My son's knowledge of these things is limited, very limited." Surprisingly, the *Ch'ul Ahau* agreed with Toucan Claw. "Yes," he said. "Very true. But that's why I want your son. You see, in my experience two people can see the same thing yet have a very different memory of what happened. What I want is for the boy to talk to everyone who was there, at least everyone important. From that he will distill the truth so that the wall reflects a diversity of memories, not just those of one man, not even if that one man is me. This is not for the public to see. This is not to perpetuate my glory in victory to the masses. This is only intended for me, so that it can help me relive and remember the memory of my triumph. Do you understand?" This time both father and son nodded in silence. "Good," said the *Ch'ul Ahau*, "thank you for coming. Gray Sky will show you out."

As if on cue, Gray Sky entered the room and beckoned them to follow, which they did. Just as they were passing through the door the *Ch'ul Ahau* called on them to stop. "One more thing," he said. "Snail said that you still need to complete your Council Book. So, every morning you need to spend at least half the morning copying the book over at Snail's workshop before working on our project. Now you may go." Gray Sky led them through a number of chambers before they were at the second floor's main door again. Just as they were about to step out into the rain, which had started while they were inside, the *Ch'ul Ahau* came running, looking relieved that he caught them. "Ah, I managed to stop you. Good. Just let Gray Sky know when you want to talk to me about the battle, and it will be arranged. I would suggest starting your research with that fiend Fireborn, who now resides in my dungeon. Gray Sky can arrange that as well." With that the *Ch'ul Ahau* disappeared into the darkness and they went into the wet night.

Chapter Five
FIREBORN

8.16.13.12.15. August 9, 370 A.D.

Jaguar Spot did not interview Fireborn until twenty days had passed from when the *Ch'ul Ahau* gave him his commission. He had spent the intervening time speaking to his father and some of the other *ahauob* who had been present at the battle, and visiting the battle site itself. Like every other battle between the two cities, stretching back as long as the records recorded, the fighting took place on a large open field approximately mid-way between Uaxactun and Tikal, which were not more than a long day's walk apart in the first place. Years before, Tikal had installed a long earthen and stone barrier to keep out prowlers and invaders from Uaxactun, and no one had developed any military tactics to overcome this obstacle. To Jaguar Spot, the barrier seemed to be somewhat of an overreaction due to the fact Uaxactun could muster no more than 300 able bodied warriors for any given battle. The actual security of Tikal and its citizens could therefore never be threatened by their neighbor to the north, but the same could not be true for the honor of the city. Battle was all about honor. Battle was an opportunity for noble men to show their true quality, and to establish among the nobility that they had courage worthy of their position.

All battles between the two cities were arranged well in advance. The *Ch'ul Ahau* of one city would send a challenge to the other, and the men of the nobility of the two cities would meet on a day agreed on by the priests of both sides. The date would be selected as that most auspicious for battle based on the common auguries from the Council Books of the two cities. The warriors would arrive at the field shortly after dawn, covered in cotton armor. The *ahauob* would lead squads of *cahelob* and other close relatives. Some of the warriors carried obsidian blades, others had wooden spears with obsidian tips. The two sides would arrive at their respective sides of the great clearing, and upon the blowing of a trumpet they would race to the center of the field and begin physical combat. The *Ch'ul Ahau* of each city was almost always carried onto the field of battle on a litter loaded with relics and images of the Gods. When the time came to fight the *Ch'ul Ahau* would step down from the litter and join in. All that mattered was courage and honor. Throughout history leaders gave little, if any, thought to tactics or strategy. A man could win honor by killing the enemy, but capturing the enemy was a far better result. Upon capture the enemy could be forced to march back to the victor's city in shame and humiliation, to be killed or kept alive for years as a trophy. In most battles each side had the opportunity to take prisoners, and both sides could claim victory. Battle thus almost always ended in a draw, a ritual designed to gain honor and praise for both sides. Actual victory was almost never the real object.

All of that had changed with the *Ch'ul Ahau*'s victory over Tikal five years before. The *Ch'ul Ahau* told Jaguar Spot that the Gods had inspired him to defeat Tikal. On the occasion of the Festival marking the winter solstice Speaking Macaw carried out his duties as leader of the city. He officiated over the traders from around the domains of Uaxactun who exchanged their wares for money. He mediated disputes. He judged ballgames. His most important duty was to journey into the Otherworld. On the fifth day of the Festival, which was the actual day of the solstice, he stood on the observatory temple with his priests and *ahauob* and watched the sun rise exactly above the structure that indicated the occasion of the solstice. He then led the men around him in a procession to the main temple of the city, which he had just re-built the year before. The original temple had been built by his ancestors ten generations in the past, and over the centuries various *Ch'ul Ahauob* had rebuilt it, renovated it, and improved it. Speaking Macaw had razed the top third of the temple and had it completely re-built, twenty foot-lengths higher. When the procession reached the base of the temple, two priests who had been waiting at the top walked down to meet the *Ch'ul Ahau*. Speaking Macaw led the way to the top, never actually facing up the temple and into the open door of the ceremonial room at the top. That door was the gateway to the Otherworld. Artisans had carved an image of the maw of the Great Vision Serpent--the god that controlled access to the sacred realm--around the opening of the gateway. The priests had left incense burning outside the door, along with a bowl of holy mushrooms and the ribosomes of the waterlily. The *Ch'ul Ahau* made his way to the top of the temple by stepping up each individual step facing sideways, walking down the length of the step, and so on. It took the span of five hundred breaths to get to the top of the temple in this fashion. Once at the top the *Ch'ul Ahau* took a handful of the mushrooms and ribosomes and ate them, and then stepped through the maw of the Great Vision Serpent to stand alone in the Otherworld. He took a stingray spine that the priests had left for him and quickly punctured the base of his penis, and then his tongue. The pain was almost unbearable, but he knew what the Gods required of him on this occasion, and he was not about to let them down. With blood trickling from his groin, he opened his mouth as wide as he could and began to spin around faster and faster. The blood flew from his groin and mouth to the walls, and to pieces of paper that the priests had left just for this purpose. He let the blood run from his mouth and it flowed down his cheeks. He quickly became dizzy from the spinning, the loss of blood, and the holy food that the priests had left for him. Finally, when the dizziness took him over, he collapsed to the floor in a trance.

In an instant he was no longer at the top of the temple. He lay on his back on the floor of a strange forest, naked. It was not the forest of home. The trees, covered with multi-colored leaves, seemed to stretch into the heavens. Strange animals, some with four legs, with six, some with ten, walked past him. He heard the calls of strange birds, almost sounding like they were speaking some kind of language. Even the sky did not look quite right, there was an odd red tinge to it. He tried to get up, but it felt like he was tied down by invisible bonds, as if a great weight pushed down on him. He could not move so much as a finger. As he struggled to get free he heard footsteps approaching. Suddenly the air was filled with a bright light. He closed his eyes, but the light was so bright that it seemed to burn his eyes through the eyelids. He desperately tried to cover his eyes with his arms, but he still could not move. All the while the footsteps kept getting louder and louder, until they stopped right next to his head. In his right ear he heard a strange voice. The voice started as a whisper, and as it became louder he heard that it was actually many voices, all saying the same thing at the same time.

Some of the voices were men, some were women, some were children, and some sounded like beasts of the forest. At first the voices spoke nothing but nonsense, some kind of jabber that Speaking Macaw had never heard before. They may have been speaking in some strange foreign language, he did not know. Suddenly the voices started speaking Yucatec. They whispered to him: "You are Speaking Macaw, the *Ch'ul Ahau* of the City of Uaxactun?"

"Yes," was all that Speaking Macaw could manage to say with the invisible weight pushing down on his chest, and even that took a supreme effort.

"Do you know who we are?"

"No."

"We are Lord Sun. We are one. We are many. We are all. We are nothing. Do you understand?"

"No."

"We are Lord Sun! Address us properly!"

"I don't understand . . . Your Lordship."

"Understanding is not necessary. All that is necessary is for you to listen, and to answer. Open your eyes." At this point the light began to dim, and the pain in Speaking Macaw's eyes diminished. Finally, when there was no longer any light coming through his eyelids, he opened his eyes and tried to look over at Lord Sun, but he could not move his head. Lord Sun spoke again. "We are going to lift the weight from your head. Do not look at us! I want you to look down at your belly. Do you understand?" The weight slowly came off of Speaking Macaw's head and he managed to croak out "Yes, Your Lordship." He looked down at his stomach and could not believe his eyes. If Lord Sun's invisible weight had not been holding him down, he would have run for his life, but he was held completely motionless except for his head. There, burrowing into his navel was a . . . he could not believe his eyes . . . but it was true. A great and multi-colored serpent was burrowing into his navel. It was a strange serpent, covered with feathers of every color that Speaking Macaw had ever remembered seeing. The body of the serpent extended into the sky, seemingly going on forever.

Just as quickly as it had been released, the weight suddenly came back, forcing his head into the ground in an instant. At the same time the painful light returned and Lord Sun spoke again. "Tell us, Speaking Macaw, *Ch'ul Ahau* of Uaxactun, what have we shown you? Speak!" The weight on his body now seemed to have increased twofold. Speaking Macaw could barely breathe, and it was hard for him to even manage a quiet whisper. "Your Lordship has shown me a great feathered serpent burrowing into my stomach." For a while the forest was completely quiet. Not even the strange birds and animals and insects made a sound. Just as Speaking Macaw thought that he would suffocate, the weight on him began to lessen. Lord Sun spoke again. "It is not just a serpent, it is *your* serpent, your *feathered vision serpent*. It is always there, but you can only see it when we wish it to be so. Do you hear us? It is *always there!*" By now the weight had so diminished that Speaking Macaw could speak easily. "I hear Your Lordship, but I don't understand." Once again the strange silence returned to the forest, and Speaking Macaw lay there in the quiet for some time. At last Lord Sun spoke again. "Your ignorance is surprising for one of so high a station. Every person of your rank, every *Ch'ul Ahau* of every city, has a feathered vision serpent. This is your umbilicus to the Otherworld. It is only through *it* that you can come here, that you can commune with the Gods and your ancestors. But it must be fed, it must be nourished. Your feathered vision serpent is hungry. It is starving. In fact it may soon die. Do you know what that would mean?"

The ramifications of Lord Sun's revelation were staggering. If Speaking Macaw lost his connection to the Otherworld, his legitimacy to rule Uaxactun as *Ch'ul Ahau* would be gone. He would be ruined. "Have I not given enough of my blood, Your Lordship?" he asked. This time Lord Sun answered without delay. "Idiot! It is not fed with blood! It is not a god! It is not your ancestor! It is a feathered vision serpent!.. It can only be fed by glory, your glory! Do you hear us? You must have glory!" Speaking Macaw did not know how to answer. He thought that he had gained a sufficient amount of glory for a *Ch'ul Ahau* with his amount of time in power. He had built monuments to the Gods and his ancestors. He had won numerous skirmishes against neighboring cities. As if reading Speaking Macaw's thoughts, Lord Sun expressed his dissatisfaction. "We have one question for you, Speaking Macaw. Have you ever defeated your enemy in battle?"

"Yes, Your Lordship."

"We don't mean taking a couple of prisoners, or killing a couple of weak old men! For that is what you have done. That is *all* that you have done! We mean utterly defeating them. Defeating them in such a way that they leave the field of battle in total, and abject, humiliation. So that they cannot hold their heads high in the halls of honor. So that their *ahauob* are captured, killed, or leave the field of battle so dispirited that they lack even the taste for revenge! You haven't done that, have you?"

"No, Your Lordship."

"Well, that is what it will take. That is the only thing that will give your feathered vision serpent enough nourishment. It is a hungry beast, more hungry than any other that we have seen in all our long life. Feed it, and you will thrive. We need not remind you of the consequences of failure. Good Bye, Speaking Macaw."

The instant that Lord Sun's voice stopped speaking, Speaking Macaw felt the world around him change. The sounds and smells of the strange forest disappeared and quickly faded from his senses. He opened his eyes and suddenly he was back on top of the temple, the incense still burning, the paper spattered with his blood still leaning against the walls. After he and the priests completed all of the required rituals, after the *ahauob* distributed the blood stained paper throughout the city so that the *cahelob* could burn it with incense in all of the public places, Speaking Macaw retired to his palace and conferred with his most cunning warriors about how he could satisfy Lord Sun's demands. Brave as they were, his men could offer him nothing better than the same old plans of action, the same old recipes for failed glory. He dismissed them and sat in his bedchamber for days and days and racked his brain. Finally he had it, inspiration struck him. He knew how he could feed the feathered vision serpent.

The very next day he sent a herald to Tikal with a battle challenge, accompanied by three priests. Three days later the herald and priests came back, and the date of battle was set. He immediately ordered all the nobility to stay in the confines of the city, and began crash training in his new military tactics. He formulated a plan for the battle, and he drilled his men on this plan, over and over. They practiced the group movements dictated by Speaking Macaw until they almost collapsed from exhaustion. When the trumpet finally blared on the morning of the battle the Tikal men rushed out of the forest on their side of the clearing in the usual disorganized mob, while the Uaxactun warriors stayed put in their lines at the forest edge. The Tikal warriors rushed onward and onward past the center of the clearing. With each step the Tikal warriors became more and more exhausted, and by the time they reached the Uaxactun line almost all of them were short of breath. Uaxactun had remained motionless, and Speaking Macaw's warriors were still fresh. At the last moment Speaking Macaw had his warriors point their spears right at the bellies of the Tikal men, spearing those whose forward momentum would not allow them to stop, and causing the rest to recoil back. Simultaneously Speaking Macaw set off two organized flanks, which quickly ran around the Tikal warriors and encircled them. These warriors then extended long spears toward the inside of the circle. Uaxactun then slowly collapsed the circle until Tikal was being harried on all sides, and began to panic. Tikal's men had no idea what to do, and there appeared to be nowhere to flee to, as there were spear points facing them in every direction. Just when it seemed that everything would be lost for Tikal, its *Ch'ul Ahau*, Great Jaguar Paw, organized his men. Even though he looked as old as the Great Tree itself, he got off of his litter and ran back and forth like a lad of fifteen years, screaming orders, having his men form a wedge, which he used to break through the weakest point in the Uaxactun encirclement. He then led his men, many of them limping, some of them being carried, across the field and back into the forests of Tikal. His litter bearers followed, leaving the royal litter and its assorted gods and other statues to be captured by the enemy as spoils of war. Speaking Macaw chose not to pursue, for he had his victory and there was little to be gained by more combat. His men had captured more Tikal prisoners in a single battle than in any battle chronicled in the history of the city, and they had killed many times more. Tikal managed to kill a few men from Uaxactun, but captured no prisoners, and left the field of battle in total humiliation, just like Lord Sun had dictated in Speaking Macaw's vision. But for the actions of Great Jaguar Paw in organizing the retreat, Tikal might very well have suffered total defeat, with the entire nobility of the city killed or captured. After fleeing in disgrace, Great Jaguar Paw would be in no mood to make any challenges to Uaxactun for the time being. Speaking Macaw had found glory like no king in the annals of the history of Uaxactun.

A few days after speaking to the *Ch'ul Ahau* Jaguar Spot appeared at the palace late one morning and asked for Gray Sky, who quickly appeared. He led Jaguar Spot into the first floor of the palace and through a dark and dank passageway, which curved throughout the building. After they walked for a while it was clear to Jaguar Spot that they were no longer in the main palace building, but had entered a subsidiary structure that was not open to public view. Jaguar Spot had the uncomfortable feeling that he was being led deeper and deeper into a cave. With each step the air became thicker and the smell fouler. If not for the light from Gray Sky's torch they would be walking in total darkness. At last there was another torch light ahead and they approached an open room about the size of a house. There were torches on the wall and two palace guards stood nearby, looking bored. At the sight of Gray Sky's approach they snapped to attention. Gray Sky had Jaguar Spot wait in the doorway to the room as he spoke to the older of the two guards. Each wall of the room had an open door exposing another room beyond. From the flickering light of the torches, Jaguar Spot could sense the presence of people in these rooms, but he could not make out who they were or what they were doing. He imagined that they were prisoners, and that they *lived* in this place, with the filth and stench that were now making a concerted assault on his nose.

The guard that Gray Sky had been speaking to barked an order to the other, who was clearly his subordinate, and who went into one of the dark rooms. He came out pulling a rope, and at the end of the rope was a man, bound at the wrists, with his feet bound so that he had to walk in short steps. The bound man was covered in filth and bruises, and Jaguar Spot immediately recognized him as Fireborn. Since the date of the ballgame that had claimed the life of his brother, Fireborn was a frequent feature of life in the city. At every festival or day of special significance the *Ch'ul Ahau* would haul him out of his dungeon, wash off the filth, and parade him around the city as a trophy of victory. Sometimes at the market children would yell insults and throw rotten food at the nobleman from Tikal. Indeed, Jaguar Spot himself had participated in these spectacles on more than one occasion. Gray Sky walked past Jaguar Spot and led him down still yet another corridor, although this one led to open air in the guise of a small courtyard bounded by single-story stone buildings. Gray Sky took a deep breath of fresh air and spoke to Jaguar Spot. "My colleague is going to give our friend a little bath, so that he is presentable to Your Lordship. Is this going to be the only time that you want to speak to him, or will you need further interviews?" Jaguar Spot had not thought of that, so he decided that he better play it safe. "I don't know," he said, "I may want to talk to him again." Gray Sky grunted in annoyance. "As you wish, Your Lordship. In the future I will bring you straight here then. There really is no need for Your Lordship to put up with that filth and stench."

After the span of about a hundred breaths had passed, the guard walked into the courtyard pulling the rope. A few breaths later, Fireborn followed him through the doorway, still bound, but cleaned of the filth that Jaguar Spot had seen before. The guard took Fireborn over to the only tree in the courtyard and tied him to it. Gray Sky told Jaguar Spot to sit on a rock that would allow him to speak to Fireborn, but which would keep him outside of Fireborn's range of movement. Fireborn sat under the tree and regarded Jaguar Spot with a bemused look on his face. "You are Jaguar Spot, son of Toucan Claw, if I am not mistaken," he said. Gray Sky immediately rushed over to Fireborn and kicked him in the ribs. "You call him 'Your Lordship,' you Tikal scum!" he screamed.

"Okay. From now on I call him 'Your Lordship,'" Fireborn struggled to say, still lying on the ground from the guard's kick. Once Fireborn had regained his composure he sat up once again, and looked at Jaguar Spot. "To what do I owe the pleasure of Your Lordship's visit?" he asked. Jaguar Spot did not quite know how to answer that question. Just looking at Fireborn he saw an impertinence that he had never seen before. As the son of an *ahau*, Jaguar Spot was used to being treated with respect from common citizens and the *cahelob*, and with a feeling of good fellowship from the *ahauob*. Fireborn's tone of voice and the look in his face showed nothing other than ridicule and scorn. Even with Gray Sky ready to give Fireborn a swift kick in the ribs for any perceived slight against his dignity, Jaguar Spot had the feeling that he would be mocked no matter what he said. In the end, he decided on the truth. "His Lordship the *Ch'ul Ahau* has commissioned me to paint a mural depicting his glorious victory over Tikal on the field of battle. I wanted to talk to you about the battle, and your role in it."

Fireborn squinted his eyes at Jaguar Spot. "Why should I want to help you, Your Lordship?" At this remark, Gray Sky started running toward Fireborn again and pulled his leg back for another kick, until Jaguar Spot stopped him. "Gray Sky," he shouted, "that is not necessary." Gray Sky aborted his kick and looked at both Fireborn and Jaguar Spot with consternation. "As Your Lordship wishes," he hissed as he walked away.

Jaguar Spot reached into a bag that he had brought with him and brought out his lunch, which consisted of some cold tortillas and roasted rabbit. He had a feeling that this was better fare than anything that Fireborn had been served in the *Ch'ul Ahau's* palace, so he offered them to Fireborn. "Will this be sufficient payment for speaking to me?" he asked. Gray Sky was incredulous. "Rabbit meat?" he whispered, his voice filled with contempt. "You give the prisoner rabbit meat?" Fireborn, obviously reveling in Gray Sky's reaction, took the food from Jaguar Spot's hand. "What would you like to ask me about, Your Lordship?" he asked before filling his mouth. Jaguar Spot started with a few general questions about the course of the battle five years before.

As everyone that he had spoken to in Uaxactun had said, Fireborn acknowledged that Tikal had been caught completely off guard when Speaking Macaw utilized his new tactics and battle plan. Tikal had expected Uaxactun to use the same normal and accepted military tactics that all Maya cities had used for the past six hundred years. Even though he acknowledged that they were wildly successful, Fireborn thought that Speaking Macaw's new military tactics were unmanly, cowardly, and perhaps even perverse. Fireborn had been part of the Tikal vanguard, and he was nearly impaled when the Uaxactun spear men lowered their weapons right into the Tikal warriors' bellies at the very last second. As it was, he escaped with a nasty cut right below his sternum. Fireborn still had a plainly visible scar on his chest from that day. Two Uaxactun men had captured Fireborn when he fell to the ground in shock from the injury. For Fireborn the battle was over before it had a chance to even start. The men immediately tied him up, and he did not remember much of the battle after that.

They kept speaking into the early afternoon, and Jaguar Spot was getting hungry. Even though he wanted take a break and continue their conversation later so that he could get some food, there was something about the way that Fireborn talked that made him want to stay and listen. When Fireborn described the battle, and the other battles he had fought in, his language painted such a vivid picture that Jaguar Spot could almost see the battle in his mind's eye. After a while Jaguar Spot did not even have to ask questions anymore, Fireborn kept talking and talking, getting more animated, and interesting, as time went on. Something about Fireborn's story, however, bothered Jaguar Spot. "Lord Fireborn," he asked, "you speak like a very brave and honorable man. You have seen battle many times before. I would like to think that you are a man who would do almost anything to avoid the disgrace and ignominy that you are suffering here as a captive. I was there at the ballgame after His Lordship the *Ch'ul Ahau* defeated Tikal." Fireborn sighed and looked to the ground. His voice, which had been so strong and engaging, now sounded strained, almost as if he were holding back tears. "I assumed that you were there, as the son of an *ahau*. So you saw my moment of public disgrace and humiliation. And now you want to ask me why, yes? You want to know why me and my brother declined your *Ch'ul Ahau's* gracious offer to die with honor? Is that what you were about to ask?" Jaguar Spot nodded, still captivated by Fireborn's words. "Well," Fireborn continued, "your *Ch'ul Ahau* taught me a very valuable lesson on the battlefield. He taught me that the days of honor are gone, that the chivalry of the nobility has come to an end. And not just here! Everywhere! This new military doctrine that your city adopted on that day will spread to all the Maya cities, until war as we have known it for all of our history is forgotten. Tell me, what do you think would have happened if your *Ch'ul Ahau* had achieved complete success on the battlefield, if he had killed off all of the male nobility of Tikal?" Before Jaguar Spot could think of a response, Fireborn answered his own question. "Interesting question, isn't it? All my life before the day of my capture I knew that the purpose of war was to give honor to a city's leadership, usually through acquiring a few sorry captives from the opposing city. Your *Ch'ul Ahau* taught me different. War can be used to dominate, to control, to *conquer* another city. If he had complete victory I have no doubt that your *Ch'ul Ahau* would have marched his *ahauob* and *cahelob* into Tikal and proclaimed himself *Ch'ul Ahau* of both cities."

Gray Sky, who was carefully listening to the conversation, scoffed at Fireborn's conclusion. "That's impossible," he said. "Why?" Fireborn shot back. Gray Sky answered instantly. "Because His Lordship's ancestors are not to be found in the temples and palaces of Tikal. The gods and other spirits connected with Tikal would reject him as the *Ch'ul Ahau*. The city of Tikal would wither and die. Our city would do the same without His Lordship being here to make the necessary bloodlettings and rituals. What you suggest simply can't be done." Fireborn acknowledged the common sense of Gray Sky's argument, but was not persuaded. "A good point," he said. "But I still think that it could be done. I guess that we will just have to wait until someone actually conquers another city to see who will win our argument."

Jaguar Spot opened his mouth to ask a question, but before he could get a word out, Fireborn provided the answer. "So, you wonder what this has to do with my decision not to accept an honorable death? I'll tell you. I decided that your *Ch'ul Ahau* fought a battle without honor, and that I would not pretend that he had won an honorable victory, even if it meant dying without honor, or worse, years in your *Ch'ul Ahau's* dungeon." Fireborn suddenly stopped speaking. Even through his hunger pangs Jaguar Spot was enthralled with Fireborn. There was nothing in the world that he wanted more than to hear him keep speaking. He decided to change the subject and ask about Fireborn's family history. "My father says that you were born on an unlucky day," he said.

"Unlucky?" responded Fireborn. "Unlucky? That's what he says?" Fireborn once again sat there silently, as if pondering Toucan Claw's apparently colossal understatement. When he started speaking again it was if he had never stopped. "I was born on the unluckiest day imaginable. The last day of the civil year, and as if that were not bad enough, it augured bad on the religious calendar as well. A double whammy, so to speak. So yes, you could say that I was born on an unlucky day."

Gray Sky started laughing. Jaguar Spot knew why. The civil calendar was divided into eighteen months of twenty days, and one "month" of five days. The last "month" was there only for the purpose of filling out the calendar so that it totaled 365 days in a civil year. Because the number twenty was considered to be the most perfect of all numbers it was unthinkable to assign additional days to any of the normal months. These last five days of the year were a time of great celebrations and festivals, but they were considered to be unusually bad days to bear a child, and the fifth day of this "month" was considered the worse possible day of all. If this were coupled with a bad augur from the religious calendar date for the same day, the result was almost as if the unlucky soul was cursed for life, and could only attain redemption by living out his days in flawless virtue and service to his city. Families in Uaxactun would usually try to hide the shame and humiliation associated with such an unfortunate birth, and would conceal all evidence of a child's delivery until the new year started, claiming that their child was born later than he or she really was. If they did otherwise, families would find it almost impossible to arrange suitable marriages for the children, and any hope of a successful career in a profitable profession would be virtually nonexistent. Because of this, anyone born in the few days near the start of the new civil year would inevitably suffer from being the brunt of rumor and innuendo about whether their birthday actually fell in the five day "month" or not. Fireborn, however, did not have to suffer rumors. Because he had been the brother of Tikal's *Ch'ul Ahau*, and a possible heir to the throne of that city should all of his older brothers die without male children, the law required that his birth had to be witnessed by all of the important priests and nobility of the city. There were so many witnesses to the shameful date of his birth that it would have been impossible to conceal.

"Is this why Great Jaguar Paw made your brother Gray Thunder his war master and not you?" Jaguar Spot asked. He knew the answer to the question before he asked it. He really could not think of anything else anything else to ask, but hoped that it would re-direct the direction of their interview. Suffering from such a bad date of birth was almost like having some kind of loathsome disease–it was not considered a polite topic for extended discussion. "Your Lordship," Fireborn answered, "I think that you are old enough to know that my brother was selected because he was the eldest brother, and a full brother at that. If I may be so bold, Your Lordship, could I ask why you are here speaking to me? Not that I object, mind you. I always appreciate some fresh air and roasted rabbit meat. You said that you were going to paint a mural of some kind, but that doesn't really answer my question. So if you wouldn't mind, Your Lordship, please satisfy my curiosity."

Ever since the *Ch'ul Ahau* had made him a full fledged scribe and commissioned him to paint the mural, Jaguar Spot had paraded around the city like a deer in rut. His father would have been aghast to hear the unseemly level of self-congratulation in his voice as he answered Fireborn. "Well, His Lordship has asked me to paint a mural depicting his glorious victory over Tikal. He wants all of the major events in the battle to be portrayed, and all of the important participants to be mentioned in the text. That is why I am here talking to you." Fireborn smiled, amused at the pride he saw in the child, which almost extended to the point of strutting around bragging. "Tell me, my young Lordship, where is this mural to be located? Outside the palace? On a wall in the market? On a shrine?"

"Oh no, it is much better than that," whispered Jaguar Spot.

"Better than that?" whispered back Fireborn, with his patronizing tone lost on the boy. "Tell me, Your Lordship, how could it be better than that?"

Now Jaguar Spot lowered his voice to make sure that Gray Sky could not hear. "It is supposed to be a secret. I don't think that I should tell you." Fireborn played along with what seemed the child's imaginary sense of self-importance. "Please tell me, Your Lordship. After all, I am a prisoner here in the palace. Who am I going to tell?" Jaguar Spot squinted over again at Gray Sky, who now seemed to be more interested in some birds that had landed in the tree than the conversation, and whispered back to Fireborn. "You see, this is a mural for the *Ch'ul Ahau's* sleeping chamber. He has there a beautiful wall of white plaster, just waiting for me to paint it. Every day when he wakes up, he will look at the wall and relive his glorious victory in his mind. No one will see it except him and his servants."

Fireborn scoffed, momentarily unable to do anything else. Finally, he whispered again. "Let me get this straight, Your Lordship. The *Ch'ul Ahau* of this city is commissioning this mural for his own private bedchamber, for his own private pleasure? No one else will see it except him. Simply for his own edification. He's not doing it for glory. Not to garner the praise of his citizens. Just for himself?" Jaguar Spot nodded. Fireborn's patronizing tone was gone as he whispered again to the boy. "Doesn't that strike you as just a little strange? Doesn't that seem to be rather unusual behavior for a *Ch'ul Ahau*? I mean, I admit that I am from Tikal where the customs might be a little different, but I thought that a *Ch'ul Ahau* was supposed to be humble in private, and only seek praise and admiration in some kind of public forum. Isn't it supposed to be the same way here?"

Fireborn had a point. Toucan Claw had expressed similar misgivings in private the evening that the *Ch'ul Ahau* had given Jaguar Spot his commission. Jaguar Spot found it difficult to continue to look Fireborn in the eye. He now whispered so quietly that Fireborn had trouble hearing him. "That's true. It is a little strange. But it is quite an honor for me and my family."

"But it's a secret. How can you have honor in secret?"

"Uh, well, I . . ."

"You can't. There is no honor in secret. Honor only exists when someone else knows about it. Tell me, who knows of this?"

"Well, there's Snail, the scribe to whom my father apprenticed me."

"But your clothes are those of a full scribe, not an apprentice. Aren't you a little young to be a full-fledged scribe?"

"Yes, that's true. But you see, the *Ch'ul Ahau* granted me the official title of scribe when he commissioned the mural."

"Commissioned? You? A young child? I know for a fact that there are many fine scribes in this city. Why do you think that your *Ch'ul Ahau* would commission you, an apprentice, before you were ready, when there were scribes of great experience who would have jumped at this commission?"

"Who says that I wasn't ready?"

"Take it easy. You can't possibly have the necessary maturity to be a full scribe at your age."

"That's what my father said when we got home. He didn't want me to stop with my apprenticeship, but His Lordship insisted."

"Your father. . . .did not want this to happen? And the *Ch'ul Ahau* overruled his judgment anyway? What kind of city do you live in where an *ahau* is not entitled to make his own decisions about the education of his own son?"

Jaguar Spot did not know how to answer. He could not deny that His Lordship's actions seemed to contrast with the traditions of the city, at least as he knew them. Yet what was the point of being the *Ch'ul Ahau* if you couldn't change traditions now and again, or if you couldn't promote a deserving apprentice to a full scribe? Even though Jaguar Spot had his doubts about what the *Ch'ul Ahau* had done, he was not about to criticize His Lordship in front of a nobleman from Tikal, much less in front of a palace guard like Gray Sky. "I don't think that is unusual at all," Jaguar Spot said, looking at the ground, unable to make eye contact. Fireborn now whispered so quietly that Jaguar Spot could hardly hear him. "I know Your Lordship is not a fool, so I have no doubt in my mind that you don't believe a word of what you just said. I don't think that you are a liar either, at least not by nature. More likely you are a loyal citizen who will not criticize his own *Ch'ul Ahau* to a foreigner, or in front of Gray Sky over there. Yes, that is it. Well done. I applaud your caution and discretion. You will go far in this city."

Jaguar Spot was stunned. Fireborn had been able to read his thoughts as if they were written on paper. "How did you know that?" he whispered. Fireborn looked him right in the eyes. At that moment Jaguar Spot almost thought that he was looking into the eyes of a god. When Fireborn spoke again it was as if his words pierced directly into Jaguar Spot's soul. "I have one bit of advice for you, my young friend," he said. "I am sure that you have studied the Great Tree, about how it connects the different realms of the universe, about how it feeds us and nourishes us. But what they probably haven't taught you is that we are all part of the Great Tree. We are all branches and leaves. You, me, Gray Sky over there, those birds on the roof, and your *Ch'ul Ahau*. Remember this, we are all parts of the same thing, all connected, all the same. Your *Ch'ul Ahau* is just a man. Loyalty to your *Ch'ul Ahau* is a noble quality. It is the foundation of society in every Maya city, like the glue that holds the leaves on the Great Tree. But there comes a day when every tree's leaves must fall. Your father is a loyal man. You will some day follow in his footsteps, and you will be a loyal *ahau* of this city. But there will come a day when your loyalty is put to the test. On that day you will have to make a choice, a choice between loyalty to your ruler, and loyalty to yourself. I can't tell you what choice you should make. You will have to make your own decision. When that happens you think it through thoroughly, make sure that the choice you make is the right one." Fireborn stood up and told Gray Sky that the interview was over for the day. Gray Sky looked down at Jaguar Spot, who nodded. The guard who had brought Fireborn untied the rope from the tree and led Fireborn back into the darkness of the palace hallway. Gray Sky led Jaguar Spot through a separate door that opened into one of the other buildings that bordered the plaza, through a series of light and airy passageways, and out of the main entrance of the palace. "Can you remember how to get into that courtyard using the route that we just took?" Gray Sky asked Jaguar Spot. "I think so," came the reply. "Good. Next time you need to speak to that villain Fireborn, just tell the guard on duty here at the door. He will let you through to that corridor, and one of the other guards will bring Fireborn. I don't see any reason that I have to be involved in these conversations."

When Jaguar Spot arrived home, he found his father and the *ahau* Buried Tapir sitting in the main hall, drinking chocolate out of large bowls. Toucan Claw snapped his fingers and a servant standing quietly against a wall came forward and poured a bowl for Jaguar Spot. "Sit with us, boy. We have to discuss some matters with you," said Toucan Claw. Jaguar Spot had known Buried Tapir for as long as he could remember. He was his father's best friend, the only *ahau* that he would trust to put loyalty and friendship above ambition. More than any of the *ahauob* Buried Tapir was truly was like an uncle to Jaguar Spot. He had taught Jaguar Spot how to haggle with the merchants in the market or at a fair. Before Toucan Claw had sent Jaguar Spot to Snail to learn to read and write, Buried Tapir had taken the boy to the temples and read the inscriptions on the hieroglyphic staircases and the other public writings to him.

Whatever conversation that the adults had been having had stopped the moment that Jaguar Spot had walked through the door. The conversation did not resume until the servant had handed Jaguar Spot his bowl of chocolate and left the room at Toucan Claw's direction. Jaguar Spot started licking the froth at the top of the bowl as Buried Tapir spoke. "Jaguar Spot, what we say here today does not leave this house. Your father and I have been discussing the *Ch'ul Ahau's* assignment to your father. You know of what I speak?" Jaguar Spot, still slurping the chocolate froth, nodded in the affirmative. Buried Tapir continued. "That is not what we are here to speak about. Your Father is still calculating the auguries for all of the girls at issue. Some of the girls augur very poorly for the *Ch'ul Ahau*, so they are out of the running. Of all the girls, Waterlily is perhaps the poorest match of all." Jaguar Spot put the bowl down and wiped his mouth with his arm. Waterlily was Buried Tapir's youngest daughter, one year younger than Jaguar Spot, who almost thought of her as a sister.

"I am sorry, Uncle. You must be very disappointed that your daughter will not be marrying the *Ch'ul Ahau*," said Jaguar Spot, trying to console Buried Tapir, who locked eyes with Toucan Claw with the barest hint of a grin. "I am not upset," he said, "In fact I am quite content. With some of the things that we have seen lately, I am not sure that I would want His Lordship to be the husband of my youngest daughter. Regardless, for some time your father and I have had our eyes on someone else to fill that position."

Jaguar Spot finished the last of the chocolate. A feeling of pride overwhelmed him. The adults had never entrusted him with this kind of intimate information before. He found it difficult to control his feelings, but ultimately he remembered that he was the son of an *ahau* and managed to restrain himself. "Who?" he asked with false calmness. "Tell me Uncle, who is it?" Buried Tapir and Toucan Claw looked at each other and started laughing. "Son," said Toucan Claw, "have you noticed that Buried Tapir and me have been meeting in private quite a bit lately?"

"Yes Father, I had noticed. But with all of the excitement lately, I haven't given it much thought" said Jaguar Spot.

"We have been negotiating, and we have reached an agreement," said Buried Tapir, "agreement on Waterlily's dowry. Of course there cannot be any *public* announcement until this . . .this . . . errand of your father's is completed and the moratorium is lifted, but there is no reason that the parties involved have to remain in the dark."

The three of them sat in silence for a while, the adults looking like they expected Jaguar Spot to have some kind of reaction, or at least to say something. At first the import of their words was lost on Jaguar Spot, then he thought through what they were saying and came to the realization that they were not only talking *to* him, they were talking *about* him. "Me?" he asked, "You are talking about me, aren't you? I am going to marry Waterlily? When?" Toucan Claw pulled a piece of paper from under a mat and showed it to Jaguar Spot, with Buried Tapir looking over his shoulder. The paper showed detailed auguries based on the birth dates of both Jaguar Spot and Waterlily. Based on these auguries, he had calculated the best date combinations to act as wedding dates. Although it would have not occurred to him until the *Ch'ul Ahau* had suggested it, Toucan Claw had used both the civil and the religious calendars to make the calculation. Because the cycle did not repeat for 52 civil years, the best possible dates were spread over several decades. Toucan Claw had calculated that the *very* best date would fall in 32 years, which everyone agreed was not practicable. The next best date fell on 5 Chuen 16 Mol, which would not occur for more than six years. Toucan Claw and Buried Tapir argued about this date for some time. They agreed this would be too long of a wait for their children, and that both of them would almost be too old to find another worthy mate if illness or another calamity would claim the life of one of them before the wedding. On the other hand, the intervening six years had no auguries that came even close to 5 Chuen 16 Mol in terms of omens for prosperity and happiness. In the end they reluctantly agreed that the benefit of the good augury outweighed the downside associated with the long wait and that the wedding would occur on 5 Chuen 16 Mol. Once the *Ch'ul Ahau's* moratorium was lifted, Waterlily would move into Toucan Claw's house and live with the women of the family. Buried Tapir agreed to pay a small dowry every twenty days to cover Toucan Claw's expenses in caring for the girl, with the larger dowry to be paid on the date of the wedding. As Buried Tapir left, Toucan Claw went back to his work for the *Ch'ul Ahau*. Jaguar Spot found his ballclothes and ran to the ballcourt for a practice match.

Chapter Six
DROUGHT

8.16.14.17.4. April 15, 371 A.D.

The next spring, calamity befell the city of Uaxactun, and all the cities of the Maya lowlands. The spring rains, essential for the crops and lives of the people, did not come. They had been due for some time. The priests had carefully monitored the path of Lord Sun through the sky, noting exactly where he rose and where he set each day against three temples set in a line across a plaza from the highest temple in the city. Lord Sun rose exactly above a particular temple on the dates of the solstices and equinoxes. By observing the place where Lord Sun rose, and by counting the days on paper or other devices, the priests could tell the farmers when to plant their crops, when to harvest their crops, and when to leave the fields to help the noble classes on other works. In living memory, the priests had never erred in their predictions of the seasons or with their advice on when to plant the crops. Yet this year the sky stubbornly refused to lose its dark blue color, and Lord Sun beamed down upon the earth without so much as a cloud to give the people respite from his light. Even the trees in the forest assumed a strange aspect. As during any dry season, their bark lost its dark color and the forest became almost white in appearance. This year the trees looked like huge dry animal bones thrust into the ground by unseen giants. The leaves started falling to the forest floor in great piles, sometimes so large that they obscured the well worn paths that had enabled the people to walk from city to city for hundreds of years. As in every year, the birds and the beasts were quiet, waiting for water or busy finding the closest water hole, but in this year there were hardly any birds to be seen at all. Hunters reported traversing great distances without seeing any game. The worst hit, however, were the farmers.

When the spring rains were more than a month late, panic began to set in among the population of Uaxactun. His Lordship the *Ch'ul Ahau* had wisely stored enough grain and dried beans so that the city could survive a year, or perhaps two years, of drought, so the citizens of the city were guaranteed full stomachs. Hunger did not panic them. What concerned them most was the possibility that the Gods had abandoned them, that Lord Sun was somehow punishing them for a transgression that they could not remember committing. Or worse. Some even whispered questions among themselves, questions that could be considered treason. Had the *Ch'ul Ahau* committed some unknown blasphemy against the denizens of the Otherworld? Had their city's holy protector lost his powers? No one would dare breathe a word of such treasonable thoughts in public, but more and more whispered their doubts to trusted friends behind closed doors. The scribes, the priests, and the city's other people of education had an even more terrifying fear: perhaps something was wrong with the Great Tree itself? They knew that the rain was the holy blood of the Great Tree, a sacrifice to humanity, made in the same way that humanity sacrificed blood to its gods and ancestors. If the Great Tree withered, or if it, Gods Forbid, died, what would happen to the people of the Earth?

Speaking Macaw was at a loss to devise a solution for the disaster. He had submitted himself to thrice daily bloodlettings, moving from temple to temple, from precinct to precinct, and to every outlying village in the realm of Uaxactun. He sometimes felt that the entire nation was painted not with red stucco, but with the blood from his offerings. He was now perpetually weak, sometimes faint, and never in a good humor. The men of the city were also expected to sacrifice blood to solve this problem. Throughout their adult lives all of them had participated in private bloodletting rituals, designed to feed their ancestors. During normal times, every few days, according to a schedule announced by the priests, they would go to a small shrine in the courtyard of their house, or in the courtyard of their family compound, and cut themselves with an obsidian blade. The blades, and the stingray spines used by the *ahauob* and other deserving men, came from the *Ch'ul Ahau*, as gifts designed to cement the city's social compact. All of the blades were first used by His Lordship, or by one of previous *Ch'ul Ahauob* of the city. Royalty would use a blade only once, after which the blades would be distributed throughout the realm by the *ahauob*, where they would become family heirlooms. Some families used the same blade for hundreds of years. The men of the city were used to these private rituals. They were an important and valued part of life, something to be cherished as a moment of blessed piety.

With the crisis Speaking Macaw had ordered a change in plans. Now all the men of the city, from the humblest laborer to the highest of the *ahauob*, was required to amass in great gatherings in the public squares and cut themselves together. Their blood, flowing in little rivulets, collected in stinking pools. Perhaps, the priests thought, such a demonstration of public sacrifice would satisfy the Gods, or would nourish the Great Tree, or would cure whatever cursed plague was besetting their city. The public was dubious, but they followed the orders of the priests and their nobles and submitted to the rituals. After a while, it was clear to everybody that bloodletting would not cure the city's problems, nor would the now daily sacrifices of animals, and as was becoming common, orphaned children. Speaking Macaw had spoken with every luminary, every wit, and every man with knowledge that the nobility could dredge up, but no one offered anything other than the pallid advice to offer the Gods more blood.

It was in the midst of this crisis that Jaguar Spot found himself staring at the unfinished mural in the *Ch'ul Ahau's* bedchamber, unable to paint. Almost seven months had passed from his first visit to Fireborn, and the work was almost halfway completed. His normal daily routine usually consisted of half a morning at Snail's workshop to work on his Council Book, an early lunch at home, and then painting the mural until mid-afternoon, when he would run off to the ballcourt.

He sat and stared at the mural. Embarrassed at his lack of modesty, he admired his own work. He picked up the brushes and wet them in paint, but something in his mind was unable to put brush to plaster. He had just finished a particularly complicated battle scene with the *Ch'ul Ahau* standing on top of a bound *ahau* from Tikal when inspiration completely abandoned him. He sat there, staring at his work, dumbstruck. After a series of increasingly fruitless attempts to start at something, he picked up his paints and brushes and left the room in a huff. Rabbit, the palace guard who had been monitoring him, silently followed him to the top of the stairway on the second floor, and they both surveyed the sorry state of the city in silence. The market was half-abandoned, and almost no traders from other cities had arrived in weeks. Some people glumly went about their work while others sat around drinking maize beer or doing nothing at all.

"Are you done for the day, Your Lordship?" the guard asked, eager to return to other duties. Jaguar Spot nodded silently and started walking down the stairs. Halfway down, he turned around and shouted to the guard, who returned to the shade inside the palace. "Rabbit?" he said, "Rabbit, are you still there?" Rabbit quickly returned to the stairway from some dark recess in the palace. "Your Lordship?" he asked. Jaguar Spot told the guard that he wanted to speak to Fireborn, that he would meet them both in the internal courtyard when it would be convenient. Rabbit was incredulous. "That Tikal scum, Your Lordship? Now why would a nice boy from a family as good as yours want to see him. I hear that there is going to be a ballgame this afternoon. Wouldn't Your Lordship rather spend his time playing ball than commiserating with that ill-augured vermin?" Jaguar Spot assured the guard that the purpose of the meeting was simply to assist him with ideas for the *Ch'ul Ahau's* mural. "Well in that case," said the guard, "I completely understand. I will make sure that he is brought to the courtyard presently, Your Lordship."

Jaguar Spot found his way to the courtyard in almost no time. The lone tree looked very much the same as it did during his last visit, although this time there were no birds to grace either it or the roofs of the surrounding structures. Jaguar Spot sat against the tree in a silence more profound than anything that he could ever remember. He heard nothing stirring. There were no shouts of people, no beasts bleating, no birds in the sky, no wind. He could hear his own breathing above all else. He could even hear the sound of his own heart. After a while a guard brought out Fireborn, tied up in the same fashion as at their last meeting. For all Jaguar Spot knew, it was the same rope, and the same knots, as before. "Where's Rabbit?" Jaguar Spot asked the guard, who responded in a huff, pointing at Fireborn and speaking with obvious sarcasm. "Rank has its privileges, Your Lordship, and His Excellency Lord Rabbit decided that he was too high born to even be in the same room as this one."

Fireborn ignored the guard and promptly sat down at Jaguar Spot's feet and started speaking: "It's been quite a while since our last little talk, Your Lordship. But I must thank you for this little bit of sunshine nonetheless. Have you finished your mural yet?" Jaguar Spot sadly admitted that he was barely halfway finished with the mural, which was becoming more and more of an undertaking as time went on. Fireborn waved Jaguar Spot's self-doubt away. "I am sure that Your Lordship will complete the job to the satisfaction of your *Ch'ul Ahau*. Anyway, self-flagellation and expressions of self-doubt can't have been the reason that you so kindly invited me here for this pleasant little chat. Or were they?" Jaguar Spot then leaned up close to Fireborn and whispered. "Sir, I must admit that I have no real purpose for talking to you. I just couldn't think of anything to paint today, and I was bored. So I asked to see you."

The guard that had brought Fireborn to the courtyard moaned a little in apparent discomfort. "Your Lordship?" he asked, almost meekly, "you and the gentleman from Tikal seem to get along all right. Would it be acceptable to Your Lordship if I just tied he gentleman up to the tree while I took care of some . . . . personal business." Fireborn laughed at his jailer's discomfort. Jaguar Spot looked at him. There was no doubt in his mind that Fireborn would escape if he could, and that he would have no qualms whatsoever about killing a young boy in the process. On the other hand, he did seem to be tied up very securely, and that chance seemed remote at best. "That's fine," Jaguar Spot finally said, and the guard quickly tied Fireborn to the tree, and then ran down the hall, almost hopping.

"My," Fireborn said, looking up at the sky, "the weather seems usually clement for this time of year. Has there been much rain?" Jaguar Spot did not answer. Even in his cell, Fireborn must have known something about what was going on in the city. At the very least, he must have picked up intelligence about the events in the outside world from listening to the guards' idle chatter. Jaguar Spot was old enough to know that Fireborn was performing the rhetorical equivalent to a probing serve in a ball game, trying to size up the opponent's skill and ability. "I expect that there hasn't been," Fireborn continued, "with what you told me about the behavior of the *Ch'ul Ahau* of this city. He must be accursed by the Gods for your city to suffer such a fate. Perhaps even the Great Tree now bestows disfavor on this place, as punishment for your leader's perversions." Jaguar Spot knew what Fireborn was doing, as sure as he knew that Lord Sun would rise the next day he knew it. Fireborn was trying to bait him into some kind of unseemly outburst, to deprive him of his self-respect. Even so, Jaguar Spot could not help himself from taking Fireborn's bait and rising to the defense of the *Ch'ul Ahau*. "Nonsense!" he said, almost losing control of himself, "this drought has struck everywhere! All the Maya cities, even Tikal, are afflicted. If anything, His Lordship has done everything he can to help us. Father says that he has never seen such devotion in a *Ch'ul Ahau* before. So you don't know what you are talking about!" Jaguar Spot was getting so angry that he stood up and started to leave. As he was about reach the door to summon a guard to take Fireborn away, Fireborn erupted into loud laughter. "Come my friend," Fireborn said in between laughs, "I know all about that. Indeed, His Lordship your *Ch'ul Ahau* has been doing everything humanly possible to stop this awful drought. I am sure that my brother in Tikal is doing something similar. I merely said that to goad you. You seemed to be a challenging boy to goad. I didn't mean it. Please, let us sit and talk as friends."

Jaguar Spot reluctantly accepted Fireborn's invitation and once again sat next to him. "Tell me," Fireborn said, "about this moratorium on marriage in the noble families that I have heard about. It seems that some people are quite upset by the whole thing, but no one knows the reason behind it. What do you know?" Before he could think about what he was doing and who he was talking to, Jaguar Spot started telling Fireborn the entire story. He told him of his father's commission to find His Lordship a new bride, about the unrest that was building in among the *ahauob* and the *cahelob* who were unable to marry off their sons and daughters, and about his own planned marriage to Waterlily. Finally, when he was near the end of his story, he began to realize that he was speaking with the *Ch'ul Ahau's* enemy, a man who might be able to use this information to somehow damage His Lordship and the city. He stopped talking and looked at Fireborn with embarrassment. "I had better not say anything more," he said quietly. "I have probably said far too much as it is." Fireborn clicked his tongue against his teeth in agreement. "Yes," he said, "Yes you have. I like you, Your Lordship. You remind me of myself when I was your age, for some reason that I can't quite describe in words. So I will give you this little bit of advice. Don't talk so much. Your father's high station in the city gives you access to some very important information. Don't worry about telling me. The only people that I get to talk to are the guards, and whenever I say anything they yell at me to shut up. Remember that the world is full of knaves and fiends. Always remember that. The knaves will use the information to advance their own interests and to discredit you. The fiends will take the information and stab you in the back. If you keep information like that to yourself, you will be much better off in the long run. Do you understand me, Your Lordship?"

"Yes."

"And will you follow that advice? Promise me that you will."

"I promise."

"Good. I expect that we don't have much time until the guard comes back. There are some things that I want to say to you, things that I would not try to say with them around. So just let me speak. I fear that Your *Ch'ul Ahau* has done something so horrific that the Gods have abandoned not only him, not only your city, but the entire Maya realm. Perhaps the people up in the Valley of Mexico are not suffering as we are, I don't know. I don't care. Your *Ch'ul Ahau* has been doing some very strange things of late. Take this nonsense of a moratorium on marriage. Consider this ridiculous practice of mass bloodletting. What about this heroic mural that you are painting in his own bedchamber.

To make matters worse, he makes you a scribe against your father's wishes. Instead of using the priests, he has your father, who I am sure is a very capable man, augur a compatible mate. All of this seems very strange. Either he is abandoning the ways of the Gods, or the Gods have abandoned him. No, no, let me talk. I know that you want to defend him, but we have no time for that. I know that the other cities are suffering from the same drought, but please, do they have the same issues with their *Ch'ul Ahau*? Even with all of this, I feel that *you* are the solution. It has something to do with you. If anyone is going to have to save the world, it is you. I don't know why I know this, but I do."

Jaguar Spot was absolutely certain that Fireborn was trying to manipulate him through flattery. At the same time he couldn't help but feel pride in Fireborn's statement that he, Jaguar Spot, son of Toucan Claw, would be the one to save the world. His mind told him to get up and walk away, but there was something that drew him to Fireborn, something that he could not put into words. "What must I do?" Jaguar Spot asked.

Fireborn laughed. "You ask me? Jaguar Spot, future *ahau* of the great city of Uaxactun, asks humble Fireborn, captive from Tikal? I have no answers for you, except that you must search within yourself for guidance. Inside you is a pathway to the Gods. Speak to the Gods. Maybe they can give you the answers. Maybe the Great Tree will speak to you, although I don't think that it has much to say. For my part I have never been able to get any information out of it, but maybe you will have better luck. The same feeling that I have about you tells me that the Gods will help you, and that you will bring peace between the cities of Tikal and Uaxactun. Perhaps peace will save our world."

Jaguar Spot thought that Fireborn had lost his mind, that the stress of captivity had dulled the edge of his thoughts. "Only His Lordship can speak to the Gods," he said, "Everybody knows that." Fireborn now gave a wry smile and looked around to make sure that no one had wandered in to overhear their conversation. "Nonsense," he whispered. "That's just what the *Ch'ul Ahau* and the priests want you to believe. The truth is that everybody, form the *Ch'ul Ahau* to the *ahauob* to the *cahelob* to the humblest citizen of this city can speak with the Gods. Perhaps the Gods listen better to royalty or nobility, I don't know, but the pathways of communication exist for everyone. All you have to do is try."

"How do I try?" Jaguar Spot asked. Fireborn started speaking very quickly, as if afraid that the guards would come back at any second.

"This is what you do," he said. "You take some holy mushrooms, and some waterlily ribosomes. You let out your blood and you eat the mixture. The gods, if they wish to speak to you, will speak to you then. Do not delay. Everyone's well being may depend on what you do." Just as Fireborn stopped speaking, Jaguar Spot heard the sound of footsteps running down the hallway. From the sound of it, there were many people running together, and in an instant Rabbit and four other guards burst into the courtyard, spears in hand. Rabbit had a look of relief on his face when he saw Jaguar Spot and Fireborn talking peacefully. "That's a relief," Rabbit said. "Your Lordship, I am sorry that my colleague endangered you by leaving you with this ruffian from Tikal. I am glad to see that you are uninjured."

Jaguar Spot touched Fireborn on his left bicep and stood up. "It was no problem," he said to Rabbit. "I will leave now." Rabbit motioned one of the other guards to untie Fireborn from the tree and they started pulling him away into the corridor. Just as he was about to disappear into the darkness, Fireborn turned around and looked Jaguar Spot in they eye. "Thank you, Your Lordship," Jaguar Spot whispered silently to Fireborn. In an instant he was alone in the courtyard.

On his way home Jaguar Spot stopped in the daily market, or what passed for the daily market during the days of the drought. It took him quite a while to find a merchant who was selling the items that he was looking for. The merchant, an elderly man with long white hair, sat in the dirt behind his wares, which were displayed on a colorful blanket. Jaguar Spot knelt down and pretended to examine the holy mushrooms like an expert. He picked up a large brown piece and held it up to Lord Sun, then squeezed it between his forefinger and thumb. He had seen his father do the same when purchasing holy mushrooms in the market. The merchant, apparently sensing Jaguar Spot's inexperience, pulled out a cloth bag and placed it on the blanket. "I believe that I have seen Your Lordship here before, with His Lordship your father. He must have sent you to get supplies for Lady Moon's festival tomorrow, yes?" The merchant waited for Jaguar Spot to answer with his hand on top of the bag. Jaguar Spot did not want to lie to the man, especially when the man regularly did business with his father. He gave a sort of non-committal throat clearing that he hoped the merchant would take for an answer. The merchant continued to stare at him, and then spoke while pointing to the stock displayed on the blanket. "You can ignore that stuff on the blanket. I leave that out for the idiots who don't know what they are buying. But I don't want Your Lordship's father to think that I chiseled you out of your money. These are my good stock. How much do you want?"

Jaguar Spot picked up the bag and opened it, still pretending to know what he was doing. "Well," he said, "um, let's see. Not that much, really. Just as much as is necessary. You know, the usual amount, and some ribosomes." The merchant looked confused but picked up the bag and poured a handful of the dried mushrooms into his hand. He replaced the bag where he had found it and pulled out another bag filled with ribosomes. "I don't get much call for ribosomes these days," the merchant said as he plucked three or four from the bag, "your father, for one, has never had any call to buy ribosomes. Who are they for?" Jaguar Spot gulped some air and regarded the merchant without speaking. He could not very well tell the truth and say that the holy mushrooms and ribosomes were for him. Boys were not supposed to eat either of them prior to their ascension ritual, which was still some time off for Jaguar Spot. As it was, Jaguar Spot thought that the merchant was suspicious, but knew that the merchant would think very hard before refusing to sell to the eldest son of an *ahau*. "Your Lordship," the merchant asked, "I am sorry, but I must know who these ribosomes are for before I can sell them to you. I am sure that His Lordship your father would understand." Jaguar Spot's mouth ran dry at the repeated references to his father. He knew that he was taking a big risk by making a purchase from this merchant, but it would be a bigger risk if is father found out that he had lied to someone in the market. "An *ahau*," Jaguar Spot finally said. "An *ahau* asked me to make this purchase." Jaguar Spot's answer was literally true, but he knew that it was misleading. He hoped that his father would respect the technicality that he told the truth, but it was a faint hope. The merchant, however, accepted his word without question. To do anything else would be seen as an insult to Jaguar Spot's father. He handed Jaguar Spot the holy mushrooms and ribosomes and asked for three cacao beans in return. Jaguar Spot was glad to give the merchant the money and be gone. He hurried through the market on his way home. He had no time to bleed himself and submit to the ritual described by Fireborn, so he chewed on the dried mushrooms as he walked. Hopefully the holy mushrooms and ribosomes would work well enough without Jaguar Spot spilling his own blood.

The holy mushrooms were hard and crunchy. They tasted horrible, like old moldy tortillas or dirty feet. He ate some of the waterlily ribosomes, in hope that they would override the flavor of the mushrooms, but that only made matters worse. They were the most bitter thing that he had ever put in his mouth. He quickly chewed the rest of the mushrooms as he walked to his home. He barely had time to rinse his mouth out with water before he had to run off to the ballcourt for that afternoon's game.

The sons of the *ahauob* usually practiced and played the ballgame together. They would usually divide up into different teams for practice each day. Sometimes they would pick the best of the boys and play the sons of the *cahelob*, or even the sons of common citizens of the city. Jaguar Spot, as one of the younger boys in his age group, usually watched such games from the sideline. Today was different. The priests said that the day augured well for a game between the sons of the *ahauob* and the citizens of the city's most southern precinct. There were almost fifty ballplayers from each side gathered in the ballcourt for the beginning of the game, which the priests had decided would have six players on each side. This was most unusual, as the game was usually played with two or three players to a side, with four at most. The sons of the *ahauob* had elected Stag, the eldest son of a minor *ahau*, as their captain. Stag was by far the best ballplayer in the city. Jaguar Spot held out little hope that Stag would call on him as he surveyed the other boys sitting down beside him. He nonetheless felt a little disappointment when Stag failed to point in his direction as he picked out the team. Stag and five other boys made their way to the playing surface, and six boys from the South Precinct did the same. Just as the priest was about to hand the ball to Stag so that it could be put into play, several of the boys sitting around Jaguar Spot let out gasps and looked to the far end of the ball court. Everyone slowly came to their feet and bowed their heads as they realized that the *Ch'ul Ahau* had entered. The *Ch'ul Ahau* walked up to Stag and patted him on the back. He did the same to the captain from the South Precinct, who was unaccustomed to personal interaction with the *Ch'ul Ahau*. The South captain fell to his knees and began to weep from the excitement. The *Ch'ul Ahau* pulled him up and wiped the tears from the boy's face. "I wish all of you a good and merry game, boys," the *Ch'ul Ahau* said. He then nodded to the priest and climbed up the wall to the ledge overlooking the ballcourt. The boys sitting there all moved to stand up. "Sit down boys," the *Ch'ul Ahau* said with a jolly voice. "I am just here to watch the game, not for some damn official ceremony. Ah, Jaguar Spot. Come, sit with me." The *Ch'ul Ahau* sat down and beckoned to Jaguar Spot, who dutifully walked over and sat down next to him.

No one spoke as the game began. Stag took the rubber ball, which was about the size of a man's head, from the priest. He took it in his left hand and hit it hard with his right forearm. The ball flew far into the South Precinct side before bouncing into the end zone. Two of the South Precinct players ran to the ball, and one of them was able to hit it with his waist before it bounced for a second time. The ball went flying back toward Stag and crossed the center line before its second bounce. The *Ch'ul Ahau* and all of the boys watching the game started to lean forward. The serve from Stag had been excellent, almost not returnable. The fact that a player from the South Precinct backcourt had returned it with such aplomb boded well for an excellent game. Stag tried to make a run at the ball, but it flew past him and into the *ahauob* back court. One of the back players was able to connect with his forearm and send the ball bouncing off the wall, back into the South Precinct side. The assembled boys watched in silence as the player who had made the previous return with his hip ran out of the South Precinct end zone and made a spectacular return with his right hip. The ball bounced high into the air before flying over Stag's head and deep into the *ahauob* end zone. One of the *ahauob* players tried to make an attempt on the ball, but it went flying backward into the rear stands. The South Precinct had scored a point.

The priest walked out onto the court and handed the ball to the South Precinct captain, who served it high into the air. The player guarding the *ahauob* end zone made a desperate play for the ball, but tripped over his own feet at the last second. The ball hit him straight on the head and he fell to the ground, unconscious. The other *ahauob* players ran over to him while the priest came to examine his head. The boy started to regain consciousness almost immediately, but the priest ordered that he sit out the rest of the game. Stag pointed to another boy from the *ahauob* ranks to take his place. Before the new boy could make his way to the field, the *Ch'ul Ahau* raised his hand, cleared his throat, and motioned with his hand for Stag to speak to him. Stag came running over and knelt next to the *Ch'ul Ahau*, who whispered in his ear. Stag got up and pointed to Jaguar Spot. "Come on," he said. "You are going to play in the back court." Jaguar Spot followed Stag down to the playing surface while the previously selected boy returned to his seat.

The South Precinct still had the serve. Jaguar Spot was in the fourth position, right in front of the end zone. Two players were behind him, strapping lads with big muscles who could hit the ball out of the end zone and back to the South Precinct side. This was the most difficult shot in the ballgame. They would have to hit the ball so that it would fly out of the wide end zone and into the narrow central playing area. The ball was heavy, but it would bounce a fair distance off of the central area's stone walls. The boys in the back had to have special skill and strength to make the shot, which they were able to make less than half the time. Jaguar Spot's job was to serve as a blocker to make sure that boys in the end zone did not have the chance to test their skills. As he stood there waiting for the serve, he noticed that things were beginning to look strange. The player standing in front of him appeared to be glowing with some kind of aura around his body. The drab walls of the ballcourt started bursting with color. There was blue and purple and orange, constantly shifting, changing from one to the other. Something else about these colors was strange, because he didn't seem to be seeing the colors with his eyes, but felt like he was *tasting* the colors on the wall. Finally the boy in front of Jaguar Spot screamed that the South Precinct had served the ball, which was already airborne. The ball appeared to be moving slowly, almost as if it were crawling through the air. The ball was coming straight toward Jaguar Spot. He turned to his side and hit the ball with his right hip, directly on his waist pad. The impact from the ball sent him staggering back, but the ball flew forward toward the South Precinct side. As he stood there awaiting the ball's return, he saw strange things moving on the playing surface. The entire ballcourt seemed to be crawling with insects and frogs. The priest officiating the game was speaking somewhere in the distance, but his voice was faint and garbled. All of the sudden the ground seemed to start spinning and flying up at Jaguar Spot. It hit him hard in the face, and the world went black.

Jaguar Spot awoke on a bed of pine needles, in a forest clearing high in the mountains. He was looking down at the top of the clouds, one of which had the shape of a jaguar. The jaguar cloud slowly moved up the mountain until it was eye to eye with Jaguar Spot. "Where am I?" Jaguar Spot asked.

The cloud seemed to speak, but his words came as whispers from all directions. "You are here. That is exactly where you are. Nowhere else."

Jaguar Spot thought about what the cloud had said to him, and decided that it was not much of an answer at all. "Why am I here?" he asked. The cloud now moved toward him and surrounded him. He could smell the cloud's moisture. The air was now an opaque fog. "Because you came here," said the cloud.

Jaguar Spot lay there in silence, unsure of what to do next. The cloud did not seem to be very forthcoming with information, so Jaguar Spot sat on the pine needles and waited. Time passed, but it passed in a strange way. The world seemed to pulse all around Jaguar Spot. One moment he would be conscious of the silence and emptiness of this place, and the next he would feel like he was wrapped in cotton, almost part of the ground, almost like he was a blade of grass. The cloud started whispering again. "Tell me, Jaguar Spot, son of Toucan Claw, why did you come to this place?"

"I don't know. I didn't seek to come here. I was playing the ballgame."

"You ate the holy mushrooms, yes?"

"Yes. Oh I see. The holy mushrooms and the ribosomes brought me here?"

"Why did you come here, Jaguar Spot, son of Toucan Claw?"

"I came to ask how what I can do to stop the horrible drought that has been afflicting my people. Fireborn mentioned something about solving it through peace, but I don't quite understand what he means by that."

"Peace is the absence of war."

"I know that. I don't think that was what he meant. What can we do to stop this horrible drought?"

"Peace is the absence of war."

"What is that supposed to mean?"

"Peace is the absence of war." The voice started to fade. The cloud became darker. The voice kept repeating itself until Jaguar Spot had to strain his ears to hear it. The air became so dark that it was as if Jaguar Spot were standing in a starless night. Finally Jaguar Spot fell asleep on the pine needles.

When Jaguar Spot woke up he had no idea how much time had elapsed since he went to sleep on the mountainside. He was on his own sleeping mat in his father's house. His vision was blurry, but he could make out the shape of four people in the room with him. The people were talking to each other, about him he imagined, but he couldn't understand what they were saying. There were four distinct voices, three men and a woman. The voices became more understandable, and he was able to make out individual words. The female voice said "idiot" followed by more nonsense words and then "don't care what you think" followed by still more nonsense words. Whomever the female was speaking to appeared to take offense with her remarks, because Jaguar Spot heard him say "insulted in my life" before he stormed out, screaming more words that Jaguar Spot could not understand. Jaguar Spot tried to whisper to get the attention of the woman. "Peace is the absence of war," he whispered. The three people remaining in the room immediately walked over to him, and he saw that they were his sister Orchid, his father, and the *Ch'ul Ahau*.

Orchid leaned over him and felt his head. "What did you say?" she asked.

All that he could do was repeat himself: "Peace is the absence of war." Before he could say anything else, light in the room went dark. When he next awoke he was alone in the room with Orchid, who sat on a stool next to his sleeping mat, sewing. "Ah, you are awake," Orchid said, and then poured him a bowl full of water. "You took a nasty blow to the head. Father has put you in my care, much to the chagrin of that hapless idiot Spirit Dog, who suggested that you had eaten too many holy mushrooms and had a bad reaction. Imagine that! You, the son of an *ahau*, eating holy mushrooms before your ascension ceremony! Father was quite insulted by the very insinuation, and His Lordship the *Ch'ul Ahau* told Spirit Dog in no uncertain terms that such an action would not be in your character. So how are you, my brother?"

Jaguar Spot couldn't believe that he was being put in another situation that tested his honesty so quickly after his experience with the merchant. It was almost as if the Gods had decreed that he be tempted in to telling lies on a daily basis. He did not want to lie to Orchid, but after his father and the *Ch'ul Ahau* had defended him, he could not just turn around and admit that, well yes, he had eaten holy mushrooms before his ascension ceremony after all. He decided to tell a half truth. "I had a vision," he said. Orchid poured him some more water and played along. "A vision?" she asked. "That sounds quite exciting, really it does. Please tell me about your vision."

"Well," Jaguar Spot started. "I was playing the game when I saw the ground start to spin and then come at me. I woke up in a forest, and there a saw a cloud in the shape of a Jaguar. I spoke to the cloud. I asked it how to end the drought. All it kept saying was 'peace is the absence of war.' I would ask for clarification, but it gave me none. I asked what it meant, but all it would say is 'peace is the absence of war.' It kept saying the same thing over and over, and then it disappeared. The next thing I know, I woke up here." Jaguar Spot took a gulp of the water that Orchid held up to his mouth. Orchid put the water bowl down and felt his head. "Hmm," she said, "no fever. You do have a nasty bump from the fall. I will go get Father and His Lordship." Orchid stood up and left the room. Jaguar Spot was just about to fall back asleep when she returned with Toucan Claw and Speaking Macaw. Toucan Claw knelt down next to Jaguar Spot and felt his head, just as Orchid had done. "The boy has no fever," he said, turning to the *Ch'ul Ahau*, who nodded and motioned for Orchid to bring him a chair. The *Ch'ul Ahau* sat down next to where Toucan Claw was kneeling with his hand still on Jaguar Spot's head.

"Your sister says that you had some kind of vision. Tell us about it," said the *Ch'ul Ahau*. Jaguar Spot repeated the story that he told Orchid. The *Ch'ul Ahau* rubbed his chin and repeated the words "peace is the absence of war" quietly to himself, thinking. "What do you make of it, my friend?" he asked Toucan Claw. Toucan Claw took his hand from Jaguar Spot's forehead and motioned for Orchid to bring him a chair so that he could sit next to His Lordship. "I don't know what to make of it, Your Lordship," he said once seated. "It could be a real vision, or just as likely it is an hallucination brought on from the boy falling down and knocking his head. It is a strange vision, though. The message seems pretty unclear." The *Ch'ul Ahau* stood up, pushed the chair away, and started pacing back and forth. He started speaking to the air more than anyone else. "Strange? Yes, it is strange. His head? Yes, he hit his head, but why? No. Not the head. He fell. Why. Hmmmm. The day was not overly hot. Hmmm. I saw him. I just watched him. He hit a good shot. The next ball came and he collapsed to the ground? Hmmmm. Very interesting. Yes. The auguries! Yes! Of course! Don't you see?" he said, finally addressing his ramblings to Toucan Claw, who was still sitting down.

"Um, I don't think that I do, Your Lordship," said Toucan Claw. The *Ch'ul Ahau* started pacing faster and faster, speaking again. "The auguries! Don't be dense! The priests did auguries for the ballgame. They said that it was an *unusually* prodigious day for a ballgame. That's why I was there. They said the most unusually prodigious day for a ballgame that they had ever seen. Do you hear me? Ever! And why? Why did the augurs grant the priests this information? I'll tell you! Because of this vision. The gods made sure that your boy was there on the ballcourt to have the vision, and here we are. This is a divine vision. Almost as divine as if he had entered the Otherworld himself. Don't you see?"

Toucan Claw thought about his answer before saying anything. "Not entirely, Your Lordship," he finally said. The *Ch'ul Ahau* now started pacing so fast that he was almost jogging. He waved off Toucan Claw's remark. "No matter. No matter," he said. "The meaning is clear. Peace will cure this drought! The absence of war will cure this drought! I must make peace with Tikal!" The *Ch'ul Ahau* stopped in his tracks and knelt next to Jaguar Spot, putting his hand on Jaguar Spot's forehead in the same way that Toucan Claw and Orchid had done. "Good," he whispered quietly to Jaguar Spot. "No fever. I just had to make sure that your sister and father were right. I wouldn't want to go and declare peace just because some boy had a fever. You have my gratitude, Jaguar Spot." Before Jaguar Spot could thank him for his kind words, Speaking Macaw stood up and stormed out of the room in a great hurry.

CHAPTER SEVEN
SAVIOR

8.16.14.17.14. April 25, 371 A.D.

Ten days later Jaguar Spot was back at work, painting the mural in the *Ch'ul Ahau's* bedchamber. Something about the experience of the ballgame and the vision had given him the inspiration he needed, and he found the work literally flowing from his fingers. Over the past five days he had almost completed the mural. All that he really had left was to show the enemy noblemen, their heads hung low, returning to Tikal in disgrace. He had never been to Tikal. His father had been there years before, but could only give him the most general description of temples so tall that they seemed to touch the sky. The guard Rabbit stood behind him, admiring the mural. "It almost looks finished, Your Lordship," Rabbit said. "You have painted quite a beautiful mural. I know for a fact that His Lordship the *Ch'ul Ahau* is very pleased."

Jaguar Spot stood next to Rabbit and admired his own work. "Only one more thing to paint and it is finished," he said. "But to do it, I think that I will need to pay another visit to Fireborn." Rabbit groaned at Jaguar Spot's mention of Fireborn's name. He began to plead with Jaguar Spot. "Oh not him, Your Lordship. Last time that you did that I got in such big trouble after my idiot underling left you alone with him. Do you have to?" Jaguar Spot answered the question without taking his eyes off of the unfinished mural. "Yes," he said. "I have to." Rabbit stormed off in a huff to get Fireborn while Jaguar Spot made his way to the courtyard where they had their previous meetings. As he got to the hallway outside the courtyard he heard voices, and when he turned the corner he saw that the courtyard was full of people. The *Ch'ul Ahau* was holding formal court in the courtyard. An *ahau* was informing Speaking Macaw of latest news of the drought from around the lowlands. None of the cities had seen any rain. Jaguar Spot heard the words, but he could not concentrate, as he had never seen His Lordship's formal court before. All of the times that he had met with Speaking Macaw had been outside of the palace or with just himself and his father. In addition to His Lordship, it looked like every single *ahau* in the city was there, along with numerous *cahelob*, guards, and attendants. He saw his father standing near the front of the *ahauob*, and he tried to stay out of his view. Standing next to the *Ch'ul Ahau* appeared to be four strange-looking small children who were wearing odd colored robes. Jaguar Spot had never seen children dressed like this before. Without thinking, he walked into the courtyard and moved to stand next to them. When he got up to them he saw they were not children, but small adults. "Dwarves!" he thought to himself. "They are dwarves!" Jaguar Spot had never seen a dwarf before, but he knew that they were considered to be children of the rain gods. Snail had once told him that the *Ch'ul Ahau* kept all the dwarves in the dominion of Uaxactun cloistered in the palace, as they were known to be harbingers of good luck. As Jaguar Spot stood there next to one of the dwarves, listening to the *ahau* speak, he suddenly realized that Rabbit, or some other guard dragooned into the task, would be bringing Fireborn into the courtyard at any moment. He tried to quickly move back to the hallway so that he could head off that disaster. Only the Gods knew what Fireborn would say if he stumbled into the *Ch'ul Ahau's* formal court. If Jaguar Spot knew anything about Fireborn, he knew that Fireborn would likely start spouting off some acerbic remarks at the expense of the *Ch'ul Ahau*. Just as Jaguar Spot was about to make it to the door, disaster struck.

Toucan Claw, who had been carefully listening to the other *ahau's* report, glanced around the room and saw his son making his way to the door. He tried to slide his way as discretely as possible through the *ahauob*, but everyone started looking at him, and the *ahau* speaking even stopped talking for two breaths before resuming his report. Toucan Claw quickly caught up with his son and pulled him off to the side by his ear. "What in the name of Lord Sun are you doing here?" Toucan Claw demanded. He spoke so loudly that the *ahau* who had been addressing His Lordship completely stopped speaking and looked over at the father and son, and the assembled audience began murmuring to each other about the unprecedented interruption of the *Ch'ul Ahau's* court.

Jaguar Spot pleaded with his father as quietly as possible. "Please Father," he whispered. "You must let me go. Otherwise . . . otherwise . . . any second now a palace guard will bring a bound prisoner to this courtyard, stinking of the dungeon." Toucan Claw did not know what to say. Had his son lost his mind? If not, what kind of mischief had he gotten himself into? Before he could inquire further, the *Ch'ul Ahau* waved his audience to silence. "Toucan Claw, my friend," he said, "please bring the boy over here. I wish to speak to him." Toucan Claw and Jaguar Spot walked over to the *Ch'ul Ahau* in silence. Jaguar Spot knew that there was now nothing he could do to stave off the disaster that was about to occur. He could not warn His Lordship or say anything. In the presence of the *Ch'ul Ahau*'s formal court, no one spoke unless they were asked to do so by His Lordship himself. The *Ch'ul Ahau* got off of his chair and walked up to Jaguar Spot. "This boy," he said to the crowd, "is the one who has given me the answer of how end this drought. Yes, he is the one who had the vision of which I spoke. Tell me, Aktak," the *Ch'ul Ahau* now directed his attention to his principal priest and advisor, "what do you think of my plan. You have been strangely quiet."

Aktak was a tall man, perhaps the tallest and thinnest man in the city. He was very old, with long, white hair. He looked at Jaguar Spot, then looked to His Lordship, and cleared his throat. "Well Your Lordship, since you have asked my advice in this forum, I would not dispute that you know best and that your plan is sure to work. On the other hand, perhaps if you did more . . ." The *Ch'ul Ahau* cut Aktak off. "Don't say it!" he screamed. Aktak stood there silently, staring at the floor. The *Ch'ul Ahau* calmed himself down and spoke again. "You were going to say that the rains might come if I only did a little more bloodletting, weren't you?" Aktak nodded. The *Ch'ul Ahau* started screaming again, this time to the assembled crowd. "I forbid any of you to speak to me of bloodletting! I forbid it! Do you hear me? I have drained more blood from my body in the last two months than my father did during his entire reign. I have given plenty of blood. More than plenty! We will go with my plan! Bring in the prisoner."

Two of the palace guards who were standing close to the door that led to the dungeon turned around and started marching out. Before they could get through the door, Rabbit came through pulling Fireborn with a rope. For a moment, His Lordship looked confused. "Rabbit," he asked, "how did you know to bring the prisoner Fireborn, I only just asked for him a mere moment ago?" Rabbit, who had not expected to walk right into the middle of the *Ch'ul Ahau*'s formal court, looked stunned. "Um, well, Your Lordship, well, to tell the truth, the boy asked me to bring Fireborn here," Rabbit said, gesturing toward Jaguar Spot. The crowd started murmuring again, this time much louder than before. "Silence!" screamed Aktak. The *Ch'ul Ahau* turned to Jaguar Spot. "Is this true, my boy?" he asked in a fatherly tone. Jaguar Spot gulped. He had no idea how His Lordship would react under these circumstances. "Yes, Your Lordship," he said. The crowd gave a collective gasp, and started furious whispering to one another. Aktak again brought everyone to silence, so the *Ch'ul Ahau* could speak to Jaguar Spot again.

"Why?" he asked. "Did you have another vision? Did the jaguar cloud once again speak to you and tell you to have this gentleman from Tikal brought here?" Before Jaguar Spot could answer, the *Ch'ul Ahau* raised his voice and spoke to everyone present. "Did you hear that?" he cried. "The boy had another vision that told him to have the prisoner brought here! The jaguar spirit spoke to him! That proves it! We will use my plan." The *Ch'ul Ahau* asked one of his guards to hand him an obsidian knife, and walked over to Fireborn. Fireborn stood as erect as he could with his hands tied behind his back. He had the same look of defiance that Jaguar Spot had seen on his face when he stood on the ballcourt years before. The *Ch'ul Ahau* walked behind Fireborn and raised the knife. Before he could strike, Fireborn spoke in a strong tone. "Is Your Lordship such a coward that he would stab a bound captive in the back? Don't you have the guts to look me in the eye as you kill me?" Everyone in the crowd except the palace guards and the *Ch'ul Ahau* dropped their jaws at Fireborn's insolence. Gray Sky, who had been standing in the background, ran up to Fireborn and reached back to punch him in the stomach when the *Ch'ul Ahau* told him to stop.

 The *Ch'ul Ahau* then proceeded to cut Fireborn free of his bonds. "You are free to return to your city," the *Ch'ul Ahau* said before snapping his fingers. Two palace servants came through a doorway bearing a large bowl of water and some rough cloth. Two more brought a fine set of cotton clothes, which they set at Fireborn's feet as the first two began bathing a stunned and bewildered Fireborn. After Fireborn was cleaned and dressed, the *Ch'ul Ahau* went back to his chair and sat down, followed by Fireborn and the guards. "You might be wondering why I have decided to free you," the *Ch'ul Ahau* said to Fireborn. "It was the boy Jaguar Spot. He had a vision of a jaguar spirit. The spirit came to him in the form of a cloud. A cloud which spoke to him. Just think about that for a moment. The spirit told the boy that peace between our cities would bring an end to the horrible drought that has plagued both my realm and yours. You are my peace offering. Go and tell your brother in Tikal that, as far as I am concerned, we are at peace. Go." A palace guard gently pulled on Fireborn's left arm and led him out of the courtyard. Fireborn gave a faint smile as he looked Jaguar Spot in the eyes on his way out. Jaguar Spot thought that he detected slight nod of thanks. He wondered if he would ever see Fireborn again.

 The *Ch'ul Ahau* then asked that Toucan Claw come up and speak to him about his long overdue project to find His Lordship the best possible second wife. Other than the drought, this was the principal issue on the minds of everyone present. The *Ch'ul Ahau's* moratorium on weddings and engagements was starting to cause real hardship and inconvenience to the nobility of Uaxactun. Months had now gone by, and the wedding season had long come and gone. For the past few months Toucan Claw had been reluctant to leave the clan compound for fear of running into one of the *ahauob* and having to answer angry questions about when such and so's daughter would finally be allowed to marry such and so's son. He had been summoned to the palace at regular intervals to report on his progress. Lately the *Ch'ul Ahau* had grown more and more impatient with the delays, which Toucan Claw explained were due to the exacting nature of the work. In truth, Toucan Claw had augured the best wife for His Lordship many months before, but he refused to accept his own conclusion, and re-did his work over and over. At first he could not believe the results. Then, after he reached the same conclusion for the twentieth time he resigned himself to the truth, and decided to delay relaying his results to the *Ch'ul Ahau* for as long as possible. Jaguar Spot knew this, and had kept the secret, much to his father's pride. It was impossible to put things off any longer. During their last meeting, three days before, the *Ch'ul Ahau* had intimated that he might give the assignment to someone else if not completed quickly, which would have brought extreme dishonor to Toucan Claw. Toucan Claw assured the *Ch'ul Ahau* that he would have his final answer in three days.

"Well," asked the *Ch'ul Ahau*, "do you have an answer to my question? Do you know who will be my future bride?" Toucan Claw, resigned to the inevitable, answered that he had determined auguries for His Lordship's best possible match. The assembled nobility collectively sighed in relief, but the *Ch'ul Ahau* showed his impatience. "Well," he demanded, "out with it!" Toucan Claw tried to hide the look of distaste from his face as he gave the answer. "The girl is Hummingbird, daughter of the *cahel* Blue Squirrel, of my clan." Jaguar Spot had known of the results of his father's research for months, so he was not surprised. The same could not be said for the assembled *ahauob* and other nobles. There had lately been much talk among the *cahelob* of Blue Squirrel's increasingly erratic behavior, they even had a nickname for him: "The Groveler." Blue Squirrel had been seen trying to curry favor with every nobleman he met. He would prostrate himself in front of every *ahau* that he came across, which was becoming such a nuisance that many of the *ahauob* would turn the other direction if they saw Blue Squirrel approaching down a public way. There were even rumors that he would sometimes go so far in his efforts to ingratiate himself with anyone that could help his desire to increase his social standing that he would call other *cahelob* "Your Lordship." Toucan Claw, who received regular reports of Blue Squirrel's doings, viewed his kinsman and underling with an attitude verging on contempt, a fact that was well known to most of the *ahauob* present at the palace. The *Ch'ul Ahau*, however, was not privy to gossip concerning a *cahel* of Blue Squirrel's lowly station. He waved to Gray Sky and told him to summon Blue Squirrel and his daughter. Gray Sky took a squad of six palace guards with him as he left, presumably to protect the body of the *Ch'ul Ahau's* future second wife.

With the assembled nobility silently feeling shock, foreboding, disgust, or some combination of all three, the *Ch'ul Ahau* began peppering Toucan Claw with questions about his Hummingbird. "How old is she?" he asked.

"She just turned twelve years, Your Lordship."

"And is she beautiful?"

"Yes indeed, Your Lordship."

"Did your auguries tell you when we should marry?"

"Yes, Your Lordship, if my calculations are correct the best possible day for you to marry, considering both the civil and the religious calendars, will be sixty days from today. Of course, she will still be twelve, and unable to bear children right away. I know that you want a male heir above all else. Because of this I also augured the best possible day for you to consummate your marriage so that it will produce a male heir."

The *Ch'ul Ahau* was having a hard time containing his excitement, so much so that he stood up and almost started pacing. "Well tell me!" he demanded. Toucan Claw pulled a small piece of paper from his tunic and read from it aloud. "The best day for consummation so that conception will result in a male child is 12 Kaban, 10 Pax. That date combination will next occur in a little less than five years." The *Ch'ul Ahau* collapsed in his chair in disappointment. "Almost five years!" he shrieked. "She will be almost seventeen years old! I need an heir, and I need an heir in less than five years. Are you absolutely certain in your calculation of the dates? Could you be wrong?" Toucan Claw shook his head. "No, Your Lordship. I doubt very much that there can be a mistake. I checked and re-checked my work twenty times. Please, have your priests do their own calculations, but they will seek guidance from the same texts that I did. The information in the Council Books is clear.

If Your Lordship desires a male heir, you will marry the girl Hummingbird in sixty days, and you will consummate your marriage on 12 Kaban, 10 Pax. If you fail to heed the advice provided by the Gods through the sacred texts, then I fear that Hummingbird will prove to be barren, or will provide you with nothing but daughters."

The *Ch'ul Ahau* stood up and began to walk out of the courtyard, his shoulders slumped. "Well," he said, his voice sounding weak and bitter, "if that's what the texts tell you, that's the way it has to be." After he disappeared into the darkness of the doorway, followed by the dwarves and the remaining palace guards, the assembled nobility and other persons attending the formal court filed out on the opposite side of the courtyard in absolute silence. Not even the birds and the insects, it seemed, had anything to say after hearing the news that day had to offer.

Chapter Eight
THE MYSTERIOUS *AHAU*

8.16.14.9.4. May 24, 371 A.D.

Three days after the *Ch'ul Ahau* released Fireborn and sent his offer of peace to Tikal, rain fell on the city of Uaxactun in a great deluge that lasted for six days. After that, the rains became more gentle and sporadic, but continued almost every day until the eve of the scheduled date for the *Ch'ul Ahau's* wedding to Hummingbird. In honor of the celebration the *Ch'ul Ahau* had called a public festival and holiday, and Jaguar Spot had spent almost the entire day walking through row after row of merchants selling special items for the celebration. The *Ch'ul Ahau* had paid him half his weight in cacao beans for the now completed mural that graced the royal bedchamber. Jaguar Spot knew that such a sum of money would feed the average family of six in the city for a year, but he still spent nearly half of it on a new set of ballgame equipment and pads sold by a merchant from Tikal. Aficionados of the ballgame generally regarded Uaxactun equipment as serviceable, but second rate compared to what the craftsmen of Tikal could produce. Since trade between the two cities had been almost non-existent for Jaguar Spot's entire life, he had never owned a set of genuine Tikal equipment. Now, because of the *Ch'ul Ahau's* peace with Tikal, trade between the two cities had burgeoned, and Jaguar Spot walked away from the Tikal merchant feeling pride in being the youngest player in Uaxactun with a set of genuine Tikal ballgame equipment.

He arrived home in the early evening, his arms full with the equipment and other purchases. Orchid met him at the door. "I'll take that," she said, grabbing at the equipment. "You have a visitor." There was something about Orchid's expression that Jaguar Spot had never seen before. He couldn't quite put his finger on it at first, but then he realized that she was smiling, and not with just any smile at that. She practically radiated happiness. Orchid usually alternated between dour and stern. He could not remember her smiling, or being happy, for as long back as he could think. "Orchid, what's wrong with you?" he asked. Orchid giggled as she took the rest of his purchases. "Me?" she asked, with a sigh, "Nothing's wrong with me. I've never felt better in my entire life."

Jaguar Spot shook his head in disbelief as he walked into the main hall. "Is Orchid in love?" he asked himself. Even though she was almost nineteen years old, Orchid had never married. Whenever their father had suggested an arrangement, and he did so often, she flew into a fit of rage until he backed down. People in the compound were beginning to whisper that perhaps she didn't like men at all, and that she would die a spinster. Yet there she was, giggling like a fourteen year old girl with a crush. Jaguar Spot walked into the main hall and saw the back of a tall man dressed in the garb of an *ahau*, apparently admiring one of Toucan Claw's artworks. "Uncle?" he asked, unsure of who it was. The man let out a soft laugh and spoke without turning around. "Uncle?" he said. "You have never called me that before. Come here boy. I want to show you something."

Jaguar Spot knew that he had heard the man's voice before, but he could not quite place it. It certainly was not one of his father's close friends, and he did not know of any *ahau* in the city that he had not called "uncle" at some time or another. He walked up to the man slowly, trying to get a glimpse of his face, but without success. The man seemed to shift his position so that his back was turned to Jaguar Spot no matter where he went, and because he wore a large feather hat that covered the back of his head, Jaguar Spot knew nothing about his physical features except that he was very tall. Right as Jaguar Spot reached the man's side, and right before he would have been able to look up and see his face, the man gently said "stop there, boy. Look at this very interesting piece of pottery that your father has in his collection." Jaguar Spot stopped. He looked at the pottery, which was a three legged bowl painted with a light red glaze. "Regard the bowl. Tell me what you see," the man said. The two of them then stared at the bowl in silence until Jaguar Spot finally spoke. "It is a three-legged bowl for burning incense and holy paper from His Lordship the *Ch'ul Ahau*. The bowl is painted with an image of Lord Sun and Lord Venus taking shelter under the Great Tree." The man did not immediately respond to Jaguar Spot's answer, and they continued to stare at the bowl in silence until Jaguar Spot could stand it no longer and had to say something. "I see nothing else. What do you see, Uncle?" he asked. The man stood there in silence. Jaguar Spot could hear his own breathing and the breathing of the man, but otherwise it seemed that there were no other sounds in the world.

Finally, after what seemed to be an eternity, the man spoke. "You do not look hard enough, Jaguar Spot, son of Toucan Claw. Not nearly hard enough. Tell me, why are they taking shelter under the Great Tree. What do the mighty Lord Sun and his brother Lord Venus have to fear from anyone, or anything? From what danger are beings of their power taking shelter?" Jaguar Spot thought about the question. He had seen this particular piece of pottery almost every day of his life, but had seldom examined it closely. He thought about what he knew of the Hero Twins, and tried to come up with an explanation. "Perhaps it is from when they were young, before they were Lord Sun and Lord Venus, when they were still the young twins who tricked the denizens of the Underworld, and when they were hiding for their life. Perhaps the Great Tree gave them shelter," he finally said. The man once again stood there, not responding. Jaguar Spot tried to inch his way forward to get a look at the side of the man's face, but the man just as slowly turned away. Like before, the silence in the room went on so long that Jaguar Spot felt compelled to say something. "Perhaps it symbolizes that the Great Tree protects and nourishes all off us, even gods like Lord Sun and Lord Venus, that we are all dependent on the sap and tears of the Great Tree." Even from behind, Jaguar Spot could see that the man nodded slightly at the statement, but he still remained silent until Jaguar Spot could not resist speaking again. "You know, almost a year ago a wise man spoke to me of the Great Tree. He told me that we are all part of the Great Tree. We are all branches and leaves. That we are all parts of the same thing, all connected, all the same. Perhaps that is what it is meant to show us."

None too soon for Jaguar Spot, the man spoke. "Tell me," he said, "who was this wise man who said these things to you? Tell me about him." Jaguar Spot eagerly stated speaking of his meetings in the courtyard with Fireborn. "The man was a captive from Tikal. The brother of Tikal's *Ch'ul Ahau*, or his half-brother at any rate. I met him here when he was a prisoner, but now he is free." The man didn't say anything, he just made sound like he was gently clearing his throat. Jaguar Spot thought that the sound was meant to signify that the man was pondering what he just said, so he continued. "His name was Fireborn. I only spoke to him twice, but I did see him a third time. In many ways he was very much like my father." The man continued to stand there, motionless, saying nothing. Jaguar Spot could not think of anything else to say about either the bowl or Fireborn, so the two of them stood together in silence, which was only broken when the man spoke after what seemed an intolerable delay. "This Fireborn," he asked, "even though he was from Tikal, was he a man that you liked and respected? It seems so, since you call him 'wise.'" Jaguar Spot did not quite know how to answer the question. He had never thought of Fireborn from that perspective before. After thinking through his feelings on the subject, he answered. "Well, yes. I respect him. Whenever he spoke to me, the words seemed to make a lot of sense, even when I had to disagree with him for appearance's sake. I have to admit that, even though he was the enemy, there was something about the man that just made me want to like him. I don't know what you call it, but whenever I was with him, I wanted to follow him, to do what he asked me to do." The man made the throat-clearing noise again before speaking. "Charisma," he said, "it is called charisma." The man then turned around to face Jaguar Spot. It was Fireborn.

Jaguar Spot stood still with the studied detachment that his father had drilled into him since he was able to walk. "It's good to see you, Uncle," he said quietly. Fireborn chuckled as he spoke. "It's good to see you, too, my young nobleman from Uaxactun. But enough of that. What a charming sister you have! And a beautiful house. I was hoping to meet your father, but he is apparently over at the palace helping plan the celebration. And your fiancé, such a charming young girl! Come, let us sit." They sat down on the main hall's comfortable chairs and Orchid looked through the door, giggling again. Jaguar Spot asked her to get one of the house servants to make some chocolate. As the servant started grinding the cacao beans into a paste, Jaguar Spot and Fireborn continued their conversation. "What are you doing here?" Jaguar Spot asked. Fireborn explained that Speaking Macaw had invited Great Jaguar Paw, Tikal's *Ch'ul Ahau*, to his wedding ceremony. Great Jaguar Paw decided to bring most of Tikal's royal court, which included Fireborn. "Does His Lordship the *Ch'ul Ahau* know that you are here in the City?" asked Jaguar Spot.

"Oh yes. He greeted me most cordially when we arrived. He said that I should feel at home in Uaxactun, that he had no hard feelings, and that he hoped I felt the same way."

"What did you say?"

"Of course I was polite, and I said that I had no hard feelings, that bygones were bygones."

The servant finally finished making their chocolate, and they sat there slurping at the froth for a while. Jaguar Spot finished his first. "Uncle," he asked, "could I come and visit you in Tikal? I hear that it is the most beautiful city in the world." Fireborn finished his chocolate and put down the bowl. "Some day," he said. "But not for a long while. A very long while. At His Lordship my brother's request I am going abroad. I will go as far as Teotihuacan to increase our trade. It is quite a long journey, and I will have to stay there for five, maybe six years. Maybe you can come and visit me when I get back." Jaguar Spot was shocked. He had heard people speak of Teotihuacan as if it were another world. It was so far away that it could take half a year to get there, and the people didn't even speak Yucatec or any other languages of the Maya. He had seen some traders from Teotihuacan when he was six years old. They brought obsidian and other rare materials, and they dressed very strangely, with large brimmed hats with hanging tassels around the edge. The traders put on an exhibition of the way that they played the ballgame, which was with long sticks. Sometimes, people said, the Teothhuanos would light the ball afire and play at night. Toucan Claw had told him the strange people from the North even had different gods than the Maya. "Different gods!" Jaguar Spot thought as he sat there with Fireborn. "Imagine going to a place so strange that they have different gods, where they play the ballgame with sticks." To Jaguar Spot, Fireborn was going to travel on a grand adventure, to see an outside world that few men even thought about visiting, much less had the desire and wherewithal to make the journey. Some days, when he had been studying the ancient Council Books, or when he was daydreaming waiting for his turn to play in the ballgame, he thought of undertaking grand adventures like the one that Fireborn was about to start. When he first spoke with his friends about this, they looked at him as if he were a babbling nincompoop. "Why," they would ask, "would anyone want to leave our city? What could you possibly find outside that you couldn't find here?" After being the brunt of this type of scorn one too many times, Jaguar Spot had learned to keep his mouth shut about his desire for adventure, but the daydreams continued.

Jaguar Spot noticed that he was getting nervous. His heart was pounding, he was sweating, his breathing became shallow. He knew that there was a question that he had to ask, that he would regret not asking it for years if he remained silent. But he was afraid–afraid of rejection, of what his father would say, about being laughed at. He pushed through he nervousness and asked the question anyway. "Lord Fireborn, will you take me with you to Teotihuacan?" Fireborn looked over Jaguar Spot's shoulder, smiled faintly, and sighed. "I had a feeling that you would ask me that question." Jaguar Spot felt his heart beating faster and faster as Fireborn spoke. From the smile, from the way that he was speaking, he thought for a second that Fireborn might say yes, that he might get to go on a great adventure. He had never felt this way before. The only thing even close was the feeling that he got when he was standing on the playing surface of the ballcourt waiting for a serve. The nervous anticipation that he felt on those occasions, though, was nothing compared to what he was feeling now. He had trouble containing his emotions as Fireborn spoke. "Unfortunately His Lordship my brother has dictated that this will be a 'Tikal only' enterprise. We can't very well bring our competitors along on trade missions, can we?"

Jaguar Spot, feeling a sense of disappointment and defeat that he had never experienced before, did his best not to show it. "I suppose not," he whispered.

The servant came back in at Jaguar Spot's request and started making another batch of chocolate. Fireborn leaned toward Jaguar Spot and spoke in the same mock conspiratorial tone that he had affected when Jaguar Spot and he spoke in the palace courtyard. "Tell me about this wonderful sister of yours. Is she not married? Why is she still living in your father's house?" Jaguar Spot thought that he detected just the faintest hint of a smile on the part of the servant who was making the chocolate, as if he had overheard the question. Discussion of such matters in front of the servants was one of Toucan Claw's pet peeves, so Jaguar Spot did not answer immediately, making a brief nod over to Fireborn while looking at the servant to explain his silence. As they sat there, he wondered why on Earth Fireborn would want to know about Orchid. "I mean," he thought, "she's just a girl. She pretty much stays in the house and doesn't ever say anything all that interesting, after all . . ." Suddenly, Jaguar Spot's bowels turned cold. "No," he thought, "that couldn't be it! But then again, what are the other alternatives? Yes, it must be so." He could reach only one rational conclusion: Fireborn had a romantic interest in his sister.

The servant finally finished making the chocolate and handed it to Fireborn and Jaguar Spot. In between licks at the foam Fireborn prodded Jaguar Spot for information.

"She's not married, right?"

"Orchid? Married? Of course not!"

"Yet she is a lovely and charming woman. She seems intelligent, interesting, and able to have an engaging conversation. She is the daughter of an *ahau*, one of the most important *ahauob* of your city at that. Why hasn't your father found her a husband."

"He has, many times."

"And?"

"She says 'no.'"

"'No?' So what if she says 'no.' He is her father! It's not her decision."

"Well, Orchid can be a little, how should I say it? Strong willed. Every time Father mentions the name of a boy, she flies into a rage, running around the house and screaming at the top of her lungs that he is ugly, or stupid, or lazy, or something else. Then she starts crying, saying that Father would sentence her to year after year of misery and pain, living with a man like that. It just goes on and on. No one is good enough for her."

Fireborn finished his chocolate, got up, and began to pull at his clothes, adjusting them. "Tell me," he asked, "what do you think that your father would say if I asked him for your sister's hand in marriage? My friend, I don't think . . ." Fireborn suddenly stopped talking and looked at the door to Jaguar Spot's left. Orchid had just walked in. Fireborn stumbled as he tried to continue his sentence on a different topic. "Yes, I don't think that I will detain you from your duties for very much longer, my young Lordship. I will go now." When Fireborn said that he was leaving, Orchid quietly exclaimed "ah" in surprise and disappointment. She instantly covered her mouth, as if to pretend that she had not said anything, and spoke, or at least tried to speak, to Fireborn. "Um, my, what I mean to say, begging your pardon, Your Lordship surely doesn't have to leave us so soon, does he? Feel free to stay as long as you like. I am sure that my brother is delighted, yes, I mean just delighted, aren't you delighted to have His Lordship give you the honor of such a visit, Jaguar Spot?" Jaguar Spot, unsure of what to say, half-whispered "delighted" and looked over at Fireborn who had. . . he would not have believed it had he not seen it with his own eyes . . . rivulets of sweat pouring down his face. "Um, well, thanks Your Ladyship." Fireborn said with obvious nervousness in his voice. "You are very. . . very . . . kind to make such an offer. But I must go. Please give your father my respects and tell him that I would like to speak to him on a matter of great importance, if he is available. I will come back around sunset." Fireborn walked past Orchid, paused for a second to look at her, and left.

Once he was gone, Orchid instantly started questioning Jaguar Spot on his conversation with Fireborn. "What did you talk about?" she asked.

"Um, I don't know, just stuff."

"Stuff? What kind of stuff."

"You know, the drought, the crops, my painting, things like that."

"Crops? You talked to Fireborn about crops. *You?* I have never heard you talk about crops with anyone, at any time. Stop lying. What did you talk about?"

"I am interested in crops. That's what we talked about."

"What crops?"

"What to you mean, what crops?"

"What crops in particular?"

"Umm, what crops in particular? That's easy. Maize! We were talking about maize."

"Liar! I can see it in your eyes. Did he mention me at all? What did he say about me?"

"You?"

"Yes, me!"

"He said that you were charming."

Orchid fell into a chair as if she had been knocked unconscious. "Charming. He said that I was charming," she kept whispering quietly. Jaguar Spot, worried that she might be suffering from a fever, walked over and touched her forehead. She barely noticed, but her skin was cool to the touch. As she sat there whispering to herself, Jaguar Spot moved quietly to one of the doors and tried to sneak out of the room. Just as he thought that he was safely into the courtyard, he heard Orchid screaming after him. "Jaguar Spot, come back here this instant! Why did he want to talk to Father? About what? And don't you dare tell me that he wanted to talk to Father about crops!" Jaguar Spot ignored his sister's screams and continued walking across the courtyard, hoping to disappear before she could chase after him. He hurried up when he heard sounds of her stirring in the main hall, and was just about to make it into another doorway when she came bursting into the courtyard, screaming at the top of her lungs. "Jaguar Spot! Stop right there and tell me what Lord Fireborn wants to talk to Father about." Jaguar Spot stopped and turned around to face Orchid, expecting her to be angry and foaming at the mouth. Instead she was crying, tears streaming from her eyes. "Please," she pleaded, "tell me what he wants to talk to Father about. Is it about me?"

Jaguar Spot stood there in the courtyard looking at his sister. He had never seen her so emotional or so needy. Usually she tried never to depend on anyone for anything, except perhaps for the money and tribute labor that their father provided to keep the household running. Now she was begging for information as if her life depended on it, like a beggar in the street asking for a scrap of meat. Jaguar Spot could not turn her down. "Orchid," he said, "Fireborn wants to talk to Father to ask him for your hand in marriage. I don't know what father will say, after all, Fireborn is a foreigner." Orchid smiled and breathed a sigh of relief. "I knew it!" she cried. "I knew that he felt the same way about me. Father can't turn him down! Lord Fireborn is an *ahau*. He's the brother of a *Ch'ul Ahau*, a man of great importance, wealthy, powerful, strong, and handsome. Father can't say no."

Either love was blinding Orchid to the obvious, or Jaguar Spot knew a lot more about their father, and Fireborn, than she did. He had strong doubts that Toucan Claw would ever agree to let Fireborn marry Orchid, and he felt obligated to share his insights. "Orchid, Father *can* say 'no.' First, Fireborn is a foreigner. Losing you to Tikal would almost be like losing you to death. How often would he get to see you, or his grandchildren? Once every four or five years? I know that it is only a day's walk away, but how often does anyone but a trader actually make the trip? Even more, Fireborn is going away on a long journey, all the way to Teotihuacan. He will be gone for several years." Orchid smiled and nodded knowingly, as if he she had thought all of these problems through and come up with fool-proof solutions. "I know that he's going away," she said. "On a grand adventure. He's so gallant. He will come back even more wealthy than before. That's why Father will say 'yes.' Plus, I want to go along with Fireborn on the journey, assuming that he would have me come."

Jaguar Spot had saved the most damning piece of information about Fireborn, hoping that he could spare Orchid from the unpleasant truth. Now he had not choice but to tell her. "Orchid, he was born on the fifth day of the rump month. Such a birthday, well it augurs poorly for any match, with anyone. Plus, since he is a prince, everyone knows the truth. How could Father let you become the object of ridicule and humiliation by marrying him?" Orchid's smile did not falter even with the bad news. "I know all about that, too," she said. "Don't worry, I think that I can deal with Father. You don't understand all this, do you?"

"Not really."

Orchid wrapped her arms around Jaguar Spot and pulled him close. He could feel he moisture from her tears against his left cheek. "I love him," she said. "Before I met Lord Fireborn this morning, I thought that I was never going to love any man. They all seemed so petty, vain, stupid, or boorish, creatures unworthy of my affection. All of that changed in an instant. Being with him was like being in another world. We sat and talked, for what seemed forever. I have never loved a man before, but from the moment that I laid eyes on him, I knew that I loved him. You don't understand. At your age you can't understand, I know that. But my brother, some day I hope that you will feel it. You meet someone, and you just know, you *know in your heart* that you love him and you can't live without him. If Father says 'no,' I don't know what I will do."

Toucan Claw came home before sunset, while the kitchen servants were preparing the evening meal. Jaguar Spot was sitting in the main hall studying an old manuscript. Orchid sat across from him, showing Waterlily, who had moved in to the house since the *Ch'ul Ahau* had lifted the moratorium, some particularly difficult sewing techniques. Toucan Claw entered from the kitchen and grunted at the three of them. "Well," he said, "at least there is a semblance of normalcy in my own house, even if the rest of the City is going stark raving mad." He sat down and asked a servant to make him some chocolate. The four of them sat in silence as the servant ground up the cacao beans and mixed the resulting paste with chilies and honey. Toucan Claw started talking again when the servant handed him a bowl of chocolate and left. "You know, it really is comforting to come home and see such a peaceful scene. My son studying the ancient texts and my eldest daughter showing my future daughter-in-law how to sew. Somewhere in the world things are as they should be. But not out there in the City. You would think that His Lordship had never had a wedding before, the way he is planning this one, to say nothing of all the cacao beans that he is spreading around to the merchants buying food and trinkets for the ceremony. I have never seen anything like it before. His Lordship even sent an invitation to Tikal's *Ch'ul Ahau*, Great Jaguar Paw himself, and his brother Fireborn to boot! And they accepted the invitation–both of them! All for the *Ch'ul Ahau*'s wedding to his second wife." Toucan Claw started licking at his chocolate bowl while Orchid nodded at Jaguar Spot. According to plan, he was to bring up the subject of Fireborn's impending visit to their house.

"Father?" Jaguar Spot asked. Toucan Claw looked up from his chocolate bowl, but kept licking at the foam, which Jaguar Spot interpreted as granting permission to speak. "Do you remember when I went to the palace and met with Fireborn to give me ideas to help me paint the mural for His Lordship?" Toucan Claw put the bowl down and looked at Jaguar Spot. "Yes, I remember." Jaguar Spot began to squirm in his seat, trying to figure out an appropriate way to broach the subject. "Well," he stuttered, "he came here to pay me a visit today."

"That was courteous of him, I imagine."

"Yes, it was. He is going to come back before sunset. He wants to speak to you."

"Me? About what?"

Jaguar Spot looked over at Orchid, who was staring at him with wide eyes and nodding her head quickly, and looked back at Toucan Claw, who appeared to merely have only a mild curiosity in Fireborn's impending visit. "He, um, met Orchid when he came by. I was out, you see. At the market, buying some equipment for the ballgame from one of the Tikal merchants who are here for the festival."

"Son, what does that have to do with anything?"

"Um, well, he met Orchid, you see."

"So?"

"And she met him."

"I gathered that."

"He wants to ask you if he can marry her."

Toucan Claw looked at the three of them in studied silence. He showed not so much as a hint of emotion. Jaguar Spot looked back at him with the same blank look that Toucan Claw had drummed into the boy since he was able to walk. Orchid looked her father straight in the eye, as if saying "I dare you to say 'no.'" Waterlily, who had not said a word since Toucan Claw had walked into the house, appeared to be concentrating on her sewing, although that was probably an affectation. Toucan Claw looked back at Orchid and saw something there that he had never seen before–desire, maybe even lust. He knew without her saying a word that she wanted this union with Fireborn more than anything she had ever wanted in her life before that moment, and that she would scream and howl the moment he said anything even the least negative about it. From past experience, he had no doubt that his daughter would make his life a living hell if he declined, and that she could maintain such living conditions almost indefinitely.

Toucan Claw also knew more about Fireborn and his family than Orchid and Jaguar Spot could possibly imagine. Even with all the fuss and heartburn that Orchid would create by the decision, his initial inclination was to reject the idea out of hand. As he sat there eye-to-eye with Orchid, he had second thoughts. Tikal was a wealthy city, perhaps the wealthiest city in the world. Fireborn's family had been in control of Tikal for generations, and the city's prosperity had grown consistently in that time. As the half-brother of the *Ch'ul Ahau*, Fireborn was one of the wealthiest men in the city, with large estates staffed by tribute labor. Toucan Claw also had Orchid to think of. She was getting close to the age where it would be impossible to find her a good man to marry her as his first wife, and the thought of her someday accepting a position as a second wife, well it was unthinkable. This might be the last chance that she would ever have for a match worthy of her background and her family. Still, he could not make up his mind. He would have to think on this. He stood up and walked into the courtyard, speaking over his shoulder as he went. "His Lordship has been keeping me occupied day and night for three days. I am going to take a nap, so that I can speak to this Fireborn with a clear mind. I have a dowry to negotiate, and I don't want to get swindled. Wake me when he arrives."

Orchid put an arm around Waterlily and they started whispering to each other, with Waterlily looking over at Jaguar Spot and smiling. Without saying anything, they both got up and walked across the courtyard to the bedchamber that the two had been sharing since Waterlily had moved into the house.

Jaguar Spot became so engrossed in the ancient text that he had been reading that he did not even notice that it was almost sunset until a servant touched him on the shoulder to let him know that Fireborn had arrived. He looked up and saw Fireborn dressed in the grandest finery that one might ever expect the brother of a *Ch'ul Ahau* to wear. Fireborn wore a tall headdress made of scarlet macaw feathers, towering more than an arm's length above his head. His shirt and skirt were made of the finest soft cotton, colored with matching geometric patterns. In both hands he held gifts of cacao, honey, and obsidian for Toucan Claw and Orchid, as was expected of a suitor under these circumstances. Fireborn stood just inside one of the doorways to the main hall. If not for the headdress, he would have been expected to stand directly in the doorway itself, but his height and the size of the headdress made that impossible. Tradition required certain ritualized language, almost a prescribed script, for courtship rituals, and Fireborn knew the words so well that he almost recited them by rote: "I am here to see Toucan Claw, father of Orchid. My name is Fireborn, *ahau* of Tikal. I come to seek the right to marry the daughter of Toucan Claw." Jaguar Spot also knew the words that tradition required like the back of his hand. He had read them in the ancient texts on more occasions than he could remember. "I am Jaguar Spot, brother of Orchid, son of Toucan Claw. I welcome you to this house. Please come in and sit. I will inform my father of your presence." Jaguar Spot walked across the courtyard to his father's bedchamber, expecting to have to wake him from his nap. Instead he found him dressed in fine clothes that rivaled even Fireborn's in their richness. If anything, Toucan Claw's headdress was even taller than Fireborn's, and was not only adorned with macaw feathers, but those of toucans and parrots. Jaguar Spot had seen his father wear many headdresses through his life. Some had been beautiful, some had probably taken a craftsman half a year to make, some were small and tasteful, but he had never seen anyone in Uaxactun, much less his father, wear a headdress like this before. The pattern of the feathers was beautiful, making it look like there were layers upon layers of feathers under the surface, almost as it were a ball of solid feathers. The combination of colors was so bright and cheerful that it was almost hard to look at.

Like the headdress, Toucan Claw's clothes were more beautiful than anything that Jaguar Spot could ever remember him wearing. Jaguar Spot touched his father's tunic, which was made of a cotton so fine, and so soft, that it was almost like touching a cloud. He had not seen fabric this fine even in the palace. Unlike Fireborn's clothes, Toucan Claw's were dyed solid red, the same color red that adorned the stucco walls of the city. "Father," Jaguar Spot whispered, "you look so beautiful. I have never seen clothes like these before, and that headdress." Toucan Claw frowned. "Yes, they are beautiful. Gifts from His Lordship the *Ch'ul Ahau*, in honor of the work I did him in selecting a bride. They are fresh out of Tikal, which is the newest fad in fashion and sophistication at the palace. I tried to tell His Lordship that this kind of thing was really not my style, but he was quite insistent that I take them and wear them at the wedding. Who am I to say 'no' to His Lordship, and I might as well get some use out of them. So, do we have a visitor?"

"Yes, Father. He is waiting in the main hall."

"Would you like to come along and watch our negotiations, my son?"

"Yes, Father. Thank you."

"You understand that these are not real negotiations at all, don't you?"

"Father?"

"It's a formality, son, a prescribed ritual as set in stone as the stilted language that this *ahau* from Tikal and I are supposed to use for this occasion. Society demands that we haggle, that we dicker over the price for the dowry. Yet for every *ahau*, in every city, the price is the same. The mere fact that I make the prescribed initial offer tells this *ahau* that I will accept him as my son in law. If I offered something different, or refused to haggle, that would show that I hold the suitor in contempt or that I reject the proposal."

"So, will you make the prescribed offer?"

"We shall see, my son, we shall see."

Toucan Claw and Jaguar Spot walked over to the main hall side by side. Fireborn rose from his seat as they entered. "I am Fireborn, *ahau* of Tikal, and friend of Jaguar Spot, son of Toucan Claw. I pray that I am welcome in your house. I come to seek your daughter Orchid as my first wife. Will you negotiate?" Toucan Claw walked up to Fireborn and put his right hand on his left shoulder before speaking. "I am Toucan Claw, father of Orchid. You are welcome in my house as my friend, and as a friend of my son. I will negotiate. My son will join us, if that is acceptable."

"Yes, that is acceptable."

The three of them sat down and Toucan Claw opened the negotiations. "Earlier today I heard His Lordship your brother Great Jaguar Paw speaking to His Lordship Speaking Macaw, *Ch'ul Ahau* of this city. He said that you were going to travel all the way to Teotihuacan on some sort of trade mission. If I accept your proposal, what will happen to my daughter when you make this journey, which I understand will take several years?" Fireborn had apparently been expecting this question, and had a quick answer. "Is she desires, she will reside in my brother's palace while I am away, or if she wants, she can travel with me to Teotihuacan. I will leave it to her, although obviously I prefer that she accompany me."

Toucan Claw sat and looked at Fireborn for a while. His face was as still as if it had been carved from stone. Jaguar Spot, who thought that he could read his father's feelings like a Council Book, had no clue what he was thinking. Toucan Claw and Fireborn stared into each other's eyes for what seemed an eternity. Jaguar Spot felt like saying something to break the silence, but he knew that his father was testing Fireborn. It was Toucan Claw's turn to speak. If Fireborn said anything, it would be seen as a sign of disrespect and the negotiations would be off. Finally, just as Jaguar Spot thought that he was going to burst, Toucan Claw spoke. "Most young women I know would certainly choose to live in the palace, with all of its comforts, but I think that my daughter is not like most young women. Perhaps this is what you find attractive in her, I do not know, nor do I desire to know. My feeling is that she would choose to go with you on this journey. So, if she chooses to take this arduous pilgrimage with you, can you guarantee her safety and comfort?"

Fireborn did not answer for some time. He knew that this was the turning point of the real negotiations, that if he gave the right answer, Toucan Claw would consent to the match. He also knew that if he said the wrong thing that the ritual negotiations would not even get started. Choosing his words carefully, he answered. "Guarantee? If I said that I could guarantee her safety, I would be a liar. I could not even guarantee her safety if she remained in her bedchamber at the palace for the rest of her life. There are no guarantees on things like this. All I can say is that I will defend her body and her honor with my life."

Toucan Claw appeared satisfied with the answer. Both Fireborn and Jaguar Spot breathed a sigh of relief as Toucan Claw moved on to the subject of the dowry. "As a dowry, I will offer you half of her weight in cacao beans." At that moment Fireborn knew that the deal was sealed. There was only one response that the ritual allowed.

"Twice her weight."

"Her weight exactly."

"Done."

Toucan Claw pulled a piece of paper out of his tunic, handing it to Fireborn as he explained its contents. "I have consulted the auguries to determine an appropriate wedding date. As you know, you were not born on a very auspicious day. There were very few days that augured well for a wedding between the two of you." Toucan Claw stopped talking while Fireborn studied the piece of paper. He handed it to Jaguar Spot after a breath had passed. Jaguar Spot read the paper and handed it back to Fireborn, who expressed bewilderment. "This says that the best possible date for our wedding is not for almost three years. Obviously, that will not be acceptable."

"Obviously. But I will not have my daughter married when it augurs poorly," Toucan Claw replied.

Fireborn nodded in agreement. "Yes, yes, I think that we can all agree on that, but there are levels of good auguries, as well as levels of bad ones. Tell me, when is the next date that you would consider to augur acceptably well?"

"Tomorrow."

"Tomorrow? And after that?"

"Not for eight months."

"In eight months I will be in Teotihuacan. I can't wait that long."

"I understand. So it will have to be tomorrow."

Fireborn threw the paper down on a table, stood up, and started pacing around the room, thinking aloud. "How can we have a wedding tomorrow? The wedding should be done in front of the nobility of Tikal, at one of the temples. Even if I could make the necessary arrangements in such a short time, here I am trapped in Uaxactun, trapped as surely as if I were still in that stinking cell in the palace. With this royal wedding tomorrow, there is no way, no way! If I left now His Lordship your *Ch'ul Ahau* would consider it a grievous insult. It might even mean a return to a state of war between our cities." Fireborn stopped pacing and faced Toucan Claw and Jaguar Spot. "Gentlemen," he said, "please help me. Please give me your thoughts on how to get out of this conundrum." Jaguar Spot looked over at his father, who rubbed his chin with his hand and appeared deep in thought, but apparently had no immediate advice for Fireborn. The easy answer was to tell Fireborn to damn tradition and get married in Uaxactun, but certain things were expected of an *ahau*, and certain obligations could not be ignored. The three of them thought in silence until Toucan Claw spoke quietly. "I think that I may have a solution to our problem, Fireborn."

"Yes? Tell me, tell me."

"His Lordship has scheduled his own wedding ceremony at sunrise, with a ritual celebration lasting some time after that. That should leave plenty of time."

Fireborn shook his head. "No, I had already thought of that. There will be no way that we can make it back in time to have a ceremony in Tikal before sunset, even if we could get the necessary nobility together. No it won't work." Toucan Claw, still without expression, slowly shook his head. "I completely agree, it wouldn't work that way, but you miss my point, I think. Tell me, my friend, what is Tikal?"

"What is Tikal?"

"Yes, what is it?"

"A city."

"Is that all? How about the areas under your brother's control, the places where he and his ancestors have inscribed Tikal's emblem glyph, where *ahauob* under his command provide tribute labor and taxes to the city. Is that also not Tikal?"

Fireborn got Toucan Claw's point. "Yes," he said. "Yes! It can work. There is a small temple barely half a morning's walk south of Uaxactun. The area is governed by an *ahau* of Tikal, the village nearby has an emblem glyph, or so I remember. Gods be praised! All we would have to do is get the Tikal's *ahauob*, or at least a majority of them, there before sunset tomorrow and we can do it. But then, there's the problem. I certainly can't leave to summon the *ahauob* and their families, nor can any the of the notables that my brother brought along. Your *Ch'ul Ahau* would feel insulted even if my brother sent back one of the *guards* he brought along, much less an *ahau* or a *cahel*. So, how do we get the necessary people to the necessary place in the time we have available?"

Jaguar Spot raised his hand and asked permission to speak, to which Toucan Claw nodded ascent. "I will go," Jaguar Spot said. Toucan Claw and Fireborn burst into laughter. "You?" Fireborn said after he calmed down. "I mean, I appreciate your offer, my future brother. I really do. It is most generous, but you are only a child, and the son of a Uaxactun *ahau* at that. Surely anyone in Tikal would think that you were leading them into some kind of trap."

Jaguar Spot fell silent, he had not thought that the people of Tikal would refuse to believe him when he bore the message. The three of them thought in silence for a while, until Toucan Claw came up with another solution. "Well, I think I have it. A while back my son relayed a message to me using a most novel innovation. I think that it can work." Jaguar Spot had no idea what his father was talking about, but was pleased to be credited with part of the solution to Fireborn's problem. "It is a way of transmitting a message accurately over a large distance," Toucan Claw continued. "You take a piece of paper, and you write a message on it, and then give it to someone to take to the message's recipient. Here, take this piece of paper, and. . .boy get Fireborn a writing brush and some ink . . you take it and write the necessary instructions to your brother's chamberlain, and my son will deliver it, along with himself to act as hostage to assure our good will." Fireborn looked at Jaguar Spot, who was busy bringing him a writing brush and ink, with something that Jaguar Spot had never seen in Fireborn's face before–respect. "That is brilliant," Fireborn whispered. "Absolutely brilliant. People have been using paper to write counsel books and sacred texts for as long as anyone can remember. How is it that no one has thought of anything like this in the past? And the idea came from the mouth of a child? Here, give me that writing brush, I think that it will work."

Jaguar Spot handed the stylus and ink to Fireborn, who took the sheet of paper offered by Toucan Claw and sat down to write. As a high noble, Fireborn had been taught to read and write as a child, but his glyph painting was atrocious. Noblemen always hired scribes to do their writing for them, and Fireborn had probably not handled a writing brush more than twenty times since he was twelve years old. After what seemed forever, he finished the letter and handed it to Toucan Claw, who squinted as he read it. Fireborn would have never seen it, but Jaguar Spot noticed the barest hint of a frown on his father's face, which for him was a strong display of disapproval. Toucan Claw, trained as a scribe, detested bad penmanship. When Jaguar Spot had begun his training with Snail, Toucan Claw had him bring his work home with him for the first few months. Toucan Claw's criticism of Jaguar Spot's work at the beginning had been so blistering that Jaguar Spot became too terrified to bring home anything but the most beautiful and well composed glyphs that he had ever seen. After a month it was clear that he was the best glyph painter in Snail's group of apprentices. Of course, Toucan Claw knew that Fireborn had never been trained as a scribe, and that he had the barest minimum training in glyph writing, just enough to allow him to write short prayers on sacrificial paper, written in blood to be burned in a temple ritual. Without saying anything, Toucan Claw handed the paper to Jaguar Spot. It read:

Fireborn Upturned Frog
Brother of *Ch'ul Ahau* Great Jaguar Paw, ruler of Tikal
Went to Uaxactun
12 Ik, 15 Pop
Betrothed to Orchid, daughter of Toucan Claw, *ahau* of Uaxactun
Married on 13 Akbal, 16 Pop
At the place of the ancestor Broken Sunlight

Two hundred breaths before sunset
All of the *ahauob* of Tikal were present.

    The message verged on gibberish. Fireborn's knowledge of writing in the future tense appeared to be nonexistent, so he wrote the entire message as if it had taken place in the past, although it had tomorrow's date, and that was simply the most noticeable of his grammatical mistakes. If Jaguar Spot had brought this kind of work home to his father, well, he shuddered to think of what the reaction would have been. Yet there was Fireborn, smiling down at the message in Jaguar Spot's hand, as if he was proud of some great accomplishment. Jaguar Spot was half tempted to suggest some revisions to the text, but when he saw Fireborn's face he said nothing, and went in search of some suitable traveling clothes.

    When Jaguar Spot came back to the main hall he found that a servant had placed some food on a table. Fireborn and Toucan Claw were deep in conversation, which stopped when Jaguar Spot set foot in the room. "Ah, I see that you are ready for your journey," Toucan Claw said. "Good. There is some food for you." Jaguar Spot went over to the food, which consisted of some fish and tortillas, and ate quickly while Fireborn and Toucan Claw resumed their conversation, more quietly than before. When he was done, he stood in front of his father and announced that he was ready to leave. Toucan Claw got up and handed Jaguar Spot a heavy moneybag, which Jaguar Spot estimated held about 50 cacao beans. "This might be useful on your journey, son, so take it. Do not spend it foolishly," he said before sitting down again. Without getting up, Fireborn took a small green object from his tunic and handed it to Jaguar Spot. It was a skull carved out of jade-stone, about the size of a baby's fist. The craftsmanship was beautiful. "Show this to the chamberlain," Fireborn said, "and he will know that the message comes from me."

    Without saying another word, Jaguar Spot turned around and walked through the kitchen and out of the house. The air outside was cooler than normal for that time of year, and a slight rain was just beginning to end. No doubt His Lordship would take credit for the day's rain when he spoke at the wedding banquet tonight, complete with a long and storied exploration of his close relationship with the Gods. The *Ch'ul Ahau* had been making more and more grandiose comments every day since the rains began, and had asked Jaguar Spot to paint murals on each and every inside wall of the palace commemorating his close and abiding relationship with the denizens of the Otherworld. The paintings would take a long time to complete, perhaps five or six years if Jaguar Spot worked full time on the job. Toucan Claw had little choice but to go along with His Lordship's demands on Jaguar Spot's time, but Jaguar Spot knew that his father secretly seethed at the request. At this point in his life Jaguar Spot was essentially supposed to be an apprentice *ahau*, spending most of his waking time with his father, observing the things that he would need to emulate when he stepped into his father's shoes. Father and son both knew that this could not be accomplished with Jaguar Spot spending all day, every day, painting murals inside the palace. As Jaguar Spot's father, Toucan Claw was supposed to have full control over the education and upbringing of his son, and many of the *ahauob* secretly thought that His Lordship came close to overstepping the boundaries of propriety as he took more and more discretion away from Toucan Claw over how his son would spend his time. Even so, it was not their place to utter any words of disagreement with His Lordship's desires. Jaguar Spot wondered what Fireborn would say when, and if, he learned how Jaguar Spot was going to spend the bulk of his teenage years.

When he left the clan compound Jaguar Spot noticed that the public streets were filled with people, which was not normal for that time in the evening, when most families sat down to eat. The wedding festival had brought many outsiders to Uaxactun—musicians, traders, acrobats, jugglers—most of whom came from Tikal. It seemed like Jaguar Spot passed people of this ilk every few steps, eating, dancing, or playing their musical instruments. Some of the Tikalese had even brought their children with them, and a group of them were playing wooden trumpets in unison, a skill that Jaguar Spot had never been able to master after many years of earnest attempts. There was so much commotion in the streets that no one noticed the passing son of an *ahau*, which suited Jaguar Spot just fine. He wanted to get out of the city as fast as possible. The quickest way out at this time of night was to cut through the main market, which would be empty. Jaguar Spot had done this hundreds of times, and he liked the solitude and quiet that the emptiness provided. Sometimes he would stand there in the moonlight and stare up at the Overworld for what seemed half the night, wondering what heroic acts the men and gods had done to earn them their enshrinement in the nighttime sky.

Solitude was not in store for Jaguar Spot that evening, however. The closer he got to the market, the more and more crowded the streets became. He actually had to push his way past people and duck under some vendors' tables just to get to the market entrance. Instead of the anticipated relief of an open and quiet space, the market square was packed full of people and tents. It seemed like half of the city of Tikal must have been there, with the other half in the streets that Jaguar Spot had just passed through. He walked around a group of musicians playing some foreign sounding music on wooden flutes and came across a group of twenty men holding their right arms outstretched into a circle, blood flowing from multiple punctures on their arms. Two other men walked in opposite circles around the group of men with stingray spines, making additional pricks on each man's arm as they passed. The blood fell to the ground in a rough circle about five paces across. This was obviously some type of sacrifice, but Jaguar Spot did not have time to stop and ask questions. He walked around the group and through the rest of the market square.

With great relief, he passed the last of the streets and houses of the city, and walked through field after field planted with maize and beans. The plants were small this time of year, and were spaced far enough apart that Jaguar Spot could cut across the fields to get to the road leading to Tikal. Lady Moon was gloaming near the horizon, so bright that Jaguar Spot cast a shadow as he walked.

The crickets and other night insects of the forest put up a loud racket when Jaguar Spot passed from the fields to the forest boundary, and he hesitated before entering the darkness in front of him. He had never been alone in the forest at night before, and the thought of encountering a jaguar or cougar in the darkness had been on his mind ever since he saw the trees looming in the distance. Still, he had an important task to accomplish, and he knew what his father's reaction would be if he returned home, afraid, having failed. There was, of course, a perfectly good path through the forest that Jaguar Spot could have taken to get to Tikal, but it curved west towards a number of outlying villages before turning south to Tikal and would have added at least almost an extra half evening to the time of his journey. Instead, he chose to take a shortcut which would allow him to re-join the path after it turned south, just as it left Uaxactun territory.

With every step that Jaguar Spot took in the forest, there seemed to be a new and ominous noise somewhere close. At one moment he would hear something that sounded like footsteps coming from just behind a large tree or bush, and would pick up his pace to get away. The next moment it seemed that he would hear strange buzzing sounds all around his head, as if he were surrounded by a giant swarm of invisible insects. Sometimes it seemed that there was an indefinable and sinister presence just hovering in the air like a bad smell that he could not quite identify. When he got about halfway through the forest, he started hearing something that sounded like soft whispers in the air all around him, but he could not make out what anyone was saying, or even if they were really whispers at all. He stopped and held his breath to listen, but the sounds went away, in fact *all* of the sounds of the forest went away, and he was standing in complete silence. He knew that this usually meant that a jaguar or cougar was in the area, and at this time of night the beasts would be hunting. His father had told him that the best thing to do when confronted by night predator was to remain as still as possible until the predator left the area, because what the cats really tracked was movement. If you stayed calm and did not move, Jaguar Spot knew, they would probably ignore you or walk right past you. He stood as still as a cacao tree on a calm day, listening for any sounds, looking for any movement. The air remained perfectly silent, without a trace of sound or wind. The cause of the silence, whatever it was, must have been very close. The sinister presence that he had felt earlier in his walk seemed to be back, and it felt like it was getting stronger. After remaining perfectly motionless for what seemed forever, Jaguar Spot heard a faint rustling coming from his right, followed by quiet footsteps. The sound was so quiet, and the footsteps so faint, that Jaguar Spot would not have heard anything had the forest not been so silent. "Stay still!" he heard his father say from memory, as real to him that moment as if Toucan Claw were standing in the forest with him. He had no idea what movement the predator would see in the darkness. He tried to keep his breaths shallow to keep his stomach from moving in and out, and he was afraid to even turn his head and look at whatever it was that was approaching. The shallow breathing became harder and harder, and he finally had to take in a deep breath followed by as faint an exhalation as he could manage. Whatever it was making the footsteps stopped immediately when Jaguar Spot made the noise. Jaguar Spot was probably more afraid now than he had ever been in his life before. He was absolutely certain that a jaguar or a cougar was stalking him and was about to pounce for the kill, and began to instinctively pull his arms up around his head to protect himself. Working up his courage, he finally mustered enough courage to turn his head slightly to the right, where the sound had been coming from before it stopped. There, crouching on the ground, its tail quietly whisking back and forth, lay a jaguar, ready to pounce. It took every last bit of restraint and self-discipline that Jaguar Spot had not to run away at that instant, but due to his father's training he was able to overcome his will to flee. Instead, he stood and stared at the jaguar, waiting for what seemed like inevitable death. The jaguar started inching forward, making slight rustling sounds as it passed over the leaves on the forest floor. Suddenly it pounced. The jaguar jumped up and flew through the air, seemingly right at Jaguar Spot, who braced for the imminent impact and subsequent death.

The impact never came. Instead the jaguar flew past Jaguar Spot and landed on a dark shape that Jaguar Spot had not noticed before. Whatever it was that the jaguar was hunting, it was some kind of animal, and they stared fighting and snarling at each other in the darkness. Jaguar Spot took off running, speeding as fast as he could past trees and bushes, branches cutting across his face, knocking his feathered hat to the ground. He didn't care. He just kept running as fast as his legs would take him, oblivious to the risks of tripping over a root or running into an unseen tree. He kept it up until his lungs felt like they were about to explode from the exertion, and he slowed down to the quickest walk that he could muster. His breaths came so hard, and so frequent, that he heard nothing of the forest around him, but he kept walking as fast as he could.

After it seemed that he had been walking through the entire night, Jaguar Spot finally came to a large clearing. It had to be the traditional battleground used by Uaxactun and Tikal, the place of the *Ch'ul Ahau*'s famous victory. If he was right, he was more than halfway to Tikal, and the path should run right through the center of the clearing. The ground in the clearing was uneven. By tradition, men from Tikal and Uaxactun came to the clearing on alternating winter solstices and pulled up any trees or large plants that might grow there. In practice, they usually waited until the plants could be seen rising above the level of the grass before they took any action, which made for the hardest walking so far. Jaguar Spot tripped over small bushes, rocks, and other plants five times before he came across the path. He rubbed his right hand along his face and head as he stared down the path to Tikal, and he felt something wet and sticky, probably blood. After all of the spills that he had taken in the field and all after running through branches and bushes in the forest, he must have looked a mess. What would they think of him when he presented himself at the palace with a message from Fireborn, he wondered.

The first glimmers of Lord Sun's appearance were visible in the East when Jaguar Spot saw a mountain looming in front of him. "A mountain?" he thought. "There are no mountains closer than twenty days' walk, but there it is." Was this another vision? Had he fallen asleep during his journey and was he now dreaming? The closer he came, the taller the mountain looked, with impossibly steep, and regular, sides. Finally he reached the base and reached out to touch it and–he could not believe it–it was not a mountain at all, but a temple, a temple that seemed to stretch all the way to the Overworld. There was enough light now for him to see that there were stairs leading to the top, where he saw that there was a small room like was found in the temples back home. Apart from that similarity, this temple bore no resemblance to any temple he had ever seen in Uaxactun. The temples back home were broad and had gentle slopes, while this temple was narrow and steep. He would never have imagined that men could ever build anything so impressive, or so beautiful. The fact that the men of Tikal had built such an object made him wonder how anyone, at any time, could ever defeat a city capable of such greatness. Perhaps the *Ch'ul Ahau* was correct after all to want to celebrate his victory every night in the privacy of his own bedchamber.

Jaguar Spot walked past the temple into a giant square that had an even taller temple on the opposite side. There were temples of almost equal majesty looming in the distance all around him. What an incredible city! The grandeur seemed to go on and on forever. By the time he got to the other side of the square and walked past the taller temple, he smelt a cook fire somewhere in the distance. He followed the smell and walked into another square, with a long two story building off to one side. The smoke seemed to be coming from the building, so he walked over to it. He knew that there was something odd about the building as he approached it, but he could not quite put his finger on it. He walked up to an open door on the ground level and only stopped when a spear appeared out from the darkness and pointed right at his chest. "Hold it right there, son," said a friendly voice from the darkness. Jaguar Spot could barely make out the shape of the man who held the spear, but he could see that the man was wearing a plumed hat that made him look like he was a giant. "Why don't you just tell me why you thought that you could just walk on into the palace like you owned the place," the voice continued.

"Um, I am Jaguar Spot, son of Toucan Claw, from Uaxactun," Jaguar Spot managed to spit out. The man pulled the spear up and walked into the brightening morning. "Well met Jaguar Spot, I am sure. Why is a young nobleman, so far from home, walking into Tikal's royal palace as if he is a resident, if you don't mind me asking. And, Your Lordship, if you don't mind me saying, you look like a mess."

"I bear a message from Lord Fireborn for the Chamberlain."

"Oh really? And why would His Lordship Fireborn entrust a message of such obvious importance to a child? Or, more importantly, a child from Uaxactun? I tell you what, why don't you just tell me the message and I will deliver it to the Chamberlain."

Jaguar Spot pulled the message from his tunic and held it out for the guard. "What's that?" the guard asked, taking it from Jaguar Spot's hand. Jaguar Spot did not answer as the guard unfolded the paper and looked at Fireborn's writing. The guard crinkled his eyebrows. "This is writing," the guard finally said.

"Yes, it is writing."

"And what about the message?"

"That's the message?"

"The writing?"

"Yes."

"I don't understand."

"Can the Chamberlain read?"

"I should think so, but what has that got to do with anything?"

"Give him the paper. Have him read it. He will understand."

The guard folded the paper and thrust it into his tunic. "Okay," he said, and then whistled into the palace. Another guard quickly came out and stared at Jaguar Spot. The first guard yelled at the second. "Idiot! I have a job that even you can do. Keep an eye on this kid. Don't let him go anywhere until I get back, and don't let him inside."

Before the second guard could say anything in response, the first guard took his spear and stormed off into the palace. Jaguar Spot and the new guard stood at the palace doorway as the morning sky brightened and Lord Sun rose above the trees to the east. Jaguar Spot tried to make conversation with the guard, asking him about the temples and the other buildings of the city that were now visible all around them, but the guard said nothing. He merely stared at him with a blank look on his face. After a while, Jaguar Spot gave up trying to talk to the guard and the two of them stood there in what was, at least for Jaguar

Spot, uncomfortable silence. After what seemed forever, the first guard came back without his spear and motioned for Jaguar Spot to follow him into the palace, yelling over his shoulder at the other guard as he disappeared into the darkness of the palace. "Idiot, you guard the door. You know what to do if there is any trouble, not that there will be."

The inside of the palace was well lit with torches and open windows, and the stone walls were bright with whitewash. Jaguar Spot followed the guard into a large room, perhaps the largest indoor space that Jaguar Spot had ever seen. As he walked into the room, Jaguar Spot suddenly realized why the palace building had looked so strange to him as he approached–there were no stairs to the second floor. Now he saw why. Off to one side of the room was a stairway, an *indoor* stairway. Jaguar Spot stopped and stared. He had never seen anything like this before. He had never even heard of a stairway being built inside, and until this moment the very idea would have been unimaginable to him. Now that he saw it, the brilliance of the idea seemed obvious. With fewer entrances to guard, the palace would be much more defensible than any other building in the world, and its denizens could go from floor to floor without anyone outside seeing. The guard stared up the stairway and Jaguar Spot had to hurry to catch up with him. They made a few twists and turns through narrow corridors until they finally came to a small bedchamber where an old man lay on a sleeping mat. Light was streaming in though a large window, and the old man was holding Fireborn's message up to the light, apparently reading it. The old man's hair was perfectly white, and from what Jaguar Spot could see, would fall down to the man's waist when he was standing. He frowned as the guard pushed Jaguar Spot up to the side of the sleeping mat. "You are the Chamberlain?" Jaguar Spot asked quietly. The old man ignored Jaguar Spot and kept looking at the message. Jaguar Spot pulled the jade-stone that Fireborn had given him and showed it to the old man. "Fireborn gave this to me to show you. He said that you would recognize it." The old man snatched the jade-stone from Jaguar Spot's hand, looked at it closely, and tossed it to the guard, who grunted.

The old man spoke with a voice that sounded like he was choking on ashes. "Am I to understand from this piece of paper that His Lordship Fireborn has gotten it into his mind to marry some trollop from Uaxactun, and that he wants the wedding to take place today?" Jaguar Spot was speechless. The old man had called Orchid a trollop! Never in his life had he heard anyone speak so insultingly about a member of his family. At home he would have run to his father and informed him of what happened, and the retribution of the clan would have been swift. But here? What was he supposed to do here? The guard prodded him in the side. "Answer the Chamberlain, son."

"The woman is my sister" was all that Jaguar Spot could say at first. "And I would appreciate it if you did not refer to her in so disrespectful a manner." The guard put a hand on Jaguar Spot's right shoulder and pulled him from the sleeping mat. "Easy there, son. I am sure that the Chamberlain meant no offense. Remember, I had to wake him up to show him that piece of paper, and he hasn't had his breakfast and his morning bowl of chocolate yet."

The Chamberlain crinkled his nose as if an unpleasant smell had entered the room. He handed the message to Jaguar Spot and sighed. "I must apologize. Sometimes I am not myself in the early morning. I am sure that your sister is an honorable woman, and that you come from an honorable house. I just don't like surprises. By the way, you look horrible. What happened to you?" Jaguar Spot told the Chamberlain and the guard the story of his journey through the forest, of his experience with the jaguar, and about how the marriage had been arranged. When he was done, the Chamberlain screamed for an attendant, and a short woman came through the door almost instantly. "Go take this boy. Wash him up. Give him a set of clothes suitable for the brother of the bride at a royal wedding. Now!" The woman pulled Jaguar Spot by the arm into another room. She washed him and then left, presumably to find him some clothes. While Jaguar Spot was still naked awaiting the woman's return the Chamberlain walked in, alone, speaking as if he were already in mid-conversation. "Just about the most difficult undertaking anyone has ever asked of me. Oh, hello there my boy, are they taking good care of you? I should hope so. You are soon to be a very important man in the city, but you probably knew that already. Like I was saying, there is much to do. In fact, there is too much to do so quickly. I need you to help. I want you to go down to the kitchen and tell them to prepare a light feast for 100 people. I need it ready to go by noon. I'm going to start rounding up the *ahauob*. They will have to carry the food for the feast themselves, and let me tell you, they are not going to be very happy about that! But wait, what are you doing here? Why aren't you in the kitchen arranging the feast, boy? Don't you know that we are in a hurry?"

Jaguar Spot looked down at his own nakedness before answering the Chamberlain, hoping that the man would notice his current state of undress, but the Chamberlain was unperturbed. "I said off with you, boy. Get to the kitchen! Go!"

"But Chamberlain, I am naked."

"What? Oh, so you are. Put some clothes on, then! We haven't got all day!"

"My clothes are ruined, Chamberlain. You told the servant to get me new ones. I am waiting for her to get back with them."

"Ruined? What? Oh yes, I remember. You looked a mess. Damn it, I don't have time for this, not at all. Not only am I expected to arrange a royal wedding without even a full day's notice, I am expected to find new clothes for a young boy? When my father was Chamberlain, he never had . . ."

The Chamberlain stopped talking when the servant came back into the room carrying a colorful set of clothes and a red macaw feather plumed hat. Before the servant could give them to Jaguar Spot, the Chamberlain bent down over them and loudly sniffed at them two or three times. He shook his head and started to the door, speaking as he went. "Well, no time to get any better clothes. These smell like they are fifty years old, but nothing we can do about it on short notice. Anyway, lots to do today. As soon as you are dressed, run down to the . . ." The Chamberlain's voice faded away as he disappeared down the hallway, oblivious to the fact that no one was listening to him anymore.

By the time that Jaguar Spot reached the kitchen, the place was bustling with activity, with servants running around four separate cook fires making mountains of tortillas and huge bowls of meat. Five or six girls knelt in a corner, apparently making some kind of confection with honey. Jaguar Spot walked up to the oldest appearing woman, who was busy running from one cook fire to another. "Ma'am," he said, tugging at her clothes.

"What is it now?" the woman screamed as she looked down at Jaguar Spot. "Oh, I am sorry, Your Lordship," she said, looking at his clothes. "I don't recognize you. Anyway, I am rather busy right now, so if you please, tell me what you want." Jaguar Spot tried to stammer out the Chamberlain's request, but was only able to utter little more than a mumble. The woman looked annoyed. "Oh come now, Your Lordship," she said. "You come in to my kitchen, pull on my clothes, interrupting my work, and you can't even tell me what you want. Well, I must get back to work." The woman turned back to the cook fire. Jaguar Spot finally found his voice. "Ma'am," he said, "the

Chamberlain instructed me to tell you to prepare a wedding feast for at least 100 people."

The woman turned back toward Jaguar Spot and stood with her arms akimbo. "Oh did he now, Your Lordship? Did he indeed? Well, why don't you go and tell the Chamberlain that I only need to be told what to do *once*, and that I understood his instructions when he came down here and gave them to me in person. Now, with all due respect to Your Lordship, get out of my kitchen!"

Jaguar Spot picked a couple of tortillas off of a pile and wandered about the palace looking for the Chamberlain, eating as he went. He found the Chamberlain upstairs, berating the servant woman who had washed him and given his clothes. "How can you not know where he is?" the Chamberlain was asking the woman. "He was just here. You washed him. You gave him clothes. And then he just disappears? Into thin air? Is he some kind of specter, a phantasm perhaps? Was I dreaming when I spoke to him just a few moments ago? I say no! This is a most serious occurrence. This young man is important. He is going to be Lord Fireborn's brother-in-law! And we have lost him. Lost him, I say! What am I going to tell Lord Fireborn?" Jaguar Spot cleared his throat, and the Chamberlain turned around. "Ah, there you are!" he said with relief. "Where have you been? We have much to do, and I don't have time to go on searches for small boys." Jaguar Spot tried to hide his confusion when he answered. "I went down to the kitchen as you requested."

The Chamberlain put his right hand to his face and shook his head. "I asked you to go to the kitchen?" he asked. "Really? Why would I do that? Oh I see, you have gotten your breakfast. Wonderful! Come with me. I have many things to do, and I want you to stick by my side so I don't lose track of you again."

Jaguar Spot followed the Chamberlain as they left the palace and called on the houses of the *ahauob* of the city. The Chamberlain explained that he had sent out messengers to most of the nobility, but that there were certain *ahauob* that would require his personal attention. They went from compound to compound, and house to house, for most of the morning. Jaguar Spot would wait outside while the Chamberlain would run in to inform the *ahau* of the impending wedding, and then leave. By the time they got back to the palace a crowd of eighty or so people had arrived, and more were coming. "Oh my oh my oh my," said the Chamberlain, "I don't think that we asked the cook to make enough food. Never mind, there is nothing that we can do about it now." Jaguar Spot followed the Chamberlain into the center of the waiting group of *ahauob, cahelob*, and their families. "Everybody listen to me!" he screamed. Some in the crowd stopped talking, but not enough for the Chamberlain's taste, so he started clapping his hands loudly together. "Listen up! I want all of the boys and women to head into the palace kitchen and pick up as much food as you can carry for the rest of the day. Don't eat it! It is for the wedding celebration. Now, young man . . ." The Chamberlain trailed off as he looked around for Jaguar Spot, who was standing right next to him. "Oh there you are, young man. Good. Everyone follow this young man to the palace kitchen, he knows the way."

Jaguar Spot led the group of noble women and children into Tikal's royal palace, where they quickly took tortillas and bags of cooked meat. Once all of the food was gone, Jaguar Spot returned to the square where the Chamberlain was in the process of berating the *ahauob*. "Oh no," he said. "This will not do! Did no one think to bring incense? Where are the musicians? You there, didn't I ask you to bring some musicians? What? I didn't? Well, nothing we can do about it now." The Chamberlain interrupted his harangue when Jaguar Spot approached. "Well young man," he said, "do we have all of the foodstuffs ready to go?"

"Yes, Chamberlain," Jaguar Spot answered.

"Good. Let's hope that we can all get there in time. Everybody listen to me! We are leaving now! This young man here is the son of an *ahau* of Uaxactun. He will be Lord Fireborn's brother-in-law before the day is out, so treat him with appropriate respect. I want us all to walk in a nice tight bunch. No stragglers. Let's go."

The Chamberlain seemed to calm down as the day progressed, although he started dragging his feet in the afternoon as it became almost unbearably hot. Most of the nobility, and the Chamberlain, would normally be taking a nap this time of day, but the length of the journey would not permit a stop. The group began to grumble audibly as the afternoon progressed, and as they grew hungry and tired from their exertions.

At last, just as Lord Sun was beginning to lower in the West, they arrived at the village. The Village Of The Ancestor Broken Sunlight (to Jaguar Spot's surprise, that was the village's actual name, not just Fireborn's description) consisted of about twenty thatch and wood houses, all surrounding a central plaza, which contained a small pyramid, barely taller than the height of three men. As they entered the village, Jaguar Spot saw a Tikal emblem glyph carved into a large stone-tree off to the side. The Chamberlain had forewarned the citizens of the village of the visitors' impending arrival by messenger, so the *cahel* who managed the village for whatever *ahau* was in charge met them at the village boundary, dressed in what amounted to impromptu finery. He had apparently had the women of the village quickly stitch together a suit adorned with feathers, but the result looked hurried and haphazard. From the aromas emanating from the houses, Jaguar Spot surmised that the *cahel* had ordered the female residents to start cooking, and the Chamberlain was greatly relieved now that he could assume that there would be adequate food for the feast.

The weary travelers found whatever shade the local trees provided and sat down to rest. The Chamberlain dragged Jaguar Spot along with him as he chased after the *cahel*, who had quickly disappeared into the temple. "I say my good man," the Chamberlain screamed into the darkness of the temple. "Have you had any word from Lord Fireborn or anyone else coming from the North?"

When there was no answer, Jaguar Spot moved to follow the *cahel* into the temple, but the Chamberlain pulled him back. "No young man," he said. "Only that *cahel* and certain priests are allowed to enter that temple."

"But what about your *Ch'ul Ahau*? Can't he go in?" asked Jaguar Spot.

The Chamberlain rolled his eyes. "Well yes, of course His Lordship can go in." The Chamberlain started screaming into the darkness once again, but the *cahel* still did not answer, although they did hear some rustling and movement from inside. "I say! Sir, we need to speak to you about the arrangements! Please come out so that we can talk." The *cahel* still did not answer the Chamberlain, who now whispered to Jaguar Spot. "Now this is mighty queer. That temple is certainly not so large that the *cahel* can't hear me. I cannot imagine why he would not answer, and why he ran into the temple so quickly after our arrival. Well, no matter. We have work to do. I am going to take the guards and walk north on the path so that Lord Fireborn can have a proper escort for his arrival, which should be soon by any account. You see to the other arrangements."

Before Jaguar Spot could ask the Chamberlain exactly what arrangements he was talking about, the older man ran off in the direction of the ten or so palace guards who had accompanied them on the journey. They moved fast, and were almost into the forest before Jaguar Spot caught up with the Chamberlain. "Chamberlain, I need to ask you a question," Jaguar Spot managed to say, although he was almost out of breath. "What are you doing here?" asked the Chamberlain. "Don't you have work to do at the village?"

"Well," said Jaguar Spot, "you asked me to see to the arrangements, but you didn't tell me what arrangements you were talking about. What exactly do you want me to do?"

"Oh must I do everything myself?" said the Chamberlain, so loud that several of the palace guards turned their heads to look. "Listen boy, I will only say this once. Go and find that *cahel* and make sure that everything is prepared. Is that so hard?"

"No, Chamberlain."

"Good. Now get going!"

Jaguar Spot turned around and raced back to the village as fast as he could. According to the *ahau* who was sitting closest to the temple, the *cahel* had not emerged during the time that Jaguar Spot had chased after the Chamberlain. Jaguar Spot walked up to the dark entrance. He spoke as loud as he could without screaming. "Sir? The Chamberlain asked me to speak with you about the arrangements. Can you come out and talk to me?" Instead of an answer, Jaguar Spot heard what sounded like several whispered conversations taking place inside. He could not make out any words, but it certainly seemed like there were several people speaking at once, and the tone of some of the whispers seemed almost emphatic. "Sir?" Jaguar Spot asked again. "Are you alright in there? I am sorry to bother you in the holy place, but I think that the Chamberlain felt that this was rather urgent." Again there was no answer, but this time Jaguar Spot heard even more whispers than before. He inched closer to the temple until he was actually standing in the doorway itself, and could see that there was some kind of wall in front of him that blocked his view of what was inside. He felt sweat beading on his forehead as he slowly inched into the temple. He was now completely inside, and the whispers became louder. Were these gods he was listening to? Were they some other kind of spirits? Was he about to disturb some kind of holy ritual? He swallowed his fear and kept moving until he reached the wall that he had seen from the entrance. He saw that there were passageways leading in two directions, but each was pitch black. He chose to go left, and he slowly moved forward until he felt the air go cool and moist. He turned a corner, and now there was no light at all. After a few steps he detected a faint light in the distance, coming from around another corner. He turned the corner as quietly as he could, when he suddenly felt something strong and painful pulling against his chest and his mouth. He tried to scream out, but could not. A rough voice spoke quietly in his ear. "Now you just stay nice and quiet, little man, and no one gets hurt. D'ya understand me?" Jaguar Spot nodded his head. "Good," the voice whispered, and then spoke louder. "Cougar, come over here and tie this little one up, and then gag him." The man who had been holding Jaguar Spot let go, and then put what felt like the tip of an obsidian blade at the base of his neck. Jaguar Spot perceived movement to his left, and all of the sudden another shape appeared out of the gloom, the shape of a child. The child grabbed Jaguar Spot's hands and pulled them behind his back and bound them so tightly that Jaguar Spot thought that they might fall off from the pressure. Someone pushed a gag into Jaguar Spot's mouth, and then pulled him backwards into the darkness, finally shoving him against the wall and forcing him to sit.

It took a while for Jaguar Spot's vision to adjust to the darkness, but ultimately he was able to discern five shapes in the room next to him, all bound and gagged like he was. One of the others was certainly the *cahel* who he and the Chamberlain had seen running into the temple. The other captives appeared to be a woman of child rearing age and four children, all bound to each other. He looked around the room and tried to pick up some clues as to who their captors were. There appeared to be only two of them–one of them a largish man, who had apparently grabbed Jaguar Spot and whispered in his ear, and the child Cougar.

The two of them were engaged in quiet conversation when suddenly the larger one raised his voice. "I know all of that, Cougar, but plans have to change. I say that we kill the lot of them right now. Then we take the money, and we get the hell out of here."

The voice that responded to the larger of the captors surprised Jaguar Spot. It was not the voice of a child, but was not quite like the voice of an adult either. Something about the voice was odd, as if it were a little high pitched for an adult. "Okay Frog, I think that I have heard enough. Didn't we agree that I was going to be the brains of this operation, and that you were going to be the brawn? My brains tell me that we ain't gonna kill this lot. We're gonna stay right here, nice and quiet like, until all of the commotion outside is over, and then we sneak out of here nice and quiet like, savvy?"

Frog was not placated by Cougar's words of wisdom. "Dammit Cougar, I didn't sign on to get my head chopped off. You said that we could make a nice take and that we could go live somewhere else. The entire royal house of Tikal is about to walk into this town, according to what the chief over there says. That makes me think that our little hidey-hole ain't all that secure no more. For all we know, the *Ch'ul Ahau* could come walking in here any moment, and what would that mean. We'd be goners for sure."

Frog apparently said something that got Cougar thinking, because they did not speak anymore for a while. "Opportunity!" Cougar said suddenly.

"What?" asked Frog

"You make a good point, my friend. We can only hope that your prediction about the *Ch'ul Ahau* comes to fruition. The opportunity for profit would be enormous."

"Opportunity for profit? Opportunity for death it sounds like to me."

"You forget who you are talking to, Frog. I have seen a thousand of these small-town ceremonies. The *Ch'ul Ahau* will enter this temple alone, or perhaps with one priest, or maybe his brother Fireborn, who knows. We kill whoever comes in with the *Ch'ul Ahau*, and then we tie His Lordship up and hold him for ransom, as much as we can carry."

"Ransom?" asked Frog dubiously. "What ransom? The guards would kill us the moment we stepped out of this temple."

"Idiot! We take the *Ch'ul Ahau* with us into the forest, and tell the people outside that we will let their ruler go the moment that we get a few thousand paces from the village."

"And then he runs and tells his guards exactly where we went, and they chase after us, and because we are carrying all of that ransom they catch up in no time at all. Doesn't sound like that great of a plan to me."

Cougar laughed a wicked little laugh. "That would be true if we actually let him go. What we will do is cut his throat and then hide him under a bush or something. By the time that they realize he is dead, we will be long gone."

Frog sounded impressed. "Not bad, not bad at all. And what about this lot, do we kill them too?"

Cougar gave his little laugh again. 'Of course we kill them, you idiot! We can't bring them along with us, and if we left them here they would tell everyone about our little plan as soon as they were freed. No my friend, we kill them before we take the *Ch'ul Ahau*, assuming he actually comes into our little slice of paradise right here. Not before though, I don't want any decaying bodies stinking up the place."

Jaguar Spot's eyes met those of the *cahel*. They had to do something to head off the catastrophe that was about to befall the royal house of Tikal, but what could they do? Jaguar Spot looked around for anything that could help him. He saw nothing, but then noticed that the *cahel* was motioning with his eyes to a spot a few paces to Jaguar Spot's right. A shadow covered the area, and Jaguar Spot could see nothing, but he decided to trust the *cahel's* judgment. As slowly as he could, he inched himself over to the dark spot. Frog and Cougar were now deeply involved in a murmured conversation, probably about how they would spend the loot from this enterprise. They did not seem to notice as Jaguar Spot moved ever so slowly to his right. When he reached the shadowed area, he felt around with is hands, and . . . ouch . . . he cut himself on a sharp object. Had he not been gagged, he probably would have whelped in pain, as he had no doubt that there was now a nasty gash on his left index finger. He felt around more slowly now, and detected the outlines of something, he wasn't quite sure what it was, but he was sure that it was sharp–sharp enough to cut rope. As quietly as he could, he rubbed his bonds back and forth over the sharp object. Every once and a while Frog would look over in his direction, and Jaguar Spot would immediately stop, afraid that he had been caught. But every time Frog would grunt and go back to talking with Cougar. Enough time had passed that it must be almost sunset outside. If the *Ch'ul Ahau* were going to wander into this temple it would probably be soon. Jaguar Spot rubbed his bonds against the sharpness as quickly as he could without being discovered, and finally he felt the bonds begin to give. Ever so slowly, he pulled the bonds off of his wrists. Now all he had to do was get past Frog–Cougar did not seem to be that much of a physical threat. He felt behind him again for whatever sharp object he had used to cut the bonds, and realized that it was a large piece of obsidian–priceless– with many sharp edges. It was probably half the size of Cougar's head, and about as heavy as a small ball for the ballgame. He gripped the rock with his right hand as hard as he could without cutting himself and studied the exact location of Frog's head.

Suddenly he began to hear some kind of commotion outside—as if somebody was about to come into the temple. Frog and Cougar stood up and turned their back to Jaguar Spot and the other prisoners. Jaguar Spot hurled the rock straight at the back of Frog's head. It impacted right on target with a loud thud, and Frog screamed "what the Hell?" Frog fell over towards Cougar and they both tumbled to the floor. In an instant Jaguar Spot started running toward the exit, jumping over his captors, who swore curses at him as he fled.

It was almost dark outside when Jaguar Spot emerged. He started screaming at the top of his lungs as soon as he cleared the temple entrance. "Bandits! Assassins! Help! Bandits!" He ran blindly, screaming. He came straight into a group of 10 or so men who were about 20 paces from the temple and heading straight for it. He had no idea who it was that he collided with, only that whoever it was, he was wearing a feather skirt and tunic. Jaguar Spot fell onto his side and kept screaming until there was the sound of many running footsteps and all of the sudden Jaguar Spot became aware that there were more than ten spear points no more than a hair's breadth from his body. "Not me! In there. In the temple," Jaguar Spot screamed. "Bandits! Don't let them get away! They mean to kidnap and kill the *Ch'ul Ahau!*"

Five or six of the guards ran over to the temple and stood at the door, but Jaguar Spot still had an unhealthy number of spear points directed at him. A loud voice told the guards to forget about the boy and surround the temple, and then someone pulled Jaguar Spot up by the shoulders. It was Speaking Macaw. "Is that you, Jaguar Spot?" Speaking Macaw asked. "Where have you been? We've had people looking all over for you. You missed your sister's wedding. What's all of this stuff you were screaming about bandits?"

Seeing that he was now surrounded by royalty and *ahauob*, Jaguar Spot suddenly became ashamed of his screaming and hysterics. He composed himself as much as he could and spoke in his best approximation of a calm voice. "Your Lordship, bandits have taken over that temple. The have taken the *cahel* of this village hostage, along with his family. When they learned of the wedding plans, they thought that His Lordship Great Jaguar Paw might enter the temple. They devised a plan to capture him, hold him for ransom, and then kill him. They also said that they would kill any priests that entered with him."

Jaguar Spot thought that he heard murmurs of skepticism from the group, but Speaking Macaw quieted them down. "Boy," he asked, "how do you know what their plans are?"

"They spoke of them openly, Your Lordship."

"And how did you manage to hear what they said?"

"I was held hostage, too. I cut my bonds and escaped. Here, I cut my hand getting lose." Jaguar Spot showed the men his hand, and suddenly the murmurs of skepticism changed to alarm. One of the Tikal *ahauob* grabbed Jaguar Spot's hand and closely examined the wound. "You say that they are still in there, boy?" the *ahau* asked. Jaguar Spot nodded. "How many are there?" another *ahau* demanded. "I saw two," Jaguar Spot said.

One of the Tikal *ahauob* ordered the town's citizens to provide the group with torches, and once they were provided, Speaking Macaw, a torch in one hand and Jaguar Spot's shoulder in another, led the group to the temple. Speaking Macaw shouted into the temple in much the same way that the Chamberlain had done. "I say! We know that you are in there, you brigands! There are currently twenty palace guards and numerous other armed men surrounding this temple. If you come out now, and leave your hostages unharmed, we might be persuaded to spare your lives, you miserable curs! If we have to come in and get you, you will not survive this night. Speak! Tell me your answer."

The assembled group of *ahauob* and guards waited in silence before Cougar answered. "You have no authority here, Speaking Macaw, so I don't even know why I am talking to you. But nevertheless, be assured that we have no intention of surrendering to you, no matter how many men you have out there. Now *you* will listen to *me*. You will let us go, and we won't kill our prisoners."

Even in the torchlight, Jaguar Spot could see that Speaking Macaw looked confused, as if he recognized Cougar's voice but could not quite place it. "Cougar?" he asked, "is that you?"

"Of course it's me!" Cougar shouted. "Tell me, how do you think that your new found friends in Tikal are going to feel about one of your pet dwarves kidnapping one of their noblemen and defiling one of their temples?"

So, Jaguar Spot thought to himself, it was a dwarf. But why would a dwarf want to leave the royal court? If anyone led a life of luxury and relaxation, it was the palace dwarves. They never had to work, never had to tend the fields, never had to do anything except be present at the palace and provide the *Ch'ul Ahau* with good luck. Sometimes, it was known, rulers would consider dwarves to be their most trusted advisors. They were known to have deep spiritual powers. Yet Jaguar Spot surmised that such was not the case with Cougar, and with Cougar's answer Speaking Macaw's demeanor hardened. "Cougar," he said, "you have betrayed me and the city of Uaxactun. You will die. Now." Without saying another word Speaking Macaw grabbed a spear from one of the guards and nonchalantly walked in to the temple. Several of the Tikal *ahauob* moved to stop him, but they were too late. Two of the guards moved to follow, but one of the more senior looking Tikal *ahauob* blocked their path, saying that he would not tolerate any further defilement of the temple. Before Jaguar Spot had breathed twenty breaths, Speaking Macaw walked out of the temple covered in blood, the spear in his right hand, dragging on the ground. He dropped the spear and turned to the sergeant of the guards. "It is done," he said. "That scoundrel Cougar and his accomplice are on their path to the Underworld. The hostages appear to be unharmed. Here, go and cut their bonds." Speaking Macaw handed the sergeant an obsidian knife from his waist, and then collapsed to the ground.

Chapter Nine
Loyalty

8.16.18.17.8. October 15, 375 A.D.

That pompous idiot Blue Squirrel was speaking to the assembled ballplayers, none of whom seemed to be paying any attention to his remonstrations, as if they were infants. The words flowed past them all like water through a rapids, and Jaguar Spot studiously avoided looking down at Blue Squirrel. He concentrated instead on examining the creases and grooves on his arm pad and other equipment. He looked across to the other edge of the ballcourt, which was filled with the married women of the city who had yet to bear children. The purpose of the ceremonial game that the men were about to play was to honor Lady Moon, the most powerful of the fertility gods, so that the women might become mothers. Lady Moon resided in the Underworld. She was closely associated with both birth and death. At the end of the ballgame, the priests would bring in a luckless orphan child who would be sacrificed to Lady Moon. The energy released by the sacrifice would hopefully be enough to draw Lady Moon out of the Underworld so that her magic would be imparted on the women who had to suffer through Blue Squirrel's remonstrations.

Hummingbird smiled at him from across the ballcourt. In the more than four years since she had married the *Ch'ul Ahau* she had grown into one of the greatest beauties in Uaxactun, with jet black hair that fell almost to her thighs. Jaguar Spot had to admit that his father had made the best possible choice for the *Ch'ul Ahau* of all the available women in the city, and he had heard His Lordship speak in a similar vein on numerous occasions. Jaguar Spot had often caught himself daydreaming about Hummingbird after she walked past him in the palace, his face to the wall, paintbrush in his hand. Her smell, or at least the smell of the perfumes applied by the palace attendants, was almost as beautiful as she was physically. Sometimes he would be painting a particularly intricate scene on one of the palace murals and she would walk into the room. It almost seemed as if her scent would proceed her, distracting him from his work so that the brush would go left instead of right, obliterating half a day of painstaking work. By the time she actually entered the room, he could think of nothing else but her. Sometimes she would say "hello" or compliment him on his work as she passed, and as a result his concentration would be ruined for the rest of the day.

Before Jaguar Spot could answer Hummingbird's smile from across the ballcourt, she looked down at her father with a contemptuous look, as if to silently say to Jaguar Spot, "Can you believe the time that my idiot father is wasting spewing out such intolerable drivel?" At last she looked back up at Jaguar Spot and gave him an even broader smile than before. His heart started racing and he started sweating. He had never felt like this before. For a moment he thought that he would start hyperventilating, so he looked back down at her father, who was now pacing back and forth, waiving his arms wildly. Over the past four years Blue Squirrel had taken on a greater and greater sense of self importance. Even the *Ch'ul Ahau* knew that Blue Squirrel lusted after power more than anything else, and that his only loyalty was to himself. Still, he was technically the *Ch'ul Ahau's* father-in-law, and though only a *cahel*, for appearances sake he had to be given a position that at least seemed important. So the *Ch'ul Ahau* had given him the responsibility of overall management of the city's ballcourts, and of the various minor ceremonial ballgames, such as the one that was about to start, that the calendar dictated. It was actually a safe move, as the real managers of the ballgames, both major and minor, were the priests and the scribes. In reality Blue Squirrel, who was originally thrilled with the appointment, barely had the power of a figurehead. He quickly came to realize that the only real prerogative he had was to speak to the ballplayers before any minor ceremonial game (the *Ch'ul Ahau* spoke at the major ones), and to officially remind them of the rules, and of the religious significance of whatever game they happened to be playing. He usually tended to drone on and on ten times longer than any previous holder of the office had ever done.

At last Blue Squirrel was done with his speech, and a priest called the men from both teams down to the center of the playing surface and had them drop their loincloths to the ground. Jaguar Spot thought that he heard giggles from some of the women, but he ignored them. This was the part of the ceremonial ballgame that Jaguar Spot hated the most. The men from each team formed a tight semi-circle facing their opponents. The priests handed stingray spines to the captains of each team. The captains took the spines and made a series of punctures at the base of their penis, and then leaned from side to side so that the blood dripped in a line. Jaguar Spot's captain handed the spine to him, and he punctured himself four times, wincing from the pain with each strike. Gritting his teeth, he handed the spine to the man standing next to him, and joined his captain in swaying from side to side. Soon the entire circle had used the spines and they swayed from side to side in unison, chanting a prayer led by the priest. Another priest walked around inspecting each man to confirm that he was still bleeding, and after several times around the circle he seemed satisfied and raised his arms. The ballplayers instantly stopped swaying and picked up their loincloths, at the same time turning around and walking to their proscribed spots on the playing surface or back to the stands to await their turn.

Jaguar Spot stood right behind his captain, who had been chosen mostly for his incredible height than for his leadership ability or playing acumen. By all rights Jaguar Spot knew that he should have led his team—he was considered by many to be the best ballplayer in the city. But the captain was a good two heads taller than anyone else of ballplaying age, and had arms so long that people whispered that he was not actually a human being at all, but some strange creature that had fallen down from the Overworld.

The priests gave the first service to the opposite team. The opposing captain took the ball in his left hand and pulled his right arm far back behind his body. He brought his arm forward with great speed, hitting the ball with his right forearm pad with a loud "thud." The ball for this match was smallish, about half the size of a man's head, and it shot up high into the air. With such a small ball, the best strategy was to shoot it up as high as possible, so that it would come down at a steep angle, which made a successful play on the ball difficult. The opposing captain's serve fit the strategy, and the ball started falling almost straight down to a point that would probably be about three paces to Jaguar Spot's right. Connecting with the ball would be a tough play, and most ballplayers would have let it bounce up so that another player would have a chance at an easier shot. Jaguar Spot thought that he could squat down to make the shot with his waist pad. He moved over to the spot where he projected that the ball would come down. If he made the play, his fellow ballplayers would regard it as an exhibition of daring and skill. If he missed, they would know that the shot was next to impossible and would not hold it against him. Just as he got set and braced for contact with the ball, the captain ran back, jumped high, and smacked the ball with his right forearm while he was in mid-air. The captain fell to the ground and did not get up quickly, but the ball shot up so high into the air that it almost came down straight, and bounced far into the other team's end zone. One of the opposing back men dove for the ball and hit it back even farther to the rear, making a return impossible. The women cheered, but the captain lay face down on the playing surface, motionless. Two priests ran over to the captain and the crowd quieted down quickly. The priests turned the captain over and one of them examined his face. Jaguar Spot and the other players from his team walked over to their captain. He was still not moving, and the priests were starting to get concerned. Jaguar Spot suspected that the captain had hit his head when he came down from the play, and had been knocked unconscious. Another priest came running over and put his ear to the captain's mouth, while yet another priest screamed for everyone else to be as quiet as possible. Just as everyone quieted down, Jaguar Spot heard heavy footsteps approaching, and turned to see Blue Squirrel storming onto the playing surface, screaming at the priests "What, what, what? I say, what are you doing to him? Move away from that man! I am in charge here, I will take care of things. What is wrong with him? We need to get him playing again. This game has to go on. Get away from that player! I will take over!" Blue Squirrel stopped next to the priest who had been listening for the captain's breath and pulled him away. One of the other priests moved over to intervene and put his hand on Blue Squirrel's shoulder, speaking softly so that Jaguar Spot could barely hear. "Sir, please let us handle this situation. I assure you that we will keep you fully informed." Blue Squirrel slapped the priest's hand away, with a scolding tone in his voice. "Shut up, I say. His Lordship has put *me* in charge of this ballcourt and *I* say what goes on here and what doesn't. You there, what did you hear when you listened to this player's breath? I can't hear a thing." The priest who Blue Squirrel had pushed away inched back to the captain and spoke. "Sir, I heard nothing. This man is dead. I expect that he suffered a broken neck when he hit the ground." Blue Squirrel recoiled from the captain's body as if it were poisonous. "Dead?" he cried. "Dead? No, no, no! Not on *my* ballcourt. Not for *this* game."

Jaguar Spot looked around at the other players, all of whom looked confused at Blue Squirrel's statement. Death on the ballcourt was honorable, even if it came at an axeman's hands to a losing player, and to actually die making a play on the ball was the most honorable death that a man could possibly attain, even more honorable than glorious death in battle. Neither Jaguar Spot nor his colleagues had any idea what Blue Squirrel was prattling on about, if anything the captain's death should be celebrated around the city. Blue Squirrel noticed everyone staring at him and raised his voice so that he was almost yelling. "What are you all staring at! I mean, there is no honor in dying in a ritual game to appease the fertility gods. This boy's father is a friend of mine. What am I to tell him? No, no, no, he is not dead. He didn't hit his head at all. And if he did die, it was not my fault, it was your fault, priest, your negligent ministrations killed him. Yes, that is it! The ballgame didn't kill him at all." While Blue Squirrel was speaking, the men who had been sitting on the edge made their way to the playing surface, and they, along with the other players and the priests, audibly gasped when Blue Squirrel said that the ballgame did not kill the captain. There was no other possibility in their minds but that Blue Squirrel was trying to deny the captain an honorable death, and they could not figure out what grudge or hatred would inspire him to do so. The captain's dishonor would be imputed not only to his family, but to his teammates, and even to the players of the opposing team. Jaguar Spot heard his fellow players murmuring to each other about their desire to kill Blue Squirrel or, at the very least, to cause him grave bodily injury. Blue Squirrel, oblivious to the murmurs, started pacing in a circle around the captain's lifeless body, waiving his hands in the air. He spotted Jaguar Spot and pointed over to the captain. "You there, check for yourself. Tell me if this priest is correct, or if, as I expect, he is an idiot and your captain is merely taking a nap." Jaguar Spot stood where he was, ignoring Blue Squirrel, who became even more aggravated, walking right up to Jaguar Spot and shouting in his face. "Didn't you hear me? I said for you to go over and check on your captain!" Jaguar Spot looked straight at Blue Squirrel and almost spit as he spoke with as much contempt as he could muster. "To whom are you speaking, *cahel*?"

"Oh it's *cahel* now, is it? No more 'Blue Squirrel,' no more calling me my name, as my rank entitles me? And you know damn well that I am speaking to you, idiot. You heard me."

Jaguar Spot had to catch himself from losing his temper, which would have been unacceptable under any circumstances, but especially so in front of all of these people. Instead, he spoke in the most calm and even-tempered voice that he could manage. "Idiot? You call me an idiot? Since when does a mere *cahel* speak to the son of an *ahau* in such a familiar and contemptuous manner. You will address me as 'Your Lordship,' and you will refrain from any personal insults directed toward me."

Blue Squirrel stared at Jaguar Spot, looked liked he was going to say something acerbic, but apparently thought the better of it. He stormed away without saying anything else, muttering something incomprehensible. A small group of players from both teams moved to follow him, certainly for no legitimate purpose. Jaguar Spot ran after them and blocked their path. "Stay," he said. "We have a game to finish, and we all know what His Lordship would say if you did anything untoward to Blue Squirrel." Probably due to Jaguar Spot's rank more than anything else, the opposing players frowned and went back to their playing positions. The priests pulled the captain's body from the ballcourt and one of them handed the ball to Jaguar Spot to serve it, appointing him captain of his team in the process. Jaguar Spot pointed to one of the boys who had returned to the edge and then pointed to the endzone.

Jaguar Spot took the ball and bounced it a few times to get a feel for its weight and shape. He took it and held it towards the opposing team as a salute, which was traditional after a fallen or injured player was removed from the court. After the opponents returned the salute, Jaguar Spot bounced the ball against the playing surface and reached his right arm far behind his body and down to the ground. Just as the ball reached the top of its bounce, he brought his right arm forward and hit the ball high into the air, so high in fact that he worried that it might leave the court entirely, resulting in a foul and a point for the opposing team. Jaguar Spot held his breath as the ball came down. It bounced in the far rear of the opponents' endzone and then bouncing into one of the endzone's corners, making any return impossible. The women in the stands stood and cheered, and Jaguar Spot looked up at Hummingbird, who was standing, clapping, and looking right at him. If anything, her smile was even more beautiful than anything that Jaguar Spot could remember, and he thought that he felt his heart skip a beat as he looked at her. As much as it pained him, he had to return his attention to the ballcourt and accept the ball from one of the priests. This time he bounced the ball high over his head and raised his right arm. As the ball came down, he struck it with his arm protector, sending it on a downward angle so that it bounced just a hair's breadth on the other side of the center line. If the ball had landed any closer, the priests would have called a foul. The opposing captain dove to hit the ball with his hip pad just as it landed, but he misjudged the angle and landed on top of the ball, trapping it. Again the women in the stands cheered. Jaguar Spot wanted to look up to see if Hummingbird was still there cheering for him, but he knew that he should not. She was, after all, one of the *Ch'ul Ahau's* two wives. She was also the daughter of that nincompoop

Blue Squirrel, who was probably at that very moment spreading malicious lies about how the captain met his fate. If that were not enough, Jaguar Spot was engaged to be married. Waterlily already ran the household even better than Orchid had, which Jaguar Spot would not have thought possible. Every morning when Jaguar Spot woke up, there was a fresh set of clothes at the foot of his sleeping mat, and the house was now kept impeccably clean. Waterlily smiled and greeted him warmly every time he came home, and she often brought him lunch when he was painting at the palace. She was also beautiful, but not in the radiant, exotic way that Hummingbird was. He knew in his heart that it would be wrong to look up at Hummingbird, he knew that it was wrong as he turned his head to do it, and he knew that it was wrong when he felt his heart race at the sight of her smiling down at him, but he did it just the same. One of the priests motioned for Jaguar Spot and the other players on his team to vacate the playing surface, and the opposite team did the same. One of the peculiar aspects of this ceremonial ballgame was to replace all the players on each team at preset intervals. Replacement players ran on to the court while Jaguar Spot ran off and sat on the edge opposite Hummingbird.

Oblivious to the progression of the game, Jaguar Spot sat and stared at Hummingbird. As much as he tried, he could not take his eyes off of her, even when he knew that he should. He had no idea how much time had passed when he heard a whisper in his ear. "Your Lordship, I am sorry to interrupt your participation in the ritual, but I have to ask that you accompany me to the palace." Jaguar Spot turned to see Gray Sky kneeling beside him with a look of concern on his face. He acknowledged Gray Sky's request with a nod and followed him away from the ballcourt and toward the palace. Gray Sky did not seem to be in a particularly talkative mood, so Jaguar Spot had to prod him for some information as to the reasons behind the rather abrupt summons. "Do you know what this is all about, Gray Sky?" Gray Sky looked over at him with the same look of concern that Jaguar Spot had seen in the stands, but said nothing, and they kept walking toward the palace. Once the palace was finally in view, Gray Sky stopped, looked at Jaguar Spot, and spoke in a whisper.

"Your Lordship, I put on no airs when I tell you that I have grown very fond of you over the years. Looking at your paintings on the walls of the palace brings me much joy, every day. It is because of that fondness that I speak to you now. I am not supposed to say anything, but if I can be so presumptuous, I would like to give Your Lordship a word of advice."

"Of course."

"Be careful. Be especially careful of Blue Squirrel. Everyone in the palace knows his character, and no one likes it. He is a buffoon. He is rude. He is stupid. He is also a liar, we all know that."

"Yes, I agree. But what does this have to do with anything?"

"More than anything else, Blue Squirrel is ruthless. He will do anything, to anybody, in order to get what he wants. You are about to see the full measure of his ambition, that he will use any tool that he might have available in order to improve his station. When we get to the palace, I will take you to His Lordship's ceremonial courtyard. At this very moment Blue Squirrel is there with him and a few *ahauob*. Be careful what you say. If you say the wrong thing it might not only have repercussions for you, but for your father. Can you remember that? Will you be careful of what you say?"

"Yes."

Gray Sky started walking again and led Jaguar Spot through the maze of passageways in the palace into a large interior courtyard, where the *Ch'ul Ahau* was sitting, flanked by Aktak and a few other *ahauob*. Blue Squirrel stood in front of the *Ch'ul Ahau* and started swearing at Jaguar Spot the moment that he walked in. "There he is, the little hellion! That little worm who conspires with the priests to deprive me of my just authority! What? Why is he not bound? Gray Sky! Bind his hands immediately He is your prisoner, treat him as such!" The *Ch'ul Ahau*, his patience with Blue Squirrel's antics apparently exhausted, cleared his throat loudly and raised an eyebrow to Aktak, who also cleared his throat. Blue Squirrel kept yelling at Jaguar Spot and Gray Sky, even with the obvious, albeit subtle, orders that he silence himself. At least Aktak was forced to speak with a raised voice to restore order. "Blue Squirrel! You will be silent! I need not remind you that His Lordship is the one that gives the orders around here, not you. Please stop making a scene and let those who are qualified to handle this situation do so." Blue Squirrel was smart enough to close his mouth and did not say another word as Gray Sky brought Jaguar Spot to stand in front of the *Ch'ul Ahau*.

After giving everyone a few moments to settle down, Speaking Macaw spoke. "Jaguar Spot, thank you for joining us. I assure you that you are not the only one whose routine was interrupted this afternoon.

Indeed, Blue Squirrel thought that his grievance with you was important enough to interrupt a discussion that I was having with the *ahauob* you see here. I understand that you were participating in the ritual ballgame, and I am sorry for the interruption. I know that I make enough demands on your time as it is. Lets just see what you have to say about Blue Squirrel's complaints. Do you know what they are?"

"Your Lordship, I honestly cannot imagine what cause I have given Blue Squirrel to complain about anything, although in my opinion he has behaved disgracefully today."

Jaguar Spot thought that he heard Blue Squirrel exclaim "Ha!" under his breath, but he could not be sure. The *Ch'ul Ahau* continued speaking. "He says that you were disrespectful to him on the ballcourt, that you undermined the authority that I have given him to manage its affairs, and that you did not comport yourself as the son of an *ahau* should." Jaguar Spot could barely believe his ears, and then Gray Sky's advice came to him: Blue Squirrel would lie, cheat, and if necessary steal to get what he desired. Jaguar Spot spoke to the *Ch'ul Ahau* in the most respectful tone that he could. "Your Lordship, I believe that Blue Squirrel slanders me." Blue Squirrel instantly started screaming something almost incomprehensible about lies, honor, and the trustworthiness of children. The *Ch'ul Ahau* pointed to two guards who were standing just on the other side of opposite courtyard entrances, and then pointed at Blue Squirrel. The guards came running into the courtyard. Each of them grabbed one of Blue Squirrel's arms, and one of them put his hand over Blue Squirrel's mouth. Jaguar Spot could still hear Blue Squirrel trying to scream beneath the guard's hand until the *Ch'ul Ahau* actually raised his voice. "My dear Blue Squirrel, you not only embarrass yourself with that outburst, you embarrass everyone else here. If you cannot promise to refrain from such insolent behavior, I will have you removed from my sight–permanently. Do you understand?" Blue Squirrel nodded, the guard's hand still over his mouth. The *Ch'ul Ahau* motioned to the guards and they released Blue Squirrel, but still stood close beside him. Aktak told Jaguar Spot to continue with his version of events, and Jaguar Spot again spoke in the most respectful tone possible. "My captain was an honorable man, Your Lordship."

"Your Captain? Was?" asked the *Ch'ul Ahau*.

"Yes, Your Lordship. My captain was an honorable man, and was the most daring ballplayer that I had ever seen."

"Why do you keep referring to this man in the past tense?"

"He is dead, Your Lordship. He died on the ballcourt after diving to make a play and landing on his head. When he dove for the ball, it was as if I was watching a bird on the wind."

The *Ch'ul Ahau* held up his hand to silence Jaguar Spot and beckoned Aktak to bend down so that they could have a whispered conversation, which lasted for quite some time. When they were done, Aktak took over the questioning. "Young man, His Lordship is confused. As I understand it, today was a ritual ballgame attended by all of the childless women of the city, even Her Ladyship Hummingbird was there."

"Yes, Uncle. That is so."

"Then why did you get into a dispute with Blue Squirrel. Surely you weren't angry at him over your friend's death?"

"I was not angry. It was Blue Squirrel who was angry. Blue Squirrel tried to deny him an honorable death." Jaguar Spot felt his voice beginning to rise and had to fight against a strong desire to turn to face Blue Squirrel and start screaming at him. After calming himself down, he continued. "Instead of honoring my captain, instead of holding a ceremony to honor his death, Blue Squirrel said that it was not the ballgame that killed him at all, rather that it was the priests who killed him through negligent ministrations. Then, in front of the assembled ballplayers, Blue Squirrel addressed me in the most familiar of possible fashions, addressing me by saying 'you there' instead of 'Your Lordship.' I reminded him of his duty to address me properly, and he stormed off, but not before he called me an idiot in front of my friends and colleagues."

The *Ch'ul Ahau* stuck his tongue between his upper lip and his teeth and moved it around, looking back and forth at Jaguar Spot and Blue Squirrel. Finally he fixed his gaze at Blue Squirrel. "More or less what happened, Blue Squirrel? Speak the truth." Blue Squirrel said nothing, but nodded his head slowly. Without saying anything else, the *Ch'ul Ahau* again nodded to Aktak, who spoke in his stead. "Why did you interrupt our discussions for such trivial nonsense, Blue Squirrel? This boy apparently behaved honorably, and now we have interrupted his ballgame. What is more, it is inconceivable that you would try to dishonor a ballplayer who died a heroic death in a ceremonial ballgame. The lad who died is destined to be his own star in the Overworld, as if he had died a violent death in combat, yet you would consign him to the Underworld for all eternity? This, Blue Squirrel, is tantamount to attempted murder. Moreover, your actions in failing to address Jaguar Spot according to his rank cannot be attributed to mere ignorance of his rank on your part. After all, he is your kinsman. You should stop and think before. . ."

Blue Squirrel suddenly turned on Aktak, shocking him into silence. "Shut up, Shut up, Shut up you pompous twit!" The guards quickly moved to grab Blue Squirrel, but were stopped by a waive from the *Ch'ul Ahau* as Blue Squirrel continued screaming. "You totally miss the point, all of you miss the point! As long as I am a mere *cahel*, this kind of thing will continue to happen, and I will continue to be denied the respect that I deserve. I deserve respect and I am constantly denied it by young pups like this child! *That* is the situation that must be remedied." Blue Squirrel began panting after he said his piece, and the *Ch'ul Ahau* responded to his outburst with a whisper filled with contempt. "And how would you have us remedy this situation, Blue Squirrel? There is one thing that everyone here but you seems to understand. Even the boy understands it! No one can make other people respect you, only you and your actions can do that. But then again, perhaps you blame me for all of this. Do you blame me?"

Blue Squirrel, unable to look the *Ch'ul Ahau* in the eye, whispered with his eyes to the ground. "No, Your Lordship."

"That is wise, father-in-law, but in any event I blame myself. I should never have put you in this situation. I have an idea on how to get you out of it, but I would rather hear your ideas first. What would you have me do to save you from this awful predicament that I have placed you in?"

Blue Squirrel breathed a few breaths before answering. "There is only one thing that will solve this 'awful predicament,' as you call it, Your Lordship. You must make me an *ahau*." Aktak and the other *ahauob* erupted into laughter, while the *Ch'ul Ahau* simply stared at Blue Squirrel with a look of stunned disbelief. Once the laughter had died down, the *Ch'ul Ahau* spoke again. "I am sorry, Blue Squirrel, I think that I misheard you, in fact I am sure of it. For a moment I thought that I heard you suggest that I make you an *ahau* of this city. That, of course, would have been a ludicrous suggestion. I have enough *ahauob* as it is, now if . . ." Blue Squirrel interrupted the *Ch'ul Ahau*, a severe breach of etiquette, but Blue Squirrel was apparently too self absorbed at the moment to care. "Your Lordship, that is the very point that I am trying to make! You do have enough *ahauob*! What I ask is that you demote my kinsman Toucan Claw from *ahau* to *cahel*, and make me *ahau* in his stead. That would kill two birds with one stone, and I would no longer be forced to call this insufferable little boy 'Your Lordship.'"

Jaguar Spot felt bile rising up his throat and was just about to start yelling insults at Blue Squirrel for being so openly disloyal to his clan leader when he felt Gray Sky's hand on his shoulder and heard him whisper ever so quietly, "not now, Your Lordship. Trust me. You must remain silent."

Jaguar Spot swallowed his bile and turned away from Blue Squirrel, refusing to look at him. The *Ch'ul Ahau* rubbed his chin and whispered something to Aktak, who in turn whispered something to a messenger and sent him away. Aktak then spoke for the *Ch'ul Ahau*. "What do you mean, 'kill two birds with one stone,' Blue Squirrel. Are you suggesting that Toucan Claw is not deserving of his rank?"

Blue Squirrel shouted again. "That is exactly what I am saying, you dope! Most of what he does a simple scribe could do. There is no need to have an *ahau* overseeing such trivial and banal activities. And moreover, I say that he and his family are traitors to His Lordship! Toucan Claw married off his eldest daughter to that trail of fetid snail slime Fireborn. This boy walked through the night, braving the beasts of the forest, to get to Tikal so that the wedding could take place as scheduled. Risking his life? For whom? Or for what? For Tikal, I tell you, for Tikal! They are traitors! All of them are traitors! This boy especially. I know that he has designs to seduce Hummingbird, and to alienate her from His Lordship."

Jaguar Spot felt Gray Sky move behind him and grab him by both shoulders as Blue Squirrel was screaming. He knelt down and whispered in Jaguar Spot's right ear. "Your Lordship, please listen to me again. Remain silent until you are asked to speak. Do nothing." Jaguar Spot listened to Gray Sky's advice and stood there, seething at Blue Squirrel's accusations against his father and his family, and wondering how Blue Squirrel knew his feelings about Hummingbird. By this point Jaguar Spot had no doubt that he loved her, but he had never acted on it, and had never told a soul. The most that they had ever done was to exchange pleasantries and smile at each other, and there was nothing wrong with that.

When Blue Squirrel was finished, the *Ch'ul Ahau* and Aktak had a whispered conversation for a long time, and then the *Ch'ul Ahau* spoke to Jaguar Spot. "There is no need for you to respond to Blue Squirrel's accusations, Jaguar Spot. I have no doubts about your father's loyalty and your loyalty. Your father is the most loyal *ahau* that I have, excepting Aktak here, of course." Aktak smiled at the *Ch'ul Ahau's* compliment and looked at the ground. The *Ch'ul Ahau* turned to Blue Squirrel. "My dear Blue Squirrel, you say that your family overlord committed treason by agreeing to allow his eldest daughter to marry a prince of Tikal? Marrying someone from Tikal is not treason, indeed it is because of me that we have peace with our friends to the south. This peace has increased trade and benefited all of our people. I remember the day of this sister's wedding quite well, as it was the day that I married your daughter. Instead of treason, I remember seeing only bravery from Jaguar Spot, who foiled the fiendish plans of that miserable slime Cougar. Without him, it is likely that I myself would have been killed that day, as I was just about to walk into Cougar's clutches, unaware that he had taken over the Tikal temple. And this nonsense about the boy coveting Hummingbird? Why, the girl is madly in love with me! Jaguar Spot, tell us, do you love my wife? Do you covet her? Is there anything to this accusation?"

Jaguar Spot tried to hide the concern in his voice. "There is nothing to it, Your Lordship. Of course, I respect Her Ladyship as the wife of Your Lordship. I knew her as a young child and, I admit, I have said 'hello' to her on occasion when she has walked into a room that I am painting in the palace. She is, of course, a beautiful woman, as befits a wife of Your Lordship, but I have a beautiful fiancé of my own, and I would never do anything to betray Your Lordship."

Blue Squirrel moved toward Jaguar Spot, his face contorted as if from absolute hatred. "Not true, Your Lordship!" he cried. "Not true! I have seen the look in his eye when he gazes at my daughter! I tell you that he covets her! And I say one more thing, Your Lordship, I can tell from the look in my daughter's eye that *she covets him as well.*" The guards pulled Blue Squirrel back to where he had been standing, and at the direction of the *Ch'ul Ahau*, brought him to his knees. The *Ch'ul Ahau* walked up to Blue Squirrel and knelt down to look at him face to face. "Did anyone ask you to speak, Blue Squirrel?"

"No, Your Lordship."

"And yet you spoke."

"Yes, Your Lordship."

"You have spoken perhaps too much today, wouldn't you say?"

"Yes, Your Lordship."

"You understand that to accuse an *ahau* of treason is no laughing matter, and that I have to take action. I will have to impose discipline."

"Yes, Your Lordship."

"And then you accuse my wife of having improper feelings toward Jaguar Spot. Do you understand that the law allows only one penalty for these transgressions? You have put me in a very embarrassing situation. I am now going to have to discipline my own father-in-law. The entire city will know what I did and why I did it."

"Me? You are going to discipline me? For what?"

"*Cahel*, there are many transgressions that you have committed today that warrant discipline from me. You tried to deny the ballplayer today an honorable death. You accused this poor boy of treason, which must have scared him half to death. You spoke in a most disrespectful and unpleasant tone in my presence today. You even accused Her Ladyship of improprieties. All of that deserves discipline, wouldn't you agree?"

"Yes, Your Lordship."

"Yes, we agree. And if your transgressions were limited to what I just described, I might have left you off with simple stripping of your rank, or of banishment from the city, I don't know. But your crimes did not stop there. You committed perhaps the worst crime of all. Do you know what that is, Blue Squirrel?"

"No, Your Lordship."

"Disloyalty. Even though you work for me, even though you live in this palace, Toucan Claw is still your *ahau*. Your loyalty to him is supposed to be almost as great as your loyalty to me, and here you were, in front of some of the most important *ahauob* in this city, accusing him and his family of treason, asking that he be demoted in his rank, and asking me to make you *ahau* in his place. I cannot have that, not in my presence at least. As far as I can see, there is only one punishment that fits this crime. Please await it like a man."

The *Ch'ul Ahau* had the guards push Blue Squirrel to the ground so that he was prone on the stone floor of the courtyard. He walked back to his chair and told one of the *ahauob* present to get an ax. Blue Squirrel began to sob, his tears falling on the floor. The *ahau* quickly returned with a large obsidian ax and handed it to the *Ch'ul Ahau*, who continued to sit silently. Everyone in the courtyard except Jaguar Spot studiously avoided looking at Blue Squirrel, whose now loud sobbing added to the overall sense of embarrassment. After a while the sobbing died down and all that Jaguar Spot could hear from Blue Squirrel was soft cries and squeaks. The *Ch'ul Ahau* got up, ax in hand, and walked to one of the entrances to the courtyard. "Ah, I think that I hear them coming," he said.

Before the *Ch'ul Ahau* could get to the doorway the messenger that Aktak had sent away returned, followed by Toucan Claw. "Ah, my friend. It is good to see you," the *Ch'ul Ahau* said to Toucan Claw.

"Your Lordship," said Toucan Claw, looking first at Jaguar Spot, and then at Blue Squirrel, "what is going on here? Why is my son being held by one of your guards, and why is my kinsman on the ground looking as if you are about to chop off his head?"

The *Ch'ul Ahau* handed the ax to Toucan Claw and sat back down in his chair before answering Toucan Claw's question. "My friend, here is the situation. Your kinsman interrupted a meeting I was having, saying that your son had been disrespectful on the ballcourt. Absolute nonsense, as it turned out. We had the boy brought here and learned the truth, which turned out to be that Blue Squirrel was making an absolute ass of himself once again. That's when things started getting weird. Blue Squirrel accused you and your family of treason, and asked that I demote you to *cahel* and promote him to *ahau* in your stead. I am sure that you agree that I cannot tolerate such a blatant example of disloyalty in my presence. When disloyalty to an *ahau* is tolerated, open disloyalty to the *Ch'ul Ahau* can't be far behind. I have decided to rid us of his foul presence once and for all. So, there is your ax, and there is your prisoner. Since it was your family's honor that he tried to sully, I give you the honor of killing him."

Jaguar Spot knew that there must have been a million questions running through his father's mind, that he wanted more details of what Blue Squirrel had done before he killed him, but when His Lordship gave you an ax and asked you to chop off a man's head, you did it without asking questions. Toucan Claw walked up to Blue Squirrel and looked over at the *Ch'ul Ahau*, who nodded. Toucan Claw began to raise the ax above his head, then stopped and turned to speak to the *Ch'ul Ahau*. "Your Lordship, if it pleases you, I would like to give the honor of this sacrifice to my son. Some day he will lead my clan, and I think that the lesson will do him well." The *Ch'ul Ahau* nodded and Toucan Claw handed the ax to Jaguar Spot. "Make it a clean hit son," Toucan Claw said. "Don't make him suffer unnecessarily. Make sure that you do it with one fell swoop, and be careful not to hit the guards."

Jaguar Spot took the ax by its wooden handle and stood next to Blue Squirrel, who had resumed his loud sobbing, and began pleading for his life. "Please don't kill me, Jaguar Spot!" he cried, tears streaming from his eyes. "Please, what of my family? What of my wife, my children? You grew up with my children! You know them well! Have mercy, boy! Don't you remember that time I went with you and your father around the farmland and we stood in the fields watching the men work? Was I not kindly to you, cousin? Have I not always been kindly to you? I'm sorry for what I said. Don't kill a man for a moment of intemperance! Please don't kill me!" Blue Squirrel then descended into incomprehensible babbling, and the *Ch'ul Ahau* nodded to Jaguar Spot and motioned his left arm quickly downward to indicate that the execution should proceed. Jaguar Spot pulled the ax above his head and let the blunt end of the blade rest against his back. He looked down at Blue Squirrel's pitiful form and at the guards, one of whom was now kneeling on Blue Squirrel's back, with the other holding Blue Squirrel's arms together from behind the first guard. Being careful not to hit the first guard, Jaguar Spot pulled on the ax as hard as he could and brought it down squarely on Blue Squirrel's neck. The impact sounded like an ax hitting wood. There was a terrific amount of blood spattered about. Jaguar Spot looked down at his handiwork and felt like he was going to be sick. He dropped the ax and ran from the courtyard and out of the palace.

Once he was safely out of sight, he found a secluded area and violently threw up. It took two tries to empty his stomach, and he continued heaving for what seemed like the rest of the day. Just as the heaves came to an end, he heard the sound of two sets of footsteps behind him, and then his father's voice. "Son, are you alright?" Jaguar Spot nodded twice, still unable to speak, and then felt hands on his right shoulder. His father kneeled down beside him. "I know that wasn't easy for you to do, son. I would have preferred not to kill Blue Squirrel, even if he was a disloyal pain in the ass. If I were up to me, I would have demoted him and then exiled him from Uaxactun. But it wasn't up to me, or you, or even poor old Aktak. It was His Lordship's decision to make, and all that we can do is obey. When you are ready, we will go back to the courtyard. They should have the mess cleaned up by then, and His Lordship said that he wanted to make sure that you were alright. Here, take this. Gray Sky brought it along." He took the offered bowl of water, most which he sipped and then spat out, cleaning the vomit taste from his mouth. He swallowed the remainder, stood up, and handed the bowl to Gray Sky, who stood directly behind Toucan Claw. "Ready?" asked his father. Jaguar Spot nodded, and the three of them walked back to the palace.

Chapter Ten
Love

8.16.19.0.11. November 7, 375 A.D.

It had been many days since Jaguar Spot had killed Blue Squirrel, and he had not had the courage to go back to the palace. He had killed Hummingbird's father.   He knew that she would hate him for what he had done. Since he had brought the ax down on Blue Squirrel's neck, he thought of little else but the beauty of Hummingbird's face as she smiled at him, and the sound of her voice as she honored him with a friendly greeting. He knew that the next time that he saw her that the smile would turn into a grimace, that her clear eyes would be framed by a scowl, and that her voice would no longer be friendly, but spitting with venom. These thoughts deeply depressed him as he sat at the table for the morning meal one day staring at his food, eating nothing. His father, his sisters, and Waterlily sat at the table with him, eating in silence.

There had been a time when mealtime in Toucan Claw's house was a joyous affair, but Jaguar Spot's funk had been contagious, and the family chewed their food in glum silence. He knew that he had not eaten in more than two days, and he was starting to feel weak, but he felt no hunger in his stomach. He stared at his food. There were tortillas, some vegetables, and some venison–a gift from the *Ch'ul Ahau*. There were also snails, six live snails to be exact, slowly moving around on Jaguar Spot's plate. The snails were Jaguar Spot's favorite food, and had been meant to be a special treat for dinner the previous night. Jaguar Spot had skipped dinner, and had remained in his bedchamber sulking in solitude, so Waterlily put them on his plate in the morning to try to cheer him up. One of the snails started to move off of his plate, so he reached to pick it up, and noticed that the entire family was staring at him, already finished with their breakfasts. He picked up the snail without eating it and put it back down on top of a tortilla, to the disappointment of Waterlily and his father.

After Jaguar Spot's sisters left, Toucan Claw was unable to maintain his silence. "Son, how old are you?" he asked.

"Father?"

"I asked you how old you are."

"You know that I am sixteen."

"Sixteen years old. You are no longer a boy. You are a man. So, what is the explanation for this behavior? Spirit Dog has examined you and says that you are not sick, and yet you don't eat. Everything is going fine with your life, and yet you sulk around this house like a thirteen year-old girl rejected by the object of a youthful crush. Why don't you eat? Why are you acting like this?"

"I don't know, Father."

"Is it because of what you did to Blue Squirrel? You did that at His Lordship's order, and plus the man was a traitor to his clan and to his *ahau*. Even though I might not have had him killed had it been my decision to make, by law he deserved to die. You know that, don't you?"

"Yes, Father."

"Have you been feeding our ancestors too much lately?"

"No, Father. I haven't been feeding them at all."

Toucan Claw picked up his plate, and Jaguar Spot thought that he was about to throw it against the wall in anger before he put it back down on the table. Waterlily, after years in Toucan Claw's household, knew that it was time for her to leave the room and silently went into the kitchen. Toucan Claw got up and grabbed Jaguar Spot by his right ear, pulling him into the main hall, and then forcing him to kneel in the center of the floor. Toucan Claw pulled a small box out of a corner, opened it, and handed Jaguar Spot a piece of paper, some paint, and a writing brush, telling him to write an apology to his ancestors. Jaguar Spot took the brush and wrote:

Beloved Ancestors

Jaguar Spot Speaks

He neglected your nourishment

Many days

He apologizes

He offers a sacrifice of his own blood

He will not forsake you again.

When Jaguar Spot was done writing, Toucan Claw picked up the paper, read it, and handed it back to Jaguar Spot, along with a stingray spine. Jaguar Spot knelt over the paper, opened his mouth, and pierced his tongue with the spine, bleeding onto the paper. The pain was unbearable, worse than any pain that Jaguar Spot had ever felt before—the ancestors must have been punishing him for his neglect. As he watched drops of his blood fall onto the paper like rain, he pierced his tongue again and again, until the blood flowed like a torrent. After he could bear the pain no more, and after the paper was totally saturated with his blood, he dropped the spine. The room suddenly became darker, and then black. The sounds of the household faded into nothingness. Jaguar Spot had never seen such perfect darkness, nor heard such a perfect silence. He could not even hear the sound of his own breathing. He called out to his father, but there was no answer, and his voice seemed strangely quiet, as if it was absorbed by the air.

He had no idea how long kneeled there in the darkness before he heard breathing. The sound terrified him. The breathing got closer and closer. "Who's there?" he asked. There was no answer, and the breathing got even louder. It sounded like the breathing was right next to him, and he thought that he felt the breath on his right ear. "Who'sethere?" he screamed again. This time there was an answer, which was more terrifying than the breathing. "It is me," the voice said.

"Who are you?"

"Oh come now, you little pipsqueak. You know exactly who I am. You don't recognize my voice, cousin? Surely you recognize the voice of good old Blue Squirrel."

"Blue Squirrel? But you're dead!"

"Dead? Yes, I suppose from your perspective I am dead. Some day you will join me in the Underworld, a day that I look forward to very much, a day that is much sooner than you think, I expect."

"Shut up! I don't want to talk to you!"

"Ah, but you have no choice. You will sit and listen to what I have to say. You know that I was right about your feelings for my daughter. Your love for her is foolish, it is based on beauty alone. Some day you might come to realize the extent of your folly, but I don't think that you will live long enough to learn that there is more to women than physical beauty."

Jaguar Spot had no answer for Blue Squirrel's voice. He saw no sense in lying to the ghost, or whatever it was that was talking to him. The breathing got even louder now, as if the voice was a hair's breadth from his ear. Even though the voice was still whispering, it sounded as if someone were shouting at him. "Very well, pipsqueak. You don't have to say anything. I'll talk. You listen. I'll tell you a little secret about my daughter, something I had known for quite some time before you killed me. For all the love that you feel towards her, she loves you twice as much. Did you hear me? Twice as much! You know that your feelings are wrong. You know that your love is a betrayal. You know that it is much worse disloyalty against the *Ch'ul Ahau* than I ever showed for your father. You know that acting on your love might mean you and my daughter suffering a public stoning, as is fitting for adulterers. You even know that it will almost certainly mean the end for your father and the disgrace of your family. You know all of this, and yet you will risk it all just to be with her. As sure as Lord Sun will show his face tomorrow, you will throw everything you hold dear away for the sake of a pretty face."

Jaguar Spot screamed. "I won't! You lie! I will never betray this city! I love His Lordship!"

The voice laughed in his ear. It was a harsh sounding, whispered laugh. "We shall see, pipsqueak, we shall see. Do you want to know why I am telling you all of this? After all, shouldn't I be the last one that gives you advice? In all respects, I loathe you. Tell me why I am telling you this. Speak!"

"No!"

"No matter, I will do the speaking for you. I have told you this because we both know that it is the truth. There will come a time, and the time will come soon, when you are forced to make a choice—a choice between this love you feel for my daughter and your loyalty to your father, to your city, and to your *Ch'ul Ahau*. Even now you know what the consequences will be, you know how easy it would be to avoid disgrace, and yet you will do nothing. You will propel yourself to that moment when you make the choice, and you, stupid boy, will choose love over loyalty. It is as if the future were already carved in stone, and you are incapable of changing it. It will be as if you will bring the ax down on your own neck. The only thing that I regret is that I will not be there to see it myself. Ah, I see that our pleasant conversation must come to an end. I will see you soon, cousin, sooner than you think."

Suddenly there was a blinding light in Jaguar Spot's eyes, and he felt the bitter taste of chocolate in his mouth, which he gulped down hungrily. He felt a bowl in his mouth with more chocolate in it, and drank it as quickly as he could. The light in the room lowered to an almost normal level, and he saw that the chocolate bowl was held by Spirit Dog, with Toucan Claw and Waterlily standing behind him. "Ah, that's more like it," said Spirit Dog, handing the bowl to Waterlily and telling her to fill it up again. When she returned, Jaguar Spot took the bowl and gulped down the chocolate as fast as he could. There was an insatiable hunger in his stomach now, as if all the days when he had refused to eat had caught up with him. "Food," he said to Waterlily, "please bring me some food." Spirit Dog was busy mixing up some kind of potion when Waterlily brought in his plate from that morning, and he quickly ate the tortillas and meat, saving the snails for last. He picked up the largest snail on his plate and put it to his mouth, sucking the live flesh out of the shell. "Do you like the snails?" Waterlily asked. Jaguar Spot nodded, and ate the rest of the snails without saying a word. Spirit Dog handed him a foul smelling bowl filled with green liquid, and he drank it as fast as possible, trying to ignore the horrible taste. "That should do you, boy," said Spirit Dog. "That should do you fine. Tell me, did you have a vision?"

"Yes."

"What did you see?"

"Nothing."

"Nothing? You had a vision and you saw nothing? That doesn't sound like much of a vision to me."

"No, it wasn't."

Spirit Dog crinkled his nose as if he had been insulted, and left the room. Toucan Claw had been standing behind Spirit Dog through the entire exchange, staring at Jaguar Spot but saying nothing. After Spirit Dog left, he turned around to follow him. He paused at the door and turned back to face Jaguar Spot. "Son, His Lordship sent a guard. He wants you back in the palace painting this afternoon. That is, if you feel up to it." Without waiting for a reply, Toucan Claw disappeared through the door, leaving Jaguar Spot alone in the room.

That afternoon he made his way to the palace, entering through a side entrance he had discovered in his years of painting the palace walls. As quietly as he could, he followed the most remote and least used corridors and made it to the residential section without running into anyone other than the guard that had let him in. He dreaded that first moment of contact with Hummingbird, and wanted to avoid it for as long as possible. He found his paints and brushes in the same place that he had left them, and went to the room that he had been working on before the day that he killed Blue Squirrel. His Lordship had asked him to paint all four walls in this room with texts and images extolling the reign of his grandfather. When he had last worked on the room, Jaguar Spot had finished three of the walls and was starting on the fourth. He wet his brush, applied some paint, and started creating an image of some temples around the city. Just when he was starting to lose himself in the work, he heard a cough behind him. He turned around, about to chastise whatever guard had interrupted him, and saw that it was the *Ch'ul Ahau*. "Good afternoon, Your Lordship," Jaguar Spot said. "I should have this room complete within a few days." The *Ch'ul Ahau* smiled at Jaguar Spot. "That's fine, my boy, just fine. You get on with your work, don't let me interrupt you. I just wanted to watch how you produced these beautiful murals, and such wonderful texts." The *Ch'ul Ahau* walked up to one of the finished walls and started examining it, so Jaguar Spot went back to his painting. After he had completed the painting of the temples and moved on to the accompanying text, he noticed that the *Ch'ul Ahau* was standing right next to him, watching every brush stroke. "It comes so easily to you, my boy," the *Ch'ul Ahau* said. "You just put your hand on the brush and it flows out effortlessly. Ah, how I envy you."

"You envy me, Your Lordship? How can that be? You are *Ch'ul Ahau*."

"I envy your talent, young man. I envy this gift that the Gods have given you. I envy your ability to create something out of nothing. I have enjoyed watching your paint. Tell me, what room to you plan on painting next?"

"I was thinking about the walls of your ceremonial courtyard, although I will have to use some special paints so the work does not get washed away in by the rain."

"I am sure that will be lovely, Jaguar Spot. But first, I would like you to paint the walls of Hummingbird's bedchamber. She has been a little down since the untimely death of her father, and I think that some beauty in her bedchamber might cheer her up. In fact, I would like you to start tomorrow."

Jaguar Spot kept painting as he spoke with the *Ch'ul Ahau*. He felt sweat beading on his face, and it took a supreme effort to control his breathing. Hummingbird's bedchamber was the last place that he wanted to be stuck in for days on end. If he wasn't careful, if he spent too much time around Hummingbird, things might unfold exactly how Blue Squirrel's voice in the vision said that they would. He tried to speak in the most natural tone that he could. "But Your Lordship, I need more time than that to finish this room. Plus, I have a grand idea for the courtyard."

The *Ch'ul Ahau* looked at the temples that Jaguar Spot had painted and smiled wistfully. "I have seldom seen such dedication in a scribe. You are a credit to your profession, my boy. I know that you have pent-up ideas that you feel that you need to express through your work, but you are going to have to put that on hold. There will be more than enough time to finish this wall, and to paint the courtyard. I want you in Hummingbird's bedchamber bright and early tomorrow morning." The *Ch'ul Ahau* took one last look at the mural, then walked out of the room, leaving Jaguar Spot alone, except for the company of his fears.

The next morning he found himself alone in Hummingbird's bedchamber, staring at the whitewashed walls. Prior to his arrival, the *Ch'ul Ahau* had arranged for all of the furniture to be removed, so Jaguar Spot had the empty room all to himself. When Gray Sky had told him that he should have the room entirely to himself for as long as he needed, he breathed a great sigh of relief. Hopefully he would be able to finish this room without even seeing Hummingbird. The room was rectangular in shape, with two small windows looking inward to a courtyard. Fiddling with his brushes, Jaguar Spot stared at the long wall opposite the windows, without any idea of what to paint on it. His Lordship had not asked Jaguar Spot to paint anything in particular in this room, only to make it beautiful. Painting propaganda about the *Ch'ul Ahau* or his ancestors just didn't seem appropriate for Her Ladyship's bedchamber. He took a brush, wet it in his mouth, and stuck it in some brown paint. Standing on a table that he had the guards bring into the room, he placed the brush tip high in the upper left corner of the wall, and then inspiration came to him in a flash. He would paint the story of the creation of the world.

Once the idea came to him, Jaguar Spot began to paint in fast and broad strokes. First, he painted the story of the first creation of the Earth, when the Gods created the dumb animals. The gods, proud of their creation, waited for the animals to fulfill their intended purpose, which was to praise their creators, to hold religious rituals, to make the required blood sacrifices so that the Gods might be fed. When the animals ignored the Gods, they realized that they had erred in their creation, and that the animals of the Earth could neither sing the Gods' praises nor sacrifice their blood so that the Gods might be nourished. Jaguar Spot painted pictures of birds, of deer, of snakes, and of the Gods looking on from the Otherworld, and then he painted the destruction of the first Earth, with the animals being sent into the forest as prey. He then painted the second creation, where the Gods first tried to make men. The gods made men with the same goal that they had when the made the beasts, to praise the Gods and make the required sacrifices. The mistake that they made this time was to construct the men out of mud, so that they said and did little, and they washed away in the rain. The third creation was little better, with the Gods deciding to make the men out of wood this time, with equally disastrous results. Running through all of these creations, he painted the image of the Great Tree, sneaking, growing, its tendrils reaching to all corners of each creation. Just as he was about to start painting the fourth creation, where the Gods had finally gotten it right and created men out of flesh and blood, he stuck his brush in the paint bowl and discovered that it was empty–in fact *all* of his paint bowls were empty. He stacked the paint bowls up and turned around to get more paint, only to see that he had been painting in near darkness. Very little light came through the windows, and he realized that it was dusk outside. Suddenly, he became acutely aware that he was extremely hungry–he had been so engrossed in his work that he had painted nonstop.

He turned around to look at his work. The murals that he had already painted had taken up most of the wall. The beauty of his own work stunned him. In all his memory, he had never seen murals so expertly painted, or so beautiful. The depth, the detail in the work, all of it made him feel that he was actually looking at history, not a painting. It was almost as if the images were painted by someone else, that an unseen force had been guiding his hand all day as he ran the brush against the wall.

He carefully packed the bowls and brushes in a sack and turned to leave the room, when he saw a shadow in one corner, a shadow that should not have been there. The room was almost completely dark by now, and as he approached the shadow, it blended into the darkness and became indistinguishable. For a moment he would have sworn that there was a person sitting in the corner. If so, that person could have been watching him all day without him knowing it, but he was so hungry by now that he didn't care. All that he could think about was dinner. As he was turning around to leave the room, he thought he heard a whisper, but he could not make out any words. He turned around and walked over to where he had seen the shadow and saw that there was in fact a person sitting on the floor. There was not enough light for him to see who it was, only that it was a small person. "Who's there?" he asked, as quietly as he could. The only answer he heard sounded like a woman sobbing, but he could not be sure. He inched closer and closer to the corner, and the faint sobbing became a little louder. Finally, when he reached the corner, he knelt down and reached his hand out to whoever was crying. "Who are you?" he asked. When his hand touched what felt like the crying face of a young woman, the sobbing became louder, and almost uncontrollable. "Who are you?" he asked. "What is wrong? Why are you crying?" Whoever was sitting the corner reached out to him and wrapped her arms around him. He felt wetness from her tears against his face as he instinctively put his own arms around whoever this was and told her that whatever was wrong, everything would turn out all right.

They stayed like that for some time, kneeling in the dark corner, she crying, he wondering who she was. During a lull in the tears, he again asked who it was, and was answered with a whisper. "It is me. Who else would it be?" the voice answered.

"Hummingbird? Is that you?"

"Yes, silly boy. Who else would it be?"

Suddenly the encounter took on a whole new meaning for Jaguar Spot. He became acutely aware of Hummingbird's breasts as they pressed against his chest. Her face, which had seemed cold and clammy when he didn't know who she was, now seemed warm and inviting. He noticed her scent, which smelled faintly of perfume, and he started feeling hot all over his body. "Why were you sitting here in the corner?" he asked her.

"I was watching you paint my wall. I have never seen anything more beautiful in my life."

He felt her face moving slowly against his, bringing her mouth ever closer to his own. "Thank you," he whispered. "I think that it is my best work." He felt her eyelashes moving against his, and realized that they were nose to nose, their lips almost touching. Her breath was hot as she whispered back. "I didn't notice the painting. I wasn't looking at the painting. I was looking at you. Kiss me."

Even though he was sixteen years old, Jaguar Spot had never kissed a girl before. He touched his lips against hers. He felt her breath in his mouth. He pulled her tight against his body, and felt her hand rubbing against his chest, then his stomach. The next thing he realized, they were lying next to each other on the floor tearing each other's clothes off. He was confused about what he should do next. He had heard his friends talking about what to do with women and about going to prostitutes in the market. He had even heard women talking about sex among themselves when they did not know that he was listening. His knowledge, though, was too limited to be of any practical effect, Hummingbird, though, seemed to know what she was doing. He had never imagined that anything would feel like this, and before he knew it the world seemed to explode inside of his head. Hummingbird moved over to his side, her arms draped over his chest. "I can't tell you how long I have been wanting to do that, Jaguar Spot," she whispered into his ear. "I've seen you walking through this palace, hardly looking at me, going about your business. I never thought that I would have the chance to even try to make it happen, with all of the guards and ladies in waiting keeping an eye on me every moment of the day. Now that it has happened, I am so happy."

Jaguar Spot did not know what to say. He had never felt as content as he did at that moment lying with Hummingbird, but he kept thinking about what the voice of Blue Squirrel had said to him in the vision, and about how he just had betrayed the *Ch'ul Ahau* and his city. He realized that he did not care about any of it. Not about His Lordship, not about his father, not about the city, or his fiancé, or his family. All he cared about was lying there with Hummingbird for as long as he could, and as much as he could. "I am happy, too," he said. For a long time they just lay together in silence. Jaguar Spot felt himself falling asleep. He woke himself up with a start. Anyone could walk in on them laying there in silence, and that would almost certainly mean death for him, and probably for her as well. Jaguar Spot had no doubt that the *Ch'ul Ahau* would consider what he had just done to be nothing less than treason, not to mention adultery—either of which was a capital offense. "I have to go," he whispered, and started reaching for his clothes. Hummingbird fumbled for her clothes as well, apparently realizing that the longer that they stayed there naked on the floor the greater the chance there was of discovery. When Jaguar Spot managed to get himself fully clothed he bumbled through the dark and put his arms around Hummingbird. "I will see you tomorrow?" he whispered. "Tomorrow!" she breathed back.

Chapter Eleven
The Choice

8.16.19.4.17. February 1, 376 A.D.

More than four *uinals* had passed since the night that Jaguar Spot and Hummingbird had given in to their desires on the empty floor of Hummingbird's bedchamber. Jaguar Spot had long since finished painting that room, and now that the dry season was in full swing he spent most of his days painting the walls of the *Ch'ul Ahau's* ceremonial courtyard. What had started on the floor had continued almost unabated since that day. Hummingbird would usually give some excuse to escape from the guards or courtiers who seemed to constantly surround her and would meet Jaguar Spot at a prearranged dark recess of the palace. Sometimes a day would pass when he would not see her, sometimes two or three, but Jaguar Spot had lost track of how many times they had been together. Lately, however, a sense of foreboding had crept into their intimate moments. The scheduled date of the consummation of Hummingbird's marriage to the *Ch'ul Ahau* was forty days away. This impending date was almost all that they had spoken of recently, even though the mere thought of it seemed to bring Hummingbird to tears. She told Jaguar Spot that she loved him, and did not want to be with anyone else, and Jaguar Spot said the same back to her. He gave little thought to Waterlily or his father at these moments, but those subjects were heavy on his mind as he stood in the courtyard finishing up his work on the second wall. His idea for the courtyard had been to paint a history of His Lordship's reign as *Ch'ul Ahau*. He had started by depicting the *Ch'ul Ahau* as a small boy learning the art of statecraft at the feet of his father, but most of the first wall was devoted to the incredible victory over Tikal. The second wall showed later aspects of the *Ch'ul Ahau's* reign, starting with an administrative restructuring he had completed and ending with the peace with Tikal. The last event that he was painting was the execution of Blue Squirrel. The remaining two walls were to be kept blank in order to someday show the history that was yet to come.

Jaguar Spot stared at his own handiwork as he drew the outlines of Blue Squirrel's death. He painted himself holding the ax. His father and the *Ch'ul Ahau* looked on. It struck him that Hummingbird had never mentioned the death of her father during any of their time together. He had no idea what feelings she had on the subject, but that only occupied a small part of his mind. Looking at the image of Blue Squirrel filled him with an overwhelming sense of shame and fear. The more he and Hummingbird kept having their illicit liaisons, the greater the chance would be that they would be discovered, and if that happened he had no doubt whatsoever whose neck would be cut next. He clutched his neck and swallowed hard as he thought about the obsidian blade plunging through his flesh, and then thought about what it would mean to his father. His father had done nothing to deserve such disloyalty in a son. If anyone ever found out, the shame and humiliation that his father would have to bear would be unthinkable. It was even possible that the *Ch'ul Ahau* would order that father and son meet the ax together. And then he thought of poor Waterlily, his loyal and devoted fiancé. She had told him many times that she loved him, and that she looked forward to the day of their marriage, which was less than a year off. She never criticized him, never raised her voice, never nagged, never cried, and never did anything to cause him the least bit of heartache or discomfort. He knew that she would be the perfect wife for him, and that by all rights he should love her, and maybe he did, but he realized that any feelings that he had for Waterlily were overpowered by the intensity of what he felt for Hummingbird. At that point he made a decision–it had to stop. He and Hummingbird would have to stop their liaisons and never speak or think of them again. This was the only way that he could protect himself and his family. He was determined to tell her this the moment he saw her next. She might cry, she might plead, she might beg with him, but he was determined to be strong. He had to be.

    He had just put the finishing touches on the second wall and stepped back to admire his handiwork when a palace guard popped his head in through one of the courtyard doors. "Ah, Your Lordship, there you are. If you are free Her Ladyship Hummingbird would like to see you. I can escort you to the garden when you are ready." The guard's breath was short as he spoke, probably from running around the palace looking for Jaguar Spot. Jaguar Spot packed up his paints and brushes and followed the guard to the garden, which was in yet another courtyard. The palace garden held a mysterious mystique to the nobility of Uaxactun, Jaguar Spot included. Only the *Ch'ul Ahau*, his immediate family, and specially selected priests were allowed there, unless someone extended a special invitation. Jaguar Spot knew where the garden was, and had even caught a glimpse of it once as he walked past. He remembered seeing what appeared to be a wall of flowers, some trees, and high grass. Unlike the other courtyards in the palace, the garden only had one door, which is where the guard came to a stop. The guard raised his arm and pointed into the garden and nodded to Jaguar Spot, who hesitated before entering. "Oh come on, boy," the guard said in an obvious effort to be as quiet as possible, "Her Ladyship is waiting for you. Go on in." The guard gave Jaguar Spot a not-so-gentle shove in the back, and Jaguar Spot walked into the garden.

Jaguar Spot had never seen, or smelt, anything like this in his life. It seemed like there were flowers everywhere, and there were birds, insects, and even hummingbirds flying around. He found Hummingbird kneeling on both knees next to a tree, her eyes closed, her hands at her side. "So you have come," she said, without opening her eyes or shifting her position.

"Yes, Your Ladyship."

"Oh stop it, it's only us. You don't need to call me 'Your Ladyship.'"

"Okay...Hummingbird. Listen, I need to tell you something."

"And I need to tell you something, who should go first?"

Jaguar Spot knelt down beside Hummingbird and noticed that even though her eyes were still closed there were tears dripping down her face. "What's wrong?" he asked. Hummingbird did not answer him, and still knelt there with her eyes closed and his hands to her side. "Are you alright?" he asked, trying to get a response. She still knelt without saying anything or moving. He felt like putting his arm around her, or trying to comfort her in some other way, but he knew that the guard would probably be watching their every move. The guard might not be able to overhear their conversation, but he certainly would report any inappropriate physical contact between Jaguar Spot and Her Ladyship to his superiors.

Unable to do anything else, Jaguar Spot decided that it would be the best thing to come right out and tell Hummingbird that their relationship must come to an end, but he had trouble making the words come out of his mouth. He could not think of the right thing to say under the circumstances—everything he thought of seemed stupid or heartless. So he waited beside her saying nothing, hoping that she would break her silence and say whatever had been on her mind. He did not have to wait long. Without shifting her position, or even opening her eyes, Hummingbird whispered so quietly that Jaguar Spot could barely hear her. "I am pregnant."

Jaguar Spot felt his heart race so fast that he thought it might explode. He suddenly had trouble breathing. His vision began to darken as if he were going to pass out. With a supreme effort, he was able to calm himself down enough to avoid unconsciousness. He managed to croak out the quietest whisper that he could. "Pregnant? Are you sure?"

"Yes, my darling, I am sure."

"Who knows?"

"Just the two of us."

"This is horrible. His Lordship will have both of us put to death by stoning in a public square when he finds out. What can we do?"

"Darling, he will only have to put me to death. There is no way that he can find out that you are the father of this child. He won't even suspect. You should hear the way he goes on and on about you. That you are the finest artist in the city. That you are the best ballplayer. That you are brave beyond measuring. No, my love, he is incapable of even forming a thought that you might have done this, and I certainly won't tell him the truth."

Jaguar checked his emotions as best he could. "No! I can't let that happen, I won't let it happen. I have overheard people say in the market that there are women, who for enough cacao beans will . ."

"No, Darling. I won't do it. I won't kill our child."

"But His Lordship will kill the child anyway! He will wait for the birth and then sacrifice the both of you. I won't let you do this to yourself."

"I don't want to die any more than you do, Darling, but I won't kill our child. I must simply await my fate. That is why I called you here. We must not see each other again–it might arise suspicion and endanger you. Even this meeting was risky, but I thought that I should tell you what was going on. Go now, and never think of me again."

"No. I won't let you do it. Listen, you say that you won't kill the child, but that is exactly what you will be doing by letting it be born. It is the same thing. There must be something that we can do. I have an idea. We will leave the city. I will sneak you out of the palace and we will flee. We will go to another city. We will build our own life there, together."

Hummingbird remained silent for some time. Jaguar Spot tried to deign a hint of emotion in her face, but could see nothing other than a faint smile. Her tears stopped, then started again in great abundance.

She spoke to Jaguar Spot for what would be the last time. "No, my darling, it cannot be. If we disappeared together your family would be in peril. Your father and your sisters might even feel the ax blade on the back of *their* necks. I cannot let that happen. You will listen to me. I am still the wife of the *Ch'ul Ahau*, and for once you will just listen to me and obey me. Leave now. Tell my husband that your work in the courtyard is finished and ask for a break in painting for a while. He will agree, I am sure of that. Speak of this to no one, ever. Now get up, bow your head in respect, say 'Yes, Your Ladyship, and thank you for the compliment on my work' loud enough for the guard to hear, and leave. Never think of me again. Go!"

Trained for a lifetime to obey those above him in the social order, Jaguar Spot felt his muscles propel him up from the ground, almost as if they acted against his will. He had to fight hard to hold back the tears that threatened to well in his eyes, and it took a heroic effort to keep his voice from cracking when he mouthed the words ordered by Hummingbird. He took one last look at her, turned around, and left the courtyard.

Chapter Twelve
Reckoning

8.16.19.17.10. October 11, 376 A.D.

    The days that followed Jaguar Spot's and Hummingbird's encounter in the garden stretched in to months. The rumors about Hummingbird's pregnancy began with furtive whispers among the *ahauob* when they met in private. No one wanted to be on the record spreading scandal about the royal household. The stories came out into the open when it was announced that Her Ladyship Hummingbird would no longer be appearing in public for the foreseeable future. Stories began to swirl around the city. Jaguar Spot kept an ear out for any hints about what was going on in the palace, but heard very little hard information from the gossip mongers in the market and on the ballcourt.

    As Hummingbird had predicted, the *Ch'ul Ahau* had graciously consented to release Jaguar Spot from his painting duties for the indefinite future, on the condition that he return to finish is work in the ceremonial courtyard at appropriate intervals. Jaguar Spot devoted as much time as he could to the ballgame, but most of days were spent with his father, watching, observing, and learning the intangibles required to be an effective *ahau* of Uaxactun. What little he did learn of the goings on in the palace came from Waterlily, who had firmly entrenched herself in the feminine gossip circles of the wives of the nobility.

    At first, when the family discussed the rumors at the evening meal, no one understood why the palace was so secretive about Hummingbird. After all, the whole purpose behind the marriage was to produce a male heir to the throne, so by all rights the palace should be rejoicing and spreading the news. Waterlily reported that most of the women that she talked to assumed that His Lordship was worried that Hummingbird might miscarry, and wanted to wait until the pregnancy was well along before making any type of public announcement. Apparently it had not occurred to any of them that someone other than His Lordship was the father of her child. The fact that the pregnancy had occurred before the planned consummation date was chalked up to the *Ch'ul Ahau* had not being able to contain his lust, or his desire for a son. Then followed reports that the mood of the palace had changed, that the *Ch'ul Ahau* was not as jolly and avuncular as he normally was, and that something very heavy was on his mind. Jaguar Spot had to bite his tongue when Waterlily told him of the gossip, and feigned disinterest, but he longed for every bit of intelligence that he could get. By the time that the scheduled date for the consummation of Hummingbird's marriage had come and gone, the rumors around the city were becoming more salacious. Some said that His Lordship had taken to sitting in a dark room, and not speaking to a soul for days on end. Others said that he wandered around the palace like a madman, mumbling under his breath, sometimes screaming at the top of his lungs to no one in particular.

Months passed, and the gossip about Hummingbird's pregnancy became more accurate. Waterlily whispered to him one afternoon that the women were saying that Hummingbird's child was not the *Ch'ul Ahau*'s, that she had betrayed him, and that His Lordship was beside himself with anger and grief.

All the while, Jaguar Spot's own wedding day with Waterlily came closer and closer, and almost every day there were stories that Hummingbird's body grew larger and larger. Waterlily busied herself in preparing for their wedding, constructing the intricate headdress and arm feathers that Jaguar Spot was to wear, and her own wedding clothes. Toucan Claw offered many times to hire some women from the clan compound to do the work, but Waterlily had decided on the particulars of her wedding ceremony when she was a small girl, and did not want anyone else to mess up her plans. Jaguar Spot would often sit with her as she worked on the garments, listening to the latest gossip and speculation in the palace. He tried as hard as he could to hide the emotions that almost tore him apart with every new piece of information that came in.

Eventually, one *uinal* before the scheduled wedding date, Toucan Claw took Jaguar Spot to a hastily called meeting of the most important *ahauob* and their eldest sons. The meeting was held in an administrative building next to the palace, and Aktak, as the highest ranking *ahau* present, presided. Jaguar Spot sat on the floor next to his father, and tried to catch the whispers that filled the air, at the same time feigning as much indifference as he could. The *ahauob* had many theories about the purpose of the meeting, ranging from a decision to go to war against Tikal to a new round of sacrifices demanded by the *Ch'ul Ahau*. All the whispering came to an abrupt stop when Aktak and his son, who himself was close to being an elderly man, walked into the room. Aktak cleared his throat before speaking.

"Friends," Aktak began, "many of you may have heard that Her Ladyship Hummingbird is pregnant. Some of you may even have heard speculation that the child is the result of a treasonous union between Her Ladyship and an individual who is not His Lordship. I am here to tell you today that those rumors are absolutely true." Everyone in the room stared at Aktak in silence. This merely confirmed what they had been hearing for months, and the information they really sought was who was the father. Aktak seemed to sense their feelings when he resumed speaking, after a short pause. "Friends, we do not know who the traitor is yet. Her Ladyship has not been forthcoming on the subject, even when we have used our most . . . persuasive means of loosening her tongue." Jaguar Spot felt sick to his stomach when he thought of the tortures that Hummingbird had been subjected to in the effort to gain the truth. He did his best to conceal his feelings as Aktak continued speaking. "We have a few suspects, but still have nothing other than vague suspicion." Jaguar Spot thought that he saw Aktak glance in his direction when he said that there were suspects, and for a moment felt like fleeing from the meeting and leaving the city as quickly as he could. He did nothing. Aktak continued. "At any rate, Hummingbird will be sacrificed to the Gods the day after she gives birth, along with her child, of course." Jaguar Spot felt a sharp pain in his stomach, as if he had been hit by a particularly vicious blow on the ballcourt. On an intellectual level, he had known that this would be Hummingbird's fate ever since their encounter in the garden, but to hear it confirmed in public, to hear Aktak say it, that was something different. He did his best to remain stoic for the rest of Aktak's speech. "If we can determine the culprit's identity he will of course be killed with his child and paramour." Jaguar Spot thought that he caught Aktak once again glancing in his direction. Aktak ended his speech. "Friends, His Lordship would like you to inform your clans of these developments, so that we can put a stop to the hateful and incessant rumor mongering that has plagued our city of late. You will, of course, be kept informed of further developments on this issue. Thank your for your attendance. You may now go, except that I would humbly request that Toucan Claw and Jaguar Spot remain so that I can discuss a personal request that His Lordship has for both of them, in private. Thank you."

Jaguar Spot and Toucan Claw remained where they were while the rest of the *ahauob* and their sons walked out of the administrative building. Aktak and his son came and sat on the floor with them. "Gentlemen," Aktak started, "I am sorry to detain you, but His Lordship was most insistent that I speak to you. Toucan Claw, because you are *ahau* of Hummingbird's clan, His Lordship believes that it would be proper for you, or if your desire, your son, to wield the ax at the sacrifice ritual." It took every bit of self discipline and training that Jaguar Spot possessed to maintain his composure at that moment, with the image of the obsidian blade plunging through Hummingbird's neck dominating his mind. He felt his lips tighten, and sweat beaded on his forehead. Aktak then spoke to Jaguar Spot in particular. "Jaguar Spot, I am sure that you know His Lordship is very fond of you, and because of that I hesitate to bring up this next subject. I imagine that His Lordship would not be very happy if he found out that I even mentioned it, but sometimes loyalty to the *Ch'ul Ahau* demands that a servant must do things that His Lordship would find unpalatable. I must tell that your name has been mentioned as one of the suspects." Toucan Claw shifted his weight and almost started shouting at Aktak. "Watch what you say, friend! This is my son you are talking about, and he is a loyal citizen! I would vouch for his innocence with my own life."

Aktak tried his best to calm Toucan Claw down. "So would I, my friend, so would I. I say this not as an accusation, but merely to inform you and your son of the vicious rumors. Who knows how long such rumors might last, and how long the taint on your son's honor might remain? If gossip pointed to me or my son, I would want to be informed."

Toucan Claw put his hand on Aktak's right shoulder and apologized. "My friend, I have wronged you. You are, of course, absolutely correct. Thank you for your loyalty and your friendship, but I ask you, what can we do? If my son or I publicly deny these rumors, it will only give them more notoriety, yet to just let them fester, that seems even worse."

The only thing that Jaguar Spot could do was watch helplessly as Aktak and Toucan Claw discussed possible solutions to the dilemma. Ultimately Aktak's son came up with what Jaguar Spot had to admit was the best possible answer–have Jaguar Spot wield the ax for the sacrifice of both Hummingbird and the baby. No man would willingly kill his lover and his child. Jaguar Spot's action would set the record straight for the gossipmongers. Toucan Claw loved the idea and immediately agreed.

Every day for the next *uinal* Jaguar Spot woke up in a cold sweat, dreading the possibility of news that Hummingbird had given birth.

The mental image of his father handing him an obsidian ax and pointing to a helpless Hummingbird and baby was impossible to erase from his thoughts. He could think of little else other than his expected role in the sacrifice, even to the exclusion of his own wedding plans. Toucan Claw or Waterlily would inform him of the items they selected for the feast, or perhaps that a certain *cahel* and his and his family would be extended an invitation, and Jaguar Spot would feign interest and walk away.

Finally, in the early morning of the day before the wedding a palace guard came to the house and summoned Jaguar Spot and Toucan Claw to Aktak's residence, which was in reality a palace to itself. Aktak and his son were eating their morning meal, consisting of venison, tapir meat, and tortillas, when Toucan Claw and Jaguar Spot arrived. Aktak invited them to sit at his table and had a servant prepare them breakfast. After the servant had placed food on the table for the visitors and left the room, Aktak spoke to them in a hushed tone. "My friends, I have grave news. Hummingbird has given birth, to a daughter. The sacrifice ceremony will take place tomorrow in the market square. All commerce and other business will be suspended so that as much of the citizenry as possible can attend. His Lordship has left it up to me to organize the particulars of the ceremony, so I wanted to see what your thoughts were on the subject. I was thinking that mid-day would be the best time. What do you think?"

Jaguar Spot finally saw a faint hope of a way out of killing Hummingbird and his own daughter. "Uncle," he said, "tomorrow is my wedding day. The ceremony is scheduled to take place at mid-morning. At mid-day we are supposed to be in the midst of the wedding feast. This sacrifice will ruin years of planning." Aktak locked his eyes on Jaguar Spot, who had to fight against a strong desire to avert his gaze. Jaguar Spot detected what he thought to be contempt on Aktak's voice when he spoke. "Boy, sometimes you have to make sacrifices for your city and for your *Ch'ul Ahau*. You and your father will have to change your wedding plans, that's all there is to it. Why don't you just move the wedding to the early afternoon, right after the sacrifice? Surely that is not too much of an imposition for His Lordship to put on you and your family."

"No, Uncle, it is not. We can change the time of the ceremony, of course," Jaguar Spot said, his voice filled with shame. Jaguar Spot walked home with his father in a deep depression. Until now the prospect of hewing an ax and killing of Hummingbird, while occupying his thoughts, was an abstraction. It was something that would happen in the indefinite future, but now it was to happen tomorrow at a specific time and place. He could almost feel the wood of the ax handle in his hands and the blood splattering on his face and body. At that moment he knew that he could not do it, he would not do it. His father might be shamed, even stripped of his position as *ahau*, but that could not be helped. He would not, he could not, kill Hummingbird. If he refused now, however, the rumors about his role in the pregnancy would be confirmed in the minds of everyone. Why else, they would ask, would a loyal citizen of Uaxactun refuse the honor of sacrificing a confirmed adulterer and traitor? "Why else indeed!" Jaguar Spot muttered to himself as he and his father walked through the entrance to the clan compound.

"Did you say something, son?" Toucan Claw asked.

"No, Father," Jaguar Spot lied.

Jaguar Spot made for his bedchamber the moment that he got into the house. In his mind he had reached the point of no return. It was as if he had already left the city and abandoned his family–that these events had already happened and there was nothing in the world that could change them. Hopefully his father and the others would put his disappearance up to foul play, or some accident, or that he just did not want to get married. Men and women occasionally left the city rather than submit to an arranged marriage that they found odious–everyone knew that. Yes, perhaps his father would not feel the wrath of the *Ch'ul Ahau* after all. Once he reached his room he found a large pack that he sometimes used to carry equipment for the ballgame and gathered some clothes, a flint blade knife, and every cacao bean that he had. His wedding clothes were laid out on a chair. Leaving like this would break poor Waterlily's heart, but what was he to do? He put the pack on his shoulder, and started making his way to the main hall. Just has he was about to enter the courtyard he heard his father coming his way, talking to a servant about the re-scheduled wedding feast. He pulled himself into an alcove and hid in the shadows as his father and the servant passed. Once they were gone, he walked as quietly as he could across the courtyard and into the main room. He peeked into the kitchen–no one was there. He made it through the kitchen and was just about to leave through the front door when he heard a soft voice behind him. "Where are you going, my beloved?"

Jaguar Spot turned around, half expecting in his heart to see Hummingbird standing there, but it was Waterlily, hiding in the shadows. "Um, I am leaving," Jaguar Spot stuttered.

"I can see that," said Waterlily, walking into the light. "Where are you going with that pack on your shoulder? There is no ballgame or practice scheduled for today, so where are you off to?"

Jaguar Spot had no answer for her. "I . . .uh . . . I. . I don't yet know. I am leaving. I am leaving for good. I am sorry, but I must go." Jaguar Spot turned back to the door, but before he could take a step Waterlily ran up to him and grabbed his right arm. "Oh no you don't!" she cried, then let go, fell to the floor and started crying. Jaguar Spot looked out through the front door, then looked back at Waterlily, out the door again, and finally put his pack down and knelt next to Waterlily, trying lamely to comfort her. "It has nothing to do with you, I just have to leave and never come back," he said. For all he knew, Waterlily did not even hear him through her own sobbing–she certainly did not respond to what he had said. He put his arms around her and put his face right up to hers. "Waterlily, please understand, it is not *you* that I am leaving, but it is this cursed city and that madman, the *Ch'ul Ahau*. If I do not leave, it will be a disaster for me, for my father, and even for you. I must go." He tried to pull away from her, but she had grabbed onto his arms so hard that it hurt. "Liar!" she spit at him. "You dare lie to me on the day before we are to wed? You don't want to get married? Then fine, leave the city and my father will find me another husband. We all know that this happens on occasion, and my humiliation will pass over time. But I still don't understand why. You know that I love you. You know it! Am I not beautiful?"

"Yes, you are beautiful."

"Am I not a good cook? A good seamstress? Is it not enjoyable to spend time with me in the evenings?"

"Yes, all of that is true. You would make the perfect wife."

"Then why? Why are you doing this to me? Have I offended you? What have I done? Tell me the truth!"

"You have done nothing. It is not because of you. Please believe me."

Waterlily looked straight into Jaguar Spot's eyes, and then grabbed his ears so hard that he thought that she would pull them off. "Liar!" she screamed again, right in his face. "Tell me what I have done or I will run screaming around this house telling everyone who has ears what you are doing. Let's see how your father feels about your plans." She let go of his ears and started to get up. Jaguar Spot grabbed at her and pulled her down to the floor. "Let me go!" she cried. Jaguar Spot pulled at her harder and put his hand over her mouth so she could no longer utter a word. "Listen to me!" he whispered in her ear. "Here's the truth. You know that Hummingbird is going to be sacrificed, along with her baby, the day after she gives birth?" Waterlily nodded, with Jaguar Spot's hand still over her mouth. "You are also aware that I am the one who is supposed to wield the ax at the sacrifice ceremony?" She nodded again. "I just found out that Hummingbird has given birth to a daughter and that the sacrifice ceremony is take place right before our wedding ceremony, which has to be moved into the afternoon. The reason I am leaving is that I can't do it."

Jaguar Spot released his grip on Waterlily's mouth. She seemed strangely calm. "Why can't you do it?" she demanded. "After all, you had no trouble killing her father."

Jaguar Spot swallowed before answering. "Because I do not wish to kill my own daughter and a woman that I have loved." Waterlily pulled free of Jaguar Spot's grip and faced him on all fours. "You?" she whispered. "You? Of all people, it was you! You would leave me, leave your father, and leave your city out of love for another woman, and for her child?" Jaguar Spot said nothing and tried not to look her in the eye, but Waterlily grabbed his face so that he had no choice but to look at her. "Answer me!" she hissed

"I cannot kill them," Jaguar Spot answered.

"You can. You must. Whatever you do, the results will be the same. If you run away, your father will wield the ax, and they will both die. If you remain and confess to His Lordship, you will die with them. If you abandon this foolish plan, if you do your duty and kill them yourself, they will die, but only that course of action will save your family from disgrace. You must protect your father's reputation and position. I know that you are not so selfish as to ignore the consequences that your plan will impose on your father. You must go through with it. You must kill them."

Jaguar Spot thought a long time about what Waterlily said. Even though she merely restated the thoughts that had raced through his mind ever since the meeting with Aktak, she made a compelling case. He was being selfish. He should think of his family and put his personal feelings aside, as his father had taught him for as long as he could remember.

He almost opened his mouth and told Waterlily that he had changed his mind, that he would ignore his conscience and go ahead with the sacrifice, but the image of the ax ripping through Blue Squirrel's flesh filled his mind. Instead of Blue Squirrel's face he saw Hummingbird's, and that of an infant. He knew that he could not bring himself to complete the act. "No," he whispered.

"No?" demanded Waterlily. "That's it? No."

For the first time that he could remember, Jaguar Spot cried. "I know that you are right, Waterlily, but I know just as strongly that I can't do it. If I stood there, with the ax in my hand, looking down at the neck of. . .of. . .Hummingbird, and my child, I know that I would not be able to cause my body to swing the ax. I would stand there as motionless as if I were carved in stone. I want to do what you suggest. I want it so bad that I can't express how much, but I . . . no . . . I can't do it. I won't. Do you remember Fireborn?"

"Of course I remember *Lord* Fireborn. Unlike you, I was at his wedding."

"Never mind that. A long time ago he told me that I would be faced with a choice. That two paths would lay before me, each leading my life into different directions, and that once I made the choice, once I took one road or another there would be no turning back, that I would have to follow the path and see where it led."

"Lord Fireborn really said that?"

"Well, not those words exactly, but something like that. It was a long time ago. The point is, when I made the choice to commit adultery with Hummingbird, from that point onward I was walking down a divergent path than the one my life would have previously taken. I didn't see it at the time, but I see it clearly now. I am on that path. I have to follow it no matter where it leads."

Waterlily looked angry now, as if she couldn't believe that she was hearing Jaguar Spot say this. "What rot!" she said. "What absolute rot! How do you know that path you are on? Who are you to say where it leads? How do you know that your path isn't to sacrifice Hummingbird and her child in front of the entire court? Why do you insist that your path has to be the one of exile and disgrace?"

Jaguar Spot got up, put the pack on his shoulder, and started for the door again. Before he left, he turned to Waterlily, and uttered what he thought would be his last words to her. "I can't explain it," he said. "I just know that I have to leave the city, and I have to do it now." He turned and stepped into the doorway.

"Wait!" Waterlily said. He turned around to face her, too embarrassed to say anything. "Where are you going?" she asked.

"Away."

"I know that. I mean where exactly. In what city will you seek refuge?"

"I don't know."

"What are you going to do?"

"I don't know."

"Are you going to Tikal?"

"No."

"Why not?"

"My father has friends there. He would eventually learn where I had gone, even if I wore the clothes of a common citizen and assumed a fictitious identity. He would bring me back so that the *Ch'ul Ahau* could have me sacrificed. I will wander until I find a city to my liking, then I will work as a scribe. Hopefully my talents will earn me a living."

Waterlily told him to wait, then went through the kitchen gathering numerous food items and putting them into a large basket that the servants normally used to bring in food from the market. When she was done, she walked up to him. "I'm ready," she said.

"Ready for what?"

"To come with you, of course. You tell me that I will make you a fine wife. I am going to hold you to that. I haven't waited to marry you all of these years simply to have you walk off into the jungle, never to be seen again."

"You can't come with me. It's too dangerous. The forest is no place for a woman."

Waterlily put both arms around the basket and took a step in front of Jaguar Spot out the door. "Try and stop me. No matter what you say, I will follow you into the forest. Once we get there, I will be at your mercy, but I will follow you as long as my strength holds me."

Jaguar Spot followed her as she walked out the door and toward the exit from the clan compound. Few people noticed them as the walked through the streets. When they reached the market Jaguar Spot bought Waterlily some clothes and shoes better suited to travel through the forest than what she had been wearing. After he was finished counting out the cacao beans with the merchant, she pulled on his hand. "Beloved, what about your father? Shouldn't you tell him the truth? Doesn't he deserve to know?"

Jaguar Spot had already thought of that. He had planned on leaving without notice to anyone. Waterlily's decision to come with him changed all that. He knew that he could not just leave the city without at least telling his father that they were going, yet by informing his father he might put his own life in danger. He had no doubt that his father would drag him over to the palace and turn him in to Aktak as the traitor who impregnated Her Ladyship, and that once he found out that Jaguar Spot was leaving the city, he would have him tracked down if he could.

Once they got out of the market, Jaguar Spot started making his way north. They passed Snail's workshop. He had Waterlily wait at the door as he went inside and found Snail sitting at his writing desk, putting the finishing touches on a ceremonial book to be burned at a sacrifice ritual. "Ah, Your Lordship," Snail said as Jaguar Spot came in, "what can I do for you?"

Jaguar Spot asked for a piece of paper, some paint, and a brush, which he took over to an empty writing table. It felt strange writing the message. As far as he was concerned, this would probably be the last that his father ever heard from him.

8.16.19.17.10

4 Ok 18 Mol

Jaguar Spot, unfaithful son of Toucan Claw

Toucan Claw, Ahau of Uaxactun

Jaguar Spot, Father of the daughter of Hummingbird

He Leaves the City, into the forest

In the forest he will meet his fate

Along with Waterlily

She joined him in the forest by choice

Never again will Jaguar Spot be seen in the City of Uaxactun.

Jaguar Spot took the paper and folded it as if it were a book, so that no one could read it unless it was opened. He took some string and tied it around the paper as tight as he could, and went back to Snail, who greeted him with sarcasm in his voice. "Ah, Your Lordship, are you finished using my humble facilities? It is an honor to have you back here after so long. Please come and join us again!" Jaguar Spot understood Snail's bitterness. Snail saw the *Ch'ul Ahau*'s decision to end Jaguar Spot's apprenticeship as a threat to his authority as master of his workshop. Plus, Jaguar Spot had not been in to see Snail in more than a year, not even to say hello. Jaguar Spot put the message to his father on Snail's desk. "What's this?" Snail asked while picking up the message and examining it as if it were a piece of rotten food.

"I need to ask a favor of you, Snail," Jaguar Spot said.

"I am, of course, at Your Lordship's service." If anything, Snail's voice had become even more sarcastic, but Jaguar Spot knew that he would not decline a request from the son of an *ahau*. "Please deliver this to my father at sunset, not before, not after. Do you understand?" Snail nodded his ascent to Jaguar Spot's request and put the message in his tunic. "At sunset, as you say, Your Lordship. It is always a pleasure to be of service to Your Lordship," Snail said before he put his nose back into the book he was working on.

Waterlily was waiting right where he left her, and easily kept up with him as he walked quickly to the northerly path out of the city. It was the same route that he had taken with his father and Blue Squirrel many years before. It was early afternoon when they reached the site where Jaguar Spot had seen Mak and his work crew working on the irrigation canal. The canal was still there, but now it stretched away as far as the eye could see. "Come on, we need to get across," he said to Waterlily as he started walking down the bank into the canal. Waterlily looked like she was about to say something, thought the better of it, and followed Jaguar Spot down into the water. They took off their clothes before entering the canal. Waterlily giggled when she saw Jaguar Spot without his clothes—she never seen a boy over the age to two years old naked before. Jaguar Spot put his pack on the shore and jumped in the water, swimming in circles. Waterlily put her basket down and jumped in after him, making the biggest splash that she could. She swam up to Jaguar Spot, put her arms around his neck, and kissed him on the cheek. "Thank you for letting me come with you," she whispered.

"You may regret it later, when we are alone in the forest," Jaguar Spot whispered back, and kissed her on the mouth. He pulled her to the other side of the canal and led her by the hand into a maize field, which was more than shoulder high. She laid down on her back and pulled him on top of her. "I have been dreaming of this moment for as long as I can remember," she said.

They fell asleep and did not wake up until Lord Sun was getting low in the sky. Jaguar Spot got up and looked around the area while Waterlily retrieved their clothing and belongings from the other side. Jaguar Spot whispered to her has she returned. "Come on, we need to get going. They may send people after us and I want to get as far off the main road as I can."

He led her along the edge of the forest. He looked for the path that Mak had used many years before when he showed Jaguar Spot the cacao plantation and the old ruined pyramid. After a short while he found it, and led Waterlily into the forest. Waterlily had never been into forest like this before. Once, when she was about seven years old, her father had taken her along the east road out of the city to some plantations he supervised for the *Ch'ul Ahau*. She had seen fields of maize and a village, but remembered little else. The forest had always been a source of fear and amazement for her. Now every sound, every creak of a tree, every buzzing insect became cause for fear and alarm. She was relieved when they arrived at the ruined pyramid and Jaguar Spot stepped off the path. "Here is where we sleep tonight," Jaguar Spot said.

Waterlily put her basket down and made them a meal of cold meat and tortillas. Jaguar Spot found a pool of water nearby and filled a gourd. They ate and drank as Lord Sun set and the forest became dark. It was a cloudy night. There was no moonlight, or even starlight, in the forest. They lay beside each other in the darkness, not getting any sleep, with Waterlily crying out in fear at every noise. It would be the first of many such nights that they spent in the forest together.

Chapter Twelve
The Forest

8.17.0.0.0. October 21, 376 A.D.

They passed the next few days staying off the paths and roads of Uaxactun, heading north away from the city as quickly as they could. Their food ran out after three days, and the meager rations that Jaguar Spot managed to secure for them out of the forest were not enough. Even finding water was sometimes a problem. Although they frequently waded through swamps, the water there had a foul smell and neither of them wanted to drink it. On the fourth day they ran out of drinkable water, and on the fifth day they had neither food nor water. In the early morning, of the sixth day they came to a break in the forest and saw a village surrounded by green fields of maize and irrigation canals filled with fresh water. The day was hot, and neither Jaguar Spot nor Waterlily thought that they could bear another day without at least a sip of water.

Jaguar Spot hoped that they had left the domains of Uaxactun, and that the inhabitants of the village would welcome them as they would any travelers. His hopes were dashed when he saw Uaxactun's emblem glyph prominently displayed atop a large stone-tree in the village square. There was still a slim chance that word of their flight from the *Ch'ul Ahau*'s domains had yet to reach this outlying area, but the risk was too great. The *cahel* of this place, if it was even big enough to be led by a *cahel*, would likely instruct the men of the village to bind Jaguar Spot and carry him to the city the moment that he found out who he had. On the other hand, he might decide to kill him right then and there–His Lordship would certainly not object to the summary execution of an adulterous traitor and his paramour. So they waited just inside the forest edge, hungry, thirsty, and waiting for nightfall. At sometime during the day they fell asleep, even though Jaguar Spot had promised to himself that he would stay awake to keep watch. When he woke up it was dusk, and he could hear the sounds of conversation coming from the village. There was no one in the fields, and no one was even visible in the village. He kissed Waterlily on the ear to wake her up, but all she did was squirm on the ground, still asleep. He took the water gourd and crept on his stomach through one of the maize fields until he reached an irrigation canal. He slid into the canal as quietly as he could and drank as he filled up the gourd. Once he had his fill he crept back to Waterlily, stealing a few ears of maize along the way. She was still sleeping when he got back, so he poured water from the gourd slowly into her mouth. Finally she woke up. "Ah, that feels good," she said as she took the gourd in her hands and drank the rest of it. "Come on," Jaguar Spot whispered, and pulled her by the hand through the maize field to the irrigation canal, where they bathed themselves and filled up the water gourd again. On their way back to the forest Waterlily busied herself with picking as much maize as she could carry.

There was a full moon that night, and Jaguar Spot led her back into the forest so that they could continue their journey and avoid the village. Once they had walked a fair distance Jaguar Spot found a grassy area under a tree and they quietly chewed on raw maize.

"Do you know what day this is?" Jaguar Spot asked. Waterlily shook her head. "Today is the new *katun*, the seventeenth *katun* of this age," he continued. To Jaguar Spot's surprise, Waterlily had no idea what a *katun* was. "Do you know what a *kin* is?" he asked.

"Of course, it is one day."

"And a *uinal*?"

"That's twenty days, everybody knows that."

"And a *tun*?"

"That's a year."

"Well, it's twenty *uinals* to be exact, three hundred and sixty days. A *katun* is twenty *tuns*. There are twenty *katuns* in a *baktun*. Eight *Baktuns* have passed since the creation of the world, plus seventeen *katuns*. Most people see three, maybe four changes of the *katun* in their life. Back home there will be feasts in the palace, and in the morning the *Ch'ul Ahau* will perform some special ceremonies, and there will be a special ceremonial ballgame."

Waterlily finished her maize and threw the cob into the trees. She moved over to Jaguar Spot and he put his arms around her. "Are you sorry that you left the city?" he asked her. She kissed him on the ear and started moving toward his mouth. "As long as I am with you, beloved, I am happy no matter where I am."

The forest grew considerably thicker over the next few days. Jaguar Spot insisted that they ration their water supply to make it last as long as possible, but they had plenty of maize. After five more days, their water once again completely ran out, and they became so thirsty that it became hard to walk. After two days without water Waterlily collapsed next to a tall tree. Jaguar Spot knelt down next to her, crying, then got angry at himself for wasting water on tears. As much as he tried, he could do nothing to revive Waterlily. She was breathing, but not doing much else. He had no idea what to do. Should he leave her there and go in search of water? But then, what if he got lost and could not find her again? What if a jaguar came upon her sleeping body? He started crying again at these thoughts, but knew that the alternative was for both of them to await their deaths helplessly. He had to do something, but what? He noticed that one of the nearby trees appeared to be much taller than the others. Maybe if he climbed the tree he could see if there was a river or other body of water nearby. If he did his, he would still be close to Waterlily and even though nothing would probably come if it, he would still be doing *something*. The problem was that the tree had very few low branches, so he had to try to climb it using nothing but the roughness in the bark for support.

    He took off his shoes and gripped the tree. It was hard going, and after he had been climbing for half the afternoon he was only seven times his own height off the ground. The branches of the three were still a good ways above him when the thought struck him: how was he going to get *down* from this tree? Climbing up had been difficult enough, but getting down the same way would be impossible. He started panicking. He felt his palms start to drip with sweat. His legs started shaking, and his hands grew weak. He was paralyzed by his fear, unable to move a muscle, unable to think. His strength gave out. The last thing he remembered was screaming at the top of his lungs as the ground raced up at him.

Chapter Thirteen
Return

8.17.0.0.10. October 31, 376 A.D.

"I think that he is coming around." Jaguar Spot heard a male voice that sounded familiar, but he could not quite place it, and then an unrecognizable voice answered. "Yes, he is moving. Quick, go get Her Ladyship." Somewhere in the periphery of his senses he heard shuffling, and then for a moment felt a sensation of sunlight on his face. There was something covering his eyes, and his head hurt like he had never felt before. He tried to raise his hands to touch his face, but his head started pounding the moment he raised his arms off the ground. The unrecognizable voice spoke again. "Easy there, son. Her Ladyship says that you need to rest, so rest you shall. Don't worry. She says that you are going to be alright, given enough time." Jaguar Spot dropped his right hand and the pain pounding in his head lessened. There was something unusual about the way that the second man was speaking, perhaps it was some kind of foreign accent, he could not be sure. Jaguar Spot tried to speak, but found it a struggle even to mouth one word. "Waterlily," he finally managed to say, with supreme effort. The second man's voice sounded again. "Waterlily? Oh yes, your lady friend. Don't you worry, she's just fine. She just needed a lot of water and a little rest. She's been up and around for days now, and has barely left your side. It took all of Her Ladyship's persuasive charms to be coax her out for a little while to take a swim in the river. Anyway, they should be back soon. I am sure that your lady friend will be most vexed that she was not here when you woke up."

After a while Jaguar Spot felt the sensation of sunlight on his face again, and heard a third voice speak, this time it sounded like a child, with the same strange way of speaking as the adult. "Uncle," the child's voice said, "mother says that she will be here soon, and not to do anything until she gets back. She says that father is out hunting with the *Teotihuacanos* and won't be back until late afternoon." Jaguar Spot heard an adult voice grunt in response to the child, but could not be sure which of the adults it was.

The next thing Jaguar Spot remembered was the sensation of sunlight again, and then squeals of delight from Waterlily. "Oh, my beloved! You are awake? They said that you woke up, can you hear me?

How do you feel?" Before he could try to answer another woman spoke. He had heard the woman's voice before, he was sure of that, but in his current condition he could not quite place it. He knew that he would feel embarrassed when he finally found out who it was. "There, there, Waterlily, remember we need to keep him calm, and distractions to a minimum. Gentleman, thank you for keeping an eye on our patient. You can go now." Jaguar Spot heard the sound of the men shuffling away and then the warm feeling of sunlight on his face again. A hand touched his neck, and then the top of his head. "Well, you don't have a fever anymore," the familiar woman's voice said. "Does your head hurt?" It took all of Jaguar Spot's strength to say "Yes." The hands moved to the side of his head, and the woman spoke again. "That's only to be expected, I'm afraid. You took quite a blow to the head. I thought that we might lose you for a while, but I think that you are probably ready for me to take this bandage off your eyes. Take my advice: open your eyes slowly. We are in a dark place, but when you have had your eyes covered as long as you have, even a dark room can seem painfully bright."

Someone, almost certainly the woman who was talking to him, started removing the bandages from his eyes. He closed his eyelids as tight as he could and waited until she was done, and then opened them as slowly as he could and looked around. As he had surmised, he appeared to be lying inside of a large tent, probably so large that it would take two men just to carry it. At one end of the tent there was a closed flap, with sunlight streaming in around the sides. The light was painful to look at. Waterlily was on both knees to his left, and he did his best to smile at her. He turned his head to the right and saw that the other woman that had been speaking was . . .Orchid!

His sister had changed a great deal in the years since he had seen her. Her hair was styled with various braids and flourishes, unlike anything that he had ever seen before outside of images on pottery from Teotihuacan. "Orchid," he whispered, finding that speaking now took less effort. "Yes, it is me," she said back to him, smiling, and putting a bowl of water to his mouth. "Here, drink some water. I think that you have had enough excitement for one day. Why don't you try to get some sleep. One of us will always be next to you if you need anything."

Jaguar Spot had no idea how long he slept, but he woke up to the smell of meat cooking and men speaking what sounded like gibberish, but must have been the tongue of Teotihuacan. How far had they carried him, he wondered. Had they taken him all the way to

Teotihuacan? He opened his eyes and saw Waterlily sleeping to his left. There was a small boy sitting cross-legged at his feet, staring at him. The boy grabbed Jaguar Spot's feet upon seeing him wake up, and spoke the same incomprehensible gibberish that the others spoke. "I am sorry, I don't understand," Jaguar Spot managed to say, the words coming much easier than they did before. "Oh, sorry. You don't speak *Teotihuac*, do you?" the boy said. "Father keeps telling me that I need to remember to speak Yucatec from now on. Mother and father say that you are my uncle Jaguar Spot, from Uaxactun. I'm supposed to ask you if you need anything."

With the smell of burning meat wafting in from outside, what Jaguar Spot wanted more than anything was something to eat. He felt like he hadn't eaten anything in almost a *uinal*. "Some food, bring me some food," he said to the boy, who got up and ran out of the tent without saying anything, and returned with some tortillas and a bowl filled with steaming venison. Jaguar Spot managed to prop himself up on an elbow and eat while the boy resumed sitting cross-legged and stared at him. "What is your name?" Jaguar Spot managed to ask between bites of meat. "Floating Crocodile," the boy answered, taking the empty meat bowl from Jaguar Spot

"That's a good name, nephew. A strong name. Tell me, where is your father? I would like to see him." Jaguar Spot found that his strength was returning now that he had eaten. Without answering, the boy ran out of the tent, bowl in hand. There was a jug of water in the tent, and Jaguar Spot managed to crawl over to it and drank until his stomach was full, and then more. He crawled over to where Waterlily was sleeping and gently caressed her head, waking her up. "Oh, beloved, you are up," she whispered. "How are you feeling?"

"I'm getting better, I think. The boy Floating Crocodile brought me some food. Is he really my nephew?"

"Oh, he's your nephew all right. I think that he is the spitting image of Lord Fireborn, but the *Teotihuacanos* say he looks more like your sister. Lord Fireborn has been most anxious to see you, but your sister would not let him in the tent, not even when we needed a man to keep watch while we swam in the river. She thought that the excitement would be too much for you if you saw him when you woke up. Do you feel up to walking around a little?"

"I think so. Let's give it a try."

Waterlily got up and helped him to his feet. He was a little wobbly at first, and had to lean on her as she opened the tent flap and stepped outside. It was almost dusk. Someone had a large fire burning about twenty paces from the tent. They were next to a large river, in a small forest clearing. There were ten or so dugout canoes pulled out of the water, many of them filled with baskets and satchels. "Traders," Jaguar Spot thought to himself, realizing that he had not been taken to Teotihuacan after all, but that Fireborn and the others had traveled to him. Waterlily led him to the fire, which was surrounded by twenty or so men, women and children. Everyone around the fire was singing a strange song in what must have been the Teotihuacan language, for Jaguar Spot could not understand a word, and the melody was unlike anything he had heard in his life. When they reached the ring of people around the fire, the singing suddenly stopped. One of the men stood up and approached him. In the twilight and firelight, it was hard to distinguish the man's features at first, and his face was also obscured by a strange hat he was wearing. The hat had a large brim going all around, and had tassels hanging down from it, obscuring the wearer's face. Most of the men around the circle, Jaguar Spot now noticed, wore similar hats. The man took off his hat. Jaguar Spot saw that it was Fireborn, who looked like he had not aged a day since they had last seen each other. Fireborn threw his hat to one of the men sitting down, and gave Jaguar Spot a hug, his arms cinching so tight that Jaguar Spot found it hard to breathe. "Brother," Fireborn breathed, "it is good to see you after all of these years. Come, we have much to discuss." Once released from Fireborn's grip, Jaguar Spot noticed that Orchid was now standing next to her husband. She had undoubtedly been one of the women sitting around the fire circle. Waterlily led him back to the tent, and Fireborn lit a small fire inside so that they could see. They all sat down in a circle. "So, you have returned from Teotihuacan," Jaguar Spot said to both Fireborn and Orchid. Fireborn nodded and Jaguar Spot detected a faint smile on his face as he spoke. "Brother, we have returned, with many goods to trade and with new knowledge that will allow Tikal to finally . . ." Fireborn caught himself before he said something that he obviously thought the better of, paused for a moment, and continued. "Well, knowledge that will help Tikal, at any rate. Now brother, both my wife and myself are most curious as to how we managed to find you and Waterlily out here in the wilderness, many days walking distance from Uaxactun, starving, dying of thirst, and you falling out of a tree like some kind of maniac. Waterlily has been most circumspect on the subject, saying only that we had to question you in order to get the information."

Jaguar Spot looked over at Waterlily, who was busy staring at the floor. He frowned. "I am embarrassed to say what has brought us here. Suffice it to say that I am now an outcast from Uaxactun, and will almost certainly be sacrificed to the Gods if I ever set foot in the *Ch'ul Ahau*'s jurisdiction again. Waterlily joined me by choice, although she could easily have remained at home with her honor intact. We have wandered through the forest for many, many days. Please do not ask me more."

Fireborn's face showed a look of shock and concern, while Orchid tilted her head to the right, then left, then scowled, then grimaced, as if she were thinking through a range of equally unpleasant possibilities that could have resulted in her brother being made an outcast from the city. Finally she spoke in a tone that Jaguar Spot had heard many times a child, when his older sister had caught him in some act of minor malfeasance. "Brother, tell me why this has happened, tell me now!"

Jaguar Spot looked at Fireborn, who looked equally as determined to get an answer as did Orchid, and once again tried not to give a straight answer. "Well, it's a very long story, and not very interesting." The "avoiding the answer gambit" did not work, and Fireborn barked out what sounded very much like an order. "Tell us now, Jaguar Spot. Leave nothing out. Nothing." So Jaguar Spot told them. He told them how he loved Hummingbird from afar for what seemed like years, of his role in the sacrifice of Blue Squirrel, of the subsequent romantic relationship with Hummingbird, of the pregnancy, of the rumors and suspicions, and of how he had to flee before being forced to kill both Hummingbird and her child in a public square. He told them of their travails in the forest, about the hunger and thirst, and about how he climbed the tree in desperation. Fireborn and Orchid listened impassively, showing little emotion. When he was finally done, Orchid started crying, and Fireborn put an arm around her to comfort her. She spoke through her tears, although her voice was so quiet that Jaguar Spot had to struggle to hear. "Brother, how could you? How could you do this to Father, and to Waterlily, and to yourself? Why did you decide to ruin your life, and the life of your family, all for sake of satisfying your animal lust for a pretty girl! And then, even when you could have easily have covered it up, and saved Father's honor, you flee the city like some kind of . . . some kind of coward. I would never have thought that my own brother would be so foolish, and so stupid. What have you to say for yourself?"

Jaguar Spot had no answer for her, just as he had no answer for himself. He hung his head in shame and stared at the floor. Fireborn finally broke the silence. "I take it from your silence that you have no excuse or justification for your actions. What are your plans? Where are you going to go? What are you going to do? Or did you have no plan other than wandering through the forest for the rest of your days?"

Jaguar Spot found it hard to answer. The words came out only with great difficulty. "I don't know. I haven't really thought about it. I can't go back to Uaxactun. I was just going to walk until I came across another city, and maybe find some work as a scribe."

"Just wander?" Fireborn asked, his voice now filled with scorn. "Through the forest? Until you found a city? With Waterlily at your side, sharing your fate? Do you have any idea how much forest there is and how few cities? No? Well let me tell you that you could wander for years and years and years and never see so much as a village unless you knew where you were looking. This 'plan' of yours, and I use that word only in the most general of senses, is a recipe only for starvation and death. And not only would you subject yourself to this foolhardy endeavor, but Waterlily as well! I am astounded at your bad judgment. Go! Both of you, go! Sit with the others at the fire. Lady Orchid and I have to discuss what to do with you. Go!"

Jaguar Spot and Waterlily left the tent and slowly made their way over to the fire, where everybody was singing another foreign-sounding song. The night was warm and humid, and the stars and Lady Moon were obscured by clouds. After they sat down one of the *Teotihuacanos* handed both Jaguar Spot and Waterlily pointed sticks, about twice the length of man's arm. The *Teotihuacano* said something in his own language and gestured to a large wooden bowl of raw meat that sat on the ground. He pointed to the bowl and to the tips of the sharp sticks and then to two women had meat on the ends of their sticks and were cooking the meat in the fire. Jaguar Spot took some meat from the bowl and handed half of it to Waterlily. During a lull in the singing, they put the meat on their sticks and cooked it on the open flames. As they worked at the meat, one of the *Teotihuacanos* handed them a bowl filled with a dark liquid and motioned for them to take a drink. Jaguar Spot put the bowl to his lips and took a sip, and his mouth felt inflamed with a hot and bitter taste. It was as if the *Teotihuacanos* had managed to fit an entire harvest of chilies into the small bowl, probably to mask whatever it was that tasted so bitter. He swallowed the almost undrinkable beverage and handed the bowl to Waterlily, who drank it down without any outward reaction. As they sat by the fire, the singing got louder and more imperative. Jaguar Spot imagined that the *Teotihuacanos* were singing as a means of praying to their gods, and lost sense of time as he stared into the flames.

Jaguar Spot had no idea how long he had been sitting there when he felt a hand on his shoulder. He looked around and saw that everybody else who had been sitting around the fire, including Waterlily, was sleeping, and that the fire was now reduced to orange and red embers. The hand on his shoulder belonged to Floating Crocodile. "Uncle," he whispered, apparently in an effort to avoid waking any of the others up, "Father and Mother would like to talk to you, follow me." Jaguar Spot followed Floating Crocodile into the tent and saw that Fireborn and Orchid were seated in the same positions as when he had left them earlier. Orchid looked rather glum and depressed, and Fireborn looked almost disinterested. Jaguar Spot knelt across from them and waited for one of them to speak. Once Floating Crocodile left, Fireborn did the talking. "You understand that you have put me and your sister in a most difficult position?" Jaguar Spot nodded without saying anything. "So, what are our choices? We could leave you out here in the forest to meet your own fate, which would almost certainly mean that you would die. Frankly, that is no more than you deserve for your crimes and the disloyalty you have shown to your family and your *Ch'ul Ahau*. Tell me, if we did that, do you think that Waterlily would come with us voluntarily or would she want to stay with you?"

"She would want to stay with me."

"We agree. Hence our problem. Waterlily is innocent. Her only crime appears to be her love for you. She does not deserve to die for that crime. She deserves to live the life that she was going to have before you created this disgraceful state of affairs. So, we can't just leave you here in the jungle. What if we took you back to Uaxactun and handed you over to Speaking Macaw? I think that all of us know that Waterlily would follow you, and I fear that Speaking Macaw would order both of you killed–you for treason, and her for being your accessory in escaping from justice. Maybe he would hold her blameless and spare her life, I don't know, but we can't take the chance. Neither me nor your sister is willing to allow your actions to result in the death of Waterlily, even indirectly.

What are we left with? What solution to do you have for our problem?"

"I have no solution."

"No, that much is obvious, so I will give you my method for solving this problem. What first came to my mind was to send you and Waterlily to Teotihuacan, and let you ply your trade as a scribe in that city. It would be difficult, but you would probably survive. Of course, they have no written language as we know it up there, in fact the priests consider writing to be an abomination to the Gods. Still, there is a Maya quarter where most people speak Yucatec, and you could probably eke out a modest living catering to those who have enough money to take on the trappings of the aristocracy back home. But there is a problem with this course of action. Do you know that the problem might be?"

"No."

"Loyalty. I would have to send you there under my personal protection. Without being there to keep an eye on you, I don't think that I could be sure that you wouldn't embarrass me, or commit some treasonous crime against the King. At any rate, I am not willing to take the risk of setting you free in such a city without supervision that I can trust. So Teotihuacan is out. That leaves taking you to Tikal along with us, which has its own host of problems. It would certainly be an embarrassment for the royal family to have a notorious traitor from another city roaming about, with all of us pretending like nothing happened. On the other hand, I could keep an eye on you and, maybe, just maybe, correct these inexplicable ethical and moral lapses that you have shown of late. What do you say to that?"

"I have nothing to say. I am at your mercy."

"Ah, so maybe you have a bit of intelligence left inside of you after all. You are correct. You are at my mercy, and you will have no choice but to do what I say. This is how it will be: you and Waterlily will come with us to Tikal. We will not hide who you are. You will live in my house under my protection, and you will not leave the confines of the city without my explicit consent. That is not meant to punish you, but it merely reflects that fact that I cannot offer you any protection if you leave the city. I will find you work as a scribe, and on occasion I will ask you to perform a special task for me. You will have no title. You will call any of the *cahelob* 'sir' and any of the *ahauob* 'Your Lordship,' including me. You will do exactly what I tell you to do on any matter, no matter what your personal thoughts are on the subject. If you agree to these conditions, you and Waterlily may come with us to Tikal. If not, we will leave you here in the forest. Both choices are open to you, but you must decide now. What is your decision?"

"I will accept Your Lordship's most generous offer and accompany you to Tikal."

"You are right. It *is* most generous, and don't you ever forget it. Now leave us."

Jaguar Spot went back to the fire circle and found Waterlily where he left her, sleeping on her side, facing the fire. He laid down behind her, put an arm over her shoulder, and went to sleep.

They spent two more days at the camp before they loaded up the canoes and paddled up river. Jaguar Spot and Waterlily shared a canoe with two large *Teotihuacanos*, who paddled to the rhythm of a song that they sung together. Jaguar Spot picked up the count of the song and paddled with them. The canoes traveled up river in a long line, each of them staying as close to the left shore as the conditions would allow. They paddled all day and did not come stop until close to nightfall, when Jaguar Spot thought that he was about to collapse from exhaustion. Before they left their original camp, Jaguar Spot noticed that all of the men traveling with Fireborn had unnaturally large shoulders and biceps. Now he knew why.

They pulled the canoes out of the water into a small clearing. Jaguar Spot noticed the stumps of a great many trees in the clearing, which was the only suitable camping area that he had seen all day. Apparently the traders who used this river to come up from the Valley of Mexico had decided to make their own permanent campsite when the Gods would not provide one. Someone started a fire and the women began busying themselves grinding corn for tortillas and preparing other food. One of the *Teotihuacanos* took some strange looking wooden objects out of a bag and handed them out to all of the men, including Jaguar Spot. Another unbundled some strange looking short spears and threw them in a pile on the ground. The spears were barely the length of a man's arm, and had a flint tip. The rear of the spears had a large notch and three sets of feathers flensed along the back. All of the men, including Fireborn, took a spear and headed into the forest. Jaguar Spot, assuming that they were going hunting, picked up one of the last remaining spears and made to follow, but Fireborn turned to Floating Crocodile and shouted something in *Teotihuac*. Floating Crocodile pulled Jaguar Spot by the arm in the opposite direction and headed to the other end of the clearing. "Uncle," he said in Yucatec, "Father says that I am to show you how to use the spear thrower." Floating Crocodile displayed a wooden object almost identical to the one that someone had handed Jaguar Spot. The object was oblong, about the same length as a man's forearm, and tapered into a handle at one end. The other end had a notch. Jaguar Spot looked at his spear thrower, and then the spear, without a clue as to how they were supposed to work together. Jaguar Spot was reasonably proficient at handling a spear, and had managed to kill several deer when hunting with groups from Uaxactun, but he was used to spears almost twice the length of these. When they reached the end of the clearing Floating Crocodile took the spear and put the feathered end in the notch of the spear thrower, at the same time explaining what he was doing. "Uncle, watch where I put the end. It is very important to get it seated correctly, or the spear can fly wildly and hurt someone. Once you have it seated, you take the spear and pull it behind you, so that you have the spear thrower here down by your backside and the spear resting on your shoulder. Now, point out a tree for me to hit and I will show you."

Jaguar Spot pointed to a smallish tree about twenty paces away, but Floating Crocodile shook his head. "No, Uncle. That's way too close. Pick something farther." Humoring the boy, Jaguar Spot pointed to another tree, about twice as far, but Floating Crocodile again shook his head. "Uncle," he said with frustration, "why are you picking these close-in targets? Do you see that tree over there? That's still kind of close, but it will do for a demonstration. Now watch." The tree that Floating Crocodile had selected was more than a hundred paces away, much farther than Jaguar Spot could ever dreamed of hitting by simply throwing a spear. Floating Crocodile leaned back until the spear was vertical and was no longer resting on his shoulder, and then in a movement faster than Jaguar Spot would have thought possible, brought his arm above his head and then forward so quickly that they seemed a blur. The spear went flying away in a graceful arc almost too fast to follow and hit the selected tree square in the middle with a loud thump. Never in his life would Jaguar Spot have imagined that anyone could hurl a spear so far, and with such accuracy. Floating Crocodile, visibly pleased with his accomplishment, flipped his spear thrower in the air, caught it, and turned to Jaguar Spot. "Uncle, your turn, here let me help you."

Jaguar Spot put the spear in the notch the same way he had seen the boy do, and rested the spear on his shoulder. Floating Crocodile examined how the spear was seated in the spear thrower and nodded to

Jaguar Spot. "Now Uncle, you must remember to follow through with the spear thrower, and keep the spear seated until the very last second, until the moment when your arm is almost horizontal to the ground," he said with concern in his voice. Jaguar Spot let the spear fall from his shoulder as he had seen and brought the spear thrower forward as fast as he could. The spear went over his shoulder and disappeared. He followed through with the spear thrower as Floating Crocodile had advised, but the spear was long since gone when his arm reached the point where it was horizontal with the ground. He looked to see where the spear had gone, but could not see it anywhere. "Uncle!" Floating Crocodile screamed, "get out of the way!" The boy pushed Jaguar Spot hard in his right side so that he fell onto the forest floor, with the boy on top of him. Just as they reached the ground Jaguar Spot heard a loud thump and saw that the spear had landed right where he had been standing and stuck straight up from the ground.

Under Floating Crocodile's guidance Jaguar Spot practiced with the spear thrower until the only light came from the torches and cook fires of the camp. By the end he could hit a tree at ten paces away with a fair degree of regularity, but the boy laughed at his horrible form. Jaguar Spot saw the advantages of hunting using this tool, but he knew that it would take him years to become as proficient as the boy, if ever. A conch shell trumpet sounded to announce that the hunters had returned to the camp with their quarry, and Jaguar Spot, his right arm sore from all of the spear thrower practice, followed the boy back to the fire.

The next day was was the last day that they traveled by canoe. Jaguar Spot rode with Fireborn and two *Teotihuacanos* who apparently did not speak a word of Yucatec. While the *Teotihuacanos* spoke animatedly to each other in their own tongue, Fireborn took the opportunity of relative privacy provided by the canoe to openly discuss subjects that he would never dream of breaching in front of the women. "Tell me about the Great Tree, Gentle Scribe. What is its nature?" he asked in a pedantic tone of voice.

Jaguar Spot, knowing that Fireborn did not really want much of an answer but was merely using the question to set up a point that he wanted to make, gave the most general reply that he could. "Your Lordship, the Great Tree is the common thread linking all of the worlds of the universe. Its roots go deep into the Underworld, and . . ."

Fireborn waved him off. "Yes, yes, yes. You give me the rote answer that you learned in your training as a scribe. Very true, quite correct, and absolutely meaningless. Tell me, Gentle Scribe, is the Great Tree a god?"

Fireborn had asked a very interesting question. Jaguar Spot had never thought of the Great Tree in these terms before. "A god, Your Lordship?" he said. "I don't know. I have never heard it discussed in such terms. But now that you ask the question, I have to say 'no.' It is not a god. It is something different."

Fireborn laughed. "Not a god? Are you sure? Isn't the rain the holy blood of the Great Tree? Does it not sustain all of us in our lives, each of us from the lowliest laborer to the rulers of great cities? Is it not responsible for our well being more than any entity that you would call a god beyond any doubt? Is not the wind the very breath of the Great Tree. Do we not see its branches in the nighttime sky? How can you say that it is not a god?"

"Well Your Lordship, if you put it like that, perhaps it is a god."

Fireborn laughed harder. "A god? You call the Great Tree a god? Tell me, does it speak? Does it think? Does it play games, or demand sacrifices the way that the denizens of the Otherworld do of us? In fact, are not the Gods just as dependent on the Great Tree for their survival and well being as we are? How can you call it a god? Have you gone mad?"

Jaguar Spot knew that any answer that he gave to Fireborn would only serve to be more fodder for whatever rhetorical challenge he would put up next. He did not answer for some time, and watched as the paddles churned the water and caused small eddies in their wake until he came up with an answer. "Perhaps, Your Lordship, you have asked a question without an answer. The Great Tree simply exists, to try to categorize the quality of its existence is, in the end, a meaningless exercise."

All that Jaguar Spot could see of Fireborn was his back as they paddled up river, so he was unable to gauge his reaction. They paddled in quiet past two bends in the river before Fireborn answered. "A good response, Gentle Scribe. In fact, not bad at all. Perhaps you are on your way to understanding the world after all. The Great Tree is everything, it is everywhere. Its shoots and streamers reach out to every spot in the universe, drawing energy and returning life. But it needs no words of thanks, it seeks no praise, it demands no sacrifice. It is as indifferent to our comings and goings and to the affairs of men as it is to the development of a single ear of maize on a farm in the deepest forest. It has the power to dominate, to control, but it never uses that power, the thought would not even enter its mind, if it has a mind. Do you see my point, Gentle Scribe?"

"I am afraid not, Your Lordship."

"Some day, if you live long enough, you will."

"I hope so, Your Lordship."

Fireborn stopped paddling momentarily. He turned around and faced Jaguar Spot with an almost menacing look on his face. "You hope so? You should not wish such enlightenment on your worst enemy. Such enlightenment comes with a heavy price. A very heavy price." Fireborn turned his back to Jaguar spot and resumed paddling.

They paddled through the rest of the day without another word exchanged between them, although Fireborn laughed occasionally at something said by one of the *Teotihuacanos*. They reached the portage to Tikal just as Lord Sun began to hide behind the trees on the western side of the river.

Chapter Thirteen
Great Jaguar Paw

8.17.0.0.14. November 4, 376 A.D.

Floating Crocodile woke Jaguar Spot up just before daybreak while almost everyone else was still asleep. He took him to a secluded place by the river where Fireborn and one of *Teotihuacanos* were getting dressed into fancy ceremonial garb and the broad brimmed tasseled hats that Jaguar Spot had seen before. In the growing light Jaguar Spot could see that the clothes were very rich, covered with rare feathers and intricate patterns on the textiles. At their feet lay two large ceramic pots, from the look of them meant to be gifts, probably filled with cacao beans. Fireborn noticed them as they walked out of the gloom. "Ah, it is our friend, the Gentle Scribe. Good. Gentle Scribe, I would like to introduce you to my nephew Curl Snout, son of His Lordship Great Jaguar Paw, *Ch'ul Ahau* of Tikal. Your job today will be to carry this piece of pottery for him until we reach the city. My son will carry mine. Can you do that?"

So the man standing next to Fireborn was not a *Teotihuacano* after all, but an heir to the throne of Tikal. At any rate, he seemed to speak *Teotihuac* well enough, because Jaguar Spot could not remember him ever uttering a word in Yucatec. Jaguar Spot looked Curl Snout in the eye and nodded. "I will be honored to carry the item for His Lordship." Curl Snout nodded back at Jaguar Spot without saying a word. Jaguar Spot had seen nods like that before, in the palace. It was a nod of dismissal, the kind of nod that the nobility would give to a lowly servant who was no longer required. In many quarters it would be considered an expression of contempt, which was the way Jaguar Spot took it. He turned around and returned to the camp in silence, leaving Floating Crocodile with his father.

When he got back to camp everyone else was waking up. The women were preparing a quick breakfast, and the *Teotihuacanos* were busy getting dressed in hugely plumed garments that Jaguar Spot recognized to be military finery. Just as he grabbed a warm tortilla and began to eat, Orchid appeared out of nowhere and handed him a set of clothes similar to what the palace guards wore in Uaxactun and explained. "We were going to have one of the *Teotihuacanos* wear these things, just for appearances sake. Both Lord Fireborn and His Lordship Curl Snout have decided to return from Teotihuacan after all these years dressed in the fashion of the nobility of that city, as a statement that they have learned and acquired much in their years abroad. Yet they are still *ahauob* of Tikal, so we will have you and Floating Crocodile dressed in these garments, to represent their ties to their home." Orchid promptly turned around and walked in the direction of where Jaguar Spot had seen Fireborn and Curl Snout getting dressed.

Jaguar Spot dressed himself and watched as the *Teotihuacanos* began to load up all of the baskets and bags of trade goods for the day's walk to Tikal. Most of the baskets were specially designed to be carried on a man or woman's back, and appeared to be filled with valuable trade goods such as obsidian, greenstone, and rare bird feathers. A conch shell trumpet sounded from the direction where Jaguar Spot had seen Fireborn and Curl Snout getting ready, and all of the *Teotihuacanos* turned in the direction of the sound and knelt on one knee. A stern look from one of the older *Teotihuacanos* was all that Jaguar Spot needed to know that he should do the same. He knelt down and watched as Fireborn, Curl Snout, Orchid, and Floating Crocodile appeared out of the foliage. The *Teotihuacanos* all bowed their heads to the ground. Jaguar Spot followed their lead, although it was an alien practice as far as Maya nobility were concerned. The trumpet sounded again and all of the *Teotihuacanos* jumped up and got back to work. Orchid came up to Jaguar Spot and handed him the ceramic container filled with cacao beans. Jaguar Spot had no idea that it would be so heavy–even heavier than the largest rubber ball for the ballgame. The thought of carrying such a weight all day without rest, and the fact that his honor and worth as a man might be judged by how good a job he did in carrying it, filled him with dread. At Orchid's direction he stood beside Floating Crocodile, who appeared to have little, if any, trouble in carrying his burden. Fireborn and Curl Snout stood three paces behind them, and the four *Teotihuacano* guards, all armed with spears and spear throwers, prepared to march to the side. Orchid stood a few paces behind her husband, and the Waterlily and rest of the *Teotihuacanos* all marched in a group behind her.

One of the *Teotihuacanos* sounded the trumpet and the column began the slow march toward Tikal. It was a hot day, and the humidity was especially oppressive, but they marched without stopping until Lord Sun was starting to get low in the West. The forest by the river was thick, lush, and filled with the sounds of birds and animals, which Jaguar Spot found cheerful as he carried his burden. As the day wore on

Jaguar Spot became exhausted. Try as he might, he could never find a comfortable way to hold the ceramic container, and it seemed to get heavier with every step. What he wanted more than anything was some water and something to eat, but apparently that was not to be permitted. By mid-day the heat was almost unbearable and Jaguar Spot's hands and forearms were raw from shifting the position of the pot from arm to arm and side to side. As his agony grew he became more and more impatient with the sounds of the birds and the animals rustling in the leaves. They seemed to be mocking him, taking pleasure in his pain. Sometime after mid-day a small troupe of monkeys, no more than four or five, came down from the trees and howled together at the side of the forest road. To Jaguar Spot's eye the monkeys were howling at him, taking delight in his suffering. He felt like throwing the cacao beans down to the ground and chasing after the damn monkeys, but kept walking, refusing to let his discomfort show. Shortly after the sound of the monkeys faded into the distance, the forest opened up into farmland, with field upon field of maize and beans as far as the eye could see. Every few thousand paces or so there would be a little hamlet or village, with four or five houses. The residents of these communities stood in front of their houses or peered through their crops to see the strange spectacle that passed them by.

Finally, just as dusk was about to set in, and when Jaguar Spot thought that he could just see the tops of the tallest temples of Tikal looming in the distance, they heard a conch trumpet sound from the front, and the *Teotihuacano* in the rear sounded his trumpet in return. Fireborn called out for them all to stop marching in both languages, so they waited on the road in silence, still in the same formation, no one moving a muscle.

The air was heavy with moisture as they waited. Everyone's body was covered with a shimmering layer of sweat from the day's hike. After a while Jaguar Spot thought that he heard the faint sounds of drums beating the distance. The sound got louder, and Jaguar Spot saw another group of people appear in the distance, apparently a delegation from Tikal. The group from Tikal was much larger than the group that Jaguar Spot had been marching with, and was led by twenty palace guards dressed much in the same way as Jaguar Spot and the boy. They were followed by about ten similarly-dressed men bearing a litter carrying a sedan chair and numerous statues of the Gods. There was a man sitting on the sedan chair. He was very old by the looks of him, and was dressed in an enormous scarlet headdress and a rich feather cloak. When the group from Tikal reached them, the guards moved over to the side of the road. Jaguar Spot saw that there were several hundred people, *ahauob, cahelob,* and their families by the look of them, bringing up the rear. The bearers placed the litter gently on the ground, and the old man stood up, walked past Jaguar Spot, and embraced Fireborn. "Brother," he said. "It is good to see you after all of these years." Fireborn said nothing as the old man, who had to be Great Jaguar Paw, *Ch'ul Ahau* of Tikal, moved over to embrace Curl Snout. "Ah, son," he said. "You are looking very well, it appears that your years living among the foreigners have done you a world of good. Come, all of you, we have a feast waiting at the palace and you must be famished." The *Ch'ul Ahau* released his son and went back to sit in his sedan chair, and then nodded at Fireborn. "Your Lordship," Fireborn said in an oddly formal manner, "thank you for your kind and generous offer to feed me and my traveling companions, but first I have gifts to present to you. Jaguar Spot, Floating Crocodile, give His Lordship his gifts." Jaguar Spot and Floating Crocodile walked up to the *Ch'ul Ahau*'s litter and placed their containers next to two statues of the Hero Twins. Jaguar Spot followed Floating Crocodile as he walked back to where they had been standing and stood at attention. Never in his life had Jaguar Spot felt such relief as when he was finally able to rid himself of the burden of carrying that container. The *Ch'ul Ahau* opened one of the pots, pulled out a handful of cacao beans, and smelt them. "Very good beans, Brother," he said, with his nose still occupied. "*Very* good indeed."

"They are a gift from the King of Teotihuacan, Your Lordship," Fireborn said. "And because we bear his gifts, we have dressed as his emissaries would on such an occasion." The *Ch'ul Ahau* clapped his hands and the litter bearers lifted him back up into the air and turned around to face the city. Without anyone saying another word the guards moved in front of the *Ch'ul Ahau* and led the procession back towards the towering temples that lay before them. The nobility that had followed the *Ch'ul Ahau* to greet the party now lined the sides of the road and shouted greetings to Fireborn and Curl Snout as they passed. They came upon the temples that Jaguar Spot had marveled at on his only previous visit to Tikal. The procession wormed its way through the city, past a market that was, if anything, five times the size of the market in Uaxactun. Every street or byway that they passed was lined with throngs of people, many cheering, some throwing flower pedals at the *Ch'ul Ahau* or Fireborn, all of them somehow paying homage to the royalty of the city. Jaguar Spot had never seen anything close to this number of people at one place–not even in a packed ballcourt or a crowded market at festival time.

After the procession passed what seemed to be endless streets lined with countless cheering faces, they arrived at the palace and the *Ch'ul Ahau* got out of his sedan chair. Fireborn, Curl Snout, Floating Crocodile, and Orchid walked with the *Ch'ul Ahau* into the palace, followed by the *ahauob* and the guards who had met them on the road. Jaguar Spot was unsure of where to go or what to do, so he wandered back to the group of *Teotihuacanos* and spied Waterlily among them, standing with the *Teotihuacano* women. He knelt to the ground in exhaustion. Waterlily rubbed his forehead in concern. "You look horrible," she said. "Do you know where we are supposed to go? I'm pretty hungry." Jaguar Spot shook his head and glanced around the area for any sign of guidance as to what was supposed to happen next, but saw nothing. Moreover, the *Teotihuacanos* looked just as unsure of what they were supposed to do as Jaguar Spot imagined that he did. Just as he was beginning to think that Fireborn had forgotten about the lot of them, a diminutive man dressed in the clothes of a *cahel* approached them and meekly came up to Jaguar Spot. "You are Jaguar Spot?" he asked with a quiet voice, his face full of fear and concern.

"I am," said Jaguar Spot. "Tell me, Sir, is there anywhere around here that we can get something to eat? We have been marching all day."

The little *cahel* groaned and looked to his feet before answering. "Eat? Yes, of course. His Lordship Fireborn said that I should look after you tonight. Come, I will have my wife cook up something to feed you." Without waiting for an answer, the *cahel*, who had still not introduced himself to Jaguar Spot, turned around and walked away from the palace. Jaguar Spot gestured to the *Teotihuacanos* and Waterlily to follow him, and they all set off after the strange *cahel*.

For a little fellow, this *cahel* seemed to be walking awfully fast, or perhaps Jaguar Spot's legs were tired after the day's march. Jaguar Spot caught up to the *cahel* and asked him his name. The *cahel* seemed taken aback. "My name? Good gracious me! Why would you want to know my name? All you need to know is to call me 'Sir.'"

"Sir, I understand. But I am sure that me and my companions will want to thank His Lordship Fireborn for offering us your gracious hospitality. After all. . ."

The *cahel* grabbed Jaguar Spot by the right arm and almost shouted. "What did you say?"

"I said that I wanted to . . ."

"No! Not that rubbish. What did you say about these companions? What companions?" Just then the *cahel* turned around and saw the hungry group of *Teotihuacanos* and Waterlily just a few paces behind them. "That rabble?" the *cahel* cried. "Oh, what I am asked to do for my country! Very well, very well," he said while turning back to Jaguar Spot. "You should have told me that I was going to have to feed half the city. Here, take these, go to the market, and buy enough maize and beans to feed this entire group. If you have any money left over, get some meat, whatever you can find. Now shoo." The *cahel* handed Jaguar Spot a sack of cacao beans and fluttered his hands in an effort to get Jaguar Spot to start moving. Jaguar Spot turned in the direction where he remembered seeing the market and stopped when he was ten paces away. The *cahel* was almost out of sight around a corner. "Sir!" Jaguar Spot shouted. The *cahel* screamed back at Jaguar Spot. "Yes? What is it now? Why aren't you at the market doing what I told you? Must I do everything myself to ensure that it is done correctly?"

Jaguar Spot felt strange shouting at the *cahel* like this, but it was the only way to get heard. "Sir, where am I to bring the food? To whose house?"

"My house, you idiot!"

"But I don't know your name, Sir. How am I to find it?"

"Otter. My name is Otter. You can find my house in Lord Fireborn's compound. Go!"

Jaguar Spot nodded to Waterlily, who had been giving him a questioning look, and set off for the market. He found it in short order, and was at once overwhelmed by the enormous variety of sensations. Outside of festival time, at this time of the evening back home in Uaxactun the market was usually shutting down and would be almost empty. Not so here. The air was full of exotic fragrances and the sound of strange music. Every few steps there seemed to be an acrobat, or juggler, or someone else capering around seeking the odd cacao bean from the patrons of the market. Pushing his way through the masses, Jaguar Spot found a reputable looking maize merchant and knelt down beside him in front of his stall. "I need four head-weight of ground maize," Jaguar Spot said. Using a stick, the merchant wrote the numerical symbol for four in the dirt and wrote a couple more numbers next to it. "Thirty-five beans," the merchant said.

"Ten beans."

"Thirty-five"

"Ten"

"Oh alright, I like the look of your face. I will sell it to you for thirty, but not a bean less."

"Fifteen, and that's my final offer."

"Twenty-five."

"Twenty."

"Done."

The merchant wrote out the number twenty next to the number four and circled it. "It'll take me a little while to get it packed up for you. If you have anymore shopping to do, you could come back a little later, but you need to give me the twenty-five beans right now."

Jaguar Spot had spent enough time in the market at home to know that he should not simply leave this man with the money. "That's alright, I'll wait. And it's twenty beans, not twenty-five," Jaguar Spot said, pointing at the numbers in the dirt. The merchant gave Jaguar Spot a wry smile and started filling up a fabric sack with the ground maize.

Chapter Fourteen
Assignment

8.17.0.5.17. February 15, 377A.D.

"Exquisite!" exclaimed Great Jaguar Paw when Fireborn presented him with the pot that Jaguar Spot had been laboring over for almost a *uinal*. Ever since his arrival in Uaxactun, Fireborn had kept Jaguar Spot busy painting pot after pot. Some pots showed the activities of Fireborn, or of Curl Snout in Teotihuacan. Some depicted the river journey back to Tikal, and the arrival at the city. Most of the pots became gifts to *ahauob, cahelob,* or common citizens of more than average importance. When he first started painting the pots, Jaguar Spot carefully wrote out glyphs explaining the context of the painting, but Fireborn quickly put the kibosh on that, telling him "less than half of the *ahauob* can read, almost none of the *cahelob* can, and none of the other men of importance will be able to read so much as a word that you paint. I need as many of these pots as possible, so cut out the writing."

After what must have been the hundredth pot that Jaguar Spot painted, Fireborn commissioned a special pot to give to the *Ch'ul Ahau* on the anniversary of a great military victory he had won many years before. The pot was to depict the journey of Fireborn and the *Teotihuacanos* from the river to the city. Jaguar Spot spent days on the painting, and in the end even he had to admit that the results were superb. Jaguar Spot felt enormous pride as the *Ch'ul Ahau* held the pot up to the light and turned it around slowly. The courtyard where the celebration was taking place was crowded with the nobility of the city, who had laid piles of rich textiles, large bags of beans, heaps of rubber, three men's weight worth of cacao beans, and an assortment of fans at the feet of the *Ch'ul Ahau*. Two important *ahauob* called the "Keepers of the Holy Books" had presented Great Jaguar Paw with a stone-tree outlining the sixty years that he had been ruler of the city. The gift that seemed to please the *Ch'ul Ahau* the most appeared to be the pot that Jaguar Spot had painted. Fireborn, who had been kneeling in front of His Lordship as he examined the pot, turned around and motioned for Jaguar Spot to step forward. Jaguar Spot went up to Fireborn and knelt down next to him. "Your Lordship," Fireborn said. "This is the artist who painted that object. I have told you about him. He is my brother-in-law from Uaxactun, and is living in my house."

Jaguar Spot had never before been this close to Great Jaguar Paw, not even when he had presented him with the pot filled with cacao beans out on the forest road. He had known that the *Ch'ul Ahau* was old, but he had never before seen anyone appearing so frail and weak. Fireborn had told him that the *Ch'ul Ahau* was in his nineties, which Jaguar Spot found to be almost farcically absurd, but now he leaned towards believing it. It was certainly true that the *Ch'ul Ahau* was so old that he had outlived most of his children, but from reading the stone-trees and monuments around the city, Jaguar Spot knew that Great Jaguar Paw had a large number of sons who had died in battle over the decades. Curl Snout and his older brother were the result of relatively recent union between the *Ch'ul Ahau* and a specially selected young woman. The express purpose of the union was to create an heir to the throne. Fireborn's relative youth had been the main reason that Jaguar Spot had not been inclined to believe the stories about the *Ch'ul Ahau*'s age, but Fireborn said that they shared a mother in common, not a father, and that his mother had given birth to Great Jaguar Paw at the age of thirteen, and had become pregnant with Fireborn in her mid-forties. Still, the ages did not add up when Jaguar Spot tried to figure them out, and he still thought it unlikely that the *Ch'ul Ahau* was really that old, even though the stone-trees said that the *Ch'ul Ahau* had ruled the city for sixty years

The *Ch'ul Ahau* put the pot down and picked up one of the fans that someone had given him. "So you are the boy from Uaxactun," he said. "Lord Fireborn says that you might be of use to us in another project we are planning. Based on this work, I am inclined to agree." The *Ch'ul Ahau* snapped his fingers and shouted to the audience. "Stone, come forward." One of the Keepers of the Holy Books came up and knelt beside Jaguar Spot. "Stone," the *Ch'ul Ahau* said, "this young man is a scribe from Uaxactun. He will be working on a special project for Lord Fireborn and myself. You will give him access to all of your records relating to astronomy, the stars, and calendars. Do you understand?"

"Yes, Your Lordship," said Stone.

"Good. It's all settled then," said the *Ch'ul Ahau* as a servant gave him a bowl of chocolate. "Thank you for the kind acts of tribute that all of you have paid me today. I appreciate your coming by, but now Lord Fireborn and myself need to have a meeting with the scribe who painted this wonderful pot."

The *Ch'ul Ahau* suddenly got up and quickly went through a doorway. Fireborn pulled Jaguar Spot to follow. They walked through the palace and out of a side entrance where a score of palace guards had a sedan chair waiting for His Lordship. The guards immediately picked up the sedan chair and set off to the south, but Fireborn pulled Jaguar Spot to the east. "We are going to take a shortcut." Fireborn said with halted breath. "We will meet up with my brother later." Jaguar Spot struggled to follow as Fireborn picked up the pace to a near run. Jaguar Spot had no idea where Fireborn was taking him. Apart from selected public events and important religious rituals, the *Ch'ul Ahau* rarely left the palace, and they were headed in the wrong direction if they were going to meet with him. They also were headed away from the administrative buildings that surrounded the palace, and away even from Fireborn's compound. Fireborn led him to the foot of the tallest Temple in Tikal. Standing at its base, the temple seemed impossibly high to Jaguar Spot–much higher even than the tallest trees of the forest. Jaguar Spot had not realized how steep the temple was until he looked right up a stairway. It seemed to shoot straight up into the sky. Fireborn started walking up the stairs, and beckoned Jaguar Spot to follow. "But Your Lordship," Jaguar Spot almost pleaded, "it is forbidden to ascend a temple without . . ."

Fireborn cut Jaguar Spot off. "Forbidden to you, Gentle Scribe, but not to me. Come, I want to show you something."

They ascended the temple stairs slowly, almost deliberately. Not only was it an exhausting climb, but the stairway was very steep, so steep that one slip might be fatal. When they got close to the top Jaguar Spot could see the beautiful temple building that capped the pyramid. The temples at Uaxactun were not nearly so tall, nor so steep, and Jaguar Spot was used to the rather plain building that topped the temples. This temple was unlike anything that Jaguar Spot had ever seen. The building itself was covered in beautifully carved glyphs, telling the story of the creation of the world, and of the career of the *Ch'ul Ahau* who had built the temple. The glyphs were carved so deep into the stone, and the craftsmen who carved them had created such clear images, that Jaguar Spot could read them from fifty paces away, notwithstanding the fact that the building was covered with red stucco. When they finally reached the top, Jaguar Spot was stunned by the view. He had never looked down on the tops of the trees before, and it seemed that he could see farther from this height than he could walk in a day. He looked North in the direction of Uaxactun, hoping to catch a glimpse of the city, but he could see only forest. He wondered about his father, and what had become of the rest of his family. Had the *Ch'ul Ahau* exacted vengeance on the family of a traitor, as he had every right to do? Was his father still alive, and still an *ahau*? He wondered what old Master Snail was doing, and who among his old friends were excelling in the ballgame. In that moment he felt an intense feeling of homesickness.

"A beautiful view, isn't it?" asked Fireborn, interrupting Jaguar Spot's train of thought. All Jaguar Spot could manage to do in return was to nod. "Tell me, Gentle Scribe, why have I brought you here?" Fireborn asked.

"I don't know, Your Lordship."

Fireborn stood next to Jaguar Spot as he looked North. "That's good," Fireborn said. "The first step to wisdom is understanding what you don't know, not what you do know. Tell me, Jaguar Spot, what do you see?"

"I see the city, I see farmland, I see the forest, Your Lordship."

"Good. Tell me this, do you see the Great Tree?"

Jaguar Spot looked upwards, thinking that the contours of the Great Tree might be visible from this dizzying height, but all he saw was blue sky and clouds. "No, Your Lordship," he said.

"I disagree. You need to look harder," said Fireborn.

Jaguar Spot was confused. "Your Lordship, I don't understand where I am to look. I just see the natural world around us, not the Great Tree."

Fireborn grunted, and turned to walk into the temple building. "Come on," he said, over his shoulder. Jaguar Spot reluctantly followed. Entering a temple building like this one was entering a sacred place, and was equivalent to actually stepping foot into the Otherworld. The room was small inside, and the inner walls were covered with even more glyphs than the outer ones. One of the walls had a giant carving of the Great Tree, showing its roots going deep into the Underworld, and its branches stretching high into the heavens. Fireborn pointed to the carving. "This is the traditional way that our society portrays the Great Tree, but I don't think that it is correct."

Jaguar Spot was almost too stunned to speak. "Your Lordship?" he said, almost choking on his words. "That's blasphemy. How can you say . ." Fireborn stomped his foot and shot Jaguar Spot a stern look. "Listen, boy. You should think long and hard before you accuse an *ahau* of blasphemy. I have traveled far and wide over the past few years. Not only to Teotihuacan, but so far north that the land turns into a desert, and there is barely a plant or tree for as far as the eye can see. I have seen pyramids so high that they make this temple look like a child's toy. I have seen the ocean, where the water stretches on forever. The Great Tree is real enough, but everyone sees it from the point of view of their surroundings. Our people have lived in the forest for *baktuns*. The forest is the world as we know it, so we see the personification of the world as a tree. But others, like the *Teotihuacanos*, like the residents of the deserts, they see the world differently. I am convinced that the Great Tree is more than the glue that binds the various worlds of the universe together. It is more than a provider of rain. It is everywhere, it is everything. When you see a tree in the forest, you are looking at such a small part of the Great Tree that it is less than a single leaf. When you see a river, you are looking at the Great Tree. The Great Tree is so big that it can't be seen, but you see it every moment of your life. Do you understand?"

"I think so, Your Lordship. But I don't see how it changes anything. After all, the form of the Great Tree is not important, so long as it is there to sustain us."

Fireborn stomped his foot again. "It is important!" he almost shouted. "It is all important. You see, we are small. In relation to the Great Tree, we are less important than the smallest mites on a fallen leaf. Tell me, would a tree in the forest care about the lives of mites on a fallen leaf?"

"I expect not, Your Lordship."

"Exactly! We are less important to the Great Tree than the mites, and less noticeable. It doesn't care what happens to us, whether we fight wars, whether we live long lives or if we all were to die. It just doesn't care. We are just insignificant specks of dust."

"And what of the Gods?"

"Ah, now you finally ask a good question. The gods are more important than us, but the Great Tree cares little about them, and the Gods care little about our affairs. And that, Gentle Scribe, is the point of our discussion. Take another look outside, imagine that you are a god, what stands out at you?"

"The temples, the city . . ."

"But what people stand out at you? Can you even see individual people if you are a god?"

"I don't know."

"You don't know. Very well. Neither do I, to tell the truth. Sometimes I think that our prayers and sacrifices to the Gods fall on deaf ears, that what we perceive as divine intervention is, in reality, nothing other than random chance. So, I propose to make the Gods take notice. I propose to do a deed that will make the entire Otherworld shudder in fear. A deed so daring, so important, that the people will still speak of it at the turning of the twelfth *baktun*. And to carry out this deed, I need your help. Will you help me?"

"Of course I will help you, Your Lordship. What, if I may be so bold as to ask, is this thing that you would like to accomplish?"

Fireborn smiled and walked out of the building. "I can't tell you that, yet," he said. "All I need to know is that I have your absolute loyalty and obedience on the matter."

"You have it," Jaguar Spot said without hesitation.

"Good," Fireborn said, and led Jaguar Spot down the temple stairs and back into the city.

They met up with the *Ch'ul Ahau* in an administrative building close to the palace. Stone was there, as were seven or eight other *ahauob*, along with two of the *Teotihuacanos*. Living in Fireborn's house, Jaguar Spot had seen the *Teotihuacanos* on an almost daily basis since his arrival in the city, but he had never heard them speak a word of Yucatec, as if Fireborn wanted to limit their ability to communicate with the people of Tikal. Indeed, Fireborn chose servants who could not speak the language to help the *Teotihuacanos* with things like food an clothing. Today the *Teotihuacanos* were dressed as if for battle, except for strange implements they wore over their eyes. Stone and the *Ch'ul Ahau* were deep in conversation when Fireborn and Jaguar Spot walked in, but immediately stopped talking. Fireborn and Jaguar Spot knelt down next to the *Teotihuacanos* and waited for the *Ch'ul Ahau* to speak. "Now that we are all here," the *Ch'ul Ahau* began, "we can start. Today we begin our plans for battle. For too many years have we lived side by side with that idiot, that midget who calls himself a *Ch'ul Ahau*, Speaking Macaw. Now, perhaps, with the help of our friends from Teotihuacan, and with the assistance of their god *Tlaloc*, we can remedy that situation for the better. As you can see, these men from Teotihuacan are wearing goggles around their eyes. These are symbols of the god *Tlaloc*, who is a powerful god of battle. In truth, he is just the *Teotihuacano* version of the same Hero Twin that we worship as the personification of the planet Venus. But up north, he is a powerful harbinger of battle and victory. Thus we will fight this war as *Tlaloc* would have us do, according to the transit of the planet Venus. That is where you, my young friend, come in." The *Ch'ul Ahau* was looking at Jaguar Spot.

"Me, Your Lordship?" asked Jaguar Spot.

"Yes you, my young friend. As I understand it, scribes in Uaxactun are well trained in astronomy, are they not?"

"Yes, Your Lordship."

"And trained in recording the movements of the heavens, and predicting the movements of the stars and planets?"

"Yes, Your Lordship."

"That is why we need you. I don't want the priests of the city to know that we are letting a *Teotihuacano* god dictate our battle plans. They might object to a foreign influence in their realm of affairs. So we can't use any of them. Stone here can read the books, but he is not really trained a scribe, and just doesn't have the knowledge to do the necessary work. So you, not being a priest, not even really knowing any of the scribes of this city, will do the work, and we will have absolute privacy. Do you understand?"

"Yes, Your Lordship, I understand the need for privacy. But, I still don't understand what you want me to do."

The *Ch'ul Ahau* locked eyes with Fireborn and nodded. "We need you to predict the transit of Lord Venus," Fireborn said. "On one day each winter, and one day only, Lord Venus rises at the exact same moment as Lord Sun. He rises at exactly the same time, not a heartbeat before or after. On that day, the Hero Twins are ready for battle together, as they were at the creation of the world. After that day, Lord Venus rises earlier in the morning each night, until it is high in the sky before sunrise. Then he feels his familial bonds with Lord Sun and begins to rise later each morning until he fails to rise before Lord Sun again and disappears from our view. Eventually, as with the changing of the seasons, he rises with Lord Sun once again. That will be the day of our battle. We need you to observe Lord Venus, to consult with the holy texts, and to predict for us the exact day next winter that Lord Venus and Lord Sun will rise together like brothers. That will be the day of our battle with Uaxactun."

Jaguar Spot looked around the room. Everyone was staring at him, as if they were waiting for him to agree to the undertaking, or at least acknowledge that he would carry it out. The request was laughably simple, so simple in fact that reference to the sacred texts would not have been necessary if Jaguar Spot were able make his own observations of the transit of Lord Venus for a full civil year. Making predictions about the movement of celestial bodies was one of the first things that Snail had taught him as a young apprentice scribe. With everyone staring at him, he felt compelled to give some kind of response to Fireborn's explanation of his task. "Of course, Your Lordship. I believe that I can accomplish this task with great efficacy. By when will you need the results of my research?"

Fireborn smiled and exchanged glances with the *Ch'ul Ahau* before putting his hand on Jaguar Spot's shoulder. "If you can come up with a firm date within the next two *uinals* or so, that would be sufficient."

Chapter Fifteen
The Book

8.17.0.5.17. March 8, 377A.D.

Even though the *Ch'ul Ahau* had instructed Lord Stone to give Jaguar Spot full access to the holy books, and even though Lord Stone appeared to be fully involved in His Lordship's plans for war against Uaxactun, Jaguar Spot found himself hamstrung in his efforts to predict the date for the transit of Lord Venus. The location where the books were kept was, to Jaguar Spot's thinking, a mess. The room was dark and damp, with holy books seemingly strewn about at random, some in piles on tables, some carelessly left on the floor. Some of the books were moldy, and some had been ruined by sitting in pools of moisture. Lord Stone seemingly had no interest in helping Jaguar Spot find the texts he needed, but Jaguar Spot put this down to ignorance of where certain sacred texts were located more than to some type of ill will or passive resistance to the *Ch'ul Ahau's* order. Without question, one of the senior scribes or priests from Tikal could have found the required volume almost instantly upon entering the room, but that was obviously not an option per the *Ch'ul Ahau's* orders.

Although Jaguar Spot was appalled by the lack of organization in Tikal's collection of holy books compared to what he had experienced in Master Snail's workshop, the act of rummaging through book after book gave Jaguar Spot an almost unique opportunity to study the holy books without being limited by time or other obligations. He read volume after volume describing the creation of the world, medicine, the stories of the Hero Twins, and countless other subjects that might interest priests and scribes.

One day, after he had spent almost an entire *uinal* in the dark repository of holy books, he came across a promising old volume lying atop a few books ruined by mold and moisture. The ruined books, sitting in a pool of water on the stone floor, were virtually a mass of green mush. Indeed, the volume that had caught Jaguar Spot's interest was in a position where it should have started to succumb to the mold, and the bottom half of it, perhaps ten or fifteen folds worth, should have been unreadable. The book, however, appeared to be in almost pristine condition. Jaguar Spot took the book to a table and carefully started examining it. The paper felt strange, as if not made from pounded tree bark and then covered with plaster. Jaguar Spot ran his fingers along one of the folds. There was something strange about the way the book felt. A normal book would normally consist of one large long piece of paper folded up into twenty or so leaves. Jaguar Spot had assumed that this book, being large, would have contained even more. The folds of the paper would be hard and almost sharp to the touch. This book, upon closer examination, had only five or six folds, although it was thicker than a normal paper book would be. How, Jaguar Spot wondered, could someone have made paper so thick? Was there something special about this book?

Lord Stone had left Jaguar Spot alone in the library, so Jaguar Spot carried the book in question over to Lord Stone's house, where the house chamberlain asked him to wait in the great hall. Jaguar Spot pulled a table over to a doorway that led to the central courtyard and started examining the strange book in the sunlight. He hesitated to begin unfolding it, worried that it might have some kind of special spiritual or ceremonial significance. All of the sudden, he heard Lord Stone's booming voice from right behind him. "That's an interesting book that you have there, young man. My chamberlain says that you want to speak to me, so speak."

Jaguar Spot handed the book to Lord Stone. "Your Lordship, I have never seen a book like this before. It looks interesting, but I wanted to show it to Your Lordship before I opened it. Have you ever seen a book like this before?"

Lord Stone closely examined the outside of the book, smelt it, and then put it down on the table. "Laddie," he said, "this is a *very* special book. I have not seen one like this in . . . well a bloody long time. This is more than just a holy book, it is the holiest of books. Where did you find it?"

"In the library, Your Lordship"

Lord Stone sat down so fast that he seemed to faint. "In *my* library? You are saying that you found this book in *my* library?"

"Yes, Your Lordship."

"Where was it?"

"On a pile of books, Your Lordship. Many of them were getting pretty moldy, but this one seemed to be in much better condition than the others."

Lord Stone sounded like he was choking. "Moldy? With other books? Just sitting there? May the Gods forgive me. Laddy, do you understand that this book is not even written on paper?"

"I thought that it looked unusual, Your Lordship."

Lord Stone pointed to the book without touching it. "This book is written on jaguar skin. I have only seen one other such book in my life, and that was buried with old Lord Frog when I was a lad not even half your age."

Jaguar Spot had heard of books written on jaguar skin, but he had never seen them. One had to kill very many jaguars to get enough skin, and then the tanning process to stabilize the skin was painstaking. Only the holiest of holy books would warrant writing on jaguar skin. "Your Lordship, may I see it. Can we read it together?"

For the first time since Jaguar Spot had met him, Lord Stone smiled. "Why not! Alright Laddie, you look over my shoulder." Jaguar Spot watched as Lord Stone carefully opened the first fold of the book. The painting was more clear, and the images more crisp, than anything that either of them had ever seen. "Breathtaking, isn't it?" whispered Lord Stone. All that Jaguar Spot could do was nod in response. Both of them instantly saw that it dealt with the general subject of celestial bodies. On the fifth leaf they finally came across a table for the movements of Venus.

Jaguar Spot gasped. "That's it! Your Lordship, we have found it!" Lord Stone smiled. "Indeed we have, Laddie. Please leave it here when you are done. I need to make sure that it doesn't get lost for hundreds of years again." Taking a small piece of paper from his tunic, and using a piece of charcoal to write, Jaguar Spot quickly used the table to calculate the date next winter that Venus and Lord Sun would rise in the morning together: 8.17.1.4.12 11Eb 14 Mak. He then left the book on the table and immediately went home to find Fireborn, but was told by Otter that he was with Curl Snout training a group of farmers at a nearby village.

"Training farmers, Sir?" Jaguar Spot asked incredulously.

"Were you listening to me, young man?" asked Otter.

"What are Their Lordships training the farmers to do?"

Otter closed his eyes, and Jaguar Spot thought that his body started shaking. He more hissed than spoke to Jaguar Spot, his eyes still closed. "I don't see how His Lordship's affairs are any business of yours, *citizen*, even if you are his brother-in-law. Please leave me, as I have business to attend to."

Otter turned to go back into his house, but Jaguar Spot did not let him leave without another question. "But Sir, I need to find His Lordship and deliver an important message. In what village will I find him?" Otter stopped, turned to look at Jaguar Spot, and walked into his house without saying a word.

Jaguar Spot walked home dejectedly. He found Floating Crocodile playing with a rubber ball in the central courtyard. Jaguar Spot joined him, and they bounced the ball to each other using their hips, their elbows, and their forearms. Floating Crocodile quickly grew bored with the game. "Your Lordship," Jaguar Spot asked him, "do you know where His Lordship your father is this afternoon? I need to speak to him."

"Oh yes, uncle. He and uncle Curl Snout have gone to a village to the east of here to be with the farmers."

"Do you know the name of the village, Your Lordship?"

Floating Crocodile furrowed his brow and thought for a while before looking up at Jaguar Spot. "I am sorry, Uncle, but I cannot remember the name. I could take you there."

Jaguar Spot accepted the offer, and followed Floating Crocodile, who had apparently had much more time than Jaguar Spot to learn the lay of the land. Even though the boy had been in Tikal for only a few *uinals*, he led the way with as much confidence as if he had lived there his entire life. They walked through the city. They walked through swampland, passing giant cisterns that had been built by the citizens of Tikal over the centuries. Jaguar Spot could not even begin to fathom how much water these cisterns held, but he imagined that they could sustain the city through many years of drought, assuming that the *Ch'ul Ahau* had arranged for enough maize to be stored.

Once they were out of the city they passed through a number of villages, all of them prominently bearing the Tikal emblem glyph, and all of them seemingly deserted. Neither Jaguar Spot nor Floating Crocodile thought that this was particularly peculiar, as villages were often deserted in the dry season, when the men, and sometimes the women and children, fulfilled their obligations of labor to their respective *ahauob*. The village where Fireborn was supposedly training the locals was the fifth that they came to, and was as deserted as the others. Neither Fireborn nor Curl Snout were anywhere to be seen. Floating Crocodile thought that his father might be somewhere to the north, and Jaguar Spot, having no information to the contrary, followed his nephew in that direction. After walking a few hundred paces they heard the sound of shouting in the distance, and came across a large open field where hundreds of men stood in a line on one side, all of them carrying spear throwers and the short *Teotihuacano* spears. Jaguar Spot estimated that these men constituted the entire male population of all of the villages that they had passed through, and might have included men and boys from other villages as well.

In the middle of the field someone had cleared away all of the grass and bushes and set up a host of mock animals made of wood, straw, and cloth. Jaguar Spot heard a loud shout, and saw Fireborn and Curl Snout standing in the center of the line of men. Fireborn had his hand raised high, and the farmers each took their spear throwers, seated a spear in the notch, and pulled their arms back behind their bodies. Curl Snout sounded a conch shell trumpet and, in an instant, hundreds of farmers let their spears fly. There were so many spears in the sky that they almost darkened the light from Lord Sun, and an instant later the spears landed almost in unison in the center of the field, many of them expertly spearing the mock animals, and the rest landing in close proximity to their targets. Without waiting for any signal, the farmers each took another spear and made ready almost before their first salvo had landed. Curl Snout quickly sounded the conch shell trumpet and the farmers again let loose their spears, all at the same time. This time very few, if any, spears missed their targets, which were ranged from fifty to two hundred paces away. The farmers continued doing this until each of them had shot twenty spears. When they had shot all of their spears the ground in the middle of the field was so thick with spear shafts that it would have been hard to walk across. Curl Snout sounded three short bursts of the trumpet and the farmers all ran out to the field to retrieve their weapons. Jaguar Spot and Floating Crocodile took advantage of the interval to approach Fireborn and Curl Snout.

"Ah, Jaguar Spot. It is good to see you out in the sunlight once again," Fireborn said as they approached. "I was afraid that you were going to get as rotten and musty as all of those old books if you stayed in that library much longer. Tell me, does your presence here indicate, as I hope, that you have accomplished your task?"

"Yes, Your Lordship," said Jaguar Spot. "I have the exact date."

"You are certain?" asked Curl Snout. "No offense intended, but the date must be exact. There is no room for any error in this calculation."

"Your Lordship, the calculation is rather simple, and I triple checked my work. As long as the holy book is correct, the date is correct, you can be sure of that."

Fireborn clapped his hands and rubbed them together. "Good. I am glad to hear it. Now you can get started with your real work on this project."

Curl Snout and Fireborn laughed at the obvious look of surprise on Jaguar Spot's face. After an entire *uinal* of work on this single project, Jaguar Spot had hoped to spend some time outside again, maybe even joining the young men of Tikal in some ballgames. Curl Snout took his trumpet and sounded five short blasts, and the spearmen, many whom had not retrieved all of their spears, ran back to the side of the field and formed the same line that Jaguar Spot had seen upon his arrival. Fireborn raised his hand again, and the entire line of spearmen repeated the process of shooting their spears at the now dilapidated targets in the center of the field in unison until their entire supply of spears was depleted. Once the men ran out to collect their spears, Curl Snout moved close to Jaguar Spot and spoke in hushed tones approaching a whisper. "We need you to get with the *Teotihuacanos*, and tell them the date. There is a series of rituals that need to be carried out in order for our battle plan to have any efficacy. These rituals must be undertaken on certain dates in relation to the day of our battle. The *Teotihuacanos* are educated men, as far as anyone in their city can truly be called educated, but like all of their countrymen, they are completely illiterate. They know the general rules for conducting the necessary rituals, but they need help achieving the required level of precision in setting the dates and laying out the steps that need to be taken. That is where you come in. You will get with the *Teotihuacanos* and help them determine the exact dates, then you will take what they say and write out all of the necessary steps for all of the rituals. Once you get that done, Lord Fireborn and I will take care of giving the instructions to our own priests and nobility, so that the rituals can be carried out."

"But Your Lordship," Jaguar Spot said, "I don't speak their language."

Curl Snout clicked his tongue in frustration and conferenced quietly with Fireborn. Once they were done, Fireborn spoke to Floating Crocodile. "Son, you will have to act as an interpreter for Jaguar Spot and the *Teotihuacanos*. At your age, I would rather you were learning the ballgame and the skills needed for battle, but this is too important, and you are the only *Teotihuac* speaking male in the city, other than myself and Lord Curl Snout here, that we can completely trust. Do you understand?"

"Yes, Father." Floating Crocodile said dejectedly, looking at his feet. "Oh cheer up, son," said Fireborn. "I don't think that your uncle's work with the *Teotihuacanos* will take more than a *uinal* at most, and after that you can get back to your normal routine. Plus, once your uncle is free of this duty, he might be able to teach you a few moves for the ballcourt. From what I hear, he is quite a talented ballplayer. Now both of you, get back to town and get with the *Teotihuacanos*. We have very little time to spare."

Jaguar Spot and Floating Crocodile walked behind the line of spearmen as they once again shot their short spears. The men had achieved an amazing degree of proficiency, not only in hitting their targets, but in moving quickly to seat a new spear in the spear thrower, and in shooting their spears in together in one fluid movement. Without question, this would be an effective means of hunting where there was a large group of deer or other large animals present, but Jaguar Spot had never heard of, much less seen, a group of animals even one-twentieth the size as the group of mock animals in the center of the field. Jaguar Spot could not see how this training would have any practical purpose— using such a large group of men to hunt beasts in the forest appeared to be a colossal waste of time.

They arrived back in the city just at twilight, so Jaguar Spot decided that they would begin their work with the *Teotihuacanos* the following morning. He sent Floating Crocodile off to find the *Teotihuacanos* in the quarters that Fireborn had provided them in his compound and went to Fireborn's house to find Waterlily and have some dinner.

Waterlily and Orchid were just starting to eat dinner when Jaguar Spot arrived, and a servant brought him a steaming place of venison and beans, with three tortillas. Apart from the usual pleasantries, neither woman had much to say to Jaguar Spot, although they seemed to be having a lot of fun whispering in each other's ear and smiling in his general direction. Finally, when they were almost done with their food, Jaguar Spot had enough. "Okay, what's so funny?" he said to both of them.

"Brother," said Orchid, "we were just wondering what your reaction to the news would be."

"News?" asked Jaguar Spot.

The women started with their giggling again, which was only aggravated when Floating Crocodile walked into the room. "Enough," said Jaguar Spot, trying to avoid losing his temper. "What is the news that you are talking about?"

"I'm pregnant," said Waterlily.

"And so am I," said Orchid.

Jaguar Spot felt his jaw drop. "Pregnant?" he asked, staring at Waterlily. "You are pregnant? Are you sure?"

The women started laughing hysterically now, and were unable to stop until Orchid managed to get control of herself. "Brother, why is it that men always ask that question when a woman tells them that she is pregnant? Believe me, a woman knows. So I am finally going to be an auntie! Isn't it wonderful news? Lets have some chocolate to celebrate." Orchid called for a servant to prepare chocolate, and Jaguar Spot smiled at Waterlily. "I am happy," he said, "that we are going to have a child. It is probably time that we had an official wedding ceremony so that the child is legitimate."

Waterlily nodded thanks to the servant as she accepted the tendered bowl of chocolate and started sucking the foam from the surface. She did not directly reply to Jaguar Spot's statement about the wedding ceremony right away, but switched to a different topic. "I was in the market today," she said. Jaguar Spot and the others looked at her over their chocolate bowls as she continued speaking. "And I saw a merchant that I recognized from home. He had information about what happened after we left the city."

At that moment, an intense feeling of dread overcame Jaguar Spot. He had wondered many times what had become of his family in Uaxactun, but had never actually sought out the information. The chances that Speaking Macaw had treated his family with forgiveness were small in the extreme, and if he really thought of it, he was fairly certain that his father and family were dead, along with Hummingbird and her child. Still, Jaguar Spot tried to keep his composure and act as disinterested as he could. "Oh?" he said.

"Yes," said Waterlily. "Hummingbird is alive. Word has it that she is pregnant with the *Ch'ul Ahau*'s child."

"How," asked Jaguar Spot with an even stronger feeling of dread than before, "could this possibly be true?"

"According to this merchant, your father went to the *Ch'ul Ahau* after he found out that you fled the city and explained that you were the father

235

of Hummingbird's child. Apparently the *Ch'ul Ahau* confronted Hummingbird with this information, and she told him that you had forced yourself on her, and that she had not previously wanted to divulge the information because she knew how fond the *Ch'ul Ahau* was of you. The *Ch'ul Ahau* forgave her, and reinstated her in her position as his second wife. They sacrificed the child, of course, as an orphan."

When he heard that his child had been killed, Jaguar Spot felt as if he had been punched in the stomach. He could not blame Hummingbird for lying to save her life, but he knew that his reputation in Uaxactun was now even worse than that of a simple traitor, and was now that that of a traitor-rapist. He had given little thought to the possibility of ever showing his face in Uaxactun again, but he now knew that it could never happen, even long after the death of Speaking Macaw. "Anyway," continued Waterlily, "the *Ch'ul Ahau*'s forgiveness was so complete that he has now impregnated Hummingbird, although she is still pretty early along."

"And what of my father?" Jaguar Spot asked. "Did this merchant have any news about my father?"

"He did," said Waterlily. "He said that the *Ch'ul Ahau* forgave your father because he came to him with the news about your being the child's father, even though it meant implicating his own son in treason. Apparently your father is now the second most important *ahau* in the city, right below Aktak himself. This trader thinks that when Aktak finally dies or is too old to continue in his office, your father will take his place."

Orchid reached for Jaguar Spot's hand. "Brother, isn't it wonderful! Father is safe and secure, and no one had to die on account of what you and Hummingbird did."

"Except for the child," said Jaguar Spot, his throat barely able to get out the words.

No one present had a response for that statement.

The meeting the next morning with the *Teotihuacanos* did not go as well as Jaguar Spot had hoped. They were initially very excited to learn the date of the upcoming battle between Tikal and Uaxactun, but that excitement seemed to wane after they worked with Jaguar Spot to determine the dates of the five required ceremonies for their god Tlaloc. When Jaguar Spot asked them what was required for a particular ceremony, all that they would say was something like "we play a ballgame" or "we give our blood." Jaguar Spot knew that Fireborn wanted more detail for the ceremonies than the *Teotihuacanos* were able to, or willing to, provide, but every time he pressed them they became more and more vague. Finally, after two full days of frustrating conversations, Jaguar Spot walked out, telling the *Teotihuacanos* that if they would not provide necessary detail for the ceremonies, that they would have to be done as the Maya would do them, not as they were performed in Teotihuacan. This seemed to please the *Teotihuacanos*, who were apparently as frustrated and impatient with the conversations as Jaguar Spot had been.

Jaguar Spot remembered reading a book in Stone's library that contained a passage describing rites and rituals associated with the preparation for battle. The book had been very old, and the ceremonies described were just different enough than what Jaguar Spot knew to be current custom that Fireborn might find them convincing as being from Teotihuacan. If Fireborn objected to the ceremonies as being different from what he had observed up North, Jaguar Spot would tell him that he had to modify them so that they would be more palatable to the priests and citizens of Tikal. It took Jaguar Spot almost four days to find the book he remembered, but once he did he was able to create a schedule of ceremonies, ballgames, and sacrifices in preparation for the upcoming battle, still almost a year off.

Chapter Sixteen
Rubber

8.17.1.0.3. October 19, 377 A.D.

"Rubber," said Fireborn, walking into Jaguar Spot's bedchamber long before sun-up, "we need fresh rubber, and we need it now."

"Your Lordship?" asked Jaguar Spot, barely managing to overcome the grogginess that stuck with him from being woken out of a sound sleep. Waterlily stirred beside him, but she was apparently not woken by Fireborn's intrusion.

"You heard me, Gentle Scribe. We need rubber, and I need you to come along and help me fetch it. Something about you being Orchid's brother. The priest says that the medicine will be a more efficacious if someone of her bloodline does the collecting, so get some clothes on and let's go." Fireborn spun around and left the room before Jaguar Spot could say "Yes, Your Lordship." Jaguar Spot groped around in the dark for some clothes and met Fireborn in the main hall. Otter walked in at the same time, and looked at Jaguar Spot with a derisive sneer. He was followed by two priests, and then a slew of palace guards. Finally, Great Jaguar Paw himself walked in and Fireborn clapped his hands. "I would have your attention. As you know, my wife is very close to giving birth to our second child. The midwife and the priest administering to her say that the pregnancy is not going well, in fact the priest says that Lady Orchid may die. He needs some fresh rubber to make the appropriate medicine, collected by her brother here, in the presence of her closest relatives. Since she has no family here other than Jaguar Spot and the boy, the priest suggested that all of us go instead. So we are off to the old rubber plantation south of town, if that meets with Your Lordship's approval." Fireborn looked at Great Jaguar Paw, who nodded.

Otter raised his hand to speak.. "What about the child?" Otter asked. "Shouldn't he be the one collect the rubber instead of this . . . this . . . foreigner, this scribe?" Fireborn waved the question away and handed everyone present a gourd. "I have no time to explain the technicalities," said Fireborn, "but the priests were most insistent that it *not* be the boy, and that he not accompany us at all. So off we go."

There were twelve more palace guards waiting outside the house, standing beside the *Ch'ul Ahau's* litter. They led the way to the old rubber plantation, flanked by the remainder of the palace guards who had accompanied Great Jaguar Paw. The party walked slowly and deliberately, stepping to a beat that one of the priests kept with a drum. Too much haste, either coming or going, would destroy the magic that the rubber possessed. They walked south out of the city and took a small forest trail, barely wide enough to allow for the passage of the *Ch'ul Ahau*'s litter. Just as Lord Sun began to rise they came to a widening of the trail, and then to a meadow of sorts, unusual in the fact that the forest canopy was almost completely intact above. The meadow was bordered by more than fifty rubber trees, and Jaguar Spot could see that there were more rubber trees in the forest behind. The guards set down the *Ch'ul Ahau*'s litter, and the priests led the way to the far side of the meadow.

There were holes cut in each of the trees, and each had a line scoured into the side which forced the sap escaping from the hole to run into a hole dug in the ground, no larger than a man's head. The hole was thus filled with raw rubber, which would dry and harden into a black mass over time. Every couple of *uinals* a tender would come and collect the rubber, which would then be boiled and processed until it could be used to make balls for the ballgame, shoes, medicine, or sundry other things. The rubber from the ground had a penetrating odor, much different than that of the rubber that Jaguar Spot was used to. Jaguar Spot bent down in front of one of the trees and reached out to take some rubber from the hole, but was shooed away by one of the priests. "Not that way," the priest whispered with menace. "You will spoil the entire ritual. Just stand back and follow our instructions."

Jaguar Spot fell back and watched as the priests began a slow dance, with Otter making a fast beat on the drum. The priests would bend their knees almost to the ground, keeping their torsos perfectly erect. They turned their heads to the side quickly, and began to let out menacing cries that slowly became musical. "Demons!" they sang, "Foul spirits! Be gone from this place. Be gone from this place and let the goodness of Lord Sun and Lord Venus grace us with its presence. Be gone, we say!" Otter stopped beating on the drum and the priests nodded to Fireborn and Great Jaguar Paw, who started dancing in the same way, this time to a beat made by one of the priests. Great Jaguar Paw danced surprisingly well for his age. "Gods" sang Great Jaguar Paw, "hear my entreaties! Do not forsake this holy place. Impart your goodness on these rubber trees! Infuse the sap with your holy powers! Bring us the power to heal the fair Lady Orchid." As Great Jaguar Paw sang, the beat from the priest got louder and louder until it stopped exactly on Great Jaguar Paw's last word. The forest was silent. Not a bird, not an insect made a noise. "It is time," said one of the priests as he pulled Jaguar Spot by the left arm toward one of the trees and whispered instructions in his ears. "Listen very carefully, boy. We need *fresh* rubber, not the rubber from the ground. The sap coming from these trees is barely a trickle. We need the full amount of rubber that we would get from one tree over an entire day, from sunrise to sunrise. Obviously you can't do that all by yourself. So put the gourd in the scoured line, and collect sap. In a little while I will take the gourd, and you will go and hold His Lordship Great Jaguar Paw's gourd, then Lord Fireborn's, then Otter's, then those of my fellow priests, then you will hold this one again. Thus your energy will be imparted to all of the rubber that we collect here today. We should be done long before sunset. Remember though, from this point onward none of us says a word. Understand me, the spirits may be frightened if we let out so much as a peep."

Jaguar Spot nodded to the priest and put the open end of the gourd into the scoured line. Like the priest had said, the sap that flowed into the gourd was barely a trickle. It would take days and days to fill up the gourd. After a while, the priest came and tapped Jaguar Spot on the shoulder, and took the gourd. Jaguar Spot walked silently over to Great Jaguar Paw and took his gourd, and then after a while on to Fireborn, and so on. By mid-afternoon he had traversed the circle twenty times, and the head priest clapped his hand. "It is now permitted for us to speak," he said quietly. "Young man," the priest said, looking at Jaguar Spot, "please stand next to me. All of the other rubber bearers will now pour the sap from their gourds into yours. We shall start with His Lordship the *Ch'ul Ahau*." The priest beckoned the *Ch'ul Ahau* forward, and then Fireborn, and then the rest of the gourd bearers. When they were finally done, the priest took the gourd from Jaguar Spot and placed it on the ground. All of the priests started dancing around it, in the same manner as before. They did not sing this time, but chanted.

As the priests danced, Jaguar Spot heard a faint creaking sound, and noticed that the wind had picked up. The leaves on the trees were now shaking. As the wind gained strength the old rubber trees in the plantation started groaning as they swayed back and forth. The wind grew so strong that Jaguar Spot had difficulty hearing the chants from the priests. The trees behind them were now making loud snapping sounds as they moved in the wind. Jaguar Spot looked around. No one else seemed to have noticed. The *Ch'ul Ahau*, Fireborn, and everyone else were transfixed by the ceremony. Jaguar Spot then heard four loud snaps in rapid succession and saw one of the trees swaying violently in the direction of the *Ch'ul Ahau*, who took no notice. The tree quickly moved away from the *Ch'ul Ahau* with an even louder groan, and then snapped six times as it moved back toward the *Ch'ul Ahau*. Jaguar Spot stared at the tree, totally ignoring the priests. He saw bark fly off from the back of it, and saw the trunk start splitting near the base. The trunk moved faster and faster toward the *Ch'ul Ahau*. Jaguar Spot ran toward Great Jaguar Paw. "Your Lordship," he yelled, "get out of the way!" Great Jaguar Paw looked at Jaguar Spot in puzzlement, but took no notice of the tree now moving quickly toward his head. The trunk was barely an arm's length from the *Ch'ul Ahau* when Jaguar Spot reached him. "The tree!" Jaguar Spot said as he pushed the *Ch'ul Ahau* to the ground.

    The rubber tree missed Jaguar Spot's legs by no more than a hair's breadth. Jaguar Spot felt wind from the fall on the bottom of his feet. The priests rushed over and tended to Great Jaguar Paw, gently raising him from the ground. Fireborn pulled Jaguar Spot off the ground and handed him a water gourd. "Gentle scribe," he said, "you never cease to amaze me. Now drink some of this water, I have a feeling that you might need it." After Jaguar Spot took a sip of the water, he and Fireborn went over to the tree-stump where the priests had sat down the *Ch'ul Ahau*. Great Jaguar Paw beckoned Jaguar Spot forward and spoke in a quiet voice. "Ah, young man, thank you for saving my life. I had no idea that the tree was about to fall on my head. You have done a great service this day, not only for me, but for all of Tikal. I will not forget it, and neither will my family. Let us go back to the city and let the priests administer this medicine to Lady Orchid." Two of the priests waved their hands and protested that the *Ch'ul Ahau* needed more rest before he could even think of making the return journey, even if it was to be made sitting in the sedan chair. Great Jaguar Paw was having none of it. "I tell you that we must go, and go now!" he said before clapping his hands and ordering his litter bearers to bring the litter into the meadow.

    In much the same way that the group left the confines of the city, they returned. Jaguar Spot carried the gourd with the collected rubber. The head priest was careful that the journey not go too quickly, lest the magic imparted in the rubber be destroyed. On the occasions when Jaguar Spot could see Fireborn's face as they walked, he thought that he spied a clenched jaw and a scowl. "Come on you idiots, hurry up! If we don't get there soon my wife will die!" he imagined Fireborn thinking.

Finally they reached Fireborn's compound, and the priests led Jaguar Spot quickly to Orchid's bedchamber.

When Jaguar Spot saw his sister, he could not believe his eyes. She was covered in sweat. Her hair was as wet as it would have been had she just been swimming in a canal. A midwife was at her right side, holding her hand, while a priest did a quiet dance in the hallway. Orchid was screaming in pain, although it sounded like gibberish. She saw Jaguar Spot and screamed louder, and became comprehensible. "Brother! You have come! Thank you!" Before Jaguar Spot could say anything in return, she looked over at the midwife and became completely incomprehensible once again. The head priest pulled Jaguar Spot over to Orchid's head and then stepped back a pace. "Okay boy," the priest said, "pour a little sip of the rubber into your sister's mouth. She may spit it out, but that's okay, just as long as it gets in her mouth. Do you understand?" Jaguar Spot nodded to the priest and put the gourd to his sister's screaming mouth. In the middle of a scream he poured a little in, and she did not spit it out, but swallowed it completely. "Good," said the priest. "Very well done indeed, young man. Now take the remainder of the rubber and pour it all over her belly. Pour it over at the highest point, and then rub it around with your hands so it gets an even coat. Do you understand?" Jaguar Spot nodded again and approached his sister's heaving belly, which was covered in a thin layer of sweat. He poured the rubber on as the priest had directed, and his sister seemed to calm down slightly. She calmed down even more when he rubbed the rubber-tree sap around to make a sticky coat over her entire belly. Just as he finished, the priest grabbed Jaguar Spot by the right arm and dragged him out of the room. "Thank you, young man," the priest whispered in his ear. "You did very well, but now you must leave everything to the priests and the midwife."

Jaguar Spot wandered into the main hall, where he found Fireborn, Great Jaguar Paw, and Otter. Fireborn looked at him with a raised eyebrow. Words were not necessary to get the point of the question across. "I don't know, Your Lordship," Jaguar Spot said in response. "She was pretty much incoherent, although the rubber did seem to calm her down when I rubbed it all over her belly. The priests seemed to think that everything went well." Fireborn nodded, and then spoke softly to Great Jaguar Paw. Jaguar Spot did not know whether he should stay or go when a house servant made the choice irrelevant. The servant tapped Jaguar Spot on the right shoulder and led him into the kitchen.

"Young man," said the servant, "I was told to come and find you. Your wife has gone in to labor. Follow me."

Instead of taking Jaguar Spot to the bedchamber that he and Waterlily shared, the servant led Jaguar Spot out of the house, and then out of Fireborn's compound entirely. "Where is my wife?" Jaguar Spot asked the servant, but received little more than a mumble in response. Finally they came to the palace. "Your wife is inside," said the servant, pointing at the palace before disappearing into the crowd in the public square.

Jaguar Spot walked up to the palace and was quickly accosted by a guard. "And just where do you think that you are going, young man?"

"I am told that my wife is inside."

"And what of it?"

"I am told that she is in labor."

"Yes?"

"I was told to come here?"

"By whom?"

"By whom? By Lord Fireborn's servant!"

"And where is this servant of Lord Fireborn?"

"I don't know, she left. She's gone. Will you please just let me in?"

"And why should I do that?"

"I just told you, my wife is in labor."

"Says you."

"Not says me, says Lord Fireborn's servant!"

"Even if your wife were inside the palace, and even if she were in labor, why would they need you? Surely she has a midwife, and if necessary, a priest or two. The husband's presence, as far as I know, is not even considered desirable when a woman is in labor, much less essential."

"I know all of that. I was told to come. Now, will you let me in or not."

"No."

"Will you at least check to see if I am needed?"

"Check?"

"Yes, check."

"With whom?"

"I don't know, maybe the Chamberlain for a start."

"Oh all right. What is the lady's name?"

"Waterlily."

The guard disappeared into the palace and another came out to join Jaguar Spot while he cooled his heels. After an interminable delay, the original guard came back. "Sorry about the wait, buddy, but it's a pretty big palace and the Chamberlain, well he ain't here. Anyway, I found your wife. She's in the garden, of all places. Follow me."

Jaguar Spot followed the guard through a maze of rooms in the palace, until he heard screaming in the distance–Waterlily's screaming. He prodded the guard to pick up to pace and they finally came to a large courtyard garden, at least five times larger than the one that he had seen at the palace in Uaxactun. The guard held out his arm at the entrance. "Listen buddy," said the guard, "you know that access to this place is limited to the *Ch'ul Ahau* and some of his closest relatives. You gotta understand that under normal circumstances I wouldn't dream of lettin' you in, and I shouldn't even be doing it now. If my memory is correct, you are Lord Fireborn's brother-in-law, correct?"

Jaguar Spot nodded. "Correct."

The guard raised his arm. "In that case, I will make an exception this one time, and one time only. Go ahead." The guard waited at the entrance while Jaguar Spot followed Waterlily's screams and found her laying on her back with two women who Jaguar Spot recognized to be first cousins of Great Jaguar Spot at her side. There was not a priest to be seen. The women looked upset, like they did not know what to do. Waterlily barely noticed him as he took her right hand. "You ladies are the midwives, I take it?" Jaguar Spot asked. They both looked at the ground and said nothing. "Are you ladies not midwives?" Jaguar Spot asked a second time, much more insistently. They both looked at the ground and said nothing, which was all the information that Jaguar Spot needed. "Why have you not summoned a midwife and a priest?" Jaguar Spot demanded. They said nothing. "Well go get them, now!" Jaguar Spot said with as much self-control as he could muster.

The older of the cousins shook her head. "We can't, you see, we can't," she said with some difficulty.

"And why not?"

"Because Waterlily wasn't supposed to be here in the first place. We brought her here because she so wanted to see the flowers, even though we knew it was against His Lordship's dictates. To bring in still others would only add insult to injury. No, we cannot bring in anyone else.

That is why we summoned you. You can carry her out of here and take her home. That way no one gets into any trouble. So get on with it."

Jaguar Spot could not believe his ears. "My wife is in labor," he hissed. "I will not carry her anywhere. If someone gets in to trouble, we can deal with that later, but one of you go and summon a midwife and a priest. Even if there are no problems with the birth, we will need someone to tend to the umbilicus. One of you go, now!" The younger of the cousins nodded her head and left, while the other looked at Jaguar Spot with apprehension. "It will not only be us ladies who get into trouble for defiling His Lordship's gardens," she said.

Jaguar Spot kneeled over Waterlily's face. She had been crying. There were tears running down her face. Her eyes were swollen, but she looked him in the eyes. "Ah, you have come," she said in between screams. "I don't think that it will be much longer now. I am afraid that you will have to deliver the child yourself." Waterlily let out her loudest scream so far. Jaguar Spot directed the remaining cousin to get a mat and some suitable fabric to hold the child after the birth. She left, and they were alone.

Jaguar Spot knelt between Waterlily's legs and watched for any sign of the baby. He prayed to the Gods over and over that it would not be a breach birth–he would have no idea how to handle that. After only a ten or so breaths passed, he saw something. It was a head. "Great Gods!" he thought, "a normal birth." He took his right hand and touched the head of his child. It was warmer than he thought that it would be. He quickly saw the face, and the arms, and then the legs. It was a girl. He took the girl in his arms just as the midwife and priest arrived. "If you don't mind, Sir," said the priest, "I'll take the little girl for just a little while. There is a small ceremony that we need to perform, as I am sure that you know." Jaguar Spot nodded and handed his daughter to the priest, who produced a small obsidian blade and proceeded to cut the umbilicus. Jaguar Spot put his right hand on Waterlily' s forehead. "We have a daughter," he said.

Waterlily smiled. "A daughter? Is she beautiful?"

"Of course, she looks like her mother," Jaguar Spot said.

"You always were a horrible liar," she laughed. "I have decided to name her Hummingbird."

"Hummingbird? Why?"

"Because it is the name of someone who survived certain death. It should bring our daughter good luck. Now ask the priest if I can hold her."

The priest overheard Waterlily's question and handed her the child. He took the umbilicus and wrapped it in a red cloth. "Leave your wife with the midwife, son," the priest told Jaguar Spot. "There is still the afterbirth to think about. We need to arrange for the umbilicus ceremony. Where is your house?"

"I live in Lord Fireborn's house."

"With Lord Fireborn? Indeed? Are you a servant of his?"

"No, I am Lady Orchid's brother."

"The scribe from Uaxactun! I have heard about you. You saved the life of His Lordship the *Ch'ul Ahau* today, if my information is correct. But enough of that, come with me. We will need to discuss this with Lord Fireborn."

Jaguar Spot kissed Waterlily on the lips, and the child on her forehead, and followed the priest out of the palace. They found Fireborn still in the main hall drinking chocolate, along with the *Ch'ul Ahau* and Otter. Fireborn beckoned Jaguar Spot to join them, and a servant began preparing another bowl of chocolate. The priest waited in the background.

"So, Gentle Scribe," Fireborn asked, "just where have you been? We haven't seen you since you administered the medicine to your sister."

His sister. Jaguar Spot had completely forgotten about Orchid's predicament. "How is she, Your Lordship?" he asked.

"Oh, she seems well enough now that she has received the medicine, according to the priests. It is, however, a very long labor that she is going through, especially for her second child. I am expecting news any moment now. But that was not an answer to my question, where have you been?"

"I was at the palace."

The *Ch'ul Ahau* sat up and appeared much more interested than he had before. "Why were you at the palace, lad?" he asked.

Jaguar Spot struggled with his answer. He had not expected to have to explain his presence in the garden just yet, much less Waterlily giving birth in the forbidden place. He decided that the only thing he could do was come clean with the entire story right then and there. "Well, Your Lordship, I was summoned to the palace right before I left here earlier. I was told that my wife was in the palace, and that she was in labor."

Fireborn and Great Jaguar Paw looked at each other in puzzlement, and it was obvious that both of them wanted to interrogate Jaguar Spot on the subject. The *Ch'ul Ahau* nodded to Fireborn, who then peppered Jaguar Spot with quick questions.

"Was this information correct?"

"Yes, Your Lordship."

"And did you find Waterlily at the palace?"

"Yes, Your Lordship."

"Where?"

"In the garden, Your Lordship."

"The . . . the . . . garden? What in the name of all that is holy was she doing in the garden?"

"My understanding is that two of His Lordship the *Ch'ul Ahau's* cousins had invited my wife into the garden to look at some flowers. She went into labor while they were there. I found her on the ground, screaming with her labor pains, the cousins were at her side. I asked them where the midwife and the priest were, and they said nothing. Finally they told me that they did not summon a midwife and a priest because they were afraid of being found out for bringing Waterlily into the garden. I insisted, and one of them left to find who we needed. Before they could get there, Waterlily gave birth to a daughter. This priest back there has her umbilicus."

Fireborn, Great Jaguar Paw, and Otter looked too stunned for words. Otter kept opening his mouth as if he were going to speak, then closed it again. The *Ch'ul Ahau* finally broke the silence. "Well, Gentle Scribe, if you hadn't saved my life earlier today, we might be in a different situation, but seeing that I owe you a blood debt, I can think of no way better to repay it than to let your wife give birth to your first child in my beautiful garden. Neither you nor your family will suffer any hardship as a result of this. My cousins on the other hand, well. . .that may be a different story."

Fireborn looked relieved, and ordered another round of chocolate, while Otter looked like there was an unpleasant smell under his nose. Just as the chocolate was arriving two of the priests who had accompanied them to the rubber trees appeared out of the courtyard, smiling.

"I hope that you two have good news," Fireborn said.

"Indeed, Your Lordship," said the older priest. "Indeed we have. I am happy to announce that Your Lordship is the proud father of a beautiful baby daughter. My colleague has the umbilicus in that red cloth."

"And Lady Orchid?" asked the *Ch'ul Ahau*.

The priest's smile broadened. "Your Lordship, I am happy to announce that she is in good health, and should make a full recovery. That rubber surely saved her, praise the Gods."

The younger priest handed the cloth to Fireborn, who immediately took the similar cloth from the priest that had accompanied Jaguar Spot. "Come, all of you, into the courtyard," he said as he turned to leave the room. Jaguar Spot waited for the *Ch'ul Ahau* and Otter to leave before he followed. Fireborn screamed for two of his more muscular house servants, who arrived almost instantly. They pulled on a large stone from the floor of the courtyard that Fireborn had ordered be specially prepared *uinals* before. The hole that the servants created in the floor was more than an arm-length deep. Fireborn got down on his knees and gently took the two umbilicuses out of the fabric and placed them in the hole. He nodded to the servants, who replaced the stone.

"Gentle Scribe," Fireborn said, "our families now are even more closely intertwined than ever before. Our children's umbilicuses share the same home, and may their destinies follow the paths of that our ancestors set out for them. No matter where they travel, no matter what location they may some day call home, they will always be bound to this place, and to each other. Now, Gentle Scribe, why don't we go and see your new niece?"

Chapter Seventeen
Preparations

8.17.1.2.12. December 7, 377 A.D.

Apart from personal bloodletting by the *Ch'ul Ahau* and his battle masters, the main preparations for the battle with Uaxactun were to begin exactly two *uinals* before the selected date, with the playing of a massive ceremonial ballgame. All the men who were supposed to fight in the battle, even the *Ch'ul Ahau* himself, had to be on the playing surface while the ball was in play for at least two points. The game started in the morning and continued into the night, as *ahauob*, *cahelob*, and other prominent citizens of the city took their turn. Jaguar Spot, as a citizen without rank or privilege, even if he was Lord Fireborn's brother-in-law, played in the second to last match. It was dark out when Jaguar Spot stepped onto the playing surface and took his place along with a squad of relatively unknown men, mostly merchants from the market whom members of the nobility had deemed sufficiently worthy of the honor of joining their master on the field of battle. The ballplay was perfunctory, with the captain of the other squad serving an easy pass to the man who stood in front of Jaguar Spot, who returned it right back to the server with an easy lob which the server made no effort to return. After Jaguar Spot's team had a serve, which was likewise returned and allowed to bounce twice, the teams were ushered off the playing surface by the priests, and the last team was put on court. Tired from sitting at the ballcourt all day waiting for his name to be called, Jaguar Spot ascended to the now almost empty ledge so that he could get home to his wife and daughter. Just as he was about to clear the top and start for home, he heard a voice calling his name from the opposite side. It was Curl Snout, who was seated with Fireborn and the *Ch'ul Ahau*. Jaguar Spot dutifully walked back down and and back up stood next front to them. "I am at Your Lordship's service," he said to Curl Snout. The *Ch'ul Ahau* invited Jaguar Spot to sit with them as the last squads from Tikal were ushered off the court and the *Teotihuacanos* were allowed on. The *Teotihuacanos* had their own peculiar version of the ballgame in these circumstances, always played at night. Instead of using their bodies to move the ball, they had large sticks, and the ball itself was set afire while it was in play. Jaguar Spot and the others sat as if in a trance as the ball streaked back and forth, sometimes flying through the air, sometimes bouncing off the walls and leaving a small residual fire where the burning rubber adhered to the stone.

Unlike the "game" that Jaguar Spot had participated in, there seemed to be no limit to the number of points that the priests let the *Teotihuacanos* score. Jaguar Spot's enjoyment of the game was interrupted when the *Ch'ul Ahau* spoke to him. "Jaguar Spot, since you have come to our city, you have been a loyal servant to me and my family. I want you to know that we appreciate that."

Jaguar Spot knew enough to realize that the word "but" was lingering in the air, but also knew that there was little he could do to head it off. "Thank you, Your Lordship" was all that he could say.

"But," The *Ch'ul Ahau* continued, "perhaps we are asking too much of you now."

"Your Lordship?" said Jaguar Spot, uncertain of where the conversation was headed. "I will serve you in whatever way I can. Please do not be troubled that you ask too much of me. I feel that it is I who have asked too much of you, in taking the hospitality of your brother and accepting the safety of your city."

Jaguar Spot could not see the expression on the *Ch'ul Ahau*'s face as he spoke again. "Jaguar Spot, we are asking you to fight in a war against Uaxactun, where you were born and where you grew up. Your father is an *ahau* of that city. You have other family in that city. You know their *Ch'ul Ahau* personally, as I understand it. I am not sure that it is morally correct for us to ask you to participate in a battle where you might have to take the life of your own father."

"Your Lordship," Jaguar Spot gulped. "There is nothing in Uaxactun for me any more. I can never go back there without having the *Ch'ul Ahau* kill me on sight. My home is Tikal now. Please let me serve you as any citizen of your city would."

In the dim light cast off by the moving fire on the playing surface Jaguar Spot could see that Fireborn and the *Ch'ul Ahau* looked at each other before Fireborn turned back to him and spoke. "I am happy to hear that answer, Jaguar Spot. We want to ask yet another service of you, if you are willing."

"I will do whatever Your Lordship asks of me," Jaguar Spot said.

"Good," said Fireborn. "As you know, the battle is two *uinals* away. Someone needs to deliver our battle challenge to Uaxactun, and we would like it to be you."

"Me?" asked Jaguar Spot. "But Speaking Macaw hates me. He holds me beneath contempt. He won't accept me as your emissary, and will kill me. Even if he doesn't, he will consider it a grievous insult to send me instead of an *ahau*."

Curl Snout answered instead of Fireborn. "He won't kill you. You will be an emissary of the *Ch'ul Ahau* of Tikal. Not even Speaking Macaw would kill someone in that position. We *want* him to be insulted. We *want* him to be filled with contempt and hatred at the thought of seeing you. That is all part of our strategy. If he is agitated, if he is so angry that he can't think straight, then his performance in battle will no doubt suffer. Of course you are right about one thing, it would be a grievous insult to send someone as an emissary who do not have the rank of *ahau*, and we wouldn't want to do that." The *Ch'ul Ahau* and Fireborn both nodded their heads at the last statement.

Jaguar Spot felt relieved that they had come to their senses and would send someone else. The last thing he wanted to do was to march straight into Speaking Macaw's palace and put himself at his mercy. He had visions of Gray Sky and the other palace guards seizing him by the arms and forcing him face down on the stone floor of the ceremonial courtyard, and of the *Ch'ul Ahau* himself wielding the ceremonial blade. Jaguar Spot waited for one of the three men sitting in front of him to say that they had changed their mind, but when Great Jaguar Paw finally spoke, what he said was completely unexpected. "Yes, quite. Congratulations. I hereby proclaim you an *ahau* of the city of Tikal. For a man in your position, Jaguar Spot, you really ought to dress better. I don't think that I have ever seen an *ahau* so shabbily attired." The three of them started laughing at Jaguar Spot.

Jaguar Spot was shocked. A thousand thoughts raced through his mind. Never in his wildest imaginings had he thought that he would ever be made even a *cahel* of Tikal, much less an *ahau*. He imagined himself leading a group of *cahelob* and common citizens in battle, and of erecting monuments to his own magnificence. Those thoughts brought him crashing quickly down to Earth. What an *ahau* needed more than anything was money, and lots of it. The cost of the clothes, which always had to be new and well presented, and of securing, maintaining, and staffing a home, and of a thousand other sundry expenses quickly piled up inside his head. Of course all *ahauob* had some type of income, usually in the form of land tilled by tribute labor, or in the form of keeping a percentage of taxes collected, or in trading monopolies. These things were almost always inherited from one's father, and had Jaguar

Spot remained in Uaxactun he would have received them when he ascended to the title of *ahau*. Here in Tikal he had none of it. He barely had a hundred cacao beans to his name, and what little money he was able to scrape together lately had come from tutoring some scribe apprentices whose master had taken ill. "What," he asked, "are to be my duties, Your Lordship?"

"A sound question, and well asked," said the *Ch'ul Ahau*. "Of course it goes without saying that you will be a minor *ahau*, and a *very* minor one at that, at least for the foreseeable future. Still, even the lowliest of the *ahauob* needs to perform some tasks for those above him in the social order, and needs a way to make a living for himself. How would you like to be a Keeper of the Holy Books?"

"What of Lord Stone?" asked Jaguar Spot.

"What indeed?" replied Great Jaguar Paw. "To tell you the truth, I am worried about old Lord Stone. I am not certain that he is a good Keeper of the Holy Books anymore. He may be slipping. From what I am led to believe, some of the oldest books are in a very sorry state of repair, and many of the books are so neglected that they are no longer readable. So, after our battle is over I will make you the Lord Keeper of the Holy Books and will 'promote' old Stone off to be governor of some outlying province where he can't do much damage. You will have a living collecting taxes and tribute from the scribes of the city, and from associated trades."

Jaguar Spot thanked the *Ch'ul Ahau* and hurried home at Fireborn's request. Upon his arrival, in the main room he found five sets of garments made for an *ahau*. The first set that he tried on fit him perfectly. It would have taken quite a while for a tailor, or even a small team of tailors, to fashion this many fancy garments. Apparently Great Jaguar Paw and the others had been planning this for quite some time. Dressed as an *ahau*, he wandered through the house in search of Waterlily, wanting to share in the excitement. Back in the days of their youth in Uaxactun, her future had been assured the day that she became betrothed to him. She would have been marrying a future *ahau*, unless death in battle or illness claimed his life before his father died. When they abandoned Uaxactun, Waterlily's future changed as much as his did. Instead of almost certainly ascending to the pinnacle of Uaxactun society some day, she had been reduced to being a refugee, living hand to mouth, only the generosity of Fireborn and Orchid saving her from death or destitution. Now the future that had been stolen from her had been revived, although her husband would now be an *ahau* of Tikal.

He found Waterlily and Orchid sewing in Orchid's bedchamber. The two infants of the house were sleeping quietly next to them. "Well look at you, Your Lordship," Waterlily joked as he entered. "Oh, I'm blinded by the brightness of the feathers," cried Orchid in mock pain, covering her eyes as if Lord Sun was shining directly in her eyes. The both of them then descended into fits of giggling, which periodically stopped, and then started again when they looked back at Jaguar Spot. After the fourth giggling fit, the women regained their composure.

"How long have the two of you known?" asked Jaguar Spot.

Just as Orchid started to answer, she broke into a giggling fit again, and was joined by Waterlily. This time the giggling woke up the babies, who instantly started wailing. The women picked up the children and shooed Jaguar Spot out of the room. He wandered throughout Fireborn's house but it was strangely empty, so he decided to go to bed. Just as he had taken off his clothes and was about to lie down to go to sleep, Fireborn entered the room without warning and started talking at a rapid clip "Ah, Jaguar Spot. Glad to see you are trying to get a good night's sleep. A sensible policy, I always say. You will leave tomorrow at sunrise. You know the operative date. Just deliver the challenge to Speaking Macaw and tell him to have his army on the traditional battlefield at sunrise. It's imperative that the battle start at sunrise on our planned date. Do you understand?"

Jaguar Spot leaned up on an elbow so that he could see Fireborn's face. "Your Lordship, I understand. But even with the clothes of an *ahau*, how am I to convince Speaking Macaw that I am really what I say I am. He might just as soon think that this is some kind of ruse or hoax on my part."

Before answering, Fireborn paced around the room, thinking. After he had walked back and forth ten or so times, he had the answer. "Orchid will accompany you. Her presence will vouch for the authenticity of the message, and I think that she would like to see her father and her sisters once again. Plus, I have taken something from your old bag of tricks. You will take this along, as well." Fireborn reached into his tunic and handed Jaguar Spot a folded piece of paper, which had writing inside. Whoever had actually written the message was certainly no scribe. The grammar and the penmanship were horrible. It read:

Great Jaguar Paw, *Ch'ul Ahau* of Tikal
Sends an emissary
Jaguar Spot, *ahau* of Tikal
The gods of battle are satisfied.

    Fireborn left the room without saying anything else, and Jaguar Spot fell asleep. He woke up the early next morning without assistance. Waterlily lay sleeping beside him, and the baby was on a small sleeping mat off to the side. Jaguar Spot moved as quietly as he could, so as not to wake Waterlily or the baby. He put on one of the new sets of clothes that he had been given, and went to find some food before the journey. The air was unusually cool that morning, and Jaguar Spot found Orchid fixing food in the kitchen. She was already dressed for the day's journey, and had packed them rations for the mid-day meal, and extra rations if necessary. Jaguar Spot gobbled down some tortillas and took a drink of water before they left.

    It was well before dawn when they entered the streets of the city, and there was barely a soul to be seen. The stars were still bright in the sky, and there was just a little bit of lightening in the east. They took the forest road north out of the city and walked throughout the day, stopping only to eat their rations and find the occasional sip of water. In the early evening they hit the outskirts of Uaxactun. Very little about the city had changed in the short time that Jaguar Spot had been away, but Jaguar Spot noticed that everyone he saw was staring at him as if he were some type of spectral manifestation. He did not know whether it was the strange clothes that he was wearing, or whether he had become such a notorious figure in the city that the people simply could not believe their eyes. When they started getting close to the palace, he noticed that there was a large group of people following him at a discrete distance. Some of the people he recognized, a few of them he knew quite well, but no one would do so much as acknowledge his greetings or return a simple nod of recognition. When they got to the palace Jaguar Spot and Orchid ascended the main stairway and were met by Gray Sky, who had a look of shock and horror on his face. "Jaguar Spot," he said, "what are you doing here dressed like that?"

    Jaguar Spot looked behind himself. He saw that there were hundreds of people standing at the bottom of the stairs. Jaguar Spot assumed that they thought that a public sacrifice was in the offing and did not want to miss it. He turned back to Gray Sky. "I come as an emissary of His Lordship the *Ch'ul Ahau* of Tikal, Great Jaguar Paw. I bear a message and a challenge to battle for the *Ch'ul Ahau* of this city, Speaking Macaw. Please notify your Lord of my presence and my purpose."

Gray Sky stood and stared at Jaguar Spot, as if unable to respond. "You may go now," Jaguar Spot said, trying to prod him into action. Gray Sky came back to life with a look of confusion and bewilderment. "You?" he said. "You are an emissary from Tikal? And an *ahau*? Why would they send you? Don't they know what His Lordship's reaction will be? There must be some mistake."

Jaguar Spot responded without hesitation. "There is no mistake. Please notify your master of my presence and purpose. Also, please tell him that we are hungry and would appreciate a meal suitable for an *ahau* of Tikal and for the wife of the *Ch'ul Ahau*'s brother. Go. Now."

Gray Sky turned around to enter the palace, stopped, looked over his shoulder at Jaguar Spot with the same look of confusion that he had before, shook his head, and then walked out of view. By the time he returned the crowd standing at the bottom of the stairs had doubled in size and was starting to become loud and boisterous. It had grown so large, in fact, that the palace guards became worried and moved out in force to push the crowd back a hundred paces or so. Gray Sky was ashen faced when he faced Jaguar Spot again. "I am told by His Lordship that I am to extend you the courtesy that your newfound rank deserves. His Lordship is in the midst of consultations with advisors at the present time, but will see you tomorrow morning. In the meantime I am to offer you the hospitality of the palace. Lord Toucan Claw has been informed of your presence, and would like to speak to Lady Orchid, if that is amenable to her. Please follow me."

They followed Gray Sky to a small room where someone had laid out a virtual feast. There were tortillas, beans, venison, tapir, fish, chocolate, and other delicacies. Gray Sky pointed to the table. "Your Lordship, this food is for you. There will be a guard waiting outside the room if you need anything. There is a sleeping mat on the floor. I will have another guard bring you some breakfast in the morning. You will be notified when the *Ch'ul Ahau* will see you. I am going to take Lady Orchid to see Lord Toucan Claw now."

Jaguar Spot stopped Gray Sky before he left. "Hold it, Gray Sky. Doesn't my father want to see me, as well?"

Gray Sky looked straight at Jaguar Spot with a look of fear as he spoke. "It was anticipated that Your Lordship might ask such a question. I have been explicitly instructed to say to Your Lordship that you have no father in this city, and that as far as anyone here is concerned, you have no family, no clan, and no lineage." Jaguar Spot did not know what to say. He had known that his father would be disappointed, that he would be angry, that he would disinherit him, but to have him refuse to acknowledge their bonds of kinship went much farther than Jaguar Spot had expected. While Jaguar Spot stood there searching for words, Gray Sky left with his sister.

Jaguar Spot was fast asleep when Orchid came back. He was awakened by sounds of her sobbing. She was sitting at the table, which was by now emptied of the food that had been provided, with her face in her hands. Jaguar Spot moved over to try to comfort her, but she pushed him away, so he went to his own chair and sat. He knew that it would do no good to try to pump her for information, and that she would only talk when she herself was good and ready. He did not have long to wait. In between the sobs, Orchid spoke. "I have just been to see Father. Apparently the *Ch'ul Ahau* and his advisors have known about your presence in Tikal almost from the moment that you arrived. Father wouldn't even speak your name, but he kept berating me for giving aid and comfort to a traitor and a criminal. He just kept screaming, over and over. He wouldn't hug me, in fact he pushed me away when I approached him. He didn't ask about my children. He just kept screaming about you."

Jaguar Spot knew better than to say anything to Orchid right then, and simply waited for her to work through what she was feeling. Before that could happen, he heard Gray Sky coughing at the door. He turned to Gray Sky and nodded, which signaled the guard that it was now permissible to speak. "Your Lordship," Gray Sky said. "His Lordship the *Ch'ul Ahau* will see you now. He said that Lady Orchid is welcome to attend, but to look at her right now, I am not certain . . ." Orchid cut him off. "Oh, I'll go along!" she said in a half-scream.

"Hold it," Jaguar Spot said, "it is the middle of the night. I thought you said that His Lordship would see us in the morning."

Gray Sky looked embarrassed. "I regret to inform Your Lordship that there has been a change in plans. You must come with me now."

Gray Sky led them down corridors, into an open area, and then into the same ceremonial courtyard, now torch-lit, where Jaguar Spot had slain Blue Squirrel. Speaking Macaw was seated in a chair flanked by about ten *ahauob*. Aktak stood at his right side, and Toucan Claw stood to the left. Orchid stayed in the background as Jaguar Spot walked in front of Speaking Macaw and knelt down on one knee. Tradition held that he should wait for Speaking Macaw to speak first. "So, my friend Great Jaguar Paw sends you, Jaguar Spot, a former citizen of this city, as his emissary. I had heard that you were working there as a scribe, doing some kind of secretive work for your new Lord and for your brother-in-law. I also hear that you have been assisting with the ritual preparations for a battle. I wonder, what does all of that mean? Why you? Don't they have their own priests and scribes who can do the work?"

Jaguar Spot's knee was starting to hurt from kneeling on the hard stone floor of the courtyard, but he temporarily stopped noticing. Speaking Macaw *knew*. Somehow he *knew everything*. What would this mean? Would Uaxactun be able to counter the magic of Tlaloc with some kind of magic of their own? Was Tikal headed for another defeat at the hands of Speaking Macaw? Protocol dictated that Jaguar Spot provide some kind of answer. "It is most gratifying that Your Lordship has chosen to honor me by paying such close attention to my professional development. I am honored, but of course my work for my supreme Lord, Great Jaguar Paw, is confidential. I am gravely sorry that I cannot share any details with Your Lordship."

Speaking Macaw smiled and opened his eyes wide. "No matter, my learned friend, as your professional development will come to violent end soon enough. I understand that you come here with a battle challenge. I ache to hear it. Go ahead, speak."

Jaguar Spot noticed that all of the *ahauob* were staring at him, except for Toucan Claw, who was studiously ignoring his presence. Jaguar Spot spoke from his kneeling position: "I bring greetings from His Lordship Great Jaguar Paw, *Ch'ul Ahau* of Tikal. I am sent to extend a challenge for Your Lordship and Your Lordship's army to meet my Lord and the army of the city of Tikal in battle, at the traditional place, at dawn on . . . ."

Speaking Macaw raised his hand, and then spoke as if to complete Jaguar Spot's sentence. "On 11Eb 14 Mak. That is 39 days away. You can report to your masters that I accept their challenge. I have known about this date for quite some time. They think that by timing their battle with the transit of Lord Venus they will gain some kind of advantage in battle. How quaint. I accept this challenge with great enthusiasm. Tell them that their pandering to the savages from

Teotihuacan will have no effect. Victory belongs to the bold, and the clever. Their plan is neither. It is a recipe for defeat. We will defeat Tikal just as we did the last time."

Speaking Macaw motioned for him and Orchid to leave, but then called them back before they could get to the door. "I admit," he said, "when I heard that it was you that my friend Great Jaguar Paw had sent as his emissary, I had thoughts about answering his challenge by sending the emissary's head back to Tikal at the end of a spear. Some of my advisors still advise me to take such a course of action." The *Ch'ul Ahau'* looked up at Toucan Claw before he continued speaking. "But in the end I must decline to do so. The rules of diplomacy must be respected, and I will do no harm to an emissary sent by another *Ch'ul Ahau*, so long as the emissary does not commit any crimes in this city. Take this answer back to your master. I will fight him any time, and at any place, that he offers. Tell him that my army will meet him at dawn on the selected day. Tell him also that it was only my respect for the rules of war, not respect for him, nor any respect for your sham title of *ahau* of Tikal, that kept me from instantly sacrificing you, an action that you richly deserve, I might add. You and your sister will leave now. You will leave this city immediately, or you will never leave it alive."

Jaguar Spot once again stood and turned to leave, but Speaking Macaw again called to him just as he was about to exit the compound. "Oh, and one more thing, boy." Jaguar Spot stopped and looked at Speaking Macaw. "Yes, Your Lordship?" he said, feeling that it was likely to be the last time in his life that the two of them exchanged words. The *Ch'ul Ahau* got up and walked so close to Jaguar Spot that he thought there would be a collision, but spoke so loud that everyone in the courtyard could hear. "We *will* meet on the field of battle in thirty-nine days. My only hope is that no one kills you before I get the chance. I will guarantee you one thing, you will not leave the field of battle alive."

Jaguar Spot bit his tongue and stared Speaking Macaw straight in the eyes. It seemed that they would continue like this until one of them fainted from fatigue or hunger, when Orchid pulled on Jaguar Spot's shoulder and they left the courtyard. Jaguar Spot heard loud laughter coming from the behind him as he left. He wasn't sure, but he though he caught his father's voice in the chorus of laughs.

Chapter Eighteen
Battle

8.17.1.4.12. January 16, 378 A.D.

At sundown on the day before the battle the religious preparations came to an end. That night the city of Tikal seemed bathed in firelight as the men prepared for the fight. The final preparations had taken an entire *uinal*, during which normal life and commerce in the city almost came to a halt. First the *ahauob* played in a series of ceremonial ballgames to determine who would lead the men in battle, and who would command various platoons. Some of the games had predetermined endings, and were played for ritual purposes more than anything else. Other games, however, were real. Such was the game that Jaguar Spot had found himself in thirteen days before the battle. Playing on various teams, he had participated in a string of six straight victories. Most of the *ahauob* were middle aged or older, and none were even close to Jaguar Spot in terms of youth and physical fitness. Thus Jaguar Spot tended to dominate any game he took part in, except, of course, when he was told that his team was supposed to lose.

The game that Jaguar Spot found himself in was scheduled dead last of all the ballgames to be played as part of the pre-battle ritual. Unlike all of the other games, it was played one-on-one. The *ahau* on the other end of the court, a tall and well muscled man named River, was the second youngest next to Jaguar Spot, at age twenty-nine. They played for the honor of leading the vanguard of the attack. The loser would act as the winner's second-in-command. Because this was a one-on-one game, the priests provided the smallest ball allowable, which was barely the size of two closed fists. River, being the oldest, was given the first serve. Jaguar Spot tried to follow his eyes to determine where the serve would go, and saw that River was looking far behind him. If he served the ball to that location it would be an easy return, as he would have to arc the ball through the air, giving Jaguar Spot ample time to run into position. Jaguar Spot readied himself to fall back quickly. River shot the ball as fast as lightning right at Jaguar Spot's feet. If Jaguar Spot had a man behind him, he would have jumped out of the way and let his teammate make the return. That was not an option in these circumstances. Instead he fell down in front of the ball, trying to put his hip pad in position to make the return. He timed it right, and the ball hit his hip at the same moment that he hit the ground. The ball went flying over River's head, hit the ground, and then quickly bounced off the wall back into the ground. There was no way that River could make a return, and Jaguar Spot got the point and the serve. The remainder of the game was like child's play, and Jaguar Spot beat River without letting him score a point.

After the game, the more serious rituals began. All the men who were to participate in the fighting had gone through days of fasting, purification, and sacrifice. They had to go without food for three days, and then, when they were at their weakest, give their blood to the Gods and to their ancestors. The men were allowed to go back to their houses and regain their strength five days before the battle. The day before the battle the men were told that they should sleep as much as they could during the afternoon, as there would be no rest that night.

Thus Jaguar Spot found himself standing with the other *ahauob* at the foot of the highest temple in the city, waiting for Great Jaguar Paw to paint his face. As the youngest, Jaguar Spot stood at the end of the line, and watched as the *Ch'ul Ahau* took charcoal, clay, and other pigments to paint lines and circles on the faces of his warriors. Across the courtyard Fireborn, Curl Snout, and the *Ch'ul Ahau*'s cousins were busy painting the faces of the *cahelob*, who in turn would paint the faces of the ordinary citizens who were lucky enough to be allowed to fight in the battle. When the *Ch'ul Ahau* finally reached Jaguar Spot, he painted lines under the eyes and along the cheekbones, almost reminiscent of a jaguar's whiskers.

Like the other *ahauob*, Jaguar Spot held a knife the color of honey in his right hand, and had a shield rolled up and strung along his back. All of the *ahauob* wore a helmet emblazoned with images of their animal protectors. Jaguar Spot's had an image of a jaguar's face painted on the front. Once everyone's face was painted, Great Jaguar Paw got into his litter, filled with idols to every god that one could think of, and the rest of the assembled army fell in behind him. Jaguar Spot stood right behind Fireborn and the other men of Great Jaguar Paw's family. River stood next to Jaguar Spot, and the forty men of their platoon would march behind them, followed by the remainder of the army. At the back of the column marched two men carrying enormous wooden trumpets, and when they sounded two blasts, the column began to march. Guided only by torchlight, the army marched through the night north to the battlefield. If all went according to plan, they would reach their destination well before sunrise.

Thoughts of battle swirled through Jaguar Spot's mind. What would happen that day? Would he live? Would he kill? Would he see his father impaled by his own spear? Jaguar Spot was not at all comforted that Speaking Macaw seemed to know everything about his calculations concerning the transit of Lord Venus, and about the rituals from Teotihuacan. Of course, he had told Great Jaguar Paw and Fireborn of this intelligence the moment he had returned to Tikal, but they did not at all seemed concerned. In fact, they laughed when they heard the news. "So, he thinks that he has an advantage, does he?" Fireborn said. "Well, let's just let him believe that he has our battle plan all figured out." Great Jaguar Spot saw the look of concern in Jaguar Spot's face and comforted him. "You see, Gentle Scribe, this is all according to plan. We *wanted* Speaking Macaw to have this overconfidence. The fact that he would reveal that he possessed this knowledge only serves to demonstrate that he is . . . how should I say it? Yes, emotionally compromised. This is also according to our plan."

"Your plan, Your Lordship?" Jaguar Spot had asked. "Does Your Lordship mean that you intentionally provided this information to Speaking Macaw?" Both Fireborn and Great Jaguar Paw nodded. Fireborn explained. "Speaking Macaw thinks that he has a spy. A certain merchant that travels back and forth from city to city has provided him with information about our plans. Our friend Speaking Macaw has found this information so valuable that he has lavished great gifts of cacao and cotton on this man."

"How do you know this, Your Lordship?" Jaguar Spot asked, incredulous that Fireborn and Great Jaguar Paw were taking this so lightly. Fireborn opened his mouth to answer, but was stopped by Great Jaguar Paw, who apparently enjoyed revealing how clever the two had been. "This man is our cousin, although I doubt that my friend Speaking Macaw knows this. It was we who asked him to approach Speaking Macaw and offer to provide this information. Do not worry. As I said before, this is all according to plan. Our adversary thinks that he has the key to victory, but all he has is a path to defeat. The *real* intelligence, the information that really matters, is still secret–secret even from you, Gentle Scribe."

This conversation was still fresh in Jaguar Spot's mind as he led his platoon out of the city. About halfway through the march Fireborn and Curl Snout fell back and spoke to Jaguar Spot and River. They had already been schooled in the plan for the battle, which called for their platoon to run forward in a wedge, followed by the rest of the army.

Fireborn gave them additional instructions. "Both of you, listen close. This is the most important order that you will receive in the battle. Make sure that all of your men know it as if by rote. During the battle, at some point, the trumpet men will blow continuous long blasts. That is a signal. When you hear that signal, you must fall back 200 or so paces. And you must do this fast. You and your men must run as fast as you can. You must do this regardless of whatever you are doing at the time, whether it is fighting, directing the other men, or carrying a wounded comrade out of the battle. You must drop everything and run back 200 paces. Do you understand?"

River appeared outraged. "Your Lordship, I must protest. This is defeatist talk. We will win an outright victory over the enemy. There will be no need for a retreat. I would rather die."

Curl Snout laughed. "And that's exactly what you will do if you don't obey orders. This is not a retreat, is not a withdrawal, it is an integral part of our battle plan. Will you obey your orders?"

River was about to make another outburst when Jaguar Spot put a hand on his arm to calm him down. "We will obey our orders, Your Lordship," Jaguar Spot said. "May we inquire as to why we will be falling back 200 paces?"

Curl Snout barked back with a hint of impatience. "Those are your orders. You will obey them. That is the only explanation. Go see to your men." Curl Snout and Fireborn abruptly turned around and walked farther back to speak to the other *ahauob* in the column. Jaguar Spot and River spoke to each member of their platoon individually, having conversations much the same as the one that they had just participated in with Curl Snout and Fireborn. To a man, the warriors expressed feelings of anger, horror, and disbelief that the leadership was even *thinking* that an order to fall back might be necessary, much less assuming that it would happen. Even though it went against everything that they knew about honor on the field of battle, all of them agreed in the end to obey their orders without question.

The army reached the edge of the battlefield early in the morning, long before the first glimmers of Lord Sun's light could be seen in the east. Fireborn, acting as Great Jaguar Paw's battle master, sent out scouts who reported back that the Uaxactun army was nowhere to be seen. This was to be expected. Very few armies would arrive at a battlefield much earlier than was absolutely necessary. Jaguar Spot watched with interest and admiration as Fireborn wandered throughout the army, making sure that every platoon was in position, and that everyone knew their role in the battle to come. The battle plan had been formulated for some time. For all Jaguar Spot knew, Fireborn had come up with it during his years of confinement in Speaking Macaw's palace, when he had plenty of time to think. In order to avoid the debacle that occurred the last time, Tikal would approach the opposing army in the shape of the wedge. Instead of rushing headlong across the field, Tikal would march slowly, like disciplined soldiers, waiting for the enemy to show its disposition, and to reveal its strategy. They would go no further than the middle of the field, and if the Uaxactun army waited in the trees on the other side, Tikal's army would hold its position until Uaxactun marched out to meet it. Upon contact, the ends of the wedge would collapse around Uaxactun, enveloping the enemy army, or so it was hoped. Jaguar Spot had grave doubts that the battle would go as planned. He knew, as did Fireborn, that Speaking Macaw would have something up his sleeve. Just when the first hints of dawn were appearing in the East, a scout reported that Uaxactun's army was approaching. Somehow, the scouts reported, Speaking Macaw had raised an army of almost 800 men, far larger than Tikal's force. Fireborn laughed these reports off, telling the assembled Tikal troops that the Uaxactun fighters would be little more than raw militia, mostly farmers who had little training in battle, and who would run away at the first sight of blood. Jaguar Spot was not so sure. Speaking Macaw was intelligent enough not to use the same battle strategy twice. This time, it seemed, he had decided to fight with superior numbers, even though Tikal was several times larger than Uaxactun in population.

 Jaguar Spot and River led their men to the edge of the forest and out into the field just as Lord Sun and Lord Venus rose above the horizon, exactly at the same time. When the first rays of daylight shone on Tikal's army, the troops cheered, and Great Jaguar Paw's litter, still covered with the statues of various gods, was brought into the midst of Jaguar Spot's platoon. The *Ch'ul Ahau*, still sitting on his sedan chair, beckoned Jaguar Spot over. "Gentle Scribe," he said, "today we fight what will be the most glorious battle in the history of our people, and by that I don't just mean the history of our city, but all of our people, everywhere, for all time. It will be my honor to fight this battle alongside you and your lieutenant. Do not be troubled by this, I am not supplanting your authority. You are the *ahau* of this platoon, not me. May I fight with you, sir?" Jaguar Spot nodded and helped the *Ch'ul Ahau* down from his litter. The doubts that had been festering in his mind grew until they consumed his thoughts. Fireborn's battle plan was good and well thought out, but the enemy already knew it, and had superior numbers. To think that this would be a glorious victory for Tikal was a delusion bordering on madness.

Somewhere in the back of the column drummers beat out a rhythm and the trumpets sounded one short blast. Tikal's army moved slowly to the center of the field, walking so slow that the ancient *Ch'ul Ahau* had no problem keeping up. Jaguar Spot's platoon took its position at the vanguard, and the rest of the army fell in behind, arrayed to each side. Fireborn took command of the right flank, and Curl Snout the left, with Great Jaguar Paw taking overall command of the platoons at the center. They were about half way to the center of the field when Jaguar Spot caught his first sight of Uaxactun's army. Speaking Macaw had arrayed his troops in a straight line, with himself in the center. They marched at roughly the same speed as Tikal's army, and Jaguar Spot estimated that the two armies would meet somewhere very close to the center of the field.

With each step the enemy army marched ever closer. Jaguar Spot and River stood at the front of their platoon, with Great Jaguar Paw walking twenty paces to the rear, surrounded by palace guards. When they got so close to the Uaxactun army that they could see facial details, the men from Uaxactun charged, spreading out so that they met the entire wedge before it had a chance to collapse and surround the enemy. Before Jaguar Spot had an opportunity to worry about the success of the battle's overall strategy, the fighting was upon him.

Jaguar Spot had trained for combat virtually from the time that he was a toddler, but he was completely unprepared for the speed at which things happened in real combat conditions. At one moment the men from Uaxactun were a good twenty paces away. At the next moment, almost before Jaguar Spot had a chance to take another breath, he was exchanging blows with a large man who he did not recognize through his face paint, and at the same time wielding off a spear thrust from a man dressed as an *ahau*. He managed to get his knife into position to stab the large man who first assaulted him, at the same time placing his shield in front of the oncoming spear thrust. Just as he was about to thrust his knife in to the large man, someone else dispatched him with a spear thrust to the neck. Jaguar Spot looked to his right and saw that Great Jaguar Paw himself had come forward and had killed the enemy. Jaguar Spot, River, and Great Jaguar Paw fought side by side for what seemed an eternity. The enemy would come at them with spears, with knives, and with fists, but they were able to keep them at bay. Whenever Jaguar Spot looked around, he saw that the entire line was involved in close combat, and that men from both sides were either dead or lying on the ground bleeding. After a while it seemed like Tikal was actually making some progress, and they started pushing Uaxactun back, first five paces, then ten paces, and then fifty. Even though Speaking Macaw had amassed a large army, like Fireborn had said, most of the men were obviously not skilled warriors, and Uaxactun's casualties outnumbered those of Tikal three to one. Just as Jaguar Spot was about to thrust his spear into an oncoming enemy warrior, he heard a scream to his right. Great Jaguar Paw had fallen to the ground and was wailing in pain, with a spear sticking out of his belly. "Your Lordship!" Jaguar Spot cried, moving to pull the *Ch'ul Ahau* back from the fighting, and telling River to take over command of the platoon. Jaguar Spot managed to pull the *Ch'ul Ahau* back sufficiently so that his litter bearers could load him up and carry him away from the battle, and then went back to re-join the fighting. By now almost everyone in his platoon had some kind of injury, whether it be a cut or an open wound. Three of his men were dead, but Jaguar Spot was so-far unscathed. He pushed his way back to the front of the fighting, just as River and the rest of the men were advancing another five or so paces, walking over the bodies of Uaxactun's dead and wounded. It seemed that victory was at hand, and that Uaxactun would soon turn tail and return to their city. Tikal's honor would be restored, and Great Jaguar Paw, along with Fireborn as his battle master, would erect monuments and stone-trees to celebrate their achievements.

Just then, just when it seemed that victory was assured, Jaguar Spot heard trumpet blasts coming from the rear–loud continuous trumpet blasts. Someone had ordered them to fall back 200 paces. Jaguar Spot looked around at the faces of his men, and there wasn't one of them that did not show shock and anger at the signal to retreat. He shouted out to so that the entire platoon could hear: "Alright men, your heard the trumpets. We fall back 200 paces. Let's go." The fighting continued as if he had said nothing, so he started pushing his men back. The *ahauob* of the other platoons seemed to be having similar problems, but Jaguar Spot suspected that if the center fell back the rest would follow in short order. He shouted again. "Your heard me. The battle master has given us an order. You will obey it! Now move! Let's go!" Jaguar Spot managed to scream with such emphasis that the men actually listened to him and fell back from the face of the enemy. He led them running backward, counting his paces as he went. Behind him, he could hear the sounds of the Uaxactun army cheering, and screaming insults at the Tikal army for being cowards and weaklings. Jaguar Spot fell back behind his men to make sure that none of them straggled, and noticed that all of the other platoons were following his lead, and that Uaxactun was holding its ground, enjoying the spectacle of seeing their enemy flee the field of battle. When he reached 200 paces, which happened very quickly, he stopped and turned to look at the enemy army. Everyone on the Uaxactun side was cheering, screaming, or jumping up and down in joy.

Suddenly the trumpets stopped, and Curl Snout moved forward from the line with a conch shell trumpet. He put the trumpet to his lips and sounded two short blasts. Jaguar Spot had no idea what the significance of this might be until one of his men pointed to the edge of the battlefield and shouted. From both the left and right sides of the field hundreds of men stepped out of the trees, each of them carrying a spear thrower in one hand, and a bundle of short spears in the other. Curl Snout sounded three long blasts on his trumpet, and the men who had just emerged from the forest each took one spear and set it in their spear thrower, leaving the other spears on the ground. By this time the men from Uaxactun had stopped their cheering and looked at the men on the sides of the field with curiosity more than anything else, completely unaware of the onslaught that was about to overtake them. Curl Snout sounded four short blasts from the trumpet, and there were suddenly hundreds of short spears flying in the air straight at the Uaxactun army. By the time that they landed, spearing and impaling the men from Uaxactun with deadly accuracy, there was already another flight of spears airborne. After the second salvo, the spears started falling in a more or less constant rain, and before the army from Uaxactun knew what hit them, virtually all of them were dead or wounded. Finally, someone on the Uaxactun side decided to call for a retreat, and the hundred or so men who were still relatively unscathed began a quick run to the forest. The rain of spears followed them, striking them down as they ran. Jaguar Spot only saw three or four men make it to the forest edge. Three or four men—out of an army of 800! The rest of the Uaxactun army lay there dead, dying, or so severely wounded that they could not get up.

Jaguar Spot looked over at River, who appeared to be as stunned as he was. He looked around at his men, and at the other platoons. Every single member of the Tikal army stood as still as if they were made of rock, speechless, staring with open mouths at the results of the slaughter that they had just witnessed. Tikal's victory had been immediate, utterly complete, and unprecedented in history as Jaguar Spot knew it. By tradition, wars were fought by the nobility and a few select citizens, and the object was honor more than anything else. The victor would go home and brag about his accomplishments, while the loser would skulk back home in shame and humiliation. The cities would go on as they did before the conflict, the loser knowing that it would have the opportunity to avenge its defeat soon enough. This war was different. Fireborn and Great Jaguar Paw had called it a Star War, and now Jaguar Spot finally understood why. He first thought that it had to do with the transit of Lord Venus. Now he know that even the stars would notice the victory, and would appreciate the nature of the change. Life in Uaxactun would not go on as it did in the past, and nor, Jaguar Spot expected, would life in Tikal. The nobility and leading citizens of the city of Uaxactun had not only been defeated, they had ceased to exist.

Even though this was complete victory, the men from Tikal remained silent. There were no cheers, no cries of joy, nothing that one would normally expect when vanquishing an enemy. Apart from the wailing of the wounded from Uaxactun, and the footsteps of the spear men as they approached the enemy to retrieve their ammunition, the battlefield was as silent as it were completely empty.

When the spearmen reached the Uaxactun army, they pulled their spears out of the dead, and out of the living, causing great cries of pain that Jaguar Spot could hear clearly from 200 paces away. When a downed man struggled with a spear man, he was quickly dispatched with a spear thrust in the neck. While this was going on, the Tikal army stood and stared, doing nothing to assist the spear men, and nothing to protect the wounded men from Uaxactun. Finally Fireborn and Curl Snout came over to Jaguar Spot's platoon and instructed the men to collect the Uaxactun dead and put them in a pile, with the *ahauob*, the *cahelob* and common citizens in separate heaps. For the wounded, they were instructed to render whatever assistance they could, except that anyone dressed as an *ahau*, and anyone associated with Speaking Macaw, such as a palace guard, was to be taken to a separate location behind Tikal's line. Jaguar Spot told River to take half the platoon and start collecting the dead. Four or five other platoons moved to help. Jaguar Spot took the other half of his platoon and started searching the field for wounded.

Their search was not easy. Almost everyone that they came across was dead or was so badly injured that they were just as good as dead.

One of Jaguar Spot's men screamed to him. At the man's feet, writhing in pain but not badly wounded, was Speaking Macaw. Jaguar Spot ordered five of his men to tie Speaking Macaw up and to take him back to the location that Fireborn had specified. As the men were carrying Speaking Macaw away, Jaguar Spot continued his search through the dead and wounded. He knew that his father would be here somewhere, and his heart stopped every time that he saw a body of an *ahau* lying on the ground, but each time it was someone other than his father. Slowly the piles of the dead grew larger, and the numbers of the wounded grew smaller. Jaguar Spot would periodically walk over to look at the dead *ahauob*, but his father was not there. Nor was he among the three surviving *ahauob*. Buried Tapir, though, was alive, and Jaguar Spot walked over to speak to him.

"Hello, father-in law," Jaguar Spot said, kneeling next to Buried Tapir. Buried Tapir looked in the other direction, paying no attention to either Jaguar Spot's presence or his words. Jaguar Spot tried a few more times to engage Buried Tapir in conversation, to no avail. He got up and went back to inspecting the few remaining bodies lying in the field. By mid-day they finished their work, and Curl Snout sounded his trumpet to assemble the army. They lined up in the same fashion as before, except that the *Ch'ul Ahau* was no longer at the front of the column, having been taken back to Tikal due to his injuries. Jaguar Spot expected to head back to Tikal, but Fireborn had the army face north toward Uaxactun. Leaving 80 men to take the wounded men from both armies back to Tikal, the army headed north in silence.

River, who was a veteran of many more battles than Jaguar Spot, commented that he had never seen an army march so quietly. Apart from the sound of footsteps, and of Fireborn and Curl Snout talking to each other, the army made no sound at all. By the time that they reached the outskirts of Uaxactun in the late afternoon, Fireborn had made it clear to the army why they were entering the enemy city–he intended to conquer it, to take it over, and to install himself as the *Ch'ul Ahau* of Uaxactun. The men of the army were to search the city for any remaining *ahauob*, and anyone associated with Speaking Macaw's palace or his family, and bring them to the palace.

Jaguar Spot heard the words that Fireborn spoke, but could not believe his ears. Never, in all of his reading of the sacred books, or in all the stories he had ever heard told as a child or as an adult, had he heard of one city conquering another and installing their own *Ch'ul Ahau*. Certainly, sometimes a *Ch'ul Ahau* would be killed or captured in battle and a successor would take his place, but that was always a successor chosen from the previous *Ch'ul Ahau*'s family, or from someone else from the *Ch'ul Ahau's* city if a direct successor did not exist. But conquest? This was completely outside of historical experience. And what, Jaguar Spot wondered, did Fireborn intend to do with the Gods of the city, or with the ancestors of the dead *Ch'ul Ahau* and of the dead or captured *ahauob*? A *Ch'ul Ahau* derived his power from his ability to communicate with the Gods, and with his ancestors. How could Fireborn expect to do that as an alien *Ch'ul Ahau*?

Since Jaguar Spot was familiar with the palace, Fireborn directed him to lead two other platoons and search it and its immediate vicinity. The streets of Uaxactun were empty as Tikal's army marched through in a long column. Periodically a platoon would sheer off from the main group and start searching a residential compound, or an administrative building, or a warehouse. By the time they reached the palace, there were only 150 or so men left in the column, and Jaguar Spot could hear occasional screaming around the city.

Jaguar Spot took 30 men with him into the palace, and had the rest of his troops guard the perimeter in case anyone inside tried to escape. He had no doubt that this search would bring him face to face with Hummingbird, and he wondered what his reaction would be. To his surprise, they found no one in the personal apartments of the *Ch'ul Ahau* and his family, he noticed that all of his murals had been covered over with a fresh coat of stucco. He was not surprised. Even though his art was beautiful, he knew that no one want to be reminded that the palace had previously had a traitor in its midst on a daily basis.

The men fanned out throughout the palace. They found many valuable objects, but Fireborn had decreed that all captured property belonged to him, and to him alone. Other than a few of Speaking Macaw's kept dwarfs, there was not a soul in the palace. Jaguar Spot stationed fifteen men to stand guard inside and took the remainder with him to find Fireborn, who was busy tearing down and crushing stone-trees. Jaguar Spot approached Fireborn and stood at his right, watching five men dig at the base of a very large stone-tree, until it toppled over and fell into pieces, almost crushing one of the diggers in the process. The men then took smaller stones and crushed the remainder of the stone-tree until it was reduced to rubble. Barely taking his eyes off of the destruction, Fireborn glanced over at Jaguar Spot. "Report," he said.

"Your Lordship," Jaguar Spot began, "We have searched the palace, and apart from four dwarfs, we found no one alive. I have posted guards inside and outside the palace to prevent looting. What would Your Lordship like us to do with the dwarfs?"

Fireborn, with his attention fixed on the destruction of the stone-trees, did not appear to be listening very closely, but he answered Jaguar Spot's question quickly. "Dwarfs you say? Well, I guess that they can't do us much harm. Tell them that they are free to go, but that they can remain in the palace and serve the new *Ch'ul Ahau* of this city if they like. Otherwise they can try to make their own way in the world."

Jaguar Spot looked at a *cahel* who was standing close behind him and nodded. The *cahel* ran off to the palace to carry out Fireborn's order. Fireborn was still mesmerized by the destruction and did not speak again for some time. When he finally did open his mouth, it almost startled Jaguar Spot. "I understand that neither Aktak nor your father were found on the battlefield, is that correct?"

"Yes, Your Lordship. That is correct."

"I saw a few men successfully flee the combat. Do you think that Aktak and your father could have been among them?"

"Possibly, Your Lordship."

"I agree. It appears that you are an indispensable commodity right now. I have matters to attend to, so I will leave you in overall command of the search of the city. I need you to find Aktak, and your father. Do you understand that?"

Jaguar Spot felt his stomach start to churn. When they found his father the end would not be pleasant, but he had no choice but to obey Fireborn. "I understand, Your Lordship."

"Do you have a problem carrying out that order?"

"No, Your Lordship."

"Well, you should! This is your own father that we are talking about, and you know all too well what end awaits him. Even more important than the *ahauob*, though, is Speaking Macaw's family. You know the members of his family, don't you?"

"Of course, Your Lordship. Many were killed in the battle."

"I know that! I understand that Lady Hummingbird gave birth to a son a few months ago. I hardly need to explain the significance of the fact that there may be a male heir to the ruling dynasty. I need you to find this boy, and to find the remainder of Speaking Macaw's family. When you find them, you are to sacrifice them immediately, except for his wives, and except for his son. I want his wives and son brought to the palace and detained in that stinking hole where Speaking Macaw kept me for all of those years. Do you understand? We need to kill everyone even remotely connected with the royal family. We will have a special sacrifice for the wives and the son later on. I don't want anyone trying to poison the minds of the citizens against their new ruler by claiming some kind of right of succession. Do you understand?"

"Yes, Your Lordship."

"Get to it then."

Jaguar Spot gathered 100 or so men and conducted a thorough search of Aktak's and Toucan Claw's compounds–they were as deserted as the palace had been. By the time they were done it was after dark, so they postponed the remainder of the search until the next day. Fireborn sent half the army back to Tikal and summoned the spear throwers, who had waited outside the city. He ordered them to stand guard around the city and to kill everyone trying to get in or out, without exception. Over the next three days Jaguar Spot and his men searched every family compound, and every other building in the city, and they got no closer to finding the two missing *ahauob* or any members of Speaking Macaw's family. If they were in the city, they were hiding exceptionally well, but Jaguar Spot expected that they were hiding somewhere in the hinterland. He went to find Fireborn to get further orders, and found him in the palace's ceremonial courtyard bleeding himself from the mouth. He was bent over, his mouth agape, with blood dripping out. He had a stingray spine in one hand. Jaguar Spot knelt down next to him, and Fireborn handed him the stingray spine. "He's dead," Fireborn said, his words difficult to understand due to the injuries that the stingray spine had inflicted on his tongue.

"Who's dead, Your Lordship?" Jaguar Spot asked.

"Great Jaguar Paw. He died of his wounds. Curl Snout's older brother likewise fell. I have sent Curl Snout back to Tikal. He is *Ch'ul Ahau* now. Join me, Gentle Scribe, in giving blood for our departed *Ch'ul Ahau*."

Jaguar Spot took the spine and stuck it hard into his tongue. The pain was so intense that he thought that he would vomit, but he maintained his composure and kept his mouth open and let his blood fall on the ground and join Fireborn's. When the blood had formed a big enough pool, Fireborn stood up, pulling Jaguar Spot up with him. "Report," Fireborn said as they walked out of the courtyard. Jaguar

Spot found it hard to speak. "Your Lordship, I am afraid that we have been unable to locate our quarry in the city. Both Aktak's and Speaking Macaw's houses are empty, and appear to have been stripped of all valuables that can be readily carried. We have searched every residential compound in the city, and found no one. I spoke to several citizens who claim to have seen Aktak and the royal ladies leave the city shortly before our army entered, but I am not convinced of their credibility. I suggest that we conduct a search of the outlying villages."

"Good," Fireborn said, nodding. "Conduct your search, but regardless of what you find, I need you to come with me to Tikal in five days. Understand?"

"Yes, Your Lordship. I understand," Jaguar Spot said, and then left to conduct his search. He found River waiting for him outside the palace with a party of fifty men. "Did His Lordship say whether we can search outside of the city?" River asked. Jaguar Spot nodded and pointed in the direction of the north road. He had a feeling that his father was hiding in the house of an old friend.

The march to the village of Ixan did not take long. While they were still out of eyesight Jaguar Spot sent half of his men on a roundabout route to the rear, so that they could surround the village before anyone was aware of their presence. When they got closer Jaguar Spot set up most of the rest of his men in wide arc until they met up with the rear column and formed a cordon around the entire town. He left River in command of the men outside the town, and took ten men with him to the house of Fifteen Crocodile, whom he had seen only rarely since he had been to the house as a young lad. He and the men ran into the town as quietly as possible, so that their approach would hopefully not be noticed. They reached Fifteen Crocodile's house quickly, and Jaguar Spot left two men outside the front door, and went into the house with the rest.

Fifteen Crocodile was sitting at a cook fire along with the rest of his family. He greeted Jaguar Spot most cordially. "Ah, Your Lordship. It is nice to see you once again. Please join us and have something to eat, both you and your men."

Jaguar Spot directed his men to search the rest of the house, and sat down with Fifteen Crocodile. As the *ahau* of an outlying town, and a man whose physique and ill health had not allowed him to participate in the war, Fifteen Crocodile had so far been allowed to keep his position of authority in Ixan, but that might not go on forever. Once Fireborn had consolidated his authority in the city, he would slowly move to exercise increasing control over the countryside. This might be accomplished in a couple of *uinals*, or it might take half a year, but there could be no doubt in anyone's mind that it was inevitable.

Jaguar Spot took the bowl of maize and beans that he was offered and ate a few bites before he engaged in conversation. "Thank you for the food, my friend. I see that you and your village are looking particularly prosperous. Tell me, what are your thoughts on recent events in the city?" Fifteen Crocodile slowly chewed his food as he looked at Jaguar Spot, taking time to carefully measure his words. "Your Lordship," he said finally, "I find one *Ch'ul Ahau* in the city much like another. As long as there is rain, as long as there is a market that wants to purchase our crops, and as long as there are plentiful trade goods for my people, I care little about politics of the city."

"So you promise your allegiance to Lord Fireborn as the sovereign of this country?" Jaguar Spot asked in between bites.

"Of course," said Fifteen Crocodile with an ironic tone in his voice. "I exist to serve. Now that we have dispensed with the pleasantries, please tell me what I can do to be of service to you and His Lordship, the *Ch'ul Ahau* of our country, Fireborn Upturned Frog?"

Jaguar Spot handed his food bowl to one of Fifteen Crocodile's children and spoke with as much menace in his voice as he could muster. "We are seeking out several fugitives, namely the *ahauob* Aktak and Toucan Claw, and the immediate family of Speaking Macaw. As a loyal citizen of Uaxactun who has pledged his allegiance to our new government, I know that you will provide us with any information you might have on this subject."

Fifteen Crocodile pointed his finger and the women shooed the children out of the room. "This is serious business, Your Lordship," he said. "I understand your position with Lord Fireborn. I know that you have sworn your loyalty to him, and I even know that your father no longer considers you to be his son. But still, he is your father nonetheless, and you know all too well what treatment he will receive at the hands of Lord Fireborn. What will your ancestors think of these actions? Will they still want to feed on your blood after all of this is over? Tell me truthfully, do you really want my help in capturing your father?"

Fifteen Crocodile's words had mirrored the thoughts that Jaguar Spot had been thinking ever since he was ordered to lead the search, but he knew that Fifteen Crocodile's question was not asked in earnest.

Fifteen Crocodile was trying to manipulate him out of doing his duty, or at the very least was testing how loyal he was to Fireborn. Jaguar Spot tried to hide his misgivings as he answered. "My father told me a long time ago that the most important thing in a man's life is loyalty. I have pledged my loyalty to Lord Fireborn, to the exclusion of all others, including, if necessary, my own family. I will follow His Lordship's orders without question, and without reservation. I know that Aktak and Toucan Claw are men who you have known and respected for your entire life. When I was a child, Lord Fireborn once told me that sometimes in life a man is faced with a moment where he must make a choice about where his allegiances lay, and the results of that choice will follow him for the rest of his days. For you, my friend, the moment for that choice has come. Right now, as we sit here having this pleasant conversation, my men are searching this village and the surrounding area. If we find who we are looking for in the area under your control, I will have you and your entire family sacrificed to the Gods. If, on the other hand, you cooperate, and you help us find them, I will tell Lord Fireborn of your act of loyalty, and suggest that your position as *ahau* of this village remain as it has been. Have I made myself sufficiently clear?"

Jaguar Spot noticed that Fifteen Crocodile had begun sweating and acting jittery as he listened. Fifteen Crocodile looked down at the ground and wiped his mouth with the back of his forearm. When he finally spoke again, his voice was quivering and difficult to hear. "Your Lordship is most persuasive," Fifteen Crocodile said, and sighed. "I will take you to what you seek." Jaguar Spot followed Fifteen Crocodile out of the house and towards the edge of the village. Jaguar Spot directed that twenty men follow him, and that the rest maintain the cordon around the town under River's command. Fifteen Crocodile led them to a small building near the edge of town, which was little more than a shed. "In there," he said as he pointed. "Your quarry is in there."

One of Jaguar Spot's most senior men, a relatively junior *cahel*, pushed his forearm against Fifteen Crocodile's neck and backed him up against the building, screaming in his face. "Why do you mock His Lordship, you Uaxactun scum? Show him what he is looking for or I will put this knife deep in your belly." Fifteen Crocodile strained his neck to look down, and saw the *cahel's* long honey colored knife held right at his navel. "I swear!" Fifteen Crocodile choked out. "Let me show you, please!"

The *cahel* looked over at Jaguar Spot, who nodded, and then released Fifteen Crocodile. "You had better be right, fat man, or my knife will taste your blood before this day is over," the *cahel* said as Fifteen Crocodile staggered away from his grip. Jaguar Spot and all of his men watched as Fifteen Crocodile bent over and entered the building. He reached down to the floor and pulled up a trap door that had been covered with dirt so as to be invisible, and shouted into whatever chamber lay below. "They've come for you. The game is over. Come on up. All of you." Fifteen Crocodile stood back from the house, and within a moment Jaguar Spot saw the figure of old Aktak rising out of the hiding place, only to be grabbed by two soldiers and thrust to the ground, face first. Next came a couple of more men from the royal household, who were likewise placed face down in the dirt, and then Toucan Claw.

Toucan Claw rose from the trap door and looked right past Jaguar Spot as if he was not even there. Two of Jaguar Spot's men grabbed him by the arms and put him next to Aktak. After Toucan Claw, Speaking Macaw's older wife came up, followed by Hummingbird, who quickly bent over and picked up a child that someone below had handed her. Jaguar Spot had been dreading the moment that he saw Hummingbird. He had no idea how he would react, whether his old love for her would be renewed, or whether he would be able to regard her simply as the wife of his enemy. Bracing himself for the onrush of feelings, he realized that they . . . were not there. He felt . . . nothing. It was as if she was a stranger that he had never met before. How, he wondered to himself, could feelings that once had such an overwhelming hold over him just disappear, as if into thin air?

Hummingbird was followed by Speaking Macaw's three daughters. Jaguar Spot quietly had the men summoned who were guarding the village, and ordered the prisoners, both men and women, bound and gagged. He ordered Fifteen Crocodile to accompany them back to the city, and to provide a woman from the village to act as wet nurse to Hummingbird's baby. As soon as she arrived, he immediately ordered a forced march to Uaxactun. By barking out orders, and by paying painstaking attention to the tasks at hand, Jaguar Spot had been able to keep the fact that he held his own father prisoner out of his mind. Once they began marching and he had time to think, the thought of his father's future preoccupied him to the point where he found it difficult to keep walking. He walked over to where the prisoners were being pushed and prodded along and ordered two of his men to separate Toucan Claw from the rest of the pack. They pulled him thirty or so paces in front of the others, and then removed his gag at Jaguar Spot's instructions.

Even though ungagged, Toucan Claw kept his mouth shut, and stared ahead into the distance as if Jaguar Spot was not there. "Aren't you going to say anything to me, Father?" Jaguar Spot asked. Toucan Claw gave no sign of reaction to Jaguar Spot's question, and kept staring forward. "Father!" Jaguar Spot shouted, now walking backwards and standing directly in front of Toucan Claw. Toucan Claw kept his gaze just as it was before, with an unfocused look in his eyes, as if unaware of what was right in front of him. "Father, answer me!" Jaguar Spot screamed. Toucan Claw made no sign that he even recognized Jaguar Spot's presence. "Take him back with the others, put his gag back in place," Jaguar Spot finally said dejectedly, and then turned around to finish the walk into Uaxactun.

When they made it back into town Jaguar Spot saw that Fireborn had two hundred men from Uaxactun busy tearing down the victory temple that Speaking Macaw had rebuilt after his victory over Tikal years before. The temple had originally been built by one of Speaking Macaw's ancestors on the occasion of some now forgotten victory in battle. Since that time it had been renovated, added on to, or rebuilt by successive leaders to celebrate their own victories. Now it was being torn down into rubble. Jaguar Spot stopped the column next to Fireborn, who was overseeing the demolition. Upon seeing Aktak and Toucan Claw in bondage, many of the nearby workers shouted as if they had won a great victory, even though they had been loyal citizens under the old regime just a few days before. Fireborn did not notice the noise, or at the very least pretended not to notice, and kept his gaze firmly fixed on the destruction. Jaguar Spot walked up to his side, with River right behind him, and waited for Fireborn to acknowledge their presence and ask for a report. Fireborn did not oblige, and kept staring at the quickly shrinking temple. Finally Jaguar Spot coughed to attract Fireborn's attention, which seemed to work. Fireborn turned to face them. "Ah, Jaguar Spot and River. I see that you have collected some prisoners for me. Report!"

"Your Lordship," Jaguar Spot said, "we have captured all of the prisoners that you directed. This man. . ." Jaguar Spot motioned for Fifteen Crocodile to come forward. "This man provided us with essential assistance in our pursuit. I recommend that he be rewarded by allowing him to remain *ahau* of his village."

Fireborn glanced quickly over at Fifteen Crocodile and then back to the demolition. "Of course, of course. Can you be loyal to me as your *Ch'ul Ahau*?"

"Yes, Your Lordship," said Fifteen Crocodile.

"It is settled then," said Fireborn. "Go back to your home. And tell your colleagues in the hinterland that I do not anticipate any disruption in their routines, and all of the *ahauob* and *cahelob* of the farmland and the forest should come to the city and swear their loyalty to me. Once they do this, they can go on as before. Do you understand? What is your name, anyway?"

"Fifteen Crocodile, Your Lordship. I understand. If you give me your leave, I will go now."

Fireborn nodded, and Fifteen Crocodile quickly disappeared into the city, glad to return to the anonymity of a country squire. For a man of his bulk, he moved much faster than Jaguar Spot had imagined would have been possible. "Jaguar Spot," Fireborn said, "I see that you have brought me Speaking Macaw's daughters alive. I thought that I said that I wanted them killed." Before Jaguar Spot could answer, Fireborn waved him off. "Oh never mind. Come to think of it, I have better plans for one of them anyway. Gentle Scribe, I would like you to stay with me. River, take the prisoners to the palace. Put them all in the old dungeon. Post as many guards as necessary to assure that no one escapes." River acknowledged his order and marched the column off in the direction of the palace.

Fireborn seemed transfixed by the destruction of the old victory temple. The workers were putting the stone into two piles, one for bricks that could be re-used as building materials, and the other for rubble that could be used as fill. When the workers took a break to eat, Fireborn and Jaguar Spot walked to the palace, protected by twenty guards. "Tell me, Gentle Scribe," Fireborn began, "what do you think of this war that we have fought and won. What is your impression?"

"Impression, Your Lordship? It is not for me to have an impression."

Fireborn snorted at Jaguar Spot's lack of an answer. "Now see here, Jaguar Spot! I expect my *ahauob* to give me straight answers, not to simply say what they think I want to hear. Everyone else in this city seems to have an opinion on the subject, so tell me yours."

277

Instead of answering, Jaguar Spot could not stop thinking about one thing that Fireborn had said. "What do you mean when you say 'my *ahauob*,' Your Lordship?"

Fireborn smiled. "Ah, Gentle Scribe, you won't avoid having to answer the question that easily. What I mean is that you are *my ahau*. From the date of our invasion, you became an *ahau* of this city, answerable to me. You will have the same duties that your father had in the past, and the same properties. From time to time I am sure that I will need you for other tasks. But enough of that. Answer my question."

A million thoughts ran through Jaguar Spot's mind, and he could not devote enough of his thinking to Fireborn's question to give him a coherent answer. Instead he stayed on the same subject as before. "Your Lordship," Jaguar Spot said, "I swore my allegiance to Great Jaguar Paw, so my allegiance now has to go to Curl Snout, as his heir. I am sorry that I will be unable..."

Fireborn cut him off. "Oh stop talking nonsense, you silly boy. I am not only *Ch'ul Ahau* of Uaxactun, I am Supreme Lord of both Uaxactun and Tikal. Curl Snout, while he is a legitimate *Ch'ul Ahau*, remains, and will always remain, subordinate to me. This is the way that Great Jaguar Paw wanted it. In a nutshell, your allegiance lies wherever I say it does, and I say that it belongs to me. So will you finally answer my question?"

It took Jaguar Spot a while to put the thoughts of his new office to the back of his mind, but he finally tried to answer Fireborn's question. "Your Lordship, I have enormous respect and admiration for your military victory, but I am afraid that in the end it may prove counterproductive."

"Why is that?" asked Fireborn.

"Well Your Lordship, you control the land of this city, and you are likely to control the loyalty of its people after a short while, but your ancestors do not live here. The gods in the temples do not know your blood, and they might not like its taste. Without your ancestors to protect you, and without the Gods on your side, I fear that the city will decline into nonexistence. I believe I spoke of this to Your Lordship shortly after the victory. You said that you had a plan to conquer the royal ancestors of this city, but I don't see how that is possible."

Fireborn answered and sounded like he was absolutely certain that his plan would work. He explained that he would bleed himself daily in the halls of his ancestors in Tikal, and beseech them to attack the ancestors of Speaking Macaw in the Otherworld. In the meantime, he told Jaguar Spot with absolute conviction that the royal ancestors of Uaxactun would wither and die in the Otherworld from lack of sustenance. After all, they would receive no blood from a descendant in the future.

"Tell me," Fireborn asked, "has this city always been here? Was there a time when this land was nothing but lonely forest? In the far past, isn't it true that there were no ancestors here, and that the Gods cared little about this place? Shouldn't that mean that I can make the same connection with the Otherworld as Speaking Macaw and his ancestors did?"

Fireborn had a good point, Jaguar Spot was forced to admit to himself, so good that it would likely convince the people of the city, but not the priests, and not the scribes. Jaguar Spot told him so. "Your Lordship, the holy books say that over time, over the span of *katuns*, the temples of a city build up a certain supernatural energy. The longer a *Ch'ul Ahau* and his family conduct sacrifices in a place the more of this energy the place acquires. In fact the energy is so strong, and its effects so powerful, that when a temple or a city is abandoned the priests must conduct a special ceremony to dissipate the energy and change the place from a holy site to normalcy. Even then the energy dissipates very slowly, over the course of *katuns*. As long as the temples remain standing that energy will still be strong, and the temples will reject your blood."

Fireborn did not respond to Jaguar Spot's words for a while, and only answered when they had almost reached the palace. "You raise a good point, Gentle Scribe. A good point indeed. I was going to be content destroying and rebuilding Speaking Macaw's victory temple, and then work on improving and expanding the holy places over the course of the years, but you have convinced me different. I must destroy them all. I will have the priests conduct these ceremonies that you speak of, and I will tear down every temple or holy place where Speaking Macaw made sacrifices to his ancestors or to the Gods. I will then rebuild them, larger than before. Will that work, Gentle Scribe? Will that allow me to bring this city to prosperity?"

Jaguar Spot was now doubly impressed by Fireborn. Never in the known history of all the Maya cities had there been a conquest like this one. No *ahau* had ever had to deal with the complex problems of literally replacing the civil and religious government of a city, or with the conundrum of how to deal with the power and anger of the departed *Ch'ul Ahau's* ancestors. And yet Fireborn had come up with not only an answer to the question, but a *perfect answer*, all in the space of the time it took them to walk two hundred paces. "I think that it will work, Your Lordship," Jaguar Spot said slowly. "I think that it will work very well indeed."

"So you will help me with what I need to do?" Fireborn asked jovially.

"I am at Your Lordship's command."

Fireborn's jovial demeanor diminished as they entered the palace and spoke with complete seriousness. "Good. Now listen, I want you to find River. You and I are going to go to Tikal with the prisoners tomorrow. We will likely be gone for most of a *uinal*. Tell him that he will be in charge while I am gone, and explain to him, in a much detail as possible, what he needs to do to have the temples decommissioned and destroyed as quickly as possible. After you do that I want you to go through all the city and give River a list of all the temples that we need to raze and rebuild. Any questions?"

"No, Your Lordship."

"Good," Fireborn said, and disappeared into the darkness of the palace.

Chapter Nineteen
Toucan Claw

8.17.1.4.12. February 5, 378 A.D.

Upon Jaguar Spot's return to Tikal with Fireborn, Curl Snout called for a great festival. Speaking Macaw, Aktak, Toucan Claw, and the other captured *ahauob* of Uaxactun played an important role. Every day at high noon, they were led through the market, their hands bound. The citizens of Tikal would spit on them, throw objects at them, and shout obscenities.

At the end of the festival Curl Snout called for a grand ceremonial ballgame, and that was where Jaguar Spot found himself exactly one *uinal* to the day after the victory. The prelude to the ballgame was much like what Jaguar Spot had observed after Uaxactun had bested Tikal many years in the past. Curl Snout and Fireborn led the procession side by side. The *ahauob* marched in two groups. By now Fireborn had appointed a sufficient number of *ahauob* necessary to run the government of Uaxactun. Many of these had been low level *ahauob* in Tikal, who would be elevated to a much higher station in their new city. Some had been *cahelob* from Tikal, and some were even *cahelob* from Uaxactun who Fireborn thought had talents that might prove useful to him. The new *ahauob* of Uaxactun walked behind Tikal's *ahauob*, and when they entered the ballcourt, they sat on opposite sides. The area behind the edges filled up with people, and musicians and acrobats provided entertainments on the playing surface. Finally, after it seemed like thousands upon thousands stood on top of the ballcourt or in the streets surrounding it, the priests sounded their conch shell trumpets and cleared the playing surface of the entertainers.

Forty men from Uaxactun were brought in to the ballcourt. Jaguar Spot almost had to cover his ears from the noise made by the shouting citizens of Tikal, and noticed that the *ahauob* on both sides of the court were seated, like him, as still as if they had been carved from solid rock. The guards first lined the prisoners up in front of Fireborn, who sat with his *ahauob*, and then in front of Curl Snout, who sat on the Tikal side. It took four guards to carry each prisoner, for they were all bound at the hands and feet and carried by means of a long pole strung between the rope. The guards carried the prisoners off to one side, except for four, who they untied and ordered to stand in the center of the ballcourt.

Jaguar Spot recognized these men as mid-level *cahelob*. They looked horrible, as if they had not eaten or had any water for days.

Curl Snout and Fireborn each chose two men, and the ceremonial ballgame began, although it was not much of a contest. In their weakened state, the men from Uaxactun could not even reach the ball to make a return, and they were quickly defeated and then sacrificed. The ballgame continued in this fashion, sometimes with two prisoners being called, sometimes six, and sometimes four. Every time a new group was untied, Jaguar Spot could hardly look for fear that his father would be one of those selected. He knew that Toucan Claw's death that day was an absolute certainty, but he had tried to put these thoughts as far as he could from his consciousness.

When there were six men left, the guards untied four of them, including old Aktak and three other *ahauob*, but Toucan Claw was not one of them. Jaguar Spot found it hard to look at Aktak as he stumbled trying to reach the ball, but when it came to the end, the old man did not show so much as a hint of emotion or fear. Finally the guards brought Speaking Macaw and Toucan Claw to the playing surface. Toucan Claw stared straight ahead into the Tikal side of the ballcourt, denying his son the opportunity even to see his face. Jaguar Spot expected Fireborn and Curl Snout to jointly take the honor of dispatching the vanquished leader, but Fireborn alone walked onto the playing surface and then walked down the court until he was right in front of Jaguar Spot. Jaguar Spot felt like closing his eyes as Fireborn raised his arm and pointed straight at him. "Jaguar Spot," he asked, "will you join me in this game?"

Jaguar Spot had little choice in the matter, but he still found it difficult to respond. "Of course, Your Lordship," he finally croaked out, and then slowly got up and joined Fireborn, who took the front position. Both Speaking Macaw and Toucan Claw looked too tired and dazed to notice much of what was going on around them, but Jaguar Spot hoped for at least a glimmer of recognition from his father. He received none. The game progressed quickly, with Fireborn shooting off six easy serves that were never in any serious danger of being returned. Guards pushed the two prisoners to the center of the court, and brought both of them to their knees. Fireborn accepted an ax handed to him by Curl Snout, and then offered it to Jaguar Spot. "You know what to do, Gentle Scribe. Just make it as painless as you can."

Jaguar Spot slowly took the ax from Fireborn and walked over to his father. The crowd, which had been roaring as loud as ever, suddenly became very quiet, as if they wanted to hear the impact of the blade more than their own shouts. Jaguar Spot looked down at his father, who was now lying prostrate on the stone, with his eyes facing away. Jaguar Spot pulled the ax over his head and let the handle rest on his right shoulder. "Father," he said, "have you nothing to say to me? Please, say something."

Toucan Claw turned his face toward Jaguar Spot. The face that Jaguar Spot saw was not filled with hate, or with fear, or with love, but was totally blank, as if his father were experiencing no emotions at all. Toucan Claw spoke in a flat and quiet voice. "Make it a clean strike, Your Lordship. Now, get on with your business."

Jaguar Spot brought the ax quickly down on his father's neck.

Chapter Twenty
Temple

8.17.1.8.14. April 13, 378 A.D.

Upon his return to Uaxactun Jaguar Spot saw that River had been very industrious, and that most of the temples of the city were well on their way to destruction. Although the temples were enormous, this task was not as difficult as a casual observer might think. In reality the temples were little more than large piles of rubble over which the builders laid layers of stone bricks and buildings. All that was necessary to destroy the temple was to remove the stone covering, leaving the rubble, which was not properly part of the temple in the first place. A new temple could then be rebuilt simply by replacing the stone facade.

Speaking Macaw's victory temple, on the other hand, was another story. Fireborn left much of the rubble intact but had the workmen build an elaborate chamber in the bottom which was reached through a passageway that they constructed leading to the top of the temple. They built most of the rest of the temple around it, covering it with beautiful works of stone and wonderful carvings. Still, there was a hole near the top that led to the inner chamber.

Finally, when Fireborn's victory temple was almost complete, he called the all of the *ahauob* and *cahelob* to the temple for a ceremony. Guards brought Hummingbird, her young son, and Speaking Macaw's older wife to stand in front of the temple. The three of them were carefully bound and then carried up to the top of the temple, after which they were taken down into the inner chamber. Fireborn followed them in with an obsidian knife in his hand. He came out a short while later with his knife covered with blood. He stood on his victory temple and spoke.

"I have just killed the wives of Speaking Macaw, along with his son. I will spare the daughters, and I will take the eldest as my second wife. The wives and the son will be entombed in this victory temple for all eternity as a reminder to the Gods, and to whatever ancestors Speaking Macaw has left, of what we have done here. Although the blood of my house may intermingle with that of Speaking Macaw's, his line dies now, and dies here. There will never again be a ruler of this city except for the descendants of Fireborn. Each of you will now climb down into the temple chamber and bear witness to this fact."

Jaguar Spot looked over at Orchid to see if she had any reaction to Fireborn's announcement that he was taking a second wife. If she had any feelings on the matter she was not letting them show, but there was no reason that it should concern her. She was the mother of Fireborn's eldest son, the boy who would some day be *Ch'ul Ahau* of the city.

Jaguar Spot watched as Fireborn led a group of *cahelob* up the stairs of the victory temple. He knew that news of Fireborn's conquest of Uaxactun would spread from one city to another. There could be no doubt Fireborn had altered the laws of warfare among the cities forever. He wondered if anyone would ever defeat Fireborn, or Floating Crocodile, or whoever might come after them, in the same way that Fireborn had gained control of the city. At that moment he finally understood what Fireborn had told him about the nature of the Great Tree. The Great Tree might take notice of Fireborn's innovation, but the chances were remote. It was far more likely that that it would spend the rest of the life of the world in blissful ignorance of the comings and goings of men.

"How lucky the Great Tree is," Jaguar Spot thought to himself as he walked up the steps of the victory temple.

NOTES ON LANGUAGE, NAMES, DATES, AND HISTORY

This novel, of course, is a work of fiction, yet it is, in part, based on real historical events. I am indebted to the scholars, professors, and Maya enthusiasts who have quite literally brought a dead and unknown world to life.

Only one pre-conquest American civilization created a true written language, at least a written language that has survived for us to know about it—the Maya. That language, which was used for at least 1400 years, if not much longer, provides us with a richness of cultural and historical detail unparalleled for pre-conquest civilizations in the New World. Modern scholars know much about the cultures, languages, and mythology of the Inca, the Aztecs, and the tribes found in the United States and Canada because Europeans encountered them as living, breathing communities. Not so for the Toltecs, the Olmecs, or the numerous civilizations in South America that preceded the Incas. We know very little about the lives that these people lived and the social institutions that governed them, and much of what appears in the history books is speculation, conjecture, or guesswork. The Maya are different—we have a written history.

The Mayan system of writing is unlike any known in the Old World. The scribes would write in different writing systems that used phonetics, conceptual symbols, or a combination of the two. Sometimes they would use these different systems simultaneously, much to the chagrin of those trying to decipher them. For decades the language was undecipherable, yet through amazing ingenuity, intelligence, and hard work, a small group of scholars has brought these words to life. The decipherment of the Mayan texts, even though still incomplete, was undoubtedly one of the most impressive intellectual achievements of twentieth century scholarship.

The story of the fourth century, A.D. conflict between the Mayan cities of Uaxactun and Tikal is told in the historical records of those cities. There really was a prince of Tikal named Fireborn Upturned Frog (sometimes referred to in earlier literature as "Smoke Frog" or "Smoking Frog"). His brother Great Jaguar Paw, according to the most accepted scholarly decipherment of the texts, died of wounds incurred in the final battle depicted in this book. Great Jaguar Paw's son Curl Snout took over the leadership of Tikal after his father's death. Fireborn, Great Jaguar Paw, and Curl Snout are the only characters in this book that are based on the historical record. We do not know the name of the ruler of Uaxactun who lost his last battle, and his life, to Fireborn. The new regime saw to it that his monuments were destroyed. If you go to Uaxactun you can see the victory temple that Fireborn constructed. Deep inside, archeologists have found the remains of two women and a young child, apparently sacrificed in the ritualistic manner of the times. The scholars' supposition, which I have used for the end of this book, is that these are the remains of the wives and heir of the deposed ruler of the city.

If you look at a map of ancient cities of the Mayan civilization, you will see the cities of Uaxactun and Tikal. These names, and those of almost every other city you would see on such a map, are the modern creations of scholars, archeologists, tourists, and local indigenous communities. The ancient name of Tikal, the name that the residents of the city would have known it by, was most likely Mutal or Yax Mutal, meaning either "Green Bundle" or "First Prophesy." The ancient name of Uaxactun was Siaan K'aan, meaning "Born in Heaven." I have chosen to use the modern names for numerous reasons, primarily so that the reader can see these places on a map, or use the names to go on the internet and search for photographs and diagrams of the actual ruined cities.

I attempted to minimize the number of Mayan words used in this book. Two Mayan words that I did use where *cahel* and *ahau*, simply because there are no accurate English equivalents. I could have used something like "duke" and "earl"--and "king" for the *ch'ul ahau*--but there were no "dukes" and "earls" in the Yucatan. I utilized the Mayan "*ob*" to indicate plural words, thus you see *cahelob* instead of *cahels*. I did this for not other reason than that I like the way it sounds better. Similarly, I chose to use the older scholarly way of spelling Mayan words. The proper pronunciation for the word *ahau* would be "ah-haw," and for this reason many anglophone scholars will spell the word with its English equivalent, so you might find the word spelt *ahaw* in some sources. I find the older spelling, based on Spanish phonetics, more evocative, so that's what I have used in this book.

Not only did the Maya have a living, breathing written language, they had very complex and accurate calendars. I say "calendars" instead of "calendar" because they had two separate systems of marking the passing of days, and both were utilized concurrently. What I have called the "religious" calendar was a cyclical manifestation of the way the Maya saw the world, and had a 260 day "year." What I have called the "civil" calendar had 18 months, each twenty days long. There was a 5 day rump month at the end of the year, so that the calendar added up to 365 days. There was no leap year or other means of accounting for the fact that a year is 365 and a quarter days long, so the start of each civil year would cycle throughout the seasons. The new year might start during the summer one year, and in winter hundreds of years in the future. The Mayan priests were certainly aware of this, but they saw no reason to make any changes with a calendar that, to them, was an embodiment of the cosmos. The civil calendar has provided scholars with a wonderful gift—historical dates. Thus, we know that the final battle between Uaxactun and Tikal occurred on 8.17.1.4.12, that is 8 *baktuns* (400 years each), seventeen *katuns* (20 years each), one *tun* (a 365 day year), four *uinals* (twenty days each), and twelve days since the date that the Maya considered to be the start of the manifestation of creation in which they lived. As can be imagined, scholars disagree as to the exact correlation between this calendar and the Gregorian calendar that is currently used worldwide. The most widely accepted scholarship puts 8.17.1.4.12 on January 16, 378 A.D.

The cities of Uaxactun and Tikal are long dead. Their people had abandoned them, and the forest had reclaimed them, centuries before the European conquest of the Americas. Yet their history, and the stories of their people, remain. They remain in the buildings, in the temples, and in the texts that the scribes carved in solid rock without the benefit of iron tools.

Made in the USA
Lexington, KY
05 August 2012